Praise for

The Devil's Dream

"Combining an unmistakable voice with an infallible sense of story . . . she writes lyric, luminous prose; her craft is so strong it becomes transparent, and, like the best of storytellers, she knows how to get out of the way so that story can tell itself."

—*San Francisco Chronicle*

"A heartbreaker . . . Judging fiddle music to be the voice of the Devil laughing, preacher's son Moses Bailey forbade his fiddle-loving wife, Kate Malone, the music she was raised on in the Virginia hills. She bore him three children, tending their lonesome cabin while Moses tramped the countryside searching in vain for God. But Kate's heritage proved too strong, and she soon began fiddling away for the children behind her husband's back. . . . This is the stuff of family legend, indeed the very soul of Lee Smith's beautifully told saga about a Southern singing family down through the ages. . . . Smith proves again in *The Devil's Dream* her keen ear for oral history as she pushes her extraordinary gift to new limits, switching deftly and imperceptibly from voice to voice to resounding voice."

—*Boston Sunday Globe*

"*The Devil's Dream* is a family quilt of a novel, stitched together from the patchwork fabric of several generations, each embroidered with its story in a distinctive, intensely personal style. Although it sweeps through 150 years and employs a variety of voices, the candor and warmth of the narrative encourage an intimacy with the characters. And the lure of music, whether simple hymns or Nashville rockabilly, is the thread that unites them all . . . Tragic, joyful, and touching."

—*The Washington Post Book World*

continued . . .

"You don't have to know country music to fall for Lee Smith's novel. . . . All you need to bring is a love of people, an ear that delights in the many flavors of language, and a decent sense of irony. Ms. Smith provides the rest, abundantly."

—*The New York Times Book Review*

"A storyteller carrying on the tradition of the Scottish and Irish pioneers who settled the Southern mountains, Ms. Smith allows her characters to speak for themselves, delivering long monologues in a conversational style and dialect appropriate to the times and place. . . . Her book begs to be read aloud. Down-home for sure, her characters nonetheless communicate to the reader with intimacy and honesty and hearts full to bursting."

—*The Atlanta Journal-Constitution*

"Smith has mined the culture of rural Appalachians to produce entertaining and satisfying stories. With *The Devil's Dream*, she marries meticulous research with her obvious affection for mountain music and mountain people. And, as in *Oral History*, she employs a number of narrators to create a book that often reads like a ballad. The voices, from that of a digressive old-timer remembering the girl of his dreams to a middle-aged woman taking a pragmatic view of her ex-daughter-in-law's antics, are distinctive and memorable." —*Orlando Sentinel*

"Smith spins a down-home tale of weddings and adulteries, many offspring—legitimate and otherwise—and thunderous 'signs from God' in every generation. Each chapter is the equivalent of a country song, combining the tragic, the hokey, the joyous, and the ironically inevitable. . . . Smith's strong, believable characters, their gossipy, matter-of-fact voices, and their affection for their rustic mountain home make this a rich, inviting multigenerational tale." —*Publishers Weekly* (starred review)

"With this book, Smith again shows us that she's lyrical as any songbird and second only to Fred Chappell when it comes to capturing the mystic sweetness of the Appalachians. . . . She deserves kudos just for her rendering of lunatics, for no Southerner has ever penned them better. Except, maybe, Faulkner."

—*Greensboro (NC) News & Record*

"You'd have to have a hole in your pea-pickin' soul not to be enchanted by Lee Smith's fictional paean to the white man's blues, *The Devil's Dream*. . . . Throughout this sprawling family saga, Smith captures music-making at its purest and show biz at its most disingenuous, offering fascinating glimpses of old-time medicine shows, radio barn dances, sleazy rockabilly joints, primitive recording sessions, the Grand Ole Opry, crass country commercialism—even a phantom backwoods fiddler. . . . Pleasures of all sizes and emotional hues abound in *The Devil's Dream* and, country music fan or not, you won't want this ambitious and rewarding novel to end."

—*The Cleveland Plain Dealer*

"Simply marvelous . . . One of the best contemporary novels I have ever read . . . In between these stories blooms an intricate knot garden of other tales, vivid with sexual and romantic passion, darkened with religion fevers, and sweetened by a love of, and talent for, music. Each narrator steps forward out of the group to sing his or her special 'song.' . . . In *The Devil's Dream* Lee Smith has written a classic, one that's fun to read."

—*The Raleigh News & Observer*

continued . . .

"If ever a subject found its perfect voice, it is surely in Lee Smith's new novel, *The Devil's Dream*. . . . Here are characters vividly animated by Smith's keen ear and rich imagination and whose lives assume a reality as solidly grounded as your next-door neighbor. . . . Lee Smith once again shows herself a storyteller of the first rank, and her characters in *The Devil's Dream* are among her most memorable."

—*The Columbia (SC) State*

"Thoroughly entertaining . . . Smith creates a vividly labyrinthine world of family ties in which music is always a part . . . a real treat."

—*Kirkus Reviews* (starred review)

The Devil's Dream

Lee Smith

BERKLEY BOOKS, NEW YORK

THE BERKLEY PUBLISHING GROUP
Published by the Penguin Group
Penguin Group (USA) Inc.
375 Hudson Street, New York, New York 10014, USA
Penguin Group (Canada), 90 Eglinton Avenue East, Suite 700, Toronto, Ontario M4P 2Y3, Canada
(a division of Pearson Penguin Canada Inc.)
Penguin Books Ltd., 80 Strand, London WC2R 0RL, England
Penguin Group Ireland, 25 St. Stephen's Green, Dublin 2, Ireland (a division of Penguin Books Ltd.)
Penguin Group (Australia), 250 Camberwell Road, Camberwell, Victoria 3124, Australia
(a division of Pearson Australia Group Pty. Ltd.)
Penguin Books India Pvt. Ltd., 11 Community Centre, Panchsheel Park, New Delhi—110 017, India
Penguin Group (NZ), 67 Apollo Drive, Rosedale, North Shore 0632, New Zealand
(a division of Pearson New Zealand Ltd.)
Penguin Books (South Africa) (Pty.) Ltd., 24 Sturdee Avenue, Rosebank, Johannesburg 2196,
South Africa

Penguin Books Ltd., Registered Offices: 80 Strand, London WC2R 0RL, England

Cover photography: *Blue Ridge Mountains* by Adam Jones/Getty Images; *Guitar* by Kick Images/Getty Images.
Cover design by Royce M. Becker.
Interior text design by Laura K. Corless.

PRINTING HISTORY
G. P. Putnam's Sons hardcover edition / July 1992
Ballantine Books trade paperback edition / July 1993
Berkley trade paperback edition / March 2011

Berkley trade paperback ISBN: 978-0-425-23971-1

The Library of Congress has cataloged the G. P. Putnam's Sons hardcover edition as follows:

Smith, Lee, date.
The devil's dream / Lee Smith.
p. cm.
ISBN 0-399-13745-9
I. Title.
PS3569.M5376D48 1992 92-1027 CIP
813'.54—dc20

PRINTED IN THE UNITED STATES OF AMERICA

10 9 8 7 6 5 4 3 2 1

This book is dedicated
to all the real country artists,
living and dead, whose music
I have loved for so long.

The author is grateful to the Lyndhurst Foundation for its generous support during the writing of this novel; to North Carolina State University for giving me leave of absence; and to the Southern Folklife Collection of the Wilson Library at the University of North Carolina at Chapel Hill.

The Family Tree

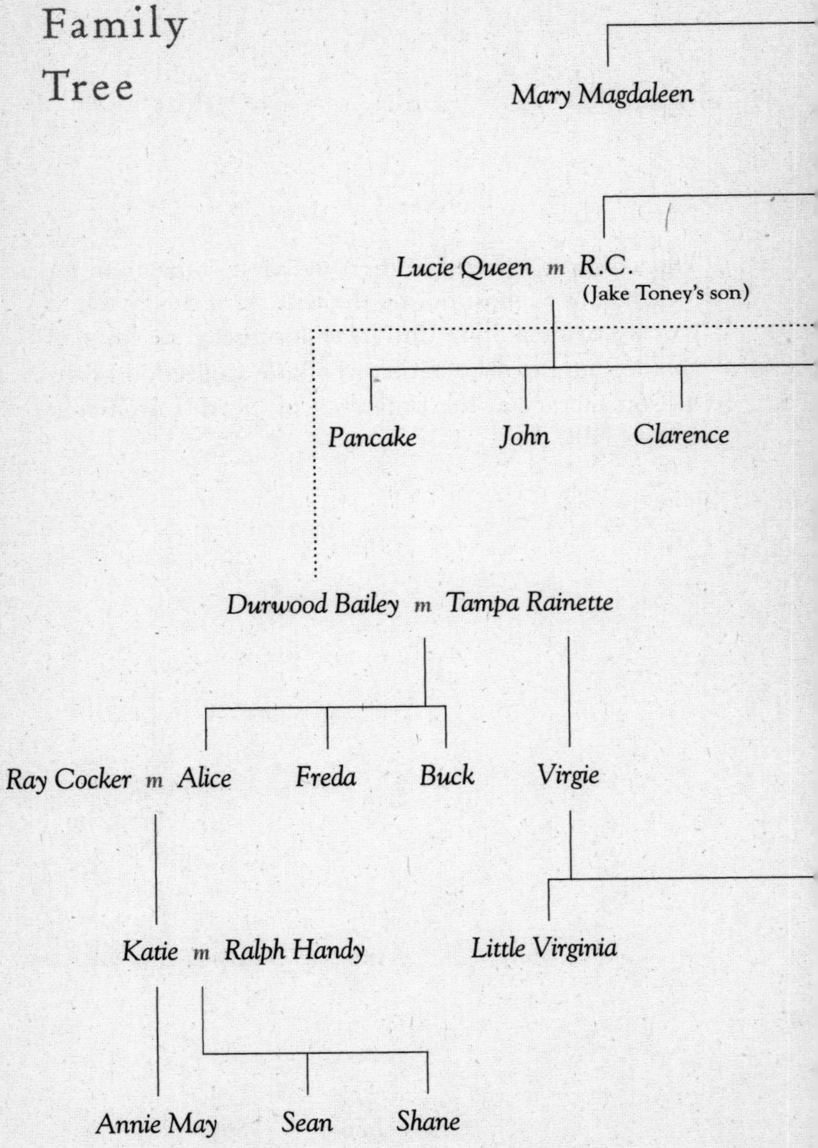
Mary Magdaleen
Lucie Queen m R.C.
(Jake Toney's son)
Pancake
John
Clarence
Durwood Bailey m Tampa Rainette
Ray Cocker m Alice
Freda
Buck
Virgie
Katie m Ralph Handy
Little Virginia
Annie May
Sean
Shane

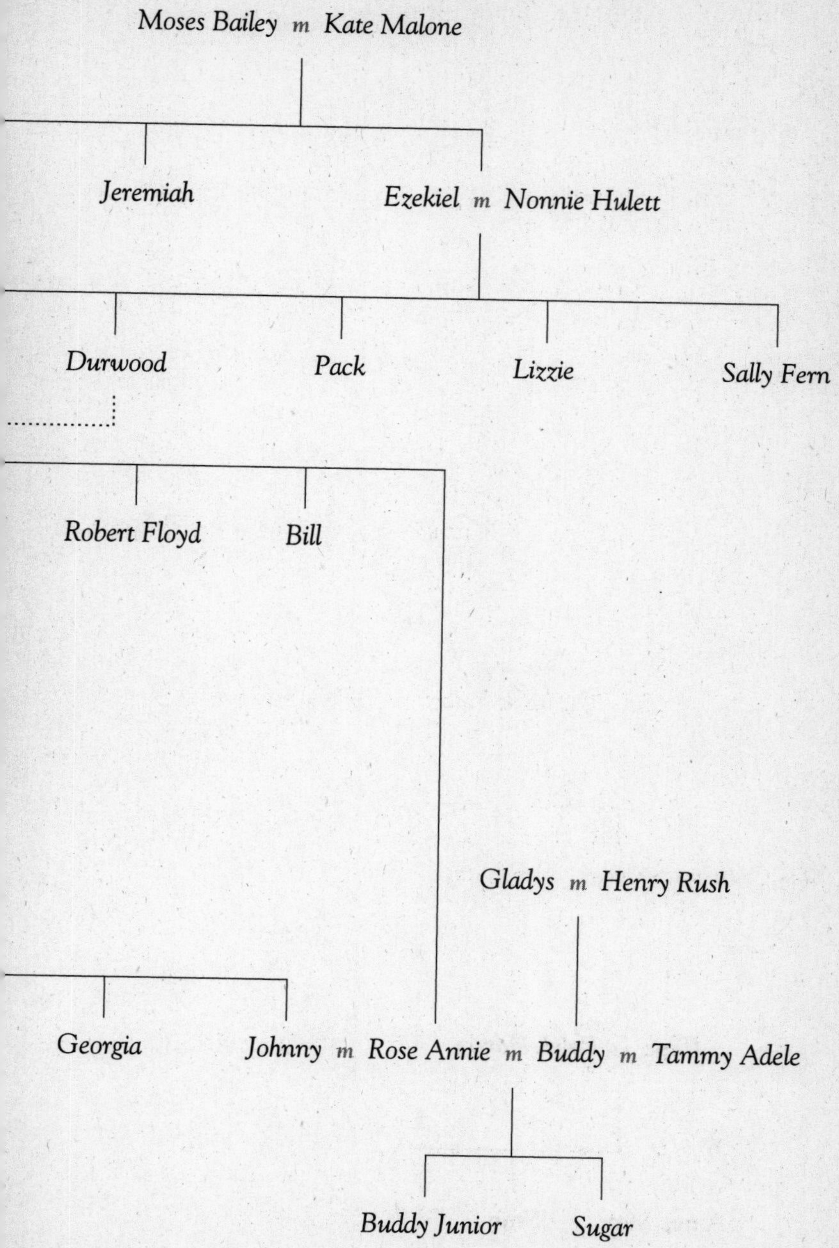
Moses Bailey m Kate Malone
Jeremiah
Ezekiel m Nonnie Hulett
Durwood
Pack
Lizzie
Sally Fern
Robert Floyd
Bill
Gladys m Henry Rush
Georgia
Johnny m Rose Annie m Buddy m Tammy Adele
Buddy Junior
Sugar

Shall We Gather at the River

It's Christmastime at the Opryland Hotel, and you never saw anything like it! Strings of the most beautiful little bitty colored lights—miles and miles of lights—are wrapped around and around every single twig on every branch on every tree, hundreds of trees, millions of lights; it must have taken them months to do it. You can't get over it! Not to mention the hotel itself, all lit up like some fairy-tale city—hell, it's as big as a city anyway, hundreds of rooms, all those restaurants, ballrooms, pools, you name it.

There's special displays, such as those darling life-size elves over there hammering away on little red high-heel shoes, or the animated ballerinas dancing Swan Lake *forever and ever on the mirror pond in the middle of the lushly blooming Conservatory. There's real strolling singers, such as the Merry Gentlemen, the Seven Singing Dwarves, a trio of snowmen, and a mysterious swashbuckling baritone in a cape singing "Silent Night." You can't quite place him. But it don't matter. Maybe he's some lunatic out here on a day trip. Maybe he's a real star. This place is full of real stars, you have to keep an eye out. You might see anybody. And if you do, it's a good bet they'll give you their autograph or maybe even the shirt off their own back. Country stars are real nice. They love their fans in a deep way. They will give of themselves till they drop. This very afternoon, Minnie Pearl is scheduled to read "The Night Before Christmas" out loud by the giant fireplace. Every child there will get a free gift, not to mention hot chocolate.*

But look—right now, right over here, flash bulbs are popping like crazy on the porch in front of the old-timey Pickin Parlor. You better hope you've got some film left, honey. It must be somebody big. . . .

And sure enough, it's Katie Cocker! One of the real superstars of country music, looking just as natural—looking just like herself! But you know they all look smaller in person than they do on TV, that's a fact. And their heads are all a little bit bigger than they ought to be, you have to have a big head to look good on TV. Of course, Katie's wearing a wig, too; they all wear a wig. Nobody's hair has got that much body. But hers is naturally blond, that's a fact, you can look back at old photographs from when she was a Raindrop with Mamma Rainette and the Raindrops, and see for yourself. Thick yellow hair, farm-girl looks—level brown eyes, honest as the day is long; a wide, full mouth; that easy smile. Red lipstick. Katie Cocker don't put on airs. She don't have to. She don't have to take off those twelve extra pounds if she don't want to, either. She looks okay. She looks fine! She's made it, and made it her own way.

God knows she's paid her dues, too. Some of the events of her life are just tragic, but she's weathered them. She's still here. She's still singing her heart out. It does seem like more things happen to country artists than to anybody else, have you ever noticed? It's like they have more events in their lives. God knows she's lived through some events. Katie Cocker is well over forty now and looks it. There's something about her that says, "Hello, honey, this is who I am, and I don't give a damn what you think about me. Take it or leave it!" she says. This sassy attitude, coupled with her down-home warmth, has made Katie a big favorite with men and women both. She wouldn't let anybody walk all over her, but she likes men, you can tell. You can always tell.

Of course, she's gotten real religious in recent years, all the big stars get religion at a certain point. In fact, that's Billy Jack Reems sitting up there at the table with her, he's the little one wearing the robe, they call him the spiritual leader of the stars.

It must be some kind of a press conference. Katie sits up on a stool, surrounded by regular reporters plus one prim, snippy virgin from the BBC, holding a microphone.

"What's the name of the album?" somebody asks.

"Shall We Gather at the River," *Katie says. "That's the name of an old hymn we used to sing in church up on Grassy Branch."*

"Is it going to be all religious songs?" somebody wants to know.

"Oh no, not at all," Katie says. "It's going to have lots of different kinds of songs on it as a matter of fact, all of them associated with my family—that's the Bailey family—down over the years.

"Well, 'Down by Grassy Branch' will be on it for sure"—Katie answers another question—"and 'Livin' on Love' and 'Melungeon Man.' R.C. Bailey wrote both of those, and they were big hits for the Grassy Branch Girls. We'll do 'White Linen,' which has always been one of my favorites. It's an old ballad that came into the family when my Grandaddy Durwood Bailey married Tampa Rainette in 1910.

"Yes, Tampa is coming! She really is! My cousin Little Virginia is bringing her and R.C., too. RCA is flying them all over here in a private plane. —Lord, I don't even know! About a hundred, I reckon. They're both bound to be pushing a hundred.

"And 'The Cuckoo Song,' it's another old ballad that goes way back—

"Yes, she is. Rose Annie is definitely coming too. They're releasing her from Brushy Mountain State Prison just to cut this album, that's one reason we're going to cut it live. —I don't know. I just don't know. I'd sure like to have 'Subdivision Wife' on here if she wants to sing it—

"No, I'm producing this one myself. Yes, that's right. I've formed my own company. This is Carole Bliss, my associate."

Heads turn toward Carole Bliss, a trim, dark-haired woman in a red business suit, but no flash bulbs pop.

Katie keeps answering questions. She's real patient with the reporters, she acts like she's got all the time in the world, but Carole Bliss keeps looking at her watch and rolling her eyes, like she's saying, "Oh, brother!" in her mind. Young RCA employees circle the scene, facilitating things. They are good at communicating and facilitating. You can tell them by their sculptured haircuts. Christmas carols float through the air. There are so many people crowded up to the porch to watch this interview that strolling hotel guests can hardly push past. A lot of them just stay, in fact, swelling the crowd.

"Any minute now," Katie says. "We're expecting them any minute."

When Katie Cocker answers a question she leans forward on her stool and speaks right to the one who asked it. She looks you dead in the eye. "That's a pretty complicated question for me to answer," she says now, slowly, to the woman from the BBC. "I have to admit, there was a time when all I wanted to do was get out of that valley. I was just dying to get away from home. What I didn't understand, all those years when I was waiting for my life to start, was that it had already started. I was already living it! Those were the most important years, and I didn't even know it. But I was real young then, and foolish, like we all are. I wanted to be somebody different, I wanted to be me, *and I thought that the way to do this was to put as much distance as possible between me and Grassy Branch. So I did that. And I took some chances, and I got knocked down flat a couple of times—I guess I'm Phi Beta Kappa at the School of Hard Knocks!—but I'd get right back up, and keep on going. I made a lot of mistakes. I thought I had to do it all by myself, see. It took me a long time to understand that not a one of us lives alone, outside of our family or our time, and that who we are depends on who we were, and who our people were. There's a lot of folks in this business that don't believe that, of course. They think you can just make yourself up as you go along. The trick is to keep on moving. But I can't do this. I come from a singing family, we go way back. I know where we're from. I know who we are. The hard part has been figuring out who I am, because I'm not like any of them, and yet they are bone of my bone. . . ."*

1

This World Is Not My Home

There once lived a fair maid named Kate Malone
You could not help but foller,
Fell in love with the preacher's son
Way down in Cold Spring Holler.

He said, "Put away your dancing shoes
If you would be my doney.
Leave your fiddle a-hangin on the wall
And cleave unto me only.

"Come lay with me on my bed of pain,
Come lay with me, my lady,
There's many a man to give you a ring,
But I'll give you salvation."

Soon Kate she lost her merry laugh,
She was like to lose her beauty
Tied back her hair of purest gold,
Bore three babes out of duty. . . .

1

Old Man Ira Keen

That the one you mean? Speak up. Well, that thar's "The Preacher's Son," and I'll play it plumb through fer you by and by, but first I'll tell ye how come I was to write it in the first place. A song don't just spring outer nowhere, ye know, hit'll grow in yer mind like a honeysuckle vine just a-wrappin itself around all the times and all the people and places that is yer life. Or that is how hit is fer me. A song will grow up in my mind unawares, and one day I'll just pick up this here dulcimore and hit'll be there whole and good, and springin to the tongue.

—Well then, I'll *sing* it, a course! And let me tell you one thing, there ain't nothin in the world to compare with the feeling that comes over you then, hit's like, Well, *this* is what happened, I see it all clear now, this is who done what, and who said what, and how it fell out in the end. Fer we go through this world with blinders on, just like that mule over yonder a-plowin in Navy Cale's newground.

Hit ain't often we are given to see.

Seems to me hit'll come to me in a song most likely, that is iffen hit comes atall, which mostly hit don't, a course. This life is a dark valley, hit's a vale of tears as the feller said, don't let nobody lie to you and try to tell you any different.

Now I know this to be a fact. Seems like I was borned knowing it, may be that is why I got along with them Baileys bettern most folks, even old Preacherman Bailey who was mean as a snake and twicet as fast, he'd come at you like lightning right in the middle of meeting, he'd grab you up and yell right in yer face. I've seed folks run outer the churchhouse just a-hollerin when he come towards em, hit was nearabout comical, but you daren't laugh, you know, nor smile, fer then he'd turn on *you*!

Big old face like a lantern he had, and a big black hat that he never took offen his head, and that hook fer a arm, it was the hook that scared folks the mostest, I reckon. He'd haul you up by your collar and say, "Ira? Ira? Air ye among the elected?" But you couldn't do nothing about it iffen you *wasn't* but wait fer a sign from the Lord. Hit weren't no use trying to lie about it neither, old Sid Bailey could smell a lie like the rest of us can smell a polecat. Hit weren't no use trying to say you hadn't done something you had done, neither, iffen he was churching you fer it. Lord, he used to church everbody when he was over here a-preaching. He'd church you fer running liquor or walking drunk or saying a bad word, or dancing, or fiddling, or shoeing yer horse on a Sunday. I weren't nothing but a shirttail boy back then when he was a-preaching, but I knowed bettern to lower my eyes not to fidget. I thought Sid Bailey was God Hisself then, and fer aught I know, he might of been.

He might of been.

Fer I haven't seed hide nor hair of Him since, I'll tell you that! Not in this here vale of tears.

But Sid Bailey was a hard man, and hit was a hard doctrine

he preached. His church was a church built betwixt a rock and a slick place.

"God don't need you," Sid Bailey used to say. "God will work His mysterious way whether or no." And God ain't necessarily *with* you, neither. As the feller said, you've got to walk that lonesome valley by yerself. You'll see temptation to the left of you and temptation to the right of you, but you've got to keep on a-going. This world is not yer home.

Now God might come down and give you a sign, or He might not. Hit don't depend on you. Hit depends on God. You ain't got a thing to do with it. You can pray till you're blue in the face, and do fer others till you're nearabout dead, but God don't give a damn. He is going to do whatever He takes a mind to. And iffen He does give you a sign, that is, a dream or a vision or such-like—well, old Price Warren that lives over there on the mountain, he swears he saw God come rolling at him outen a laurel slick in the form of a great hoop snake—well, then you can be baptized, you can join the church, *iffen* you could convince old Sid Bailey you was not telling a tale, that is. And then hit mought be, hit just *mought* be, mind you, that after you're dead and buried, and iffen Jesus Christ comes in the air like he's supposed to on Resurrection Day, and *iffen* he calls out yer name, why then you can rise up outer the dirt and fly straight up to Heaven like a jaybird.

Hit's a long shot, ain't it?

But that is what Sid Bailey preached, and what he believed, and all them hard-shell Baptists down at Bee church believe it to this day, you just go down there and ax them. Hit ain't no different today, nor will hit be no different tomorrow, for they is some folks that wants a doctrine they can't live with, that's a fact. Human beings is nothing if not contrary. They don't want nothing easy, and this is hard, hard.

But I can kindly see it, in a way, even iffen I never could

hold to it too good myself. What I figger is, any God worth His salt is not going to have no truck with me, nohow.

Well, hit was in the year 1833 or 1834, as I figger it, that Moses Bailey, now that's old Sid's least son, brung young Kate Malone over here to live in that little cabin right down there in Cold Spring Holler. *Hell* yes, that's what I'm a-telling you, right down this here hill and acrost Paint Creek yonder, and back in that little bitty cove. You could see the cabin right from this porch where we're a-sitting, iffen it weren't fer them cedar trees that has growed up so high over there. That cabin is hanted now, make no mistake about it. Won't nobody venture near it on a bet. I wouldn't go over there fer nothing. You stay round here long enough, you'll hear the music when it comes true dark. —*Fiddle* music, a course, what I wrote the song about. Hit don't happen ever night, mind, but when it does, Lord amercy! Hit's the sweetest, awfullest sound you ever heard in all yer life.

I used to could see that cabin real clear, as I was a-telling you, I used to could see pretty Kate out there of a morning with a baby on her knee, playing "This is the way the lady rides," or long towards noon, a-churning. She'd be barefoot with her yeller hair all over her head, a-churning and singing to beat the band, *"Hush, little baby, don't say a word, Pappy's gonna get you a talkin bird. And if that talkin bird don't sing, Pappy's gonna get you a diamond ring."*

—Well now, I'm a-getting to it. I'm getting to it. Anything worth hearing is worth waiting to hear, as the feller says. Why don't you go in there and reach yer hand behind the woodbox and bring me out that pint bottle of tonic I've got in there? You can get yerself some of it, I reckon, iffen you can search up something to put it in. Hit's a mess in there, ain't it? My widder sister, she set her mind on coming over here to keep house fer me after old Piney died, but I done run her off. "I don't need yer fooling around here," says I, "nor yer infernal messing, you go on," says I, "and leave me alone in my mind. I ain't worried with a mess in the kitchen," I says. "I ain't studying the here and now." In fact if you was to ax me what I et fer dinner yestiddy, I'd be hard-pressed to answer ye. Yet when I think on Kate Malone, the years slide away like a pretty lady letting her dressing gown fall to the floor, and I see her ever clear in my mind's eye, and ever young as she was then.

I loved her, a course.

But hit was a love as pure as the driven snow, with never a hope of *having*, and all the sweeter fer it.

Kate Malone was fifteen, may be sixteen, when Moses Bailey married her and brung her over there to Cold Spring Holler to live. Sid Bailey had died preaching at a brush-arbor meeting over in Madison County, the old lady had died previous, and the younguns had scattered every whichway.

I was twelve years old, a-living right here on Crow Hill with my mamma and my daddy, they was Hazel and Jesse Keen, and three sisters, and my daddy's Uncle Gabe, and my brother that weren't quite right, Dummy, he allus lived on the place here, first with Mamma and Daddy and then with me and Piney, until he died. Dummy was *sweet*, ye know, but he couldn't hold nothing in his mind. Never did work, *couldn't* work, used to sit right over there in that little rocking chair and whistle. Whistled like a bird.

Pour me a leetle bit more of that, if you will. Jest a sweetener.

The first time I saw Kate I thought to myself, Now that is the prettiest gal I will ever lay eyes on in my life, and it remains so to this day. Fer we had seed her daddy's wagon come, and trunks and general bustlement, and now smoke was a-rising outen the chimbley again. So I says to myself, "Well, I'll go. I'll go on over there, and see what they is to see."

I recollect hit was October. The sky was as blue as Mamma's Dutch plate, and red and yeller leaves was a-blowing crazy. Kate set out on the porch in a little rocker, wearing a green dress and a brown shawl, with a cameo pin at her neck, a-playing with a baby doll that she had brung with her from home, and singing, "*Go to sleep, little baby, fore the booger-man gets you! When you wake, you'll have a piece of cake, and all the pretty little horses.*" She was rocking the baby doll. Her hair fell down past her shoulders, all gold and merry-wild. Her eyes was big and wide apart and gray, the softest gray, like kitten fur. Her lips they was full and pouty and cherry red. She kept right on singing.

"Air you a girl or a missus?" I axed her finally, and she liked to died laughing.

Then, "I am the missus here," she said. "I married Moses Bailey."

"Morning," another voice said then, and outen the cabin door stepped Moses Bailey. Well, he *was* handsome, I'll grant him that, curly black hair and blue eyes and well set up, a stout strapping young man. He come out on the porch and I said who I was, Ira Keen from over on Crow Hill, and he made some manners, but I could tell he weren't studying me atall in that moment. His eyes never left her face. He had eyes kindly like his daddy, sharp as the point of a knife. Kate sung on, a-rocking.

"Hit won't be long and I'll give you a baby doll sure enough," Moses said, and Kate laughed her merry laugh at him, but it was true.

Come next August, they had them a little baby girl, and Kate thought the world of her. She thought the sun rose and set on that child, which was all to the good since by then hit was clear that everything was not sweetness and light in that cabin in Cold Spring Holler.

Fer Moses was one of them that will not be satisfied, one of them that is always hankering after something that is just around the next bend. He couldn't never settle down, seemed like. He'd farm a leetle bit, but not serious like, not enough to do no good, and then he'd be running a raft of logs down the Mononagh fer somebody, or trading some horses fer somebody else. But most times he was off at a preaching someplace, or traipsing the woods alone. See, Moses wanted to make a preacher the worst in the world, just like his daddy had done. But God wouldn't give him no sign. So Moses, he kept on a-looking fer one. He used to go to meetings all around, and offer up the prayer. Other times he'd go off in the woods by hisself, hankering after his sign.

Kate and the children was jest living hand to mouth whilst he was gone. For they'd been two more babes since that first one, which was Mary Magdaleen, they was now Jeremiah and little Ezekiel besides. It like to worried my mamma to death, I couldn't count you the number of times she sent me over there with a turn of meal, or a sack of taters, fer Kate and them little children.

One time when I was carrying them a mess of beans, I axed Kate pint-blank, I said, "Whar is yer old man, anyway?"

And Kate jest smiled her sunny smile, a-taking the cookpot from me, and said, "Well, Ira, he is off wrassling with the angel."

Come to find out this was the truth, and the whole truth, of it. Now iffen hit's a woman yer old man is gone off after, at least you've got a shape to set yerself up against, and somebody to get mad at.

But iffen hit's God, well, yer hands is plumb tied, ain't they?

Pretty Kate was stymied fer sure. And Moses being as muleheaded as ever his daddy was, he wouldn't give it up fer nothing. The more God denied him a sign, the more determined

Moses was to git one. He figgered that the more he prayed, and run the woods a-looking, the more likely he was to find his sign. Moses went from being a big husky feller to a scarecrow, and the bones in his face stuck out in a way that called old Sid to mind.

But Moses had got to where nobody could beat him a-praying, that's fer damn sure, he give out the prayer in meeting oncet a month, which is however often they helt it then, and he prayed everbody else under the table. That leetle old mealy-mouth circuit rider that was a-coming over here then, that leetle Mister Graves I think it was, could not hold a candle to Moses Bailey. He had a voice like the Bible, Moses had.

Why, we could hear him plumb over here sometimes of a evening, iffen the wind was right, praying over their supper till you know hit had growed stone cold.

Now hit would of been hard on anybody, a course, to have their old man git turned thataway, but hit was particular hard on Kate Malone. Fer she was nought but a gal, and she had come from the fun-lovingest family you ever seed. They lived on the other side of Lone Bald Mountain there, at Cana. As Kate was the only gal left at home, they all doted on her, and waited on her hand and foot. She was not raised to bear the life that she fell into, Kate was not. Her daddy, Pink Malone, was the bestest fiddler around those parts, and every one of them boys fiddled, too. Hit was always music and laughing and frolics over at Cana. They'd run a set at the drop of a hat, they'd still be a-dancing when the sun come up. So you couldn't of found two families more different-like than the Baileys and the Malones.

Moses didn't make no bones about it. When he axed old Pink fer to marry Kate, he said right out that they was to be no music at the wedding. Then Pink looked over at Kate, and she cried and said, "Oh please, Daddy, this is the man I want with all my heart," so they wasn't nothing that Pink could say or do to stop them. They was married indeed, though it is said that Kate's mamma took to her bed the day of the wedding, she was that upset about it, and hit is further said that all Kate's brothers fell on the ground a-crying when Moses took her away.

Moses wouldn't hardly let her go back over there to visit, neither. He said that the Devil walked in that house, and that fiddle music was the voice of the Devil laughing.

Well, time passed and I growed up to be about as sorry and wild as any young buck in the county, but when it come to Missus Kate Malone, I would of laid down at her feet and died if she'd of axed me to. I was keeping company with first one gal and then the other, but couldn't none of them lay a glove on Kate Malone, to my way of thinking. Sometimes I'd get all hot and bothered thinking about her over there in that holler, and how Moses Bailey done her, and one day I determined to speak up about it. I believe I must of been about eighteen year old at the time, so ye can reckon about how much *I* knowed! Kate, she would of been in her early twenties by then, and she was already losing her bloom like so many gals does around here, wore out by work and children. I swear, hit's a sight what all a woman puts up with. I tell you this *now*, but I never give it a thought back then when I was as heedless and unthoughtless as any critter in the forest, back when hit might of done somebody some good.

No, Kate was not as pretty as she was when she come over the mountain from her daddy's house at Cana, but she did not appear to have lost all her spirit, neither, despite of her sad lot. "Do ye reckon Kate *knows* that she is ill used?" I mused to myself, a-crossing Paint Creek on my horse. For iffen a body don't know something, hit won't worry them atall, a course. Hit's knowledge that is the root of all evil, as the feller said.

Hit was late November when I rode over there this time.

Daddy and me had killed two hogs three or four days previous. I was taking Kate some hog meat and cracklings. That was jest my *excuse*, don't ye know. Fer I had determined to see how things set with her. I had been sparking a girl over at Hanging Rock, and somehow I felt I could not do no real business over there afore I ascertained the state of things with Kate.

From the creek I seed smoke rising, and when I rode into the Baileys' clearing I seed Kate herself out there in a man's black coat a-stirring something in a big black kettle over the cookfire.

"Ira!" she said. She *allus* said my name like she was glad to see me. "I am just stirring up some apple butter," she said, "Hitch and light," she said. "Hit is nearabout done, and I will send some home to yer mamma, who has been so kind to me. How is yer mamma?" she said, and I said that Mamma was tolerable, all the time studying Kate real close-like. Her cheeks was red from the heat of the fire, and her hair had tumbled down. She kept it tied back all the time. She tried to put it back now, but she couldn't afford to quit stirring the apple butter.

"Jest set down and wait a minute," she said, and I hunkered down right where I was and smoked a cigarette.

I looked around good. Hit struck me how lonesome the cabin was, set back in the cedar trees thataway, despite her children a-playing all around the steps. Hit was kindly dark back in there, and the cold wind come a-blowing through them cedar trees with a sighing sound, a crying sound, real mournful-like. The feel of the forest was all around. With the leaves offen the trees, you could see how close the mountain rose up there behind the cabin, and how rocky and mean it looked. Now that is Lone Bald Mountain, ye see it over there, hit is not a pretty mountain, neither. They is a cropping-out of rocks yonder, right afore ye reach the bald where the ravens stay, and hit used to be in them days that bears was frequent on Lone Bald, too. Kate's cabin was mighty close to the mountain, to my mind, and mighty far removed from the rest of usuns living around here.

"Jeremiah! Get me some water, honey!" Kate said, and the eldest boy run up to the spring with the bucket. They loved their mamma. You could jest tell it, and they was never any back talk nor squabbling amongst them. Them and Kate was all kids together, hit appeared.

Jeremiah come back with the bucket, and Kate doused the fire. She licked the end of the sassafras stick she was stirring the apple butter with, and grinned at me. My heart liked to leap outen my chest. "This'll eat real good," she said, "come on over here and try it," and I rose up like I was in a dream and went over there where she was. I felt like my legs was lead, but my heart was a-beating double time, and she helt out the stick and giggled, and I licked the apple butter offen it, and then I dipped the stick down and helt it fer her whilst she licked it. It was real hot and real sweet. It burned my tongue. I looked at Kate in the old black coat, and I looked at her raggedy younguns barefoot despite of the cold, and I listened to the wind a-moaning and a-sighing through them cedar trees, and a resolve took aholt of me.

"Kate Bailey," I says, "how come you to stay over here this-away when yer man ain't never home? You ought to have better," says I, all hot in the face, and to her credit, Kate did not laugh at me.

"Why, Ira Keen!" she says. "Why, Ira." And fer just a minute she laid her hand upside of my face. Fer just a minute she stopped stock-still and stared straight in my eyes. We stayed like that fer a while. The cold wind blowed her hair around.

Then, "Moses needs me," she says, real soft-like. "He needs me so much," she says. Now I didn't know nothing about that then, being nought but eighteen, but I do now. For need is the powerfullest tie that they is, it seems to me now, fer a woman in particular.

But at the time Kate said it, it fair broke my heart. I reckon I got on my horse someway, and made it back acrost Paint Creek someway, but whether I carried Mamma any of that apple butter or not, I couldn't tell ye. I do know I got knee-walking drunk that night out in the smokehouse, where Pappy thought he had hid his liquor so good, and Pappy whupped me fer it. To tell you the truth, I didn't keer iffen he whupped me or not. I *wanted* him to whup me, iffen I couldn't have Kate Malone. My heart was broke fer sure.

Now this was what? Sixty, seventy year ago? And yet I can see her still a-standing by that cookfire in the wind, her skirts and her hair a-blowing, giving me that sassafras stick to lick. I see her rosy cheeks. And yet hit weren't long after that that I taken Piney Wilfong down to Bee fer somebody's wedding, and the axle broke and the horse run off, and there we was, out all night long, and hit was said I ought to marry her to make it right. Which I done. And brung her up here, and she was as good as gold to Dummy, and give me nine children to boot. Which is all gone now, finely and fectually. Two boys dead in the war and two more I have done lost track of, and another boy and four gals that lives here and there. They bring their younguns up here to see me infrequent. I ain't got no use fer younguns. And Piney dead in the ground these twenty year. It seems to me a quare thing that I lived with that old woman nearabout fifty year—and she was a *good* wife, mind ye—and yet I cannot now recall her face, fer the life of me! Not the way I recall Kate Malone the day she made the apple butter when we was young.

Anyway, I had done been caught and trussed by Piney when all the trouble started up over there in Cold Spring Holler. Hit commenced when Kate's ma took sick at Cana and they sent fer Kate, so Moses Bailey *had* to let her go. She taken Jeremiah with her, leaving Mary Magdaleen to watch little Zeke and do fer their daddy, who prayed over them out in the yard afore they left, riding on two white mules. Well, hit was two days a-riding over Lone Bald Mountain in those days, and when they got there, come to find out that Kate's mamma had took a up-turn. So Kate and her mamma just fell on each other's necks a-crying, it is said, and they was muching over Jeremiah, that they had not seed since he was a babe. So Kate and Jeremiah stayed on a few days to visit.

And one night Jeremiah noted a fiddle hanging on the wall and said, "Grandaddy, what is that?" and Pink took it down and played it fer him. And Jeremiah fair loved it! He took to the fiddle like a duck to water, and when they got back home, hit was the first thing he told his daddy about the trip.

"Now you hark me," Moses said, his voice deep and terrible. "The fiddle is a instrument of the Devil, and iffen you ever take it up you will have to leave home. Fer you won't be my boy no more, you'll be the Devil's boy." And then he put both hands on Jeremiah's head and prayed on him.

So that was the end of that, until the follering summer, when Kate's mamma took sick again, and this time Moses was off a-running a raft of logs down the Monongah River fer a feller, so Kate just up and lit a rag fer home without so much as a by-your-leave to Moses, and got there just in time to see her mamma buried.

Now I don't know but what this might of made Kate kindly reckless, fer when Jeremiah axed fer the fiddle again, Kate allowed it, and she allowed Pink to play it fer him. And then it is said that Kate herself took her own little fiddle down from the wall where it had been hanging ever since she went off to Cold Spring Holler. She took it out on the porch of her daddy's fine big cabin over at Cana, and set out there all night long a-fiddling. Everything she had ever knowed come back to her—"Barbry Allen," "Cripple Creek," "Shady Grove," "The Devil's Dream," "I gave my love a cherry that had no stone"—Jeremiah, he couldn't get over his mamma a-playing thataway. But come morning, she put her little fiddle back up on the wall and busted out a-crying.

"I tell you what," old Pink Malone says to Kate when they are saddled up to leave, "honey, you take this fiddle, it is yourn, on home with you, wrapped up in these here gunny sacks, and you teach the boy to play whenever his daddy is away. The boy has got a ear fer it," Pink said. "Besides, hit's a sin to put your talent under a bushel," Pink said. You know a feller can quote Scripture to make it come out however suits him.

Well, Kate she looked at the fiddle, and she looked at Jeremiah's face, and she looked at the fiddle again, and her whole heart was filled with longing. So she taken the fiddle.

And from then on, every time Moses was away, why we could hear them out there making music on the porch. Even the littlun was learning, that leetle Zeke. And Mary had the sweetest high thin voice. *"Down in the valley, valley so low,"* she'd sing, *"hang yer head over, hear the wind blow."* They didn't have no way of knowing how good the sound carried up here, I reckon, since they hadn't hardly ever ventured offen that place.

Well, hit used to give Mamma the all-overs and Piney, too, that singing. "No good will come of this," Mamma said. But Dummy loved it. He used to tap his foot and pat his knee in time.

Winter come, and we didn't hear no fiddling, and then spring come, with a big early thaw. Now Moses' garden never done much, and the previous summer wasn't no exception. So by spring they was about out of everything that Kate had put by to eat, they was living on apples and taters, so Moses he resolved to run a raft of logs down the river fer old man Higgins, and get him some cash money. Hit was a lot more water around here then. The Monongah was a big mighty river in them days.

"Hit might take me longern usual to get back up here," Moses warned Kate. "I might have trouble crossing them little streams on the way back, fer some of them is all swole up now and busting over their banks. I'll be aiming fer about six days," Moses says. So then he kissed her, and set out afore the sunrise.

Well, that day, don't ye know, Kate and Jeremiah took the fiddle outen the hidey-hole in the corncrib where they'd been a-keeping it, and tuned it up, and that night they set out on the porch a-fiddling and a-singing. They sung and sung. They sung the moon up.

They didn't have no way of knowing that Moses' raft had broke into smithereens right soon after he set out, when he come to a big curve with some sharp rocks over to the left of it, that he was aware of, but this year the Monongah was so high Moses couldn't get his bearings. So he run right smack into them rocks and the raft busted all to pieces, throwing Moses into the river and the logs ever whichaway. Moses was lucky not to drown. In point of fact he liked to of drowned, but he managed to cling onto one of the logs fer dear life, and come around. He stopped at a house to dry hisself, and set out walking fer home.

Now who knows what Moses was a-thinking on that long dark walk home? Fer his pretty wife and his children had nothing but taters to eat, and he was coming home with nothing in his pockets, and it must have seemed to him that God, who Moses had been looking fer all his days, was just a-mocking him. God had flung him in the river and left him fer dead.

Is hit a sign? He must have wondered. *Is hit a test?* So Moses was a-walking through the dark dripping trees alongside of Paint Creek, and pondering on God and His ways, when all of a sudden he heerd the Devil's laughter on the wind.

Now what hit was, a course, was his own wife Kate, a-fiddling a frolic tune and singing, "*Good-bye, girls, I'm goin to Boston, ear-lye in the morning.*"

Moses hastened on.

And when he come to the edge of the clearing he could see them as good as anything, in the light of the risen moon. They didn't even need no lantern. Hit was Kate with Mary Magdaleen and Jeremiah gathered round her. Little Zeke had fell asleep on a pallet at her feet.

Then Kate handed Jeremiah the fiddle.

"*Saddle up, girls, and let's go with em, saddle up, girls, and let's go with em.*" Jeremiah had a fine, light touch.

Now who knows what went on in Moses' head whilst he stood there a-listening? Who can say what drives a man to do the things he does? Fer what Moses done was awful. He come busting outen them woods like God Hisself, a-hollering, snatched that fiddle and broke it over the front porch rail, then beat all of them, Jeremiah and Ezekiel and Mary and Kate, too, until the children run off in the woods to get away from him. At the last, he throwed hisself down on the floor and cried like a baby the rest of the whole night long, or so Kate told it to Mamma, who went over there the next day and larned the whole sorry story.

One side of Kate's pretty face was black and blue, and her eye was swole shut. But Moses was the one in torment, Mamma said, gnashing his teeth over what he had done, and moaning deep moans, and a-praying out loud to God. Kate never left his side, Mamma said, nor took a thought fer herself, and it appeared to Mamma that Kate loved Moses more than ever, despite of what he done. She said Kate's face gave off a light that calmed all who come around her that day, and so before long, Moses hisself calmed down, and Mary and Zeke come back and Moses kissed them, and then Mamma come on home. Hit fair broke my heart to hear what she had to say.

But Jeremiah never come back home.

One, two days passed.

"He was right there with us," Mary and Zeke said. "We was all together in the woods," they said. But he never come back home. Moses felt awful about it, fer Jeremiah was his eldest son, and if the truth be told, his favorite.

And then Kate remembered how Moses had told Jeremiah he'd have to leave iffen he ever took up the fiddle, and they determined that Jeremiah must of gone over Lone Bald Mountain by hisself to stay with Kate's family at Cana.

So Moses saddled up his horse and went over there to get Jeremiah and bring him back. But when he got halfway up the mountain, Moses seen all these ravens around the rock cave, wheeling and dipping in the sky. He rode over there to take a look. And sure enough it was his own son Jeremiah, two days dead, having fell down the rocky clift in the dark a-trying to get to Cana. And the ravens had et out his eyes.

Well, a course Moses put his son's body acrost his saddle and brung him back, and we buried him there under the cedar trees, for Kate would not let us taken him back up the mountain where the Bailey burying ground lays. "I want him home," Kate said. She said it real calm, too calm, and her eyes was too big in her head. But everything was done as she desired. And then she appeared to go on as usual, cooking and churning and gathering eggs and such-like, and speaking reasonable to all the neighbor folks that come by bringing this or that to help out. Kate never said nothing about Jeremiah whose grave you could see from the porch, nor yet about Moses who had gone off again, wandering the mountains, it is said, praying out loud and mournful at all hours of the day and night. Some said they had seed him down on the Monongah, or over at White Oak, or at Bee. Two fellers swore they heerd Moses a-praying as they rode through Flat Gap going toward Sisterville, but they couldn't roust him outen the forest.

Well, time passed, and hit was full summer, and finally Moses come on back home. But he come home only to die. We reckoned hit was the pneumonia, fer he laid there thin as a rail with a rattle in his chest and coughed hisself to death. But whenever he weren't coughing, Moses continued to pray aloud.

I questioned Kate on this.

"Oh no, he has not lost his faith," Kate said, bright as a new penny. "He has bent hisself to the rule of God, which we cannot hope to fathom," she said. "He hopes he may hold out faithful to the end."

Now as you might imagine, word got out, and folks come from all around to hear Moses pray and to see him thataway, and they was some several folks converted on the spot. But they wasn't nobody present excepting Kate when Moses coughed his last and died. Or as Piney used to say, "when he crossed over to the other side." Piney was a good old woman. I wish I had loved her better, I wish I hadn't give her such a time. I reckon she's on the other side now, old Piney is, iffen they is one. I don't reckon I'll be joining her over there, neither. I tell ye, I hold with old Sid Bailey on that, "Ye've got to walk that lonesome valley by yerself," and I ain't looking fer company.

Now I'll admit to ye, I might of had some idea of going around Cold Spring Holler and seeing what all I could do fer Kate after Moses died, but the pure fact was that Kate died too, finely and factually, when Moses went. The Kate that I had knowed and loved, I mean, that Kate so merry and spiritous, that sung on the porch whilst she churned, and danced with her babes in the yard.

Kate Malone went plumb outen her head then, hit is sad to say.

You couldn't get her to speak a word of sense, she was so busy a-talking with them people in her mind, Moses and Jeremiah and Lord knows who else, and singing little bitty snatches of songs. Sometimes she'd wrap up her head in a shawl, and say the ravens was after her. Sometimes she'd be laughing and laughing. Sometimes she'd shush you, and say the ravens was a-whispering in her ear. Well, hit weren't long afore they come over here from Cana, some of her daddy's people, and taken her children away. Seemed like she didn't hardly miss em, neither. Now they tried to take Kate, too, but she refused to go. She would not leave that cabin.

I seen Kate one more time afore she died. She'd been a-living all alone fer a year or more, and hit was summer again, jest about dusk, when I walked over there.

Kate set on the porch in her rocking chair where I had seed her so many times, rocking and singing just like she used to, *"Go to sleep, little baby, fore the booger-man gets you! When you wake, you'll have a piece of cake, and all the pretty little horses."* Her hair had gone plumb white, but her voice was as sweet as ever. She looked real peaceful.

"Kate," I says. "Hit's Ira."

"A black and a bay and a dapple and a gray," she sung.

"Kate Malone!" I says.

"So go to sleep, little baby," Kate sung, and I seed hit was hopeless. I don't think she even knowed me. I left her there whilst the lightning bugs was a-rising from the tall grass that had growed up all around the cabin, and a leetle wind was a-singing through the cedar trees. I thought I heerd a whisper in the breeze. And when I looked back at the cabin from the

edge of the forest, I couldn't even see Kate there on the porch, I couldn't do nought but hear her, a-singing in the dark.

I believe I will take a leetle more of that there. Jest a drop, iffen ye don't mind.—What'd *I* do? Well, I'll tell ye.

I left there that night with my heart like to busting, fer a young man is a sorry wild thing, truth to tell, he don't even know what he wants, but he wants it so bad hit is like to kill him all the time. Nor did I go home to that good wife of mine. No, I walked down the creek past Bee to Reece Stiltner bottom, where a woman I knowed named Becky Trent lived, and she was glad to see me. She was allus glad to see me. But she weren't nothing like Kate Malone.

That's why hit don't bother me none to stay up here the way I do now, hit don't bother me having that hanted cabin acrost the way there. Hell, that fiddle music don't even bother me, most times. Now I won't go over there, mind ye, on a bet, but I kindly like to hear that music. Most times hit'll start up about now, jest about dark, and iffen hit's a dance tune, why sometimes I'll lean my head back and close these old eyes and listen, and them times hit'll seem like I can fair see us, Kate and me together as we never was in life, a-waltzing in the dark.

2

Ezekiel Bailey

Small wonder, then, that Zeke grew up so muley-hawed and closemouthed, a big boy with a face as fair and blank as the full moon. It wasn't that he was obstinate or contrary. It was simply that he had nothing to say. And he could sit still for hours, and not do a blessed thing. It was unnatural. Everybody said so. Zeke was passed around his mamma's family at Cana like a hot potato, staying with first these cousins, then those cousins, then his lonely old Great-aunt Edith over at Honey Camp, but nobody would keep him long, not even Edith. They'd make some excuse and pass him on.

For the pure fact was, Zeke spooked them. He spooked them all. They were not used to a big old boy that wouldn't say a word. It made them feel bad, like they ought to do something about him, but they couldn't think what. For he wouldn't work, he wouldn't play, he didn't even want to shoot a gun! Finally they got tired of thinking up things for him to do. Finally they grew to hate the very sight of him sitting hunched on the floor thataway, staring into the fire. Ain't nothing to see, in a fire.

And they couldn't stand the way he kept his head cocked like a robin all the time either, like he was listening out for something. For what? It wasn't natural.

Finally Zeke ended up living with his Aunt Dot, his mother's older sister, and her husband, Clovis Kincaid, and their eleven children in that tumbledown place at Frog Level, out from Cana. Zeke had never seen so many kids. All of them all the time laughing and crying and fighting, snot-nosed and gap-toothed, running, running here and there. They all looked alike, fair and tow-headed, just like Zeke. He fit right in, or appeared to. So he liked it there.

It was loud and rough over at Frog Level, and sometimes the boys ganged up on him, and sometimes there was not enough food to go around at supper, but Zeke liked it fine over there. Nobody paid him any mind. They'd say, "Go down there and get the cow," or "Watch this littlun, honey," or "Chop me some wood now." They did not say, "What air ye a-thinking, honey?" or "What air ye a-listening out fer?" like his Great-aunt Edith used to. They never asked him any questions at all. Which was a good thing.

For even as a child, Zeke had sense enough not to tell anybody about the voices in his head, or that other sound he always heard, like wind through a cave. The only way Zeke knew to shut off that sound was to sit still. Real still.

But then they sent him over to Frog Level, where the Kincaids drowned it out. So Zeke could relax a little bit now. He could grow up some. He could shoot marbles with his cousin Tom or get in a wrestling match with Dan or play house with Jane and Pansy or hidey-go-seek in the woods until it got too dark to see, and then he could fall on the bed tick exhausted, and sleep in a smelly pile of boys. Girls in the front room, boys in the back room, Aunt Dot and Uncle Clovis in the middle room with the babies, kitchen just a jerry-built leanto against the side of the house. Sometimes Dot would kiss you and sometimes she'd slap you. She was a good cook, who grew fatter and sassier as the years wore on.

And Dot was a Malone through and through when it came to singing, with a high nasal voice that sent a chill up and down Zeke's backbone. After supper she'd rare back and close her eyes and set to singing by the fire or on the porch, depending on the season, and the children that wanted to would join in while Clovis sat with his arms folded and his mouth in a line and did not sing, but didn't leave either. Clovis seemed to enjoy the singing, but you never could tell about him, famous for silence. Cousin Willie or Uncle Cornelius came by sometimes with their fiddles. Dan was taking up the fiddle too, but Zeke refused to learn it, and when he said *no* to Cousin Willie's offer, his other cousins all stopped dead in their tracks and looked at each other, and Willie never asked him again.

But Zeke liked music and he liked to sing, *"Oh get around, Jenny, get around, oh get around I say,"* while Cousin Willie bit his lip and perspired and the fiddles went faster and faster, *"Oh get around, Jenny, get around, long summer day."* Zeke would spin in the yard like a whirligig, faster and faster and faster until all the world was a green blur that looked like the sound in his head. When he finally fell to ground, his head would be completely clear, like the summer sky with no cloud in sight.

Sometimes, right then, he could remember his mother. He remembered her gray eyes and her clear voice and how she smoothed the hair back from his forehead when he ran in from the yard and grabbed her skirts. He remembered her saying "Now I lay me down to sleep" at night.

But most times he could not remember his mother, so that when Great-aunt Edith told him she was dead, that first summer they took him away from her, it meant nothing, nothing to him at all. He just looked up at Great-aunt Edith, whose chins started quivering like jelly when she told him, before she started to cry. Then Edith stood there on the porch staring at the boy for the longest time. Then she flung her apron up over her face and ran back in the cabin crying. Zeke stood right where he was and did not think about her, or about his mother, or about anything. It was hot on the porch. Red roses bloomed, climbing up over the porch rail of Edith's cabin at Honey Camp.

Later that day, Edith gave him a special marble, a steelie, which was exactly the kind Zeke had always wanted, and how did she know that? How could she possibly know? "Where did this come from?" he asked, holding it, and Edith said it had belonged to a dead boy. Then she started up crying again. Later she put on her bonnet and walked him down to the store and got him some horehound candy.

Zeke kept the steelie in his pocket always, and sometimes he'd roll it around and around in his fingers, and no one knew. He never traded it, or shot with it, or even took it out of his pocket. The only person he showed it to was his big cousin Tom, his favorite.

Ezekiel himself would grow up after all, or if he did not grow up exactly, he would at least change from a too solemn child to a too solemn young man. He would stay on at Frog Level, working the hard rock ground with Clovis, who was a man that did not talk to women and children and never appeared to notice Ezekiel at all, so that Zeke wondered at first if his uncle even knew he was present in the house. Until it came time to clear the field that first year, that is. Then his uncle let on that he knew it, all right. For Zeke was a large, strong lad, and Clovis aimed to make him earn his keep.

Zeke did not mind working, truth to tell. He was never much for school, where he sat like a bump on a log and refused to recite. Zeke would bite his lip and stare through the open schoolhouse door at the mountains while Mr. Green caned him unmercifully, until Zeke's face grew fiery red, and Pansy started crying. "Is this yet enough, Ezekiel?" Mr. Green would gasp, the slick yellow strands of his oily hair stuck to his head with perspiration. Mr. Green was a slight young fellow with pale skin, spectacles, and a constant cough. It was harder for him to beat Ezekiel than it was for Ezekiel to take the beating.

Both Zeke and Mr. Green were relieved when Clovis sent word that he'd need the boys, that it was time to clear the fields for planting. And Zeke loved it out there on the long hillside that rose gradually above Frog Level to the steeper incline of Cherokee Mountain; he loved the feel and smell of the dirt on his hands as they grabbled out the rocks, the ghosty look of the bare trees in the morning fog, the faint pink mist of the first redbud, then the purple sarvis, then the white blur of dogwood as spring came on and the birds showed up and the woods grew green again. One famous day when he was twelve, Zeke put himself in harness with Buck, the mule, when they couldn't for the life of them pull a particularly recalcitrant stump out of the stony newground they were clearing. Zeke strained forward as hard as ever he could. The other kids pushed on the back of the stump. Tom beat the mule. Finally, with a long, wrenching, sucking sound, the stump pulled free, spewing pebbles everyplace, and lay upended there on the hill for days, looking for all the world like a witchhead with big spiky root-hairs sticking out.

Then came the day when they burned it, and all the other brush besides, in a great wildfire on the hillside that caused Zeke's heart to beat so fast. He loved the acrid smell of the woodsmoke and the way it looked disappearing into the cloudy sky; he stayed up there on the hill all night long and watched the fire burn itself out, and then worked all the next day too with the rest of them, and never missed the sleep.

Later, Zeke was the one that walked behind Buck holding the bull-tongued plow to a furrow as straight as any man's, so that Clovis, watching him, hit upon the notion of renting Zeke out to whoever needed him in the field. Clovis told Zeke that he would not have to go back to school. Zeke liked this idea fine.

So Zeke settles into his life. He gets up in the morning and eats his Aunt Dot's good biscuits and her red-eye gravy, he walks to work, he works, he talks some to the people he's working for, he walks back to Frog Level, he eats, he sleeps. He gives the money he makes to his Uncle Clovis, who gives him back some. Zeke doesn't need much. It has not occurred to him to ask for more. It has not occurred to him to do anything else, or to go anyplace else. He wears overalls, brogans, and a plaid shirt, winter and summer. He fucks a widder woman over at Cana that he works for regular, it seems to be part of his job. She cuts his hair for him too. And be loves to dance. He is known for it. On Saturday nights he'll go anywhere, travel any distance to find a dance, and he'll dance as long as anybody will fiddle. He'll dance all night if he can.

At these dances he treats all the girls in the same courtly, old-fashioned manner, even the girls that are known to go back of the barn with you, the girls Tom has told him about. Ezekiel is a serious, dedicated, trancelike dancer. Sometimes a girl will start to look at him in another way, but usually this does not last long, for there is something in his face—or there is a *lack* of something in his face—that puts them off. They stop flirting. Oh, they like Ezekiel fine, they'll tease him and dance with him, but it isn't serious flirting. They wouldn't walk with him on Sunday if he asked them, which he does not. They don't treat Ezekiel like a man, somehow.

Sometimes Ezekiel goes with his uncles if they are running

a set someplace away from here, at Sisterville or Little Africa or Ash Holler or even as far away as Holly Grove. One time, at a dance over in Sistersville, a pretty woman comes up to Zeke and grabs him away from his partner, grabs him off the floor. She is slight, with curly flyaway hair. She wears a frilly red dress with puff sleeves. She pulls him away from the dancing.

"Zekey?" she says. "Zekey?"

The fiddles saw away, the air is close in there, and Zeke wipes sweat off his face and looks at her. There is something about her.

"Zekey, is it you?" she says.

Zeke keeps looking at her, but he can't think what to say. While he watches, her big eyes fill with tears. Then she puts her hand up to her mouth and pushes past him roughly, through the throng of people, out the door. Zeke follows after her. He makes it to the door just in time to see her start off into the night hanging on the arm of the big feller who is waiting for her there.

"Mary!" Zeke calls out, his voice rusty and odd, so that everybody out there stops drinking and smoking and talking, and turns to look at the enormous boy silhouetted by the light pouring out of the dance-hall door. His hair glows fiery pale, like bright angel hair, in that light.

But Mary Magdaleen and the man she is with have already disappeared into the darkness beyond the dance; all you can see of them is the glow of the man's cigarette in the dark, and it is his voice that calls back to Zeke from wherever they are going to, "Sorry, buddy," as if there has been some mistake.

Ezekiel will not see Mary again. A restless, wild girl, she will move eventually from Sistersville to Knoxville, where she will get in trouble.

And Zeke, standing in the doorway, has already forgotten her, her very name *Mary* drowned out by the sound in his head. He goes down the steps and buys some liquor from a man. After the dance is over, he goes with his cousins Willie and Tom to a whorehouse in Sistersville, where a girl takes off her clothes slow for him, stopping at the black garter belt and stockings. Zeke has never seen such a contraption. When he shoots off inside her, the noise in his head goes away, and then he sleeps. The next day, Willie keeps vomiting as they ride back over to Cana under the blazing noon sky, and Tom keeps laughing. "How's yer hammer hanging, Zeke?" Tom asks him, and Zeke says fine.

The other thing that Zeke likes is meeting; it helps him the way a woman and a fiddle tune help him. It quiets his head. Even though the Malones are widely known as backsliders, they all attend the Old Pisgah Primitive Baptist Church set back on the ridge toward Cana. This church, raised by its congregation in 1831, is nothing but a square cabin made of notched and chinked logs, with a puncheon floor, a single small window on each side, and a plain pine door. It stands in a high clearing on the hill, with a good view of the road to Cana and the Frog Level bottom and a glimpse of the Dismal River beyond. There's always a breeze up on that hill. Having the graveyard right next to the church keeps things in the proper perspective. There's no steeple, no sign, no bell to indicate that this small, plain cabin is in fact a church, but the stern lonesome air of holiness hangs everywhere about it, like fog on the ridge of a morning.

Ezekiel walks up here every third Sunday with the rest. Other Sundays, some of them go to other meetings, often traveling miles. For many of them, especially the women, this is the only time they ever go anywhere. They approach the churchhouse soberly and quietly, eyes cast down. Horses and mules and wagon teams are hitched in the woods. Some of the wagons have little children sleeping on pallets inside, or sucking quietly on a sugar tit. Newborns are carried into meeting.

Older children are left at home; meeting is not the place for children.

The women go on in. Most of the men stand around outside the churchhouse, smoking or chewing tobacco, until the singing starts. Then they throw their cigarettes down on the ground and spit out their chaws and file in too, men to the right, women to the left. They sit on hard plank benches. Meeting is not supposed to be comfortable.

Inside, the Pisgah churchhouse is as plain as it is outside, nothing but a potbellied stove in the back and a homemade table to lay your coats on in the wintertime, nothing up front but the rough-hewn pulpit in the center and the Amen corner over to the side, a wood platform with chairs on it for visiting elders to sit on. No cross, no pictures, no ornamentation of any kind. "Christ don't need no fancy cross," as old Elder Stump has been heard to say. No choir, no hymnbooks, no organ, no piano—no instruments of any kind. *Christ don't have no truck with the things of this world.* Cornelius Malone leads the singing by just flat starting out with it all of a sudden, his high nasal voice almost like an assault on the rustling hush in the meetinghouse.

"Hit's the old ship of Zion as she comes." Cornelius lines out the hymn and the others follow. *"Hit's the old ship of Zion as she comes."* The first line is repeated for the rest of the verse, and each hymn has many verses. *"She'll be loaded with bright angels as she comes."* Cornelius remains seated while he sings, leaning forward a little from the waist with his rough hands placed on his knees, no emotion at all on his face.

When that hymn is finally over, Aunt Dot starts another, *"O Lord, remember me, now in the bowels of Thy love."* It is straight-out tuneless singing, yet Ezekiel finds it beautiful, as his Aunt Dot does.

One time years back, when she was sitting on the porch

hooking a rug and singing one of these mournful old hymns, as she frequently did, little Ezekiel asked her, "Aunt Dot, how come you to sing that old song? How come you don't sing something pretty?" For he knew full well how pretty his Aunt Dot could sing if she took a mind to, and how many songs she knew. She turned to look at him, pursing her mouth, and said, "Honey, they is pretty singing, and then they is true singing," and although Ezekiel didn't know what she meant by that then, he does now. He loves the high hard plaintive singing too and joins in energetically, face blank and eyes closed, sometimes lining out a hymn himself.

Ezekiel likes singing as much as he likes fiddle music and black garter belts and dancing, and he makes no distinction among these things, which all comfort him. He does not care so much for the rest of the service.

The singing goes on for about an hour, and then one of the elders lifts up a prayer, and it goes on awhile too. People pride themselves on how long and how loud they can pray. Then there's some more singing, then another scripture read out by another elder, then Billy Looney giving the sermon in his unemotional singsong voice that comes to be punctuated halfway through his sermon by the "ah!" at the end of each sentence. "Jesus will come in the night, ah! And He will find you where you're hid, ah!" Billy Looney didn't even start preaching until he was an old man. You can't prepare to preach. If God wants you, He will let you know. It will come upon you unawares. Billy Looney was called in the spring of his forty-sixth year one rainy day when he was hauling a wagonload of lumber over to a man in Sistersville. He's been preaching ever since. He preaches frequently that man is a lonesome traveler on a long road, and whenever he takes this text, a thrill shoots through Ezekiel.

Once Billy Looney gets to really horating, he will go on an

hour or more, and then a visiting elder might preach some too, and if things get going good, if Billy Looney or one of them others gets to what Aunt Dot calls his weaving way, why then some folks might start to holler out "Amen" and Missus Clara Bellow might suffer palpitations of the heart and have to lay down on the bench while they sing the invitation hymn. By the end of meeting, the singers still appear detached, yet tears run down their cheeks as they continue to sing. Even some of the men are crying, but none of them wipe off their tears or appear to notice. Then the closing hymn, with parting handshakes all around.

And once again, as always, hearts are somehow strengthened and lifted as all leave meeting and go outside, where the women spread dinner on the ground, everything good you can think of to eat—chicken and dumplings, shucky beans and fatback, pork roast, sweet potatoes baked in their jackets, corn pudding, applesauce, cornbread, watermelon pickle, vinegar pie, apple stack cake. The women wait on the men and children first, then they eat too. Then there's more singing out on the hill, and the sun is low on the mountain when it's time to go. And if a horse or two gets sold behind the churchhouse, or a boy steals a kiss from a girl back in the trees there, or one woman tells another what to do when her baby won't take no titty, what is that? God has been served today.

And there will be other days too, for foot-washings and protracted meetings and brush-arbor meetings on the ground, where emotions will run so high that you have to get out of the way sometimes and let the Spirit work, or you might get trampled by them that is crying out and rushing forward in the hope of glory and flailing around on the floor and jerking ever whichaway with their eyes rolled back in their heads. A girl named Lois Ellen Buie died of religion over at Bee, right in the meetinghouse. But nobody tries to stop it, for if you die shouting happy you go to Heaven for sure, and everybody knows it.

Those remaining don't know no such thing, however. You might go to Heaven or you might not, and don't nobody know but Jesus. He likes to keep you in the dark about it too, your only light being that transitory glorious shot of rapture He grants you sometimes, as He must have done to Lois Ellen Buie down on the churchhouse floor at Bee, or in that moment at the end of meeting when all press hands, or when God appears to you wherever you are, out plowing or laid up sick in the bed or at the springhouse or just anyplace, and vouchsafes you a sign.

But who ever thought Ezekiel Bailey would get one? Or that he would have enough sense to know a sign when it came?

It all goes to show you how mysterious are the ways of God Almighty in all His doings, God who would not give Moses Bailey a sign for all his searching and heartbreak and wandering those woods around Cold Spring Holler in prayer unceasing, God who then decided to give Ezekiel one when he wasn't even expecting it or looking for it, one night when he was walking the road home from Cana drunk.

It was a wild, stormy summer night, a night full of black puffy blowing clouds and rushing winds and flashes of lightning that lit up the whole sky. Little squalls of rain would race down the Cana road and then pass over, each one leaving Zeke a more sober man.

He had been over at a house party in Cana where the liquor was pretty good, and after it he had gone down the road with Horse Hicks's fat daughter Ada. Ezekiel was singing, as he often did when he walked back drunk, *"Muskrat, oh muskrat, what makes your head so red?"* when suddenly there came a long, low rumble of thunder that was somehow different from the rest, an ominous slow roll a lot like the sound Ezekiel had heard in his head since childhood.

But now he heard it *outside* him, and it was suddenly as if his head had split and parted and poured Ezekiel himself out in the world like a pail of water, like there was nothing left of him at all.

Ezekiel dropped his bottle and shrieked and clapped his hands over his ears to hold his head together, staggering on the Cana road. The thunder boomed. A huge fork of lightning split the sky, striking so close that Ezekiel felt it race all through his body, electrifying him, knocking him down on the side of the road, where he lay jerking and crying while the thunder rolled on and on, each long rumble greater than the last, shaking the whole earth. Ezekiel peed his pants from terror as he lay trembling in the mud, and then, all of a sudden, things quieted down. The thunder ceased. The rain stopped. The wind stopped. The moon grew visible behind the fast-moving clouds. Ezekiel took his hands down from his face. Nothing happened. He sat up. Then he stood up, wobbly. What a storm, a bodacious storm! Gingerly, Ezekiel retrieved his hat from the mud. He looked around. The whole world was still. It seemed that he had been spared something. Ezekiel slapped his muddy hat against his muddy knee and prepared to walk on home, dead sober now; but as he started out, the words of that song he'd been singing earlier came back unbidden to his mind. *Muskrat, oh muskrat, what makes your head so red?*

And then a clap of thunder sounded that was louder than all the previous thunder piled together, a clap of Judgment Day thunder, and though the moon remained mostly obscured by clouds, a wild pale greeny light spread over the earth all around, so that everything, *everything* along the Cana road began to glow softly, and a kind of sparkling light danced along the edges of things. All the familiar sights and objects of the world were transformed utterly—the shining split-rail fence along the side of the road, a glowing stump in the field, three tall pine trees burning with green fire against the dark mountain, the Cana road itself, each pebble on it lit up, so that

Zeke stood among stars looking down a starry road that shone on forever, over the gleaming ridge.

And God said, "Don't be a-singing that song, boy." Then He said, "This un's yer song." Then God sang,

"Must Jesus bear the cross alone,
And all the world go free?
No, there's a cross for everyone,
And there's a cross for me."

The minute God had done singing, the light faded off the earth all around, the wind picked back up, and a small steady rain started that would last the rest of the night. Ezekiel walked on home with his face turned up to the misty rain and let it wash down over him like a benediction, singing his song.

Ezekiel Bailey was baptized in the Dismal River the following Sunday by Billy Looney, who took off only his black shoes, wading in fully clothed in his dark suit and starched white shirt. Ezekiel wore dark pants and a white shirt that his Aunt Dot had ironed the night before.

Prior to Ezekiel's baptism, nobody had ever seen him without his overalls. The way he looked on that June morning of his baptism made all the girls suck in their breath, and made some of the women feel a way they had not felt in years. With all that bright hair, Ezekiel looked pretty as an angel, solemn as a judge. He waded out into the river, brogans sticking in the sucky mud, blinded by the morning sun off the water. Billy Looney stood hip-deep in the swirling current and waited for him.

Ezekiel's heart was about to beat right out of his chest as the words of his gift hymn ran through his mind. Over on the riverbank they were singing "Amazing Grace," and Ezekiel could hear Aunt Dot's piercing voice above all the rest. Billy Looney held out one arm in a magisterial gesture in the air and put his other hand on the small of Ezekiel's back. Ezekiel was so much bigger than Billy Looney that the baptizing looked almost comical. Ezekiel stood like a huge tree in the fast-flowing river, the water dividing and eddying away from him on either side in little swirls. Billy Looney said some words, but Ezekiel didn't take them in. *"I once was lost, but now am found,"* they sang on the bank, shading their eyes from the sun blazing off the water.

Still keeping his right arm around the small of Ezekiel's back, Billy Looney smote him suddenly on the chest with his other hand, said something loud, and Ezekiel fell back into the water. He lost his footing and flailed around for a minute, panicked because he couldn't swim. He swallowed water—*half the river*, he would claim later. The white shirt pulled free of his pants and billowed toward the surface, up around his head, and the preacher had to struggle mightily to get him back up. *"Was blind but now I see,"* the crowd sang lustily yet in the old slow mournful cadence, as Ezekiel waded out spewing and dripping, saved.

He was a changed man from that day on—not that he'd been so bad before, you understand. But now Ezekiel gave up liquor and girls and even dancing. Tom soon grew disgusted with him and told him that he acted like he'd got a poker stuck up his ass, but Ezekiel didn't even care what Tom thought. He set about the business of being saved as if he'd invented it, praying out loud when he walked the Cana road home, or singing hymns.

Some people said it was like there'd been a feud over Ezekiel's soul, the Malones versus the Baileys, and the Baileys had won out in spite of him living over here all these years among Malones.

Blood will tell, in the end.

Ezekiel went to meeting every time they cracked the door

now, and walked long distances to other meetings. He got *too* good, in the Malones' opinion. He started doing things free for other people all the time, such as planting and plowing for old Elder Stump. Finally Clovis grew plumb disgusted with Ezekiel, who continued to eat prodigious amounts of his aunt's good cooking but never brought home any money. Ezekiel just sat around the Malones' place at Frog Level like a bump on a log, enjoying the silence in his head, for God had taken away the sound when He gave him his gift song.

Eventually, sensing that his long welcome on Frog Level was worn out, Ezekiel answered the prayers of the childless Elder Stump and his sick wife Garnet by moving into their double cabin at the foot of Cemetery Mountain, overlooking a clear little twisty creek called Grassy Branch.

In exchange for a place to live, Zeke would work the Stumps' land for them, since the arthuritis was fast crippling up Elder Stump too bad for him to do it. Elder Stump didn't pay him, but Zeke didn't mind, since money had never been much to him but a worry and a distraction anyway. He liked Elder Stump too, who would pray out loud whenever the mood hit him, in the field or anyplace. Elder Stump spent long hours agonizing over his Scripture. ("Do ye reckon, Ezekiel, that a suicide can find a place in Heaven?" To which Ezekiel had no opinion, but he liked to be asked.) And Ezekiel liked the place, a long narrow pretty bottom sliced through by Grassy Branch. The cabin was close enough to the creek that you could hear its gurgle as you fell asleep. A bad road, not more than a trace really, ran along the creek, coming from Cana, heading off in the direction of Oak Hill, but Zeke never went down that road, so he didn't know where it went exactly. He never had any reason to go anywhere except back and forth from Cana sometimes, or to meeting at the Pisgah church, or to other meetings.

He hardly ever went over to Frog Level to visit his cousins.

"I declare, I don't know what ails that boy," his Aunt Dot would say. "Stone for a heart." He would have gone to visit her more if he'd known he was hurting her feelings, or if it had occurred to him, but it didn't. Zeke liked people when he was with them, but if he wasn't with them, he didn't think about them. He didn't think about anything. He liked to sit on the porch and smoke a cigarette and watch the summer rains sweep down the long bottom toward the house. He liked the smoky purple possum grapes that grew in the old man's arbor, and the tart taste of the little apples that grew on the hill behind the cabin.

He was tickled by the antics of excitable old Elder Stump, who continued to get more and more riled up over Scripture; and when the Old Pisgah Primitive Baptist Church at Cana, the church that had baptized him, busted up over those same issues which so concerned Elder Stump, Ezekiel joined with him and some others to form another church, a church that would hold to the old ways which Preacher Billy Looney seemed bent on getting away from. Ezekiel did not understand the issues that split, finally, the Primitive Baptists from the Missionary Baptists, but he figured that if Elder Stump was against missionary movements and infant baptism and Sunday schools and church choirs and instruments in the church, why then Ezekiel was against these things too.

The new churchhouse they built was just like the old one, which was the point, except that they used lumber this time instead of logs, and it was closer to Grassy Branch—this side of Cana, on a little point of land called Chicken Rise. The actual name of the new church was Hebron Old Primitive Baptist, a name that Preacher Stump got out of the Bible someplace, but over the years it came to be called simply the Chicken Rise church. By 1880 it had sixty-four members, and Ezekiel had become an elder in it. He did not take his turn at reading the Scriptures, since he couldn't read, or at praying aloud, since he always got too tongue-tied to do this in the presence of other people, but he lined out the hymns and sang lustily, always experiencing a deep secret thrill when they sang his gift hymn, and he took good care of the graveyard and the church itself, often doing something extra like adding pegs at the back where you could hang your coat, or cleaning out the spring in the nearby woods, or putting up a hitching post out back.

When Garnet Stump died, Ezekiel dug her grave, then helped to lower her coffin down in it. She was light as a feather by the time she died. Old Preacher Stump was bent near double from the arthuritis by then. He used two canes to walk.

But one cold December day after her death, when Ezekiel was out in the yard boiling the wash in the old black kettle, Preacher Stump came out of the cabin and made his tortuous way around to where Ezekiel hunkered by the fire, having fallen into the kind of blank blue reverie he was prone to. Ezekiel Bailey was thirty-nine years old at this time, hale and strong. He had a slow, deliberate gait, a permanent squint, and a child's sweet heart. Preacher Stump came up behind him and said right out what was on his mind, startling Ezekiel so much that he almost pitched forward into the fire. "Boy," the old man barked abruptly, "hit's time you got you a wife." Ezekiel turned to stare at the little bent-over preacher. He remembered some things. Slowly, a big grin spread across his face.

3

Nonnie and the Melungeon

Zinnia Hulett Talking

I never did know what ailed Nonnie. Don't know to this day! But she had ever chance for happiness, *ever chance in the world*, mind you, which it is not given to all of us to have, and stomped ever one of them chances down in the dirt like a bug. It seemed that Nonnie was bent on destruction, from the womb.

Why, the very first thing she ever done was kill Mamma!

I will not forget that night as long as ever I live. It was a cold snowy night in the middle of wintertime. Old Granny Horn had been with us going on a week, Daddy had went up her holler to fetch her when it commenced to snowing so bad, so she'd be here when it come Mamma's time. Now it had snowed to where you could not even see the boxwood bush by the front steps, nor that big huge rock there by the gate, nor yet the gate itself nor the fence neither. The snow had blowed hither and you to where it had covered up what ought to have been, and made new hills and valleys all around.

I stood on the porch looking out, as I recall, while Mamma moaned inside of the house and Daddy chopped wood out back even though it was the middle of the night. Granny Horn had sent him out there finely, she said he was nought but a bother in the house. I stood still on the porch and looked out at the snow.

It was a new world out there! I didn't know nothing I saw. And white—Lord, it was white! So white it stayed kindly light all night long, and all the shadders was blue. It was scary. It would be days and days before a soul could get in or out through Flat Gap.

And I looked at that snow and felt glad for all them mason jars of applesauce and peas and such as that which me and Mamma had put up last summer, and for the sweet taters down in the grabbling hole under the porch, and for the shucky-bean leather-britches hanging up in the rafters over the loft, and the chest full of cornmeal—"cornmeal enough to last till the baby is toothing," Mamma had said.

The first time I heerd about this baby was back last summer when Mamma and me was out in the yard putting up butter beans. We had boiled the jars and lined them out in the sun, and the sun looked real pretty shining off of them. Mamma stirred the butter beans with a wooden paddle and wiped at her face with her apron.

"Honey, you don't have to stay out here and help me," she said. "You can go over and play with Mickey if you've got a mind to."

"No, Mamma," I said then. "I like to help you." And it was true. For I was the best little girl! And I loved nothing more than helping my mamma, her voice was a song in my ears.

"Zinnia," she said that day, straightening up, "now I have some news for you. Come wintertime, we will have a baby in this house."

"Where are we going to get it?" I asked, for I did not know. I had heerd that you found them under a cabbage leaf, or that a great owl brung them.

Mamma smiled real nice and stroked my hair. "God will

bring it," she said, and so I didn't think nothing of it when she growed so fat and got so tired, not until this neighbor girl come up and tole me after meeting that the baby was in Mamma's fat stomach, and then I *hated* the baby, for it had made my sweet mamma grow so big and sick she wouldn't hardly play with me no more, and she cried all the time.

I had heerd her crying at night and saying, "No, Claude," and "They is something the matter," and such as that. He said, "It is God's will, Effie," which is just like him, he bowed always to the will of God.

And Mamma bowed always to Daddy's will, which is how the Bible says it should be. In fact the only time I ever recall Mamma acting any way but dutiful was when that baby was in her, and I say it was all due to the nature of the baby.

For Nonnie had a troublesome nature from a child.

Things was never the same after the day we were out front canning, so that as I stood on the porch that winter night six months later and heerd Mamma screaming out in the house behind me, I was not surprised to look out and see the world all different, all changed before my eyes, nor to feel the wind blow offen the snow and chill me to the bone.

Granny Horn would say something, and then Mamma would scream, and then Granny would say something else, and then Mamma would scream again. Out back I heerd Daddy, *chop chop chop.* I went through the breezeway to see him. "Daddy," I said. "Daddy." I couldn't see nothing out there but his big dark form in the pale blue light. I could see it when he raised the ax, black against the snow. I heerd it when he brung it down. *Chop. Chop. Chop.*

"Daddy," I said, but he kept right on. *Chop. Chop. Chop.* I stood out there wrapped up in a coverlet, hugging myself. Wasn't nobody else going to hug me, that was for sure! They was all too busy borning the baby to care about me.

And yet I had done all the work, for Granny Horn had said her old self was wore out, and axed me would I be her extry hands, and like a fool I said yes, so she had set me to fetching and carrying for her, what all she needed—the scissors, the string, the borning quilt, water a-boiling in the big black pot. While I done all this, Mamma just laid up in the bed staring out over her great stomach at me with her dark eyes real big in her thin face.

"Now come here, Zinnia," she said. This was right before the sun went down. And I went over there, and Mamma smoothed back my hair and touched the mark on my face real gentle, the way she always done, and pulled me down to her, and kissed me.

"Now you be a good girl," Mamma said, and so I was, and did not cry.

But it galled me standing out there in the freezing cold in the middle of the night, why I could of froze to death for all they knowed, or cared! I was just a little girl. Too little to see what happened next, which was awful. For Mamma had a britches baby that wouldn't come out, Granny Horn had to cut it out of her. But it looked so awful I didn't have no sense that it was a baby. Granny slapped it until it cried. Then she flung it down in the cradle that they had there, *my* cradle, mind you, that Daddy had made for me, and left it squalling while she worked on Mamma, and this gone on all night, them packing every cloth they could find in there, and even using snow finely to try and stop the bleeding, but nothing worked.

Daylight come and the whole cabin was a wet bloody mess and Mamma was going, she did not know us. The baby whined in its cradle but Mamma did not appear to hear it. For a long time her hands was still clutching and clutching at the air, but then she stopped that. Her hands closed up, her fingers curled like fiddlehead ferns. Her eyes was wide and staring until Granny Horn closed them. Granny Horn stood up then, finely. She must of been six feet tall.

"Claude, where is yer likker at?" she said, but Daddy would not leave Mamma, he was laid acrost her bosom weeping like a child.

"Claude!" Granny Horn said sharp.

"I'll git it," I said then, for I knew where he kept it in the loft, and I clumb up there and found a jar and brung it down to her. Granny Horn took a big swig of it, it was white likker, and looked at me directly for the first time.

"Honey, you go and lay down now," she said, and I done it. No sooner did I hit the bed tick than I was fast asleep, the soundest sleep in the world, I reckon, for I slept all that day until night again, and when I woke it was dark and the fire was going and Mamma was not there, nor Daddy, and Granny Horn was cleaning with a great pot of water and the baby was crying hard. Granny Horn gave me some johnnycake then and said to eat it and then said to go back to bed, and I done so, and when I woke again it was morning, another day, and the sun was shining offen the snow all around, but it would be some several more days afore you could get in or out through the gap.

I do not remember these days too good, to tell the truth. They seem to me now as a blaze of light, sun offen the snow. I know what happened, though.

Granny Horn laid Mamma out on a plank they rigged up in the springhouse, and we kept her there until it thawed enough to bury her. So Mamma was laid out and froze, finely and fectually, in the springhouse.

When it got to where Granny Horn could get through the gap, she done so, taking the baby, as Daddy would not leave Mamma. Granny Horn took the baby to a woman that had one, so it could get some titty, and while Nonnie was gone, I played like she had never been borned. I played like I was the baby.

Then Granny Horn come back, which I hated, for she was so big and rough, she was the furtherest thing in the world from my sweet mamma.

Sometimes I would go out to the springhouse and see my mamma, although they had said not to, but I had figgered out the latch and sometimes I'd steal out there and talk to Mamma laying on the plank. They had covered her face with a camphor rag which smelt terrible; in fact you could not stay in the springhouse long because of it, you'd start choking. Once I helt Mamma's hand, but it was so cold I let go of it directly.

I don't have no memory now of exactly how long Mamma stayed in the springhouse, but it was a good long while. I got used to having her there, and was sorry when it thawed enough to where the neighbor folks come up and buried her.

Now Daddy acted awful all this while, he would not look at nobody, nor talk to them, and when the neighbor folks left, he would not talk to me either, not for the longest time. Then one time when I brung him some food, he said, "Well, Zinnia, I reckon you will have to be the little wife around here now," and I said I would, and I have done for him the best I could, ever since. Nobody could have done better.

But now it seems to me that the one who is *there* all the time, the one who is cooking and mending and fetching water and just doing in general what needs to be done, well, *that* one gets precious little attention. It is the squeaky wheel that gets the grease every time. And I have gotten mighty little appreciation over the years, all because of that hateful little Nonnie.

I say hateful. And she *was* hateful, but she had everybody fooled but me. She had them all eating right out of her hand, by acting so sweet. I know acting when I see it. And I was the one that had to go around picking up after her and saying,

"Did you eat yer supper, Nonnie?" and "Don't play in the rain, Nonnie" and such as that.

For Nonnie was the silliest, mooniest child you ever saw, not one grain of sense in her head! She would of starved to death or killed herself a hundred times if it hadn't of been for me. She would have killed herself over and over doing the crazy things she done, such as swinging on grapevines and playing with snakes. She never had a thought in the world for what might happen to her.

And was lazy to boot! If you asked her to churn, she might start out a-churning, then she'd be churning and singing, then she'd just be singing, and wander off singing, and allow the cream to clabber in the churn. Many's the time she done that, and many's the slap I give her for it. Oh, I done my duty, rest assured of it, but I just couldn't get through to her, so it done no good in the end. As a littlun, Nonnie was all the time a-singing. She used to go off down the road by herself to the Bevins sisters' house and learn songs offen them, and I'd have to fetch her home.

I could not carry a tune in a bucket myself, and don't give a damn to. For what good does it do you in the end? What good did it do Nonnie? When she was a girl, her favorite song was that crazy little cuckoo song. And to this day, it reminds me of Nonnie and how silly she was. But Daddy was plumb fooled by her, and when she was little he used to carry her to town on the front of his saddle and then set her up on the counter in the store to sing for folks. Daddy never took *me* to town on his saddle, I might add. Of course I would not have cared to be displayed thataway nohow, but you ought to treat children equal, I say, and not favor one over the other so.

Well, in all fairness, I know that Daddy did not favor Nonnie because of Nonnie her ownself. No, he favored Nonnie because she was the spitting image of Mamma. Everybody said so. So it was not Nonnie's fault, in a way, but she got spoiled rotten all the same. And she was not all that pretty neither, never mind what folks said. She was kind of dreamy and dish-faced if you ask me. Not to mention contrary. Now we all know what a woman's lot is, but Nonnie wouldn't have no part of it! We'd be sitting by the fire of a night, for an instance, and I'd be doing piecework on my lap, but Nonnie she'd of flung herself flat down on the floor and be a-staring and a-staring into the fire, and not doing a blessed thing with her hands. When you'd call her it was like she was off in the clouds someplace.

"Nonnie," I said one time, then, "*Nonnie,*" real loud and sharp. Oh, she looked up then.

"Nonnie, what air ye a-looking at, anyway?" I axed her, and do you know what she said? She said she'd seen figures a-dancing, dancing in the flames!

Of course later I remembered her answer real good, in light of the awful thing that would come to pass, but at the time it just hit me as more of her foolishness.

And as she got older, she got worser. She started in a-wanting to go to play-parties with the big gals and fellers when she was not but about twelve years old, just ragging Daddy to let her go, and of course he done it finely, for he always let Nonnie do exactly what she pleased.

"Zinnia, you go with her and watch out for her," Daddy told me the first time he let her go, but I would not do it.

"I don't care to go," was all I said. Hadn't Daddy seed that I hadn't never gone to a play-party myself in all them years? For I am no fool. And I knowed them boys would pass me by, a-stepping Charley, and I refused pint-blank to give them the satisfaction.

I didn't care for boys then, and I don't care for men now. They are nothing but a vexation and a distraction, and can't none of them hold a candle to Daddy anyhow.

But Nonnie, she'd go or die, and then she'd be mooning around over first one and then another. She used to sing this little song, "*Oh I wonder when I shall be married, oh be married, oh be married, oh I wonder when I shall be married, or am I beginning to fade?*" It was the dumbest little song I ever heerd, and she was the dumbest little girl I ever saw to sing it, and I said so. Didn't faze Nonnie, though. She'd swat away my words like they was flies.

And when we would go anyplace, if it was meeting or the store or anyplace at all, why she would flirt with the boys till it was shameful. But didn't none of them come up here, for Daddy had said that they was not to, and most folks was kindly afeared of Daddy. Daddy thought none of them boys was good enough for our Nonnie, she had really pulled the wool over his eyes.

"Anyway, Zinnia must have a husband first," Daddy said at the table one night just to devil us. Since I knowed he didn't mean it, I just laughed and said, "The last thing in the world I need is a husband. I need a husband like I need a hole in the wall," I said. "And whatever would you all do without me, anyway, if I was to leave?" I axed them, for we were eating supper which *I* had cooked, mind you. "You-uns would starve to death," I said.

And do you know what Daddy done? Why, he reached over acrost the table and took Nonnie's hand. "Why, Nonnie will be the little housewife, then," he said, grinning. He was just funning her, because he would not have let me go for the world, mind you, but silly little Nonnie busted into tears and ran out of the house a-blubbering.

"Oh, I will never get married," she wailed. "You all won't let me," she wailed. "If I have to wait for Zinnia, I'll be a old maid," she wailed out in the yard while Daddy and me sat on at the table and finished eating supper.

The truth of it was, Daddy wanted Nonnie to stay in school

as long as ever she would. I believe he had kindly a hankering for Nonnie to make a teacher like one of Daddy's aunts done, over in Tennessee. Oh, he wanted the world for our Nonnie! And she could of had it too; it was hers for the taking. And it was all right with me, mind you, for Nonnie to get all that schooling, as I couldn't get nothing at all done with her mooning around underfoot day in and day out. I was plumb glad to see her go flouncing out that door to school. She used to ride her little pony down to the schoolhouse every day, this was a white pony Daddy had bought for her over in Sparta, which she named Snowy. I had not took to school too good myself, truth to tell. It seemed like a waste of time to me. But Nonnie, she liked it fine, and the schoolteacher, Mister Harkness, set a big store by her. She had him wrapped around her little finger too.

I recall one time when our preacher, Mister Cisco Estep, was questioning Daddy about Nonnie's schooling and what did Daddy mean by it, for the Bible itself says that too many books is a sin. I will not forget what Daddy answered him.

"Cisco," he said, putting his hands on Cisco Estep's shoulders, "Nonnie is a soft girl, like her mother. I do not want her to get all wore out by hard work like her mother done. I feel real bad about her mother," Daddy said.

This is the only time I ever heerd Daddy say anything about Mamma, or saw him look so mushy in the face.

"I want Nonnie to have a better life," Daddy said.

But Nonnie, she didn't care nothing about that, all she wanted was a feller. Nonnie was just a fool waiting to happen.

And one day, sure enough, she came back from going down into Cana with some of the neighbor people, looking like she had a fine mist of moondust laid all over her. Her black eyes was as shiny as coal.

"Well, who is he?" I axed straightaway, for I knowed immediately what was up.

Nonnie would always answer you right back, and truthful too. She was too dumb to do otherwise. "Oh, Zinnia," she said, "I was just standing in the road talking to some folks when this man rode in on a gray horse. He was a man that none of us had ever seed before, and not from around here. He is real different-looking, real handsome, like a man in a song. Anyway, he looked at me good as he rode past," she said. "I looked at him and he looked at me," Nonnie said all dreamy, and I said, "So?" for this did not sound like much to me. "Well, then he got off and hitched the horse up at the rail there and come right over to where I was standing in the road talking to Missus Black, and he takes off his hat and kindly bows down like a prince, you never saw the beat of it. Then he says, 'What is yer name?' and I told him, and, 'Where do you live?' and I told him that too."

"Oh, Nonnie," I said. "He can't come up here. You don't know a thing about him."

Nonnie flashed her eyes at me and bit her pouty lip. "He has got some money from a previous venture," she said, real highfalutin. "And he aims to settle in these parts."

Well, sure enough, here he come, and sure enough, Daddy run him off. He met with the man, whose name was Jake Toney, in private afore he run him off. Nonnie sat on a chair out in the yard, just tapping her foot, while Daddy talked to Jake Toney. Then she saw fit to keep quiet for the length of time it took Jake Toney to get back on his gray horse and ride out of sight, but as soon as he was gone, she just throwed herself on Daddy like a wildcat from Hell, crying and clawing at his eyes and hitting at him, and Daddy just helt her out at arm's length and let her fight.

"Now listen here, girls," he said, when Nonnie had finely quit fighting. "That man there is a Melungeon, and he won't be coming up here again. I knowed it as soon as I saw him," Daddy said.

"A what?" Nonnie said, and then Daddy told us about the Melungeons, that is a race of people which nobody knows where they came from, with real pale light eyes, and dark skin, and frizzy hair like sheep's wool. Sure enough, this was what Jake Toney looked like, all right.

"Niggers won't claim a Melungeon," Daddy told us. "Injuns won't claim them neither.

"The Melungeon is alone in all the world," Daddy said, and at these words, Nonnie ran off crying. She was so spoilt by then, she couldn't believe she couldn't have anything she wanted.

Well, Nonnie cried for some several days after that, but then Daddy made her go back to school, and just about as soon as she started back, she cheered up considerable. In fact she cheered up *too* fast, and I don't know, there was just something about her that made me feel funny, not funny ha-ha, but funny peculiar. They was something there that did not meet the eye. So one day when Nonnie rode off to school, I determined to ride over toward Cana myself, not an hour behind her. I told Daddy I was going to the store.

I can't say that I was surprised when I come riding around the bend there where that little old falling-down cabin is, that used to belong to the widder woman, and seed the gray horse and the little white pony hitched up in front of it. I got off my horse and tethered her back there in the woods and then walked kindly tippytoe over to the cabin, but I need not have gone to the trouble. For they were making the shamefullest, awfullest racket you ever heerd in there, laughing and giggling and moaning and crying out, and then he'd be breathing and groaning at the same time, and then he hollered out, and then she did.

School, my foot!

You had better believe I told our daddy what was going on in that cabin!

So he was waiting on the front porch that afternoon when Nonnie came riding home on her little pony. He did not let on, though.

"Evening, honey," Daddy says.

"Evening, Daddy," says Nonnie, as sweet as ever you please.

"How was school?" Daddy axed, and Nonnie said, "Fine, sir," and when he axed her what did they do today, why she commenced upon some big lie about geography, but before she got halfway done with it Daddy had struck her on the shoulder with his riding crop and knocked her on the ground, and then he beat her acrost the back with it until she cried for mercy with her hands before her face. I did not lift a finger to help her neither, for she deserved it. Nor did I comfort Nonnie when she lay crying in the bed, not until way up in the night when finely I brung her some tea and some biscuit. Which she did not touch, hateful as ever.

And in the morning she was gone.

She had lit out in the dead of night on her pony, gone down to find her Melungeon at Missus Rice's boardinghouse, where he stayed, and I couldn't tell you what passed betwixt the two of them when she got there, but the next day he was up and gone before daybreak, alone. And then what did that silly Nonnie do? Why, she locked herself up in Jake Toney's room all broken-hearted, wouldn't come out for nothing. Missus Rice had to send up to the house for me to come and get her.

Jake Toney left owing money all over town, as it turned out, one jump ahead of the law. He owed a lot of people due to the poker game he had been running regular in the back of the livery stable. Missus Rice was fit to be tied, as he left owing her considerable, also old Baldy McClain that ran the livery stable and was supposed to have gotten a cut on the game.

They *all* liked to have died when they found out that Jake Toney was a Melungeon to boot, which I told Missus Rice first thing when I went down there to get Nonnie. Missus Rice's jaw dropped down about a foot. The news was all over town inside of a hour.

As for our Nonnie, she was mighty pale and mighty quiet, riding home. For once she had nothing to say. She was not a bit like herself after that, and would not go back to school for love nor money, but stayed at home not doing a thing but crying and looking out at the mountains from time to time. This liked to have killed Daddy, for deep down in secret, he is real softhearted. He brung Nonnie everything he could think of to cheer her up, including a silver hairbrush and a silk scarf.

"Iffen I was to go off in the bushes with every Tom, Dick, and Harry that come along," I axed Daddy, "do ye reckon I could get me one of them scarves?"

Whereupon Nonnie turned right around and gave it to me, of all things. I was not too proud to take it neither. In fact I felt gratified to take it, after all the trouble she had put me to. For Nonnie owed me, and that's a fact.

Well, we never seed hide nor hair of the Melungeon again, but Nonnie continued grieving him for weeks on end, and laying up in the bed all day long doing it. Then one day I looked at her good, and all of a sudden it come to me that she was going to have a baby.

"No I ain't," she lied to Daddy, flashing her eyes, but we sent for Granny Horn, who found out the truth of it soon enough.

And then here comes Preacher Cisco Estep, hat in hand, a-knocking on the door.

"I'll tell you what's the truth," he said to Daddy, when the two of them had set down. "I would send her off someplace if hit was me."

"But whar'd she go? She belongs here," Daddy said real pitiful. His eyes was all red from crying and staying up late.

"Well now, Claude, think about it," Preacher Estep said.

"If she tried to come to meeting in her condition and unwed, I'd be forced to church her, as ye know. And around here, everybody knows who she is and what she done, and won't nobody take a Melungeon's leavings around here neither, not to mention the child. This is the long and short of it," Preacher Estep said. "But if she was to go somewheres else, say, she might have a chance for a new life. In fact," Preacher Estep said real forceful, "in fact, Claude, I have got a proposition for you." Preacher Estep took out a handkerchief and wiped at his big red fleshy nose, that looks like a sweet tater.

"Well, what is it?" Daddy said without no hope.

"Well, they is a man I heerd about at the past Association meeting that needs a wife the worst in the world," Preacher Estep said. "He is in a fair way to come into quite a parcel of land over at Grassy Branch, what is now Preacher Stump's place, but he don't have no wife, nor no children to work it. He is a elder in the Chicken Rise church too. So Preacher Stump has let it out to all and evry that he hisself ain't long fer this world, and he would like to see this feller settled down regular on his land. Hit's a nice piece of land," Preacher Estep said, "and I don't believe this feller is too particular neither."

Daddy looked at him. You could tell he was considering it.

"I wouldn't see no reason to mention the Melungeon," Preacher Estep said.

"Done," Daddy said.

And so this is how Nonnie come out smelling like a rose one more time, and got a great prize for being bad. For that land over at Grassy Branch turned out to be among the prettiest I have ever seed, and hit turned out to be a fine big double cabin over there—finer and biggern our own, I might add—and I was further surprised to find that Ezekiel Bailey hisself was not so bad to look at neither. He come out to the wagon grinning when we drove up, and he was just as nice to me as ever he was to that silly Nonnie who done nothing but cry and cry, and he did not even appear to notice my face none. I remarked upon how tight he helt my arm when he helped me down off the wagon, and how much he appeared to like the fried apple pies we had brung them—which *I* had made!—and I knowed in my heart of hearts that Ezekiel Bailey preferred me over Nonnie. Yet I resolved not to act on this, nor to tell no one, for I would not disappoint Daddy by leaving him, he needs me so.

Daddy said as much too when me and him was driving back through Flat Gap late that night after leaving Nonnie over on Grassy Branch with old bent-over Preacher Stump and Ezekiel Bailey her husband-to-be.

It was too dark for me to see good even though the stars was out, because of how the mountains rise up there directly in the gap. It was black as tar in the gap, but I could tell that Daddy was crying, and when he spoke, his voice was irregular. "If I ever lay eyes on him again, I'll kill him," Daddy said after a while, meaning the Melungeon. Then after another while, he said, "Well, hit's just you and me now, ain't it, Zinnia girl?" and so I took his old work-hard hand and helt it in mine, and so it has been ever since, just me and him, the way it ought to be, ever since that very night when we was riding home through Flat Gap in the pitch-black night, the night so dark I didn't have no birthmark, and I was just as pretty as Nonnie.

4

Nonnie and the Big Talker

When Nonnie Hulett climbed down off her daddy's wagon to stand before him at Grassy Branch, Ezekiel Bailey thought she was just about the prettiest thing he had ever seen in his whole life. It made him happy to look at her, and he stood there looking at her for the longest time. Nonnie had tied her dark hair back as severely as possible, but the jolting wagon had loosened it, so that black curls framed her face, red and swollen from crying. When she finally looked up at Ezekiel, her brown eyes had yellow sun-bursts in them, like cat eyes. Nonnie's eyes reassured Ezekiel somehow. He liked cats, such as Garnet Stump's old tomcat Henry Boy, laying over there in the sunshine right now. And Zeke knew how to take good care of things—the animals, the house, the church, the land and what grew there. He took good care of everything. Nonnie would be his wife. He would take good care of her too. Slowly, he smiled at her. Nonnie did not smile back. She balled up her handkerchief in her little fist and ground it into her face, crying even harder.

Zeke did not know what to do then. He turned around to look at old Preacher Stump, up on the porch, for guidance, but Preacher Stump just shrugged and puffed on one of his asthma cigarettes, peering down at them all through the smoke. It looked like trouble to him. Meantime Nonnie's grim-faced daddy was unloading her things from the wagon without a word, box after box, leaving them piled in the yard. She sure had a lot of things. Her ugly sister had presented Ezekiel with a little bag of fried pies which he ate automatically, one after the other, watching Nonnie. Ezekiel did not look at the sister, who was poking around the yard and exclaiming over this and that and acting the fool in general. Nonnie sobbed louder and stamped her little foot.

Preacher Stump sighed. *This will be a hard row to hoe*, he thought. May be he had made a mistake. May be he should of knowed enough not to meddle with nature, should of knowed to leave well enough alone. If God had wanted Ezekiel to have a wife, may be He would of got him one His Ownself.

Nonnie's daddy took off his hat and kissed her and then put his hat on again and got back in the wagon. The ugly sister got back in the wagon too. Nonnie's daddy slapped the reins and said, "Giddap," and before you knew it, they were gone around the bend of Grassy Branch and out of sight, stirring up dust which hung for a long long time in the still hot air.

Nonnie and Ezekiel just stood there. Joe-pye weed and black-eyed Susans bloomed all along the road, bleeding hearts by the gate. Little yellow butterflies flew everywhere.

Preacher Stump felt old and foolish, surveying this scene from his porch. It was not a thing like the time when Garnet had come to him, a young girl not yet sixteen, full-figured and trembling, with a look on her face that he knew. Bent double, barely breathing, Preacher Stump could see her still, his bride of sixty years before, could feel a stirring of the heavy passion he felt then. He had to go lay down. Without a word he turned and disappeared through the open door, leaving Ezekiel Bailey and Nonnie Hulett standing out in the sun in the heat of the day like their feet had growed roots and planted them there at Grassy Branch. It was August 10, 1880.

For about a week, Nonnie Hulett continued to cry. She tried to cook, and do the chores, for she was a good girl and knew she had done wrong and knew that this was to be her lot; but to her surprise, Ezekiel would not let her do much, coming up behind her to take the skillet out of her hand, to carry the pail of water, to feed the chickens that fluttered around the yard. Nonnie couldn't get over it. She had never seen a man do such things. Once when Zeke grabbed the broom and was sweeping the porch off himself, Nonnie raised her eyebrows and looked questioningly at old Preacher Stump, who sat wreathed in smoke in his rocking chair, and for the first time, Preacher Stump smiled back at her, his mouth full of black teeth, but then he fell to coughing, and failed to answer the question which she hadn't really asked.

Preacher Stump was smoking as many of his asthma cigarettes as he could manage, trying hard to stay alive. Several times lately in a dream he had seen a great golden angel flying down from Heaven like a chicken hawk, swooping down low to get him, but so far Preacher Stump had managed to hold off this angel, for he intended to stay alive long enough to see how things would turn out.

One time when Zeke had taken the bucket from her and set off for the springhouse, Nonnie faced the old man and said, "He don't talk much, I reckon," and Preacher Stump said, "No, he don't." This was the only question Nonnie ever asked about him, as blue cloudless day after day came and went, and she got used to life on Grassy Branch. Truth to tell, it was a relief to be shut of that bossy Zinnia! Gradually it dawned on

Nonnie that she would be the mistress here, and since Ezekiel seemed disposed to spoil her just as much as her father had ever done, she could have her way without working her fingers to the bone like all the other women she'd ever known. Nonnie had time to wash her long hair and sit out in the sun to let it dry, she had time to dream in the slow afternoons while Ezekiel hoed corn and the old man dozed on the porch. Nonnie had time for herself, golden and slow and sweet as the thick honey that came from Ezekiel's hives up on the mountain behind the house. She kept crying, dedicated to grief, but it grew harder and harder to remember exactly what she was crying about.

The old man slept on one side of the double cabin, she and Ezekiel on the other side. Ezekiel had his bed tick and she had hers, and her own quilt, and her own two feather pillows that she had brought from home.

Every night, Ezekiel waited until she had put on her nightdress and taken down her hair and stretched out on the bed tick and closed her eyes before he came into the cabin. Then he entered as quietly as ever he could, yet the whole cabin would shake with his step. While Nonnie feigned sleep, he went to the foot of her bed and left a present there, something he thought was pretty—a piece of crystal quartz he'd found one time up on Cemetery Mountain, a pearl button, cornflowers from the field, an iridescent snake-skin, finally his beloved steelie marble. Nonnie's presents were lined up on the floor at the foot of her bed. Alone in the cabin, she had to smile in spite of herself, looking at them. She did not know what to make of this big, gentle man. But she was tired of tears, and one day she found herself humming a tune.

Then finally there came the night when a screech owl woke her. It sounded like the screech owl called her name. Nonnie sat up in bed and looked at Ezekiel, who always slept like a child or a dead man, flat on his back, hands clasped on his chest, breathing audibly. It seemed to Nonnie that he never dreamed; at least he never gave the appearance of dreaming. Moonlight streamed in the open door that night and made a silver path across the cabin floor, right across Ezekiel, who looked like an angel sleeping there.

Idly, Nonnie held out her hand, so that the moonlight fell upon it too, silvering her whole arm. Then suddenly Nonnie got that powerful feeling she got sometimes, that feeling she had gotten ever since she was a little girl, when all of a sudden she just *had* to do something—never mind what!—she just had to make something happen.

Nonnie stood up and took off her nightgown and stepped into the moonlight, looking down at her silver body. Her breasts were large now because of the pregnancy, and her navel stuck out on her firm high belly. She felt like she was bursting right out of her skin. She stood in the moonlight admiring herself, breathing hard, waiting to see exactly what she would do next. Then she walked over to Ezekiel and knelt beside his bed tick and leaned over him, brushing his chest with her hair. The screech owl called out to her again, clear as could be, and even if she couldn't quite make out what he said, she knew what he meant all right.

"Wake up," she said to Ezekiel. She poked him in the side.

Zeke stirred but did not wake. Even the hair on his chest was silver in the light of the moon.

"Zeke," Nonnie said. "Wake up." She poked him again, harder.

Zeke opened his eyes and looked at her. "God Almighty," he said.

For the first time since her arrival on Grassy Branch, Nonnie started to giggle.

"Why, looky here," she said.

R.C. Bailey, Nonnie's Melungeon baby, was born on February 14, 1881, about a month after Ezekiel and Nonnie were married in Preacher Stump's cabin by Dr. Paul Trott, a traveling evangelist on his way to Knoxville. Dr. Paul Trott had red hair and a little red mustache. "Man and wife," he said. Ezekiel heard him say it. Ezekiel had a wife now. Then Dr. Paul Trott rode off in the rain, and Nonnie kissed Ezekiel, and Preacher Stump died, just like that. He took a little shallow rattling breath, tried to say something, and died. It was like he had put it off to see them wed.

When folks came to the house for the laying out, they were surprised to find that Ezekiel had such a pretty, pregnant wife. They told it up and down the hollers until they got tired of saying it: "Did you ever feature Ezekiel Bailey wed, now?" and "Whar did she come from?" and "Who do you reckon her people are?" They buried Preacher Stump in the Chicken Rise graveyard not forty feet from the church he had started himself and built with his own hands, and when the first shovelful of red dirt hit the pine coffin, Ezekiel felt as though he too would die; but this feeling passed quickly, as most feelings did with him, and by the time R.C. was born, he had almost forgotten the old man although they named the baby for him, Reese, because the granny woman said they ought to, and so did some people at church. Ezekiel had not known that Preacher Stump had this first name, Reese, or any first name at all.

Then Nonnie cried because she had wanted to name the baby for her father, so the baby's name turned out to be Reese Claude Bailey, too much name for such a little baby, and they took to calling him R.C. He was a colicky baby who had a high, thin cry like a cat mewing. Nonnie had been real curious to see whether he would look like Jake Toney or not. R.C. did have curly hair like Jake Toney, but fair skin like Ezekiel Bailey. He wouldn't sleep at all. One night, sitting up with him by the fire, Nonnie got so tired and so mad that she kicked at the chimbley in disgust, the way she often stamped her little foot, and lo and behold, one of the chimbley rocks fell out as neat as you please, and she saw that there was something stuck in the hole. Nonnie plopped the crying baby down in its cradle and leaned forward to see what she'd found.

It was a burlap bag full of money, saved by Garnet and Preacher Stump for a rainy day. Nonnie, terribly excited, sifted through old silver dollars and paper money while the fire leaped up in the hearth and the March wind wailed outside. Just beyond the circle of firelight, Ezekiel slept on. Nonnie would not wake him; she'd wait until morning to give him this news which would not mean much to him anyway, she knew it wouldn't. He didn't give a damn about money. Meanwhile she would hold her baby in one arm and run the fingers of her other hand through this money, and think what she might do with it.

Later, some people would say that it was this money which spoilt Nonnie Bailey finely and fectually, that she would not have gone and done what she done if she hadn't kicked in the chimbley and found that little burlap bag. But others held that Nonnie Bailey was obviously spoilt long before she came over to Grassy Branch, that what we will do is buried deep inside us all anyway, like a dark seed. Be that as it may, the burlap bag contained just enough money—not much, actually—to give Nonnie Bailey a sense of what she could not have. It contained just enough money for her to order off for some silky rose-colored cloth and some pink mother-of-pearl buttons, some tortoiseshell combs and some magazines. It might be that the magazines were the most damaging of all, for in them Nonnie could see page after page of women dressed to the nines (bustles and mutton sleeves and tiny waists and huge plumed hats, in the fashion of the day, which Nonnie would have given her eyeteeth to model).

"Can't none of em hold a candle to you," Zeke said, looking at a magazine with her.

Nonnie knew this was true. She had always been beautiful. Now she realized that she was more beautiful than the ladies in the magazines, and since she was the missus here and could do as she pleased, she sewed a dress from her bolt of rosy silk cloth and put the mother-of-pearl buttons up the front of it, lace at the neck. But then she just sat on the porch wearing the dress and rocking R.C., with noplace to go. She wore the dress to the Chicken Rise church once, then never again, because of how the other women looked at her. She was the prettiest woman in the county, but it didn't matter. She would rot here in these mountains and be damned.

When Nonnie knew she was pregnant again, she folded the rose silk dress away carefully, regretfully, and stored it in a special place in the loft even as she stored that image of herself away in a special place in her mind where she would take it out and look at it sometimes as the years passed.

Durwood, her funny baby, was born in 1884, all smiles and giggles and kicking feet from the first, it seemed, as different from whiny R.C. as day from night. Durwood looked exactly like his daddy, but Nonnie got his name out of a magazine.

It tickled Ezekiel to death to have the two little boys around; he was always playing with them, doing "Eeny meeny miney mo, catch a nigger by the toe" over and over until R.C. shrieked with joy. You would think nobody in the whole world had ever been a daddy before, to watch Ezekiel Bailey with his boys, and folks talked it up and down the creek, how he acted, for most men would not have a thing to do with a child, leaving it all up to the womenfolks, as is proper. Zeke's behavior was unmanly. But it allowed Nonnie to primp and preen and pleasure herself, so that she didn't resemble a missus at all, in a way that made the other men cast an envious eye at Zeke and a more lingering look at Nonnie, a look that made the other womenfolks downright uneasy. "They was something quare about them from the start," they'd say later. "I knowed it was something wrong over thar," they'd say.

Then in 1885 came the baby that was born dead, and after they buried him, Nonnie dreamed for seven nights running that they had buried her too, down in the cold black ground. Every night she woke up choking, with the taste of dirt in her mouth.

Ezekiel took this to be her sign.

And because Ezekiel knew about such things—signs and portents, how God reveals himself to men—Nonnie believed him.

They had to break the ice in the river in order to baptize her right away. Nonnie stood shivering and terrified on the riverbank in the cutting wind, still weak from loss of blood, clinging to Ezekiel's strong arm beside her, hoping her sign was a true one, hoping she would not die when the preacher plunged her beneath the icy water. She could still taste the dirt of the grave in her mouth. Behind her, the folks from the Chicken Rise church were singing in the old high sad way. Suddenly Nonnie felt completely alone, and it was as if the world and all its bright trappings streamed past her like the wind and were gone forever, and she was left on the bleak brown shore of the Dismal River by herself, with the dirty grayish ice before her, the sluggish dark river moving mysteriously beneath it where they had broken the ice, and for the first time Nonnie was lifted out of the moment of her life and thrust toward something beyond herself. The others seemed far, far away, as they sang, *"Shall we gather at the river, where bright angel feet have trod? With its crystal tide forever flowing by the throne of God."*

At that very moment the sun came out from the mass of leaden clouds which covered half the sky, and the ice on the river changed instantly from gray to silver, to diamonds spread out sparkling before their eyes. Ezekiel squeezed her hand.

"Hit looks like Heaven, don't it?" he said, and then the preacher took her and then she was under, frozen solid and dead, and then she was up sputtering and resurrected, and as soon as it was done, the choking dream stopped forever.

Now Nonnie could go on about her life, her good life as it came to pass, for she grew accustomed to Ezekiel's limitations and learned to compensate for them, handling all the money, for instance, doing the things Ezekiel was not cut out to do, while he did the things he could. Under his hands, the farm prospered. Hired girls came in to help Nonnie with the work as time went on and more children were born, Pack Bailey in 1886; little Elizabeth, called Lizzie, in 1890; Sally Fern in 1898.

These were the blurred and busy years, the good years, when Nonnie got so caught up in the great tumble and roar of her life that she never even thought of the rose silk dress folded away in the loft, nor of Jake Toney, nor of how she used to dance up on the counter of the store in Cana when she was a little girl and sing, *"The cuckoo she's a pretty bird, she sings as she flies"*—

Oh, Nonnie still sang, while she carded the wool or rocked the baby or shelled the beans, but now she mostly sang the hymns that Ezekiel loved, or the old bloody ballads like "Barbry Allen" and "Brown Girl" and "The Gypsy Laddie." It gave Nonnie the strangest feeling to sing that one, all about a woman who left her house and baby to run away with a gypsy. For how could a woman do such as that? Men might wander, but women were meant to stay home, and during those years when the house on Grassy Branch was brimming over with babies, Nonnie could not imagine anywhere else she might even *want* to be, whirled round as she was in the great spinning wheel of the seasons, as implacable as the stars. *Plant now pull the fodder now hoe the corn now dig the newground the baby is crying she wants to be fed the cow is lost Mamma my throat hurts Mamma whar is the hairbrush Mamma he hurt me it is time to buy the seed corn Mamma he it is time to Mamma it is time mamma mamma mamma.*

Ezekiel loved the children and played with them by the hour, rolling down the hill behind the house with them, making cat's cradles with string and chains with daisies, singing to them swinging them chucking them under their chins tickling them, "Tickle, tickle, on your knee, if you laugh you don't love me," which made Lizzie, fat little yellow-haired Lizzie, dissolve in laughter every time.

Once when Ezekiel and the boys were wrestling on the floor at her feet while she mended their clothes, Ezekiel grabbed Nonnie's leg, as shapely as ever, and said, "Tickle, tickle, on your knee, if you laugh you don't love me," and all the children giggled expectantly, but Nonnie looked at him and did not laugh, as anger, like a bolt of lightning and just as unexpected, cut through her body like a knife.

"Ezekiel Bailey," she said, "you ought to get up from there"; for she wanted a man suddenly, and not another child on the floor. And furthermore, as Nonnie looked down at them all in a roiling heap, it hit her that she did not want to be everybody's mamma, which she was. All of a sudden Nonnie was in a temper, the way she used to get. She was still pretty, she was still young, she was furious. But when Zeke tickled her knee again she managed to laugh, even though it was not real laughter, not like back when she was a silly girl and everything was funny.

Was this the moment that marked the change, that signaled what the rest of her life with Ezekiel would be like? Or was there ever such a moment, or only a slow slipping away, a long estrangement so gradual that in the later years of the marriage Nonnie could not even remember what it used to be like in those busy, busy years? . . . Had Zeke *ever* talked more? It seemed so, but maybe it was just that the children made so much noise . . . and how Nonnie loved to chatter along with them! But at seventeen, R.C. left home to work at a lumber camp near Holly Grove, and then Durwood got on at the sawmill. Only Pack, Lizzie, and the baby, Sally, were still at home, but Pack was mostly gone already, and Lizzie lived for school and had already announced her intentions of going on to the Methodist school in Cana, once Missus Black had taught her everything she knew. Dimly, Nonnie remembered being a smart girl herself. But she couldn't really remember herself as a child, not really, and now her own children were growing up before her very eyes, their childish features sharpening and stretching and changing them into people she scarcely knew.

Only Zeke remained the same, and he remained *exactly* the same, which infuriated Nonnie. She had given up her girlhood, her beauty, and for what? For children bent on leaving like thieves in the night, stealing her youth and her heart, for an old man with nothing to say.

But Nonnie was not yet an old woman when she went to the medicine show.

Lizzie talked her into it. "Oh, come on, Mamma, everybody is going, everybody from school," Lizzie said, arms and legs flying everywhere at once as she chased her puppy around the yard. It made Nonnie tired just to watch her.

"What do you think, Zeke?" she asked her husband, who sat in his chair and smoked and stared down the valley.

"Zeke!" Nonnie said sharply, but once she got his attention, he merely asked why in the world she would want to go see something like that, and mentioned that God was against it, for it had been so preached from the pulpit Sunday past.

This made Nonnie see red. It was not like Zeke to lay down the law, it had something to do with that new preacherman that Nonnie didn't like anyway, and speaking of *him*, she could tell a thing or two about him just from the way he looked at her after church, not that she would, of course. Nonnie never told Zeke anything that would bother him, or that he wouldn't understand. But she determined, then and there, to go to the medicine show, and by the end of the week, she had cajoled Zeke into acquiescing. She got a neighbor woman to come over and stay with Sally.

Nonnie and Lizzie set out on horseback for Cana, Lizzie leading. They stopped once to water the horses and once to eat their snack of dried beef and cornbread, and pulled up at the Streets' boardinghouse just as the sun went down. "You all better hurry up," old Birdie Street said, fixing her hat. "Hit's fixing to start. Hit's starting in a minute." Then off she went toward the court-house square, followed by Nonnie and Lizzie as soon as they'd washed their faces and beat the road dust out of their clothes.

Even before they turned the corner into the square, Nonnie heard the fiddle, and as they pushed through the crowd toward the makeshift stage that had been set up in front of the statue, Nonnie's step grew lighter and lighter, until she was almost dancing to the tune. It had been years since she'd heard a fiddle—*years*, for in keeping with his position as an elder in the Chicken Rise church, Ezekiel didn't hold with dancing or dance music. Nonnie didn't know how much she'd missed it until now. She dropped years with each step as they approached the elevated stage, draped in bunting, ringed by coal-oil lamps.

Great torches flickered at each side of the stage, while large, lurid placards promised gypsy fortune-tellers and Indian dances and touted the virtues of Chief Thunder Cloud's Old-fashioned Indian Vegetable Compound for Scalp Renewal, and of Apache Indian Sagwa, the Bowel, Liver, and Stomach Renovator, and of Dr. Harry Sharp's Celebrated Nervine. Maybe Nonnie needed some of *that*. Her nerves had not been too good lately. She looked at the crowd and did not see a soul from the Chicken Rise congregation, thank goodness, for she feared she'd be churched for coming.

But it was beginning now—Dr. Harry Sharp's Celebrated Medicine Show, starring a real medicine man, Indian Jack himself, who was privy to the secrets of the ages whispered in his ear by the famous Apache medicine man Flying Black Bear on his deathbed in mountainous Colorado. A blackface-nigger dancer came out wearing a tattered coat, tails, and a top hat. He promptly fell flat, causing a huge puff of dust to blossom from the seat of his pants and a great roar of merriment to burst from the crowd. Then he started dancing to the strains of the string band which promptly joined him, and then here came two exotic gypsy women with gold scarves and tambourines, and then finally the medicine man himself, Indian Jack, a big imposing fellow wearing an Indian headdress and war paint.

As soon as the opening number was done, Indian Jack addressed the dancer. "How do you feel tonight, Sambo?" he asked.

"I feels just like a dishrag," said the blackface nigger, rolling his eyes.

"What do you mean, you feel just like a dishrag?" asked Indian Jack.

"I needs to be squeezed!" said Sambo, and everybody laughed.

Then one of the gypsy girls flounced across the stage and Sambo followed her, only to be hauled back by Indian Jack. "Don't you be follering no women offa here, Sambo," Indian Jack ordered. "Don't you forget you are supposed to be working for me."

"Yessuh! Yessuh!" Sambo grinned, nodding his head energetically. "But this redheaded nigger done come around here last night and sprinkled dis here peedee root and love powders all over me, dat's what is inducing me to commit love." The gypsy girl walked by again, and this time Sambo ran off after her, chased by Indian Jack. After the string band played two numbers, Sambo came back and stretched out full length on the stage and fell asleep, snoring loudly.

Indian Jack, annoyed at the interruption, went over and kicked him. "Sambo! I say, Sambo!" Indian Jack yelled. "Can't you be useful as well as ornamental?" This sally was met by appreciative chuckles from the crowd as Sambo droned on, the loudest snoring imaginable. Lizzie, holding tight to Nonnie's hand, was crying from laughing so hard.

"I tell you," Indian Jack said to the crowd, "that nigger ain't scared of work—he'll lay down beside the biggest kind of job and go to sleep."

After several more jokes, Sambo jumped up and ran off-stage as Indian Jack stepped forward and launched into a talk about Chief Thunder Cloud's Old-fashioned Indian Vegetable Compound. "Have you ever noticed, ladies and gentlemen, that there are no bald Indians? Now just think about it. The fact is, ladies and gentlemen, that the Indians of long ago, guided always by the Great Spirit, found curative herbs that can be of immense value to the white man's civilization. When applied directly to the scalp, this powerful compound will stimulate the nerves which produce the growth of new hair roots and invigorate those yet present, instilling not only a luxurious growth of healthy, lustrous hair but also a clarity of thought reflective of those High Plains Indians who gather these precious little herbs. I myself, ladies and gentlemen, was once plagued by a receding hairline and a consequent loss of self-esteem. But after only one year of repeated applications of Chief Thunder Cloud's Old-fashioned Indian Vegetable Compound, only one year, mind you, I have the perfectly healthy hair of a much younger man." Here Indian Jack took off his huge feathered headdress and bowed low to the audience, allowing them a closer look at his full head of shiny black hair.

"That feller weren't never bald, I'll warrant ye," somebody said right behind Nonnie, and Nonnie herself knew this was probably true, yet she couldn't take her eyes off Indian Jack, up there on the lamplit stage. He sure was one good-looking Indian. But mean? He looked like he might be mean. Indian Jack had a jutting nose and thick black brows which nearly met in the middle of his forehead, and dark eyes which flashed in the torchlight.

"Aw-right!" Indian Jack yelled, holding up a jar of the miraculous compound. "Aw-right! Puts hair on your head and hair on your chest, only fifty cents for new vigor and manliness! Boys, you'll have to beat the girls off with a stick!"

Hands went up, folks surged forward.

"Mamma, I wanna go back to Birdie's now. I'm tired," Lizzie said, but Nonnie said, "Just a minute, honey. Just a minute, I want to hear them play one more time."

"Daddy wouldn't like it," Lizzie said. "I didn't know what hit would be like when I said I wanted to come here," and she started to cry, for the noise and the crowd and the Indian man had scared her.

But Nonnie tossed her head and stamped her little foot and said, "Oh, who cares what he'd like? Old stick-in-the-mud!"

Lizzie stood looking up at her mamma and opened her mouth in an O.

"Go on, then," Nonnie told her. "Just run on back to Birdie's, and I'll be along directly. You know the way." And Lizzie ran, not looking back.

The compound sale was followed by the Gypsy Mind Readers, then a buck dancer named Dancing Henry Hayes, then a thin, sickly-looking redheaded boy who sang "Leave the Light On for Me, Mother" in such a high, sad voice that it brought a tear to every eye, and then the string band returned for a couple of rousing dance tunes.

By this time it had grown completely dark and the coal-oil lamps were lit all around the edge of the stage, giving the performers a heightened, dramatic appearance. Even the familiar faces in the audience—storekeepers, townspeople Nonnie had known by sight for years—took on a new aspect in the flickering firelight. They didn't look like themselves at all. They didn't look like anybody Nonnie had ever known. She wondered whether she looked that way to them—exotic, foreign.

And it was at this precise moment that Nonnie felt it stealing over her, that feeling from long ago, that quivering mixture of excitement and longing and dread which meant *Now: Right now. Something is going to happen.* The moment opened up, flared. Then the drums rolled and Dr. Harry Sharp ascended the stage wearing a stovepipe hat and a fake black beard, looking somewhat like Abraham Lincoln and a lot more like Indian Jack. He held up a bottle of Apache Indian Sagwa, the Bowel, Liver, and Stomach Renovator. "Now we don't have a cure-all, ladies and gentlemen," Dr. Harry Sharp announced in his deep, beguiling voice. "Far from it." Nonnie stared hard at Dr. Harry Sharp as he went on with his speech. She had never heard a man talk so much in her whole life. It made her dizzy and weak in the knees to hear him go on and on like that. "Our product is good for three things and three things only: the bowels, the stomach, the liver, and any diseases arising therefrom. . . ."

Nonnie closed her eyes and swayed to the rhythm of Dr. Sharp's voice as though it were music. The wind came up a little bit. The torches blew wildly, scattering light. The crowd drew back. The thin boy came out to sing "Letter Edged in Black" in his high piteous voice, accompanied by the old fiddler, as the wind rose steadily. People were leaving.

Then Pete the Tramp, who looked suspiciously like both Indian Jack and Dr. Harry Sharp, put a lighted cigar backward into his mouth and did a whistling imitation of a freight train rounding a curve while the band played "Little Red Caboose Behind the Train." Smoke poured out of Pete's mouth and wreathed his head while he whistled, and the wind tore the bunting loose.

"Looks like we're in for a shower, folks," he said when that act was done. "But it don't bother me none. I'm used to sleeping out here in the great outdoors. So if you'll bear with us, we'll go right on with the show until the great God Almighty pulls the curtain down. And now for a little audience participation!"

Old man Bart Willifong fiddled, and a boy did imitation birdcalls, and then Nonnie found herself walking forward, right up to the edge of the stage. She said she'd like to sing. She was doing this and watching herself do it, both at once.

"Why, yes ma'am!" Pete the Tramp, even more handsome up close, was beaming at her.

And so Nonnie sang the song she'd sung when her daddy put her up on the counter as a little girl, all those years ago, her high, pretty voice trilling on the last line, *"And she never sings cuckoo till the spring of the year,"* and for a minute, she *was* that little girl again, so silly and so good. The audience clapped and cheered as Pete the Tramp led her up onstage to take a bow. Nonnie curtsied deeply, prettily, as if she'd been doing it all her life. It was amazing how natural she felt up there. Then the thunder cracked and the first big drops of rain splattered in the dirt, round as silver dollars. The wind rose. Some of the coal-oil lamps guttered, and others turned over. "Goddamnit, Charley," somebody said in the sudden dark. Pete the Tramp turned to Nonnie and kissed her. His mouth tasted fiery as the pit of Hell itself. Nonnie stood on tiptoe on the floppy toes of his big, big shoes and kissed him back.

That was Thursday, or Stomach Night, at Dr. Harry Sharp's Celebrated Medicine Show. Friday morning, Nonnie and

Lizzie went home. Friday night was Catarrh Night at the medicine show. Saturday was Rheumatism Night. On Sunday, the medicine show left town, and Nonnie went with it, taking nothing but her rose silk dress.

For the next three years, Nonnie and Harry Sharp traveled all over Tennessee and Alabama in a wire-wheeled buggy, followed by Charley Stamper (Sambo), the singer Dennis O'Grady, and the Barnett Sisters in two wagons with DR. HARRY SHARP'S CELEBRATED MEDICINE SHOW, OR PHYSIC OPERA painted in gilt and red letters on the sides. Various musicians, dancers, and magicians traveled with them for a time along the way. They carried a hammer and a saw to build the platform in each town. Sometimes they were forced to sneak out of these towns before dawn, if business had been bad and they couldn't pay their bills.

Nonnie learned to testify movingly to the amazing curative powers of Dr. Harry Sharp's Celebrated Nervine, stating that she had been completely incapacitated by nervousness, prostrate between the bedsheets for three long years, until just four bottles of Nervine had restored her to herself.

Accompanied by Harry on guitar, she learned to sing "The House of the Rising Sun" in a soulful way, never connecting the words with her own downfall as she sang, *"It's been the ruin of many a poor girl, and God, I know I'm one."* For this number, Nonnie wore a low-cut red velvet dress with black net stockings and gloves, *in order to create the proper illusion*, as Harry said. Nonnie learned fast that nearly everything about the medicine show was illusion, including the medicine itself, which Harry mixed up as needed. Once, in Knoxville, she watched as he made up an entirely new product before her very eyes, using flour and water to form a paste which he colored green somehow and rolled into hundreds of tiny pills. "These Vital Sparks pills, derived from an amazingly virile Oriental turtle, have proved to be a remarkable remedy for male weakness," Harry announced. He said that they "rescued the Chinese from the threat of extinction when their manhood had lost the strength to perpetrate the race." Nonnie, behind the curtain, giggled and giggled the first time she heard him pushing the Vital Sparks pills, but they were all gone in a week's time. There was a lot of male weakness out there. Soon, rolling up the Vital Sparks pills was a regular part of her job.

When she questioned Harry, ever so tactfully, about the ethics involved in selling his medications to the gullible public, he just laughed. "Honey," he said, "since the public insists on being poisoned, we may as well give them a good time too."

It was impossible for Nonnie to argue with Harry, since he could talk rings around her, or anybody. Nonnie couldn't get enough of his talking. Those first months, they'd sit up late into the night in a rented room in whatever town they were in, smoking cigarettes and drinking rye whiskey and talking, talking, talking. Nonnie never knew she had so much to say. She told him her whole life, which grew in the telling until she found herself going on and on about things she never knew she'd noticed. Talking to Harry, Nonnie became more and more interesting; Nonnie became her own story. Harry's story was more tragic and more complicated although it too involved his mother's early death . . . then his stepfather's terrible cruelty, Harry's running away, his life on the road, a job in a Baltimore whorehouse, an early stint in vaudeville, time spent on a riverboat, many passionate though unwise affairs of the heart, many misunderstandings and unfair accusations. . . . Harry talked on and on into all those hot southern nights. Nonnie didn't mention it when he contradicted himself. She didn't care if all of it was true or not, or if any of it was true. She had been starved for talking. Harry was *such* a talker! Why, it was plain to see that he could have done *anything*, been *anybody*—politician, actor, lawyer, president. And he knew the biggest words, and he never used just one of them when six would do.

They worked Chattanooga, Scottsboro, Huntsville, and Decatur, then headed down toward Birmingham through Hartselle and Cullman, for Nonnie had taken it into her head to see the ocean, and Harry had promised he'd take her to Mobile. But Dennis O'Grady's tuberculosis worsened in Birmingham and they had to leave him there, and Nonnie was not comfortable with the promises Harry made to Dennis when they left him in the hospital charity ward. He looked like a mouse lying in that bed, she thought, with such great big eyes. She knew she would never see him again. One of the Barnett Sisters was swept off her feet by a rich widowed store owner in Prattville and stayed there, so they took on a new girl, Dottie Ballou. She was a plump young thing with a big voice and a kind of sparkle and recklessness about her. Charley Stamper found her singing at a café in Montgomery, and she was happy to leave there—anxious, so she said, to see the world.

For some reason, just about the time Dottie Ballou joined the show, Nonnie suddenly began to think about Grassy Branch. She thought about Durwood's funny lopsided grin and Lizzie's rosy red cheeks, and a lot of silly little things—the way the mist clung to Cemetery Mountain in the mornings, the twining ivy pattern on the oilcloth that covered the old kitchen table. She could close her eyes and trace that ivy with her fingers, even in Mobile. When Harry drove her out to see the ocean, it was not much, finally, just a lot of water. "I don't know what the hell else you might have been expecting," Harry said angrily. By then he was beginning to get short with her.

Nonnie was not really surprised when she came back to the hotel room early one afternoon and caught Harry in their bed with Dottie Ballou. Dottie Ballou's white thighs were real fat. "Excuse me!" Nonnie said, slamming the door. When she came back later, Dottie was gone, but nothing was ever the same again. Harry couldn't talk his way out of this one so fast, although he made a damn good stab at it, deriding monogamy as contrary to nature and stating that his inconsequential dalliance with Dottie Ballou was pathetic in its insignificance, and had only made him appreciate Nonnie all the more. Nonnie still loved the sound of his voice, but she listened with half a mind now, knowing—in that way she knew things—that another change was on the way. She hung out over the ironwork grille of their window in Mobile, smoking cigarettes, wearing a red Chinese silk robe with nothing on underneath, watching the bustling, brawling life in the street below, and wondered when it would happen, and what it would be. The night the hotel burned, Harry wasn't even with her. Nonnie woke up with the sheets on fire. The last thing she saw before she lost consciousness was the wide blank gaze of Ezekiel's blue-blue eyes as he led the high cold singing in the church at Chicken Rise. "Oh God," Nonnie said. "Oh God," for she really had loved him. Then her mouth was full of dirt and she was dead.

2

Down by Grassy Branch

The cuckoo she's a pretty bird,
She sings as she flies,
She brings us glad tidings,
And she tells us no lies.

She sucks all the pretty flowers
To make her voice clear,
And she never sings cuckoo
Till the spring of the year.

1

R.C. Bailey

When Mamma run off with the medicine show, I was working days at that lumber camp out from Holly Grove, old man Beady Nolan's outfit, and fiddling someplace nearabout every night. I could fiddle all night and work all day and never think a thing of it. I was wild as any young buck, but I never let on to it when I'd go back over there on Grassy Branch and see the folks. Why, I'd go right along to meeting with the rest of em, and sit in a row on them old hard benches, and sing them old high hymnsongs. What Daddy and Mamma don't know don't hurt em, I figured then, for Daddy didn't hold with fiddle music nor with dancing, and I didn't have no intention of running up again him iffen I didn't have to.

Nor Mamma neither, for I helt Mamma up in my mind as a flat-out angel in them days, her always so nice and sweet and pretty and all, not a thing like them other old women around here. Why, you could of knocked me over with a feather when she run off.

Durwood was the one told me. He come over to the camp

a-purpose to do so, and then me and him got good and drunk, and I laid out of work the next day while Durwood went on back home. Somehow I couldn't go over there just yet, I couldn't look Daddy in the face, and I had to play for a dance in town that night anyhow.

I reckon I had been drinking some when I got there. I was bad to drink back then. Well, they was this purty little redheaded gal that caught my eye. She was dancing up a storm. And I could tell that she was cottoning up to me, making eyes and such, so when me and the boys took a break, I says to her, "Let's you and me take us a little walk, honey," and we done so.

We walked off from the hall a little ways, and we was just commencing to get acquainted good when I felt of somebody a-grabbing me around the neck, liked to choke me. "What the hell air ye a-doing?" I heerd and hit turned out to be this great big old boy that was that little redheaded gal's regular feller. Right then I knowed I wasn't going to fight him, for he would of made two of me.

"Now Lonnie, now Lonnie," she was a-crying. Her name was Shirley Hash. "He didn't know no better," she said to Lonnie, and I'll give her credit for it, so then he let go of me and grabbed *her*, twisting her pore little arm up behind her back.

I was not too drunk to say I thought he ought to turn loose of her.

"I reckon you do," he said, "and just who the hell might you be, anyhow, over here a-rubbing on my girl?"

So I said who I was, and then Lord if he didn't start up laughing. "Oh, so you are that Melungeon feller," he said. "I reckon I know about you."

"What the hell are you talking about?" I axed him, and then he liked to bust a gut laughing. They was some several fellers gathered up about us by now, a-listening to all of this.

"Shirley, this here is a woods colt that don't even know it," he says, and at least he lets go of her arm. "My grandma was Missus Rice that used to run the boardinghouse in Cana, the one that stood where the lumberyard is now," he goes on to say, "and she tole it for a fact that yer mamma done tuck up with a Melungeon man that was staying up there in her boardinghouse, and yer mamma tried to run off with him too, but he wouldn't have her, and then she had his baby. Hell, it weren't no big secret at the time. Everybody around there knowed it."

"Liar," I hollered, and I lit into him, and he liked to change my looks afore they pulled him offen me.

Well, it seemed like I couldn't work no more after that, or do nothing afore I got to the bottom of it. We was paid two days prior to this dance I am telling you about, so what I done, I just tuck my pay and lit off from there, and the firstest one I went to see was Tom Kincaid that taught me to play the fiddle, and knowed me since I was a boy. He was some kind of a cousin of Daddy's. He run the dry goods store in Cana.

I reckon I looked pretty rough when I come in there, for Tom jest laid down this roll of oilcloth he was a-measuring, and said, "R.C., let's me and you go in the back here and eat us some lunch," and he tuck my elbow and brung me back there, where he doctored up my face some and give me some hoop cheese and crackers to eat and got us some sweet milk to drink, and said, "Son, it's a mighty hard thing, I'll grant ye," for he thought I was all in a swivet over Mamma running off with the show.

Then I told Tom what all that old boy had said about Mamma and the Melungeon, and his thin face got kind of a cagey look.

"Well, is it true or not?" I axed him pint-blank, but he jest shook his head. He tuck off his glasses and polished em and then he put em back on. He had these little bitty gold glasses.

"I heard something oncet to that effect," he allowed finely. "But if you live long enough, you are likely to hear anything oncet."

"I reckon I could jest an Daddy," I said, but Tom said he

didn't believe I ought to do that, that Daddy had moren plenty to bear and there wasn't no reason for me to ax him nothing about that Melungeon. Tom said this real forceful.

"So you are telling me hit's the truth," I said, for even if I was a fool, I wasn't a tee-total fool.

"I am not telling you nothing," Tom Kincaid said. "I am not telling you but what's the God's truth, you had best fergit this whole business, and get on back home and help yer pa," he said.

"I can't do that, Tom," I said. "I am bound to go around here axing some more folks, I reckon, iffen you won't tell me."

"You will do nothing of the kind," Tom said. He was getting all riled up. "Listen here, boy. Hit is best to leave well enough alone. Hit is best to keep yer goddamn mouth shut, if you foller me."

"Well, I don't foller you," I said. I stood up, I was fixing to go.

Tom kept pacing back and forth in his little office there, with the door shut. "All right," he said. "All right, Goddamnit. I tell you what. If you are bound and determined to ax somebody, go up there on Cherokee Mountain and ax old Willie. Tell him I sent you up that to ax him."

"I will," I said, and I done so, fer I was bound to get the straight of it oncet and fer all. I got up there about dark the next day.

I found old man Willie Malone a-setting out on his porch all wrapped up in a quilt, and hit August. But old folks gets cold real easy. He was so little and dried up he put me in mind of a grasshopper a-setting there.

"Howdy," I said, and said who I was, fer I knowed he couldn't see nothing there in the dark.

"Zeke's boy?" he said, and I said, well, that's what I had come up that to ax him about, and I allowed as how Tom had sent me up that. I knowed him and Tom used to be running mates, and my daddy with em afore he got religion so bad, for many's the story Tom had told me about them and what all they used to get into. I had knowed *Daddy* weren't no saint, but I had never knowed no such of a thing about Mamma.

So then Uncle Willie Malone told me what folks said about Mamma and the Melungeon, and by then it had growed so dark that it was like I wasn't talking to a man atall, jest a old voice coming from noplace, from the night and the mountain itself. "And now, if I was you, I'd fergit the whole thing," Uncle Willie said when he had got done telling it. "Fer yer daddy raised you as hisn, and used to trot you on his knee and walk you of a night and play with you by the hour," Uncle Willie said. "They is not many men that had a daddy to set so much store by a baby as yourn done you," he said.

But I was young and hotheaded then, and three or four days drunk on top of it. I had heerd what I'd come to hear, all right, and I splunged off down that mountain hollering in the middle of the night, I didn't give a damn. I went over to the camp and got my stuff and then I went over to Grassy Branch and gathered up what I had left there, and told em I was leaving for a while.

They said that that strawberry-face ugly old sister of Mamma's had come around wanting to stay and help out, and Daddy had run her off. I reckon I was still drunk, for when Durwood told me this, I says to Daddy, "Daddy, if I was you, I would of let her stay on here, I would of just put a bag over her head," I says, "for hit's all the same in the dark. I bet she wouldn't of felt no different from Mamma," I said.

Well, Daddy whupped me good then, and after he whupped me, he gone to praying over me, and I raised up long enough to say, "Quit that praying over me, for there ain't nothing to it. Hit ain't nothing to Heaven, nor nothing to Hell. Hit ain't nothing, period," I tole Daddy, for it seemed to me like that was the bare-bone facts of it all. Then I passed out finely and slept all that next day through, and woked up to see Lizzie thar by the bed crying. "What are you looking at?" I said.

Then I left. I didn't never mean to darken that door again. I went over around Bluefield, then up in West Virginia, doing first one thing and then another, fiddling here and there and drinking steady. Best I can recall, my thinking run kindly along these lines. *Mamma is a whore, and I am a bastard*, and so by God I set out to prove it. It seemed like a great storm was raging in me. I figgered I might as well get out there and fuck my brains out or do whatever the hell else I could think of, for it wasn't no pleasure in this life nor nothing beyond it, nothing, nothing, nothing.

I didn't want nothing but pussy. I'd tell a girl anything just to get in her pants, and you'd be surprised how easy that is, iffen you go projecting around with nothing but that on your mind. *They're all whores*, I says to myself, and I proved it pretty good too.

I stayed gone for some several years, drunk moren not, beat up frequent, in jail a couple of times too. Then come a pretty spring morning when I woke up in a woman's bed in Huntington, West Virginia, and didn't have no memory atall of who she was, or how I had got there, or where we was. Hit looked to be a room in a cheap hotel, or may be a boardinghouse. I could hear somebody walking overhead, and then I couldn't hardly hear nothing, fer the sound of this little old baby that started up crying to beat the band. It was in a dresser drawer over there in the corner, I reckon it didn't have no crib. And Lord, it could holler! It just cried and cried.

I rolled over and looked at the woman that was laying there in the bed with me. She didn't look too good. Matter of fact, I couldn't tell if she was breathing or not. She had dried vomit all over her face and was laying on her back with her mouth open. She was a curly-headed blond woman, vomit in her hair too. She looked awful. I felt of her arm, which was warm, but I swear I couldn't see her breathing. I don't know to this day if she was dead or not. I don't know if she was a whore or not. I don't know how I got there. I couldn't remember nothing about the baby. I couldn't remember nothing about the whole week prior, in fact. I got up and pulled on my pants, I was shaking so bad all over I couldn't hardly buckle my belt. The baby had set into a hard thin wail, like it was hopeless or something. The room was a wreck, liquor bottles and drinking glasses and cigarette butts and clothes throwed all over the place. They was a gun on the floor by the bed that was not mine, it did not look much like a lady's gun neither. The woman on the bed was not moving. She was a big woman. I reached down and got something to cover her with, or part of her anyway. Then I got out of there. I remember standing on the street in the blazing sunshine and looking back up at that window. I could still hear the baby wailing, but it sounded real far away, like a baby in another world.

Then I heerd my mamma speaking to me, plain as that blazing sun.

"Go on home now, son," she told me, and so I did.

I got back to find that Daddy had had a stroke and couldn't say a thing, nor move his left leg. He would walk after while, he got some better, but he dragged his left foot the rest of his life. Durwood and Lizzie and me figgered out later that Daddy had had the stroke just right about the time that I had heerd Mamma speaking to me up in West Virginia. Somehow it didn't surprise me none to learn this.

"I am home for good," I told them, and even though Daddy couldn't talk none, he could understand me. Tears came up in his old blue eyes. I hugged him as hard as I could. "You took good care of usuns," I told him, "and now I aim to take good care of you."

2

Lizzie Bailey

We depart for Europe within a fortnight, as soon as the *Red Cross* is completely stocked and outfitted. Caroline and I have been down to the harbor to see it more than once, of course, and I must say it is a fine sight, the great white ship brilliant in the sunlight, the broad band of red and the fluttering flag proclaiming to the world our mission of mercy. In fact, the newspapers are calling it the "Mercy Ship," and there is a write-up daily concerning these preparations. I have to pinch myself to assure myself that this is actually happening. Events have moved with such swiftness! First the Archduke Ferdinand's assassination at Sarajevo in June. Then in eight astonishing days, comprising July 28 through August 4, Austria, Germany, Serbia, Belgium, France, Russia, and Great Britain threw themselves into the war. Of course there is a lot of sentiment in this country for us to do likewise, with feelings against Germany running high at this time. Yet *our mission is mercy*, and a hospital unit of surgeons and nurses will go to each country involved in the war, myself to France, for I have a smattering of that language. "Neutrality" and "Humanity" are engraved upon the great seal of our ship, but I foresee that maintaining this position will become increasingly difficult if the war continues. Here at the Nurses Settlement, I busy myself with the routine that has occupied me for several years, yet my mind skips about in such an alarming fashion that I fear I will dispense the wrong medication to some unlucky patient!

Caroline and I have several books about France. We read them nightly, and practice the language . . . and yet, and yet—oh! Here is a riddle worthy of any of our new practitioners of this so-called science of the mind: How can it be, I wonder, that the closer our date of departure draws, the less I am able to even *imagine* France, and the more I find myself travelling back through time and circumstance, back to my Virginia childhood? In my current heightened state of mind, I remember everything—the painful and the pleasant alike, and I feel, oddly, such a need to set these reminiscences down on paper. Indeed, I feel a sense of urgency to do so. Perhaps it is always thus, for those departing—as I am—upon a great journey.

As if it were yesterday, I see our house set on the gentle hill, a large double cabin, two cabins really, connected by the breezeway in between, the wide porch overlooking the yard and the little road, hardly more than a path, which winds around that bend following Grassy Branch itself. Impossible to say how many hours I spent just sitting on that porch, looking down the road, wondering who might come along.

I can still see the wildflowers that grow in profusion all along the road, the burning bush that grows by the gate; I can smell the sweet wild perfume of the honeysuckle whenever I close my eyes; I taste the tart little apples that grow on the gnarled trees behind the barn; and I still hear Grassy Branch itself, running and gurgling along over the big rocks where I sit in the sun and dangle my feet in the clear, cold water. Even in the house, we can hear Grassy Branch—it sings us to sleep each night. And over all, of course, behind and above everything, stands Cemetery Mountain, gentle and sloping at its lower elevations, where we farm, austere and forbidding as it rises sharply to its mysterious craggy peak (which my brother Durwood nicknamed "Witch's Tit"!). How well I remember the taste of the cressy greens that grow wild in the creek, the coffee smell of early morning, Daddy's crooked black hat, Durwood's old dog Ruth that lay up under the house, Daddy saying "Now I lay me down to sleep, pray the Lord my soul to keep" with me and little Sally every night, and how the rain swept up our valley—you could see it coming from a long way off.

In my mind's eye I see so clearly that little girl I was then—miserable and motherless, to be sure, yet full of life and longing, full of belief that sometime, somewhere, there would come a better day. Lord knows whence it derives, the foolish, innate optimism of youth. . . . I was nearly ten when Mother left us, twelve when we learned of her death, and fourteen when Daddy had the stroke and R.C. returned to us from whatever dark and mysterious realms of the spirit he'd travelled through in those lost years. (Try as I might, I was never able to persuade him to tell me anything at all about that time in his tortured life.)

I say "tortured"—for I am persuaded that R.C.'s anguish is habitual with him and has always been so, that it was not simply the result of our mother's abrupt departure. R.C. has been a person of extremes for as long as I can remember. Even as a boy, nobody laughed harder, or ran faster, or yelled louder—or sulked longer, or acted meaner, or was sweeter . . . or more tenderhearted! Yet he was quick to anger, and many was the fistfight to the death which he and Durwood waged in the yard, with me crying and imploring them to stop it, stop it! Other times, he and Durwood would act the fool until they had me rolling on the floor breathless from laughter. And no boy could sing nicer or play a sweeter fiddle than R.C., either, though he had to hide his talent from Daddy in the early days. I remember he kept his fiddle out in the barn, in a special dry space he'd built up under the corncrib, and many were the afternoons I saw him sneak and grab it, wrap it up in a gunny sack, and set off for town or wherever it was that he went, grinning and sitting tall on his big black horse. How I missed R.C. when he went off to work at Beady Nolan's! For there was an intensity about him which is difficult to describe.

Let me put it this way—everyone felt more alive when R.C. came in the room. There was something about R.C. that put an edge on things.

It was not so much the way he looked, although Lord knows he was good-looking—at least, the girls thought so! He had the curliest, prettiest fair hair, which never turned dark as so often happens, yet his once fair skin was now nearly swarthy. He had a big nose, high cheekbones, and a large, mobile mouth. In form he was big and hulking, he seemed to loom over you as he spoke, and his dark eyes burned out in his face. Yet his voice was deep and gentle, almost halting. He hardly spoke, or else he spoke too much. R.C. was a young man of extremes. Often he seemed abstracted, brooding, lost in thought.

I believe he was a kind of genius, for he could build anything, make anything he chose to. Once he conceived of it, there was simply *nothing* R.C. couldn't do. I've heard that even as a little boy he made bread trays from buckeye wood and sold them downtown on Court Day—along with biscuit boards, rolling pins, rocking horses, deadfalls for catching animals, you name it. One time Judge Reckless's wife rode all the way out to Grassy Branch to find out if R.C. could fashion a newel post and a gazebo for the fine new house she was building.

After he came back, he used to go up on Cemetery Mountain

regularly to trap muskrats, minks, coons, skunks, and possums, and then he'd trade the skins for shoes for us—as well as for sugar, flour, salt, and coffee—whatever we didn't grow. We always had plenty of everything after R.C. came back. He was the best trapper in our mountains by far, because of some secret trapping device he'd invented, which he would show to no one.

I believe, thinking now in retrospect, that R.C. could have gone anywhere and done anything he chose, and been successful at it, too—even if he never would be happy. The only time he was truly happy, I believe, was when he was actually playing music. The rest of the time he was driven by a great restlessness—yet I suppose we were lucky for it, as it led him into scheme after scheme, and we were the beneficiaries.

I will never forget the day, soon after R.C.'s return, when a man came by our house with a banjo. It was certainly the first banjo I had ever seen, and it may have been the first that R.C. ever saw as well. The fellow sat down, at our request, and played a few tunes—I remember his playing "Get Along Home, Cindy" for one, and "John Hardy." Then he handed the banjo over to R.C., who took it and played it instantly. The fellow was amazed, but Durwood and I were not, well aware of R.C.'s talents.

Of course, had our visitor happened by Grassy Branch *before* Daddy's stroke, Daddy would not have permitted such music in the house, but after the stroke, all that righteous fire went out of him, to be replaced by a sweetness and light that would make you weep. I don't believe that Daddy lost his faculties, mind you, upon losing his speech; I believe rather that a finer, more tempered nature came to him. But in any case, R.C. was fascinated with the banjo from that time on, fashioning several and ordering others from a mail-order catalogue. I dearly loved to sing along, especially on the old ballads and lullabies, for they reminded me so of Mamma. I'd sing "Barbry Allen" and "Brown Girl," "Down in the Valley," and the cuckoo song. Sally especially loved "All the Pretty Little Horses." When she was a baby, I had sung it to her every night to put her to sleep.

In more recent years, friends have remarked upon how difficult it must have been for me—just a child myself—to raise Sally. And yet, as I've answered in all honesty, it was not hard at all! For Sally was a sweet-natured, easy baby, and a docile little girl. Actually, she gave me a great deal of pleasure at a time in my life when pleasure was in scant supply. And I derived real satisfaction from the knowledge that this—taking care of Sally, I mean—was something I could do which would make a real difference in the world. For I felt *helpless*, you understand, as indeed I was helpless to control the situation which had placed her in my charge, just as so many, many children—God help them!—are helpless, trapped within the circumstances of their lives.

I think I knew, even then, that I would have no children of my own—and though events may yet prove me wrong, for Heavens! it is not too late—I suspect this will turn out to be the case. To date, I have not been able to envision combining marriage and vocation satisfactorily, or indeed, at all.

For mine is not a profession to adopt lightly, or casually, and I have felt—ever since that day in 1904, after Daddy's stroke, when Miss Covington came out to Grassy Branch—a sense of real vocation. Perhaps "mission" is the more exact word.

I shan't forget my first glimpse of Miss Covington as she rounded the bend of Grassy Branch on her little mare, wearing a gray cloak over her gray split skirt, the little white cap perched firmly atop her pale blond hair, which she wore in a careful bun at the nape of her neck. Her cap sported the little red cross, and on the snowy breast of her white blouse she wore a smaller gold pin bearing the caduceus. My schoolteacher, I knew, had sent her to us—Miss Covington had only just come to Cana at that time, the public health program being in its very infancy, and strongly resisted by most folks in our community, who swore by the granny women and the old remedies. Miss Covington came riding along by Grassy Branch looking pretty as a picture, sitting straight up. For some reason, she put me in mind of a little soldier. I went out and opened the gate.

For there was something in me, I see it now, which needed Miss Covington—which *craved* her.

Since Mamma left, I'd been doing the best I could, of course, for I always felt her departure was my fault, in a way—after all, I was the one who wanted to go to the medicine show! I can never forget this. So I have always done the very best I can, dedicated to erasing some of the *harm* done by those who run loose about the world doing just whatever pleases them at any given moment, those who are messy and heedless, prisoners of their passions, unmindful of all others save themselves. *I will not be like that*, I had told myself over and over, and so I had worked my little fingers to the bone, especially in those years before R.C. came back to us. Of course Daddy was strong then, doing the farm work of several men, yet Durwood was shiftless, Pack had gone off to work on the railroad. Sally needed my constant attention, and I was all alone, the only girl in the house, the only girl—I often felt—alive in all the world!

For we were very isolated there at Grassy Branch. And Daddy, hard as he worked, did not talk much except to pray. Durwood stayed gone for days and weeks at a time, or lay out under the apple trees in a dreamy stupor when he was home. Sally, though a good child, was of course too little for conversation. So I did what I had to—cooking, milking, feeding the animals, running after Sally, churning, patching, washing, ironing, cleaning . . . well, there is no end to it. A woman's lot is a terrible one, and I realized it early, even before the age of twelve, yet I had no alternatives, it seemed—if I wished to be good and do my duty. And this *is* what I wished, above all things.

"You take good care of your daddy and your little sister, now," Preacher Johnson had said to me. I tried my best. But I was a mere child, a slip of a girl, and oftentimes I grew so exhausted I felt I might die, and oftentimes I wished I *would* die! And yet, still other times, my soul would rise up like a bird and beat its wings, flying high into the blue sky above Cemetery Mountain, wild, wild with longing—for what, I knew not. I'd be seized with emotion then, and often I'd fall weeping on the ground.

I'd been quite a fine student, yet when Mamma left and I had to stay at home with Sally, all my "book learning" seemed to fly right out of my head. My studies, which I had loved, struck me then as useless, wasted. I imagined all the books I'd read as lined up on a huge bookshelf suspended somehow in the air, separate from me, separate from my life as it was then on Grassy Branch. I yearned so for *something*, yet I could not even name my yearning—until, as I say, that day in 1904 when Miss Covington rode around the bend of Grassy Branch.

She seemed so—how shall I put it? So *all of a piece*. For when I thought of Mamma, I thought of her as falling apart, somehow—the combs flying out of her hair, her hair curling down around her face in an untidy mass; her petticoat hanging; her bodice unbuttoned as she went singing about the house, the milky-white curve of her breast showing. I thought of our household as falling apart, too, especially now in her absence—goods scattered, dishes broken, chores undone, the laundry left out in the rain—for of course I could not keep up with anything but Sally after Daddy's stroke.

And as for myself, I felt, I was not only falling apart—why, I was literally *flying* apart, with great velocity, little bits of me spinning off to every known corner of the universe.

Then Miss Covington came out to Grassy Branch, and bandaged Daddy's arm.

The day before, not understanding at first the limitations which the stroke had delivered to him, Daddy had tried to go out to the woodshed—or I *suppose* this was where he had intended to go, Heaven knows what he had actually had in mind—and he'd slipped and cut his arm on the ax blade, not deeply, but it was a jagged, messy cut.

First Miss Covington tethered her mare. Then she took her nurse's kit out of her saddlebag, set Daddy down in a chair, and proceeded to clean out his wound and bind it, wrapping the white bandage round and round his arm while Sally and I watched. I admired Miss Covington's kindness, her gentleness, her quick efficiency.

"There now," she said when she was done. "I will leave some of these bandages with you, and every day you must wash the arm with soap and water just as I have done, and wrap a new bandage around it just so. It should heal up nicely in two weeks' time. But if it does not, if any redness or puffiness or red streaking develops around the cut, you must have him come in to see Dr. Potter immediately. *Immediately.* Do you understand?"

"Yes ma'am," I said. She looked at me steadily for a moment with her soft gray eyes.

"Why, yes, I believe you do," she said. "I believe you will make a splendid little nurse. Now how old are you, dear?" she asked further.

"Fourteen," I said.

"And the little one?"

"This is Sally," I said. "She is five now."

"And how are you getting along out here?" she asked, looking all around and into the messy house, which embarrassed me.

"Just fine," I said, and then I burst into tears.

Miss Covington held me while I cried for what seemed hours, until Sally started crying, too, just to keep me company. Daddy sat right there in his chair in the midst of all this crying, his face as blank and expectant as ever, registering *nothing*. Once I thought I was finally through with crying, but then I looked over at him and started up again. At length I was done. Miss Covington made me blow my nose and sniff some smelling salts, and said that on second thought she would come back the following week herself, to check on Daddy's progress.

Thus it began, the friendship which was to change my life, as faithfully she visited us during the next several years, through Sally's measles, Daddy's cough, R.C.'s stomach troubles (*Ulcer, quit drinking*, Miss Covington said), and the birth of R.C. and Lucie's first child, the one they call "Pancake" now.

I see I am getting ahead of myself—I am always getting ahead of myself, it seems!

R.C. met Lucie Queen when he was off on one of his numerous money-making schemes, selling furniture to farmers around Oak Hill. He had bought a wagonload of furniture on the cheap, from a man in Bluefield who needed some cash money fast to pay off a debt.

The first time he saw Lucie Queen, R.C. always said, she was sitting in her aunt and uncle's kitchen playing the autoharp and singing. She had long red hair, freckles, a deep strong voice, and an easy laugh. And R.C., who had "sworn off women for good," or so he said, was so smitten with Lucie Queen that he failed to sell her aunt and uncle a single chair—and instead bought a whole set of china dishes that *she* was selling, for Lucie Queen was every bit as enterprising as R.C. Bailey!

I imagine they are using those dishes still, up on Grassy Branch—thick white china with a bouquet of purple violets in the center and a ring of violets around the edge. I imagine they've seen some rough use, with all the children up there now—I lose track! But those dishes were made to last, and so was Lucie Queen. I loved her from the minute I set eyes on her. She was just my age, sixteen.

I loved her, but I did not want her to marry R.C., though that would mean I'd have a friend at last. I did not even want her to love him, because the very notion of love terrified me, bringing to mind all the old ballads, which show love as a kind of sickness, or a temptation unto death, a temptation which destroys women, even as it destroyed Mamma. To me, "falling in love" was like falling in death—and one time, when R.C. had brought Lucie Queen over to Grassy Branch for a visit, I tried to talk to her about this.

R.C. had gone off to town to pick up something or other, which was unusual—mostly, he wouldn't leave Lucie's side when she came over to visit, since she never stayed long. Her aunt and uncle wouldn't let her spend the night, so she and R.C. would have to leave at sunset to get her back across Cemetery Mountain before midnight, and it would be near dawn when R.C.'d come dragging home again, grinning the silliest grin.

It was hot as blazes that July day, as I recall. Lucie had hiked up her skirts and wrapped her strong legs around little Sally, who stood still for once and let Lucie braid her pigtails. We sat out on the porch. Sally was just as crazy about Lucie as the rest of us were.

"Listen here, Lucie," I said all of a sudden, "are you going to marry R.C.?"

Lucie laughed her merry, musical laugh. "I reckon so," she said, "whenever I take a final mind to, which I reckon I will before long. It don't do to say yes too quick. They'll think they've got more if it's a little bit harder to get."

As I said, it was very hot and still that day—dog days, it

was—and the heat made my head hurt and my dress stick to my back while I sat in the rocker mending. Her answer infuriated me.

"Lucie," I said, though in truth it was none of my business and I knew it. "Lucie, it is not a game. It is not a play-party," I said between my teeth. "You are fooling with fire," I said. I felt so angry.

Lucie just threw back her head and laughed and laughed. "Why, it *is* a game, too!" she said. "Don't you know a thing?" I fell silent then, for I sensed that I knew too many things altogether. I felt far, far older than she.

Then it began to thunder, and lightning shot through the heavy clouds. The air smelled the way it always does right before a storm. The wind picked up and the leaves on the trees turned inside out, showing their silvery undersides.

"Oh, where *is* he?" Lucie wailed, peering down the darkening road, but just then R.C. came galloping right up to the porch and thrust a big box at her. "Here, honey!" he hollered, then wheeled his horse and headed for the barn just as the drops began to fall in earnest.

Lucie opened the box. It was a brand-new little Gibson guitar that he'd sent off for—she'd told R.C. she'd always wanted a guitar. As it turned out, this would be Lucie's wedding present—no ring, but a new guitar, and it would be just fine with her, too. That's how she was.

"Oh!" gasped Lucie then. She jumped off the porch and ran out toward the barn in the pouring rain, calling his name.

"Come on, Sally," I said, and we went inside, for the rain came down so hard and fast that we were getting splattered even on the porch. I picked up the guitar and took it inside with me. Sally went to play with the paper dolls Lucie had brought her.

But something made me walk through the front room and into the dark kitchen, and stand at the open door looking out through the rain, where I could see my brother pushing Lucie Queen against the side of the barn and kissing her, putting his hands all over her body, finally pulling up her skirts behind and putting his hands there, too. I felt hot and terrible, watching this, yet I could not stop watching. I could hear Daddy snoring in the other room, and Sally making her paper dolls talk to each other. Then lightning flashed so bright it looked like day outside, and I could clearly see Lucie Queen down on her knees in the barnyard mud. Thunder crashed, followed by a deluge, and when the lightning came again, they were gone, inside the barn I supposed. I felt sick. I went and finished the mending.

Much later they came dripping into the house and said that they had gone for a walk in the rain. They looked flushed, intoxicated, as if they'd contracted a fever. I pretended to believe them. I gave Lucie a dress of mine to wear, although she had to leave most of the back unbuttoned as she was so much bigger than I.

R.C. did not take her back across Cemetery Mountain that night or the next, and the day after that he took her over to Holly Grove and brought her back married, waving the certificate to prove it. I don't believe Lucie Queen's aunt and uncle ever forgave them for that. But Lucie didn't seem to care. She had eyes only for R.C., and I must add that he fast became a different individual altogether, a great deal less difficult and much happier as a result.

At first it angered me that he had been so difficult, so moody and temperamental, with *us*, and was now found so much easier to live with. I felt that we had had the worst of the deal! But I soon realized I should be grateful, for Lucie's presence there on Grassy Branch gave me leave to help Miss Covington, and I dearly loved to accompany her as she went about the county trying (in vain, or so it often seemed to me!) to educate people about basic sanitary procedures and nutrition, tending to their illnesses and complaints. We delivered many a baby and wormed many a child. Miss Covington, I firmly believe, was a saint, never betraying any dismay at anyone's ignorance or prejudice or lack of standards, maintaining always her calm, cheerful demeanor. Her felicitous manner is transmitted even now in the letters she occasionally writes, from the hospital training school in Cincinnati which she directs—and I imagine she is very good at it, too! Never again did Cana have a home health nurse as effective as she, and her successor, Gertrude Blivens, a horse-faced, bossy type of person, actually *undid*, or so I believe, much of the good Miss Covington had done. For we mountain people are a peculiar, proud lot, and must be approached correctly if we are to be approached at all. We will not brook contempt, or being talked down to—"biggetyness," as Lucie would say. Nor will we accept charity in any form. Miss Covington's practical manner always made it seem that she was just there to do a "job of work"—the only manner, I believe, which could have assured her entry into those remote homes.

So although I'd been forced to cease attending the Methodist school at Cana, I received an education all the same, from my dear Miss Covington. I learned not to drink water from springs or shallow wells when they are situated close by the outhouse—if there *is* an outhouse, which often, in the far-off areas, there is *not*! (They use the woods, like animals.) I learned that a baby should not be allowed to eat and drink just anything it can manage to bring to its mouth, that tomatoes are not poison, that measles will "come out" whether the unfortunate sufferer is fed sheep-dropping tea or not, that precautions should be taken against rain, as wet clothing is conducive to respiratory infection, that gargling with salt *does* help sore throat, but that a piece of smooth creek gravel placed inside a woman will not keep her from conceiving a child and is, in fact, very dangerous for her; also that putting butter on a sore and getting a dog to lick it is *not* a good idea, nor is there any reason for a woman not to bake a cake while menstruating. I could go on and on. I learned these lessons not from lectures, for Miss Covington never lectured, but on the spot, as these issues of health presented themselves during our time together.

And when the end of this time drew nigh—for Miss Covington stayed with us only four years before returning to Cincinnati to teach, this decision prompted by her mother's illness—when her departure was imminent, she asked me whether or not I should like to go to nursing school, if she could find one that would waive the normal entrance requirements, for she felt that they would be unnecessary in my case.

She broached this idea one fall day when we'd been over to Frog Level and I was leaving for home. At first I did not want to let her see my excitement over the prospect, for instantly I felt disloyal to my family.

"I'll think about it," I said carefully, and I mulled it over as I rode the colorful trail along Grassy Branch on my way home.

For much as I'd enjoyed and profited from my time with Miss Covington, I had come to love Lucie Queen, and even R.C. in his new, more pleasant guise. They had had their first baby by then—little Reese. We all called him Pancake because he loved to eat pancakes so much. And Lucie was already pregnant again! I thought about her as I rode home. I had explained to her all the precautions Miss Covington had explained to me, and I had emphasized that nursing a baby will *not* prevent another pregnancy, as commonly believed, and yet, and yet . . . Look at her! I thought, full of fury. My words had gone in one ear and out the other, obviously. So often I wanted to take Lucie by the shoulders and shake her until her teeth rattled. "Lucie, Lucie, Lucie!" I imagined saying. "Life is hard . . . *hard!* Don't you know it? Don't you know anything? Life is so precious, so easily lost. . . . You must be more serious, Lucie. Life is meant to be *serious.*"

But I had never found it in my heart to speak those words. They *did* seem happy, R.C. and Lucie. I had to grant them that. They had begun to sing in public, often accompanied by Durwood. It had come about accidentally, and now afforded all of them the greatest pleasure in the world.

Lucie liked to be the one to tell the story of how she and R.C. had gone into Cana shopping and had already spent all their money (on a new store-bought dress for her!) when the wagon broke down on their way home. But a blacksmith, Shorty Roberts, lived back toward town a ways, and when they walked back there to see him about it, he said yes indeed he could fix the wagon and shoe the horse besides, but it couldn't be done until the morrow and he'd have to have cash money for it.

"Why don't you-uns go to the bank?" Shorty had inquired, looking at them.

But of course they had no money in the bank. R.C. didn't believe in banks. They went by Tom Kincaid's store to borrow the money but found that he had gone off on a hunting trip, so they couldn't think what to do next. They had twenty-five cents left between them.

Then, as Lucie tells it, "we gone into the drugstore and got us a dope, and whilst we was a-setting there, looking up at the front of the store where they was bills of all kinds posted, meetings and sales and such as that, why, all of a sudden I took this notion.

"'R.C.,' says I, 'R.C., I reckon we will have to do something to get us some cash money, and there's not but one thing I can think of to do to get it quick.' And R.C. he was jest a-looking at me, for as a rule *he* was the one with all the big ideas. 'Well, do you want to know it or don't you?' I says, and then he says,

'Well, all right, Lucie, what in the hell *is* it?' and I says, big as you please, '*Sing!* Hit's the only thing I know how to do that wouldn't make you mad or get the law on us.' And R.C. is jest a-looking at me. Then he starts laughing. 'Well,' he says after a while, 'just where do you propose we do all this singing?' and I point straight out Mr. Sutton's screen door at the square. 'Right over there on the courthouse steps,' says I, 'but we had best get on with it, for it is late in the day and most folks is fixing to head on home.' R.C. jest looks at me. He never did say yes. Then he puts his hat on and stands up. 'Why don't you go back over to Tom's and put on that purty new dress?' he says, and then I knew we were going to do it. I jumped right up and kissed him on the spot," Lucie reported, "and we gone and done it all."

This was Lucie and R.C.'s first public appearance. They took in more than enough to fix the wagon and shoe the horse. They took in enough to spend the night at the Mountain Inn, the only fancy hotel in Cana, and order breakfast in their room. "You never saw nothing like it!" according to Lucie, who never tired of describing either the room or the breakfast—the rolling table that the boy brought to their door, the white tablecloth, the sugar in little paper packages, and the silver covers that hid the food.

After that, given their enterprising natures, there was no stopping them. R.C. took it upon himself to have bills printed up and hire a hall or a schoolhouse. Then he'd post the bills himself wherever they were playing—Oak Hill, Holly Grove, Cana, etc. I have kept one bill as a souvenir. It says: "Look! The Bailey Family Will Offer a Musical Program at Pig Branch School on Saturday, August 1. The Program is Morally Good. Admission is Ten Cents. Posted by Mr. R.C. Bailey, Grassy Branch, Va."

They played at square dances, play-parties, candy parties, house raisings, bean stringings, too. They played wherever anybody would pay them. After Pancake was born, they took him along and would put him down on a pallet on the floor; then later they took Sally along to hold him. They did not play at many dances, since R.C. was enough our father's son to be uncomfortable with dancing, although it is my own private hunch that Lucie would have loved to dance if she'd been allowed to. But R.C., always tortured, forbade her, and the family never missed meeting at the Chicken Rise church, not even when R.C. and Lucie had to drive most of the night to get back for it. R.C. took Daddy to church every time they held the meeting at Chicken Rise, rain or shine, summer or winter, regular as clockwork. It made my heart swell to see the two of them sitting there. Ever since R.C. came home, he has been devoted to Daddy.

Although I can't vouch for their programme's being "morally good" or not, I must say it was altogether entertaining, and everyone seemed to find it so. The secret of their success, I feel, was Lucie—so unaffected, so guileless, she demonstrated absolutely no embarrassment or stage fright, and sang straight to the audience, looking at them all the while. She sang each song as if she believed it, and of course her voice really is remarkable—low, full, rich, almost *smoky* somehow, yet she is capable of hitting any note effortlessly. How I thrilled to hear her sing Mamma's favorites, which *I* had taught her!—"Barbry Allen," the cuckoo song, "The Gypsy Laddie," "Brown Girl," and the riddle song I used to love so much as a child: *How can there be a cherry that has no stone? How can there be a chicken that has no bone?* Finally the riddles are answered: *A cherry when it's blooming, it has no stone; a chicken when it's pipping, it has no bone*, and so forth. I always experienced a deep satisfaction upon hearing Lucie sing this song. For I feel in general that the world is a mystery, I suppose, one vast riddle, and it is good to think that there are a few answers, even though they be fleeting—only the words of a song.

Initially, Lucie accompanied herself upon the autoharp, but as she gained in proficiency on her guitar, she began to employ it more and more frequently. Durwood started performing with them as well, alternating among fiddle, autoharp, and mandolin, and at these public appearances he became virtually a new man, I must admit: neatly shaven, all spruced up, he took on an alacrity heretofore missing in his life. The act of public performance, which encouraged Lucie to be *more herself*, seemed to produce a brand-new Durwood altogether, a Durwood who emerged as the spokesman of the group, telling corny jokes, acting the fool—a regular crowd-pleaser!

R.C., eccentric to his bones, was oddly less professional. Sometimes he sang with the other two and sometimes not, rising abruptly to pace round the stage whenever he chose. But instead of distracting from the programme, R.C.'s sudden mysterious movements added a sense of drama and unexpectedness to the proceedings. And when he wished to, of course, he could fiddle like a house afire—"Bonaparte's Retreat," "Sally Goodin," "The Devil's Dream," "Arkansas Traveller," "Sourwood Mountain"—oh, nobody could fiddle like R.C. when the mood was on him! Or play the banjo, either. I suppose it goes without saying that R.C. was the presiding genius of the group. It was he who "worked up," as he called it, the songs, figuring out new arrangements for even such old classics as "Shall We Gather at the River" and "Shady Grove"; it was he who found new songs for them to sing. Indeed, some of these turned out to be among the most requested—such as that haunting ballad "Preacher's Son," which R.C. picked up from an old man over at Bee, or his own "Melungeon Man," its title referring to a mysterious strain of folks scattered through the mountains, which some believe to be descendants of this country's first Roanoke Island settlers. Regardless of the origin of the Melungeons, that ballad captures such a feeling of *otherness*, of being outside, cut off from the rest of humanity, that I never heard them sing it without feeling a chill.

I was thinking of "Melungeon Man," in fact, on the night I alluded to earlier, the night when I was returning to Grassy Branch with Miss Covington's suggestion of nursing school filling all my mind. Yet I thought I could never do it, I could never leave Grassy Branch, as I was so sorely needed at home—and too, I'd never been anyplace else. I simply could not envision another life.

It was fairly late as I returned. They had long since finished supper and were sitting now around the fire in various postures of abandon and repose—Lucie and R.C. and the child, I mean, Durwood being off on one of his jaunts. They did not expect me, nor did they notice my arrival. The door was open, as doors are always left open in those mountains. I stood there with my foot poised over the threshold, ready to say "Hello," but something bade me hold my tongue. It was such a lovely scene I gazed upon! R.C. sat in Daddy's old rocking chair with a guitar, looking down at several little scraps of paper on his lap; clearly, he was in the process of "working up" something. Lucie half sat, half lay against his knees, her face flushed by the fire, her red hair tumbling in a cataract nearly to her waist. Lucie was huge and beautiful in her second pregnancy, daydreaming there. Little Pancake, wearing only a light shift, lay sprawled on Lucie's lap, nearly asleep, sucking his thumb, while my own sweet Sally slept on a pallet beside them, thin but pink-cheeked, not appearing nearly as fragile, in that moment, as I feared she truly was. Everybody, then, was asleep, or nearly so, excepting R.C., driven by his relentless genius. (There were nights when R.C. didn't sleep *at all*; I knew this for a fact.) With the other lamps extinguished, the firelight bathed them all in a rosy glow, it held them suspended in a round warm circle of light. While I watched, Lucie sighed and moved a bit; R.C., still absentmindedly picking the guitar with one hand, put his other hand on her breast. Pancake was sucking his little thumb.

They don't need me, I realized suddenly.

I experienced the most profound sense of loss, followed quickly by a deep relief. For the longer I looked at this little family scene, the more uncomfortable I felt—uncomfortable about R.C.'s hand on Lucie's breast, about Pancake's little penis, now curled like a caterpillar, about Lucie's big belly, full of another baby, about her slack, flushed, dreaming face. "Wake up!" I wanted to scream at her. "Watch out!" for just beyond the warm circle of firelight, the darkness, full of danger and desire, seemed to wait malevolently, patiently, for them all.

I began to cry. Without a word, I turned and went to my own bed in the other side of the house, where I lay awake far into the night. At some point the words of that old tune ran through my mind:

I never will marry,
I'll be no man's wife,
I intend to live single
All the days of my life.

Two months later, the necessary arrangements having been made by Miss Covington, I departed for the Boston City Hospital Training School, where I earned my nursing degree and remained to assist in the training of others. I found I really liked the orderly life at the training school. In addition, I found time to "catch up" on my regular education, attending many lectures, concerts, plays, etc. I have found the world beyond Grassy Branch to be wide beyond my imagining. Boston was much to my liking. But three years ago, I moved here to the

Nurses Settlement in New York City after I found it necessary to reject the marriage proposal of Dr. Richard Llewellyn, a brilliant surgeon. I simply was *not able* to marry him: frankly, his physical advances produced the strangest, most unpleasant sensations—light-headedness, nausea, shortness of breath. I did not want to hurt his feelings, of course. So I told him simply that I could not marry him because I did not love him. Now, I wonder whether that was true. In any case I have never married, nor—except in a few unexpected moments of random, piercing sadness—have I wished to do so. For family life still seems to me somehow clotted, messy, tangled—as opposed to the life I live now, this room which is my own and nobody else's, neat as a pin, which I share with nobody.

I have returned to Grassy Branch from time to time, of course, ever more conscious of the widening gap between myself and my family. (It is only at this instant, in the *very moment* of writing this account, that I am able to see myself as even vaguely the same person I was then: *only now* am I able to do this.)

Ever since Durwood married that woman, I have been even less comfortable at home, though they built their own house "down the road apiece," as Lucie says. I always felt that woman was not quite wholesome, not to mention her so-called *child*! Also, Daddy has continued to grow more remote than ever—on my last visit home, he reminded me of one of those large life-size dummies we use to demonstrate various techniques to our girls.

But it was Sally's death last year which cut me to the quick. Of course I deal with death daily, and Sally had a weak heart ever since she was a baby, so you may think it should not have affected me so drastically—but I confess I have been unable to return to Virginia since they buried her. I've a new little niece I haven't even seen: Alice, Durwood and Tampa's little girl. Yet somehow I haven't had the energy for the visit, I haven't the stomach for it—the babies, the mess, the sheer *work* of feeding and clothing so many, the cooking, the eating—I don't know. It wears me out to think of it. Far better to take a child who is sick and help it to get better, then *send it home*, far better than raising it up only to die and break your heart. So on the whole, I prefer a more professional involvement with the human race. I prefer situations I can at least *hope* to control: a bone to set, an arm to bandage, a cut to stitch up, a set of instruments to sterilize. I have not Miss Covington's capacity for emotional attachment, perhaps regrettably.

And yet, on the eve of departure, I find myself buffeted by a great storm of just the emotions I have so long sought to avoid! I believe it has something to do with a newsreel Caroline and I saw last night at the cinema—Belgian soldiers marching bravely, row on row. It filled my heart to bursting. I began to sniffle then, and have not stopped. Or perhaps it is simply the writing of this account which has transported me back in time and place to Grassy Branch, to the little girl who lived there then with her old father and her little sister, trying to be good. Her heart was often filled to bursting, too. *What has become of her*? I believe this is the question I've been asking as I've written my way back through the years, and now the answer comes to me, for I see that *we are one* after all, she and I, a life as continuous as anybody's, as that marching file, row on row, up the avenue and out of sight. The soldiers are so young, so earnest. It is glorious.

3

Not the Marrying Kind

R.C. Talking

I knowed she was trouble from the minute I laid eyes on her. Durwood don't have the sense God gave a jaybird, never did. He don't have the sense to come in out of the rain. The only kind of sense Durwood's got is the kind of sense that allows a man to play a good game of poker, judge a horse, or figger out a song. He couldn't make a living if he had to—he couldn't make a living atall if it wasn't for Daddy or me. He'd be up shit creek and that's the truth.

And women—hellfire! Durwood wouldn't know a good woman if he tripped over one. He wouldn't think of going out looking for one, neither. He's too damn lazy. He just lays around and lets them pick *him*. Anybody that wants Durwood can have him, if they work at it hard enough. He's easy that way. Now this didn't use to worry me none, for the ones that picked him dropped him fast enough, once they figgered him out. Durwood had his fancy lady friends all over—Knoxville, Bristol, Holly Springs, you name it—and I reckon they was glad to see him come, and I reckon they was glad to see him go. It wasn't no skin off my back whatever Durwood did when he was away from here. I had done my own share of helling around, too, I'll grant you. I ain't the man to throw stones.

But after Mamma called me back to Grassy Branch and I give over to God, I have tried to walk the straight and narrow from that day forth. And God has blessed me for it, giving me Lucie, the sweetest woman on this green earth, and Pancake and John, my little sons, besides.

Old Durwood, he'd come and he'd go. We was used to it. He usually had him some big deal he was working on, or so he said. I knowed he was mostly gambling and drinking and womanizing, but it wasn't no skin off my back as I said. I've got my work cut out for me, what with the farm and Daddy and all. But I did think we had got it kindly figgered out between us, Durwood and me, and that he wouldn't bring none of his trash back home.

So I was kindly discomfited, you might say, when he come over to Grassy Branch bringing Tampa Rainette. They walked right up to the field where I was hoeing corn, and I quit hoeing to watch them walk up there. I could see trouble coming in the way she walked.

"I'd like for you to meet my wife Tampa," says Durwood, proud as punch. "This here is R.C.," he says.

"Howdy," I says. I looked at her good. She did not look like the marrying kind. In fact she looked like she might of been a fancy woman, and I could tell from the way she was biting her lip and fidgeting around that she was worried somebody was going to catch on to her.

"Tampa," I said. "Where'd you get that name?"

"Florida," she said, looking at me. She didn't say nothing else about her name. She just stared at me real bold, then dropped her eyes and then raised them and stared at me again. She had big dark eyes with thick black eyelashes and little painted-on eyebrows that swooped up like wings. She had the kind of eyes a man could fall into, all right. She had a heart-shaped face with sharp little features and a rosebud

Kewpie-doll mouth. I looked at her good and kept looking at her. She was about ten years older than Durwood, I judged. I wondered if he knowed it.

"You reckon to like farming?" I asked her.

"I reckon I'll like it fine," she said.

I doubted it.

"We'll go on to the house, then," Durwood said. They walked off down the field and through the orchard, him with his arm around her waist. He couldn't keep his hands off her, it was plain to see.

At first, they stayed up at the house with us, them plus her daughter Virginia that she had brung along, which cramped us up and throwed us up in each other's faces all the time. Lucie liked Tampa all right, but I didn't trust her. I couldn't figger out why she would of picked Durwood out of all the men she must of had her pick of, and I damn sure couldn't figger out why she had married him. Tampa Rainette was a mystery to me. Likewise that daughter of hers, that whiny little Virginia, who didn't do nothing at first but cry and throw up. Sally tried to be real nice to Virginia, but nothing doing. And Sally is real sweet.

It was Lucie that figgered it out. "Why, she's going to have a baby," Lucie said all of a sudden one day when we were standing on the porch watching Virginia and her mamma walk down the road. "You wait and see."

"That little girl?" I said, for Virginia seemed real young to me. I didn't know how old she was, for Tampa was so close-mouthed about everything, with me anyway. I guess she wasn't so close-mouthed with Durwood, though. You could hear the two of them over there in the other side of the house talking and giggling way up into the night. I wouldn't put nothing past Tampa Rainette. It made me real nervous. I couldn't wait for them to get that old cabin down the road fixed up and get out of here. But all this time, Durwood looked like the cat that ate the mouse. He went around grinning like a fool, everbody remarked on it. I reckon he didn't need no sleep. *Living on love*, I thought. I sat down and wrote a song about it, but I didn't show it to nobody right then. "Living on Love," I called it.

After they had been up there with us a day or so, I had to go into town to see a man about something, and when I come back it was after supper and I heerd them all singing, from the road. They sounded good, too. That Tampa—for it must be Tampa, I figured—had one of them real high hopeless shaking kind of voices, that went good with Lucie's lower one. Tampa Rainette knew what she was doing, for sure, and I wondered just where she had been singing previous, and for who. Not that I figured she was likely to say. Hers was a voice you don't hardly hear in a lifetime, though. Hers was a voice that said she had been places, and seen things, and done things past the telling.

All right, I thought. *All right.*

I went in there and got my banjo off the wall and joined them. Lucie's face was flushed, you could tell she was having the time of her life. They sounded real good together, and that's when it hit me—a sister act. But I didn't say nothing yet.

"Do 'White Linen' for R.C.," Durwood told Tampa. "Go on, do it. I bet he don't know that one."

"I don't," I said.

"She does this one real good," he said.

Tampa was playing her own guitar and I noticed how unusual she had it tuned. We were open-tuning up to that point, Lucie and Durwood and me.

As soon as Tampa started singing that song, I knew we had got aholt of something big. *"One morning, one morning, one morning in May, I spied this young lady all wrapped in white linen,"* she began. Tampa Rainette's voice would break your heart. She sang it straight through to the end. *"My poor head is aching, my sad heart is breaking, my body's salivated, and I'm bound to die."*

"Where did you larn that?" I asked her when she was done.

"Why, I don't rightly remember," she says real sweet.

"I reckon you've been a lot of places," I says.

"R.C., be nice," Lucie says to me.

"Well, that's a real pretty song," I said. I went out on the porch to smoke me a cigarette. I was all wrought up. I know I get too wrought up, I can't do nothing about it though, I have been like that since a child. Just high-strung, I reckon.

Tampa Rainette followed me out there.

"You got another smoke?" she asked me.

Now this surprised me, as women don't smoke around here, not unlessen it is one of them old granny women with a little pipe. So I give her a cigarette and helt the match for her to light it. She took a deep drag on it.

"You don't like me, do you, R.C.?" she said, blowing out smoke.

"I don't hardly know you," I said.

I felt something else catch and flare up between us. *Be careful*, I says to myself. I turned and walked to the edge of the porch, studying the sky. I could still hear Lucie and Durwood and them in the house. But Tampa Rainette come up behind me, real close. She rubbed her breasts acrost my back in a way that I wouldn't hardly call accidental.

"You don't have to do that, nor nothing like it," I said, for all of a sudden I thought about that woman I had left laying in the bed up in West Virginia. "You don't have to do nothing to stay here," I said. "As long as Durwood wants you, you're welcome. Don't pay no attention to me. I'm half crazy, anybody will tell you that," I said without turning around. I could tell she was crying, which surprised me. "Besides," I said, trying to make a little joke of it, to lighten her up some, "Lucie has done told me to be nice."

Tampa Rainette started laughing, and I felt like we had come to an understanding. "Nice," she said. "Oh, hell," she said. "Who knows who's nice?"

4

Alice Bailey

First Daddy said he wouldn't let us go up there, but Freda started whining and crying and all, and then Mamma said, "Oh, take them then, for God's sake, Durwood," as she had a migraine headache.

"If you are going with me," Daddy said as we started off that evening, "I don't want to hear no whining, nor no muley-mouthing, nor nothing like it, from either one of you girls. I don't want to hear nobody say, 'Daddy, I'm so tired.' Nor do I want to hear nothing spoke about nobody taking a little sip."

"Yes sir," I say, and Daddy says, "All right, then," and so we set off, walking along by Grassy Branch where it was fast coming on for night already, dark shadders laying out behind everything, lightning bugs rising.

We stopped for Daddy to light the lantern, and then I got to carry it. Daddy was carrying a old quilt and Freda was carrying a sack of cold pork biscuits. We walked along the creek and then we tuck off on this path that went up by old man

Isom Daughtry's cane patch, and kept on going up into the trees. It wasn't too hard walking, for Daddy went first, and he'd stop right frequent to take a little drink, so we could catch our breath then and look around. Me and Freda held hands. It was scary up there in them big trees. We never played up on Cemetery Mountain, me nor the others, not even Robert Floyd who is so wild. We never said nothing about it, but we never went up there neither. And then there we were with Daddy, and it dark besides. I swung the lantern side to side, looking around real careful-like, for it seemed to me that I could see faces behind them trees, awful old scary hant-faces, keeping just beyond the light. But I knowed better than to say nothing to Daddy about it.

Daddy put the cap back on the jar and we went on, me still looking real careful to one side and then the other, for I felt those hants was trying to reach out and grab me, I felt like they might of wanted me to come and be their little girl. I said a prayer in my head. I was real glad when we come out of the trees and got on a real road.

I seen first one lantern, then another. Then another, all of them swinging along, just like I was swinging mine. It was like being in a big parade of fairy-lights, moving slow up the mountain. As we went on, I looked back, and I saw more and more lanterns coming. I felt like I was part of something then. I felt big—I've always been real little for my age—and I walked bigger.

Before long we got up there to a grassy bald where it appeared that the road ended, and I could tell this was where we were coming to, for it was a lot of people up there already, and lanterns, and talking and laughing.

It was Uncle R.C. who had the first radio in that part of the county, and he had it rigged up to run off a car battery. He had got this idea, he was telling everybody, because they had like to got trampled in their house by all the folks coming over to hear that new show out of Nashville on it. Everybody on Grassy Branch knew Uncle R.C., who was all the time coming up with crazy ideas. He was not ever mean, and it seemed like he was not hardly working either; he had all the time in the world to set down in the road with you and talk about what makes clouds or tell you about the brownies that live in the woods and come out only at night. Mamma said he made that up, but I don't know.

Uncle R.C. was talking a mile a minute that night, all excited about this contraption he had rigged up. Daddy peered at it for a while and then bade us put the quilt down and get on it, so he would know where we was at, and then he went off with some of his buddies. I ate a biscuit and laid back on the quilt and looked up at the stars, which was real big up there over the mountain, and before long the radio come on sure enough, all the way from Nashville, Tennessee, and you could hear them talking and singing real loud just like they was *here*. I couldn't get over it.

At nine o'clock the Grand Ole Opry come on, and Daddy come back and set down on the quilt real heavy-like, and everybody was listening to the Opry. This was the first time I heard a radio. But we was to go up there some several more times that summer, until R.C. got tired of rigging it up that-away, and by then we had got our own radio anyway. Mamma was not *about* to climb up any mountain to listen to a radio, as she said.

But listening to the radio in our house was *nothing* like listening to it on that grassy bald, laying out on a quit looking up at the stars and eating biscuits. I felt like I was all alone in the world, and also like I was a part of something big, all at the same time. I felt like I was a part of my family too, and a part of that music they loved so. See, they always left us behind when they went off someplace to sing. I didn't hardly know Mamma at all.

Me and Freda got so tickled listening to the radio that night, to Sarie and Sadie, who were funny as could be. I couldn't get over this one Opry member that Judge Hay called the Harmonica Wizard, he could make that harmonica sound ever bit like a train coming around a bend, and then passing right by you, and then going off in the distance again. Some of them up there on the bald said that the Harmonica Wizard was a nigger, but I don't know about that. I ain't never seen a nigger. We listened to Uncle Jimmy Thompson, who was real old and claimed he could fiddle the bugs off a tater vine. He tickled everybody by saying he wanted to have a fiddling contest with some champeen he got to talking about. "Let him come to Tennessee, and I'll lie with him like a bulldog," Uncle Jimmy said. We heard Sam and Kirk McGee, Obed Pickard and the Pickard Family, and Dr. Humphrey Bate and his Possum Hunters, who were real funny. The Solemn Ole Judge was funny too. And it was just fine to be laying out there under the stars and watch the moon come up, big and beautiful, over the top of the mountain. I reckon everybody's favorite singer was Uncle Dave Macon, who could sing up a storm, every now and then hollering out "Ding dong!" or "Kill yo' self!" which got us all to laughing. But even Daddy allowed, "He can frail that banjo for sure."

We sat up there on the mountain and listened to WSM until the Grand Ole Opry went off the air after midnight. It ended ever time with the Judge saying:

> That's all for now, friends,
> Because the tall pines pine
> And the paw-paws pause
> And the bumblebees bumble all around.

The grasshopper hops,
And the eavesdropper drops—
While gently the old cow slips away.
This is George D. Hay saying *So long.*

Daddy was snoring that last half-hour, and I sure did hate to wake him up. But then everbody was gathering up their things, and leaving, and I figgered he would be maddest of all if we walked on back with the others and just left him laying on the ground all night and the dew fell on him.

So finely I roused him. He looked all around real wild-like at first, and said where was he, and then he started off after the rest. Freda and me picked up our stuff and follered. But then I got afraid he was going to fall and hurt himself for sure, he was stumbling so bad, so after a while I caught up to him and said, "Hey, Daddy," and put my arm around him, carrying the quilt and the lantern in my other hand.

The three of us walked the long way back, and even after all the bad stuff that was to happen later, this is what I remember best about Daddy, walking that mountain road along by Grassy Branch with my head full of music and his arm laid across my shoulders. It was way, way late when we got home.

5

The Bristol Sessions

R.C. Bailey paces back and forth on the Tennessee side of State Street—the street that splits Bristol in two like a knife. Tennessee or Virginia: take your pick. It's ninety-five degrees in the shade, humid and overcast. The sidewalk is hot enough to fry eggs on. Yet R.C. is all dressed up—dark blue suit, boiled white shirt, somber tie, his unruly hair parted in the middle, pulled straight back, and plastered flat down to his head. His ears stick out. He looks like he's going to a funeral. From time to time he consults his pocket watch—3:10, 3:12, 3:15. Their appointment is set for 3:30. From time to time he looks up at 408 State Street. *This is it, all right.* The abandoned building does not look promising. It once held a hat factory, then a furniture store. Now its dirty plate-glass windows look into empty rooms with here and there a pile of trash, a shipping box, a broken chair. There seems to be some activity on the second and third floors, however. While R.C. watches, someone passes in front of a window. Then he notices the door at the side, where several people are coming out. One man carries a banjo. Another man looks real familiar to R.C., like somebody he's seen someplace. It is the harmonica player Henry Whitter. R.C. finally recognizes him from the picture on his record, the one that features "Wreck on the Southern Old 97" on one side and "Lonesome Road Blues" on the other. Holy smoke! Henry Whitter!

R.C. thumps on the dusty top of the Model T so hard the women all jump. "All right!" he says. "This here's the place! Get a move on!"

"Just a minute, *sir*!" Lucie answers with some aggravation in her tone, unusual for her. "You just hold your horses!" for she is still nursing her youngest child, Bill, ten months old. She switches him from one breast to the other while R.C. smokes and paces and Virgie primps, pursing her red-red mouth and pushing at her curly hair, unable to see the full effect in her compact mirror. Finally Bill stops sucking and lapses off into sleep, his milky mouth slack. He is as relaxed and as heavy as a sack of meal. Lucie hands him over to Tampa while she adjusts her bodice and buttons herself back up. Bill is an easy baby, a good sleeper, like Clarence was. Clarence is eight now. Robert Floyd is seven, a little devil if there ever was one . . . and John and Pancake are almost growed, God help them, nineteen and twenty year old. It sure don't seem like twenty years since Pancake was borned. *Well, they are good boys, all of them.* Looking down at Bill's fat red cheeks, Lucie shakes her head and wonders, *Where did the time go?* For it seems like no time atall since R.C. came in her aunt's kitchen selling furniture and she came over to live at Grassy Branch.

No time atall since Lucie was a girl herself, and sometimes she still feels like that girl she was then. Why, sometimes she stops dead still in the middle of whatever she's doing and looks around at her family and thinks, *Who* are *all these people? Where did they all come from, anyhow?* She's got moren enough children, that's for sure, yet Lucie still yearns for a girl, seems like a girl would keep you more company . . . like Lizzie, like Sally, Lord help us all. Lucie still can't hardly stand to think of little Sally, dead at fourteen of a rapid heart. Of course they had all knowed it might happen ever since she had the measles; Miss Covington had discovered then that her heartbeat was too fast and said she'd have to take it easy all her life, but Lord, you couldn't slow that youngun down any moren you could slow down the rest of them. Lucie will never forget the day of Sally's death. March 21, 1913. One minute she looked out the kitchen door and there was Sally, hanging out clothes; the next minute, she looked out and all she seen was the sheets and the bedspreads billowing on the line in the high wind, and by the time she got out there, Sally was dead on the ground. Sally had a thin face and a big wide crooked smile—Lucie will never forget her. She sure would like to have a little girl like Sally sometime.

Losing Lizzie was awful, too, but that was different because Lizzie was a grown woman and she'd been gone from home so long. In a way it was like they'd lost Lizzie when she first left Grassy Branch. Also, it's hard to believe somebody is dead if you don't set up with them and bury them, and Lizzie was buried over there in France, which bothered R.C. something terrible. He couldn't see why they wouldn't ship her back and bury her here, but they said it was against the law. Lizzie died of romantic fever and they buried her quick. So Lizzie is laying in foreign soil, which is real hard on R.C., who takes things hard anyway. It's all or nothing with R.C. Sometimes he's a ball of fire, other times he's distant as the moon. There's not another one like R.C., that's for sure!

Sometimes he pays Lucie a lot of attention and sometimes none atall, depending on whatever mood has seized him. One day Tampa came right out and said to Lucie, "I don't know how you can stand it, I really don't," and all Lucie could do was smile at her. How can she say she'd rather have one hour of R.C.'s undivided attention than a whole year with poor old broken-down Durwood? How can she say what it's like in the bed with R.C.? For a good woman like Lucie can't say those things.

"We better go on in there afore he kills us all," Virgie says, meaning R.C. She snaps her compact shut and puts it inside her purse.

"Where do you reckon he's got to, though?" Tampa asks, meaning Durwood, who took off lickety-split the minute they parked the car. Everybody knows he's out someplace taking a drink. Tampa doesn't sound mad, though. In fact, Tampa Rainette has surprised everybody by how good she's been to Durwood after all. It is not any easier being married to Durwood than it is being married to R.C., in Lucie's opinion anyway. It may be true that you never know what R.C. is going to do next, but you know for sure that Durwood isn't going to do a damn thing. *Nothing.* He didn't do a thing before he got sick, either. R.C. sees to the farm and always has. Durwood sits on the porch playing music or listening to the radio. Durwood sick is not any different from Durwood well. "Durwood has moved taking it easy up to a fine art," Tampa always said. Still, he's sweet. He's real sweet. And this apparently is what Tampa was after, all along. She'd had it with men that are mean to you, and men had been real mean to her, so she fell in love with Durwood purely for being so sweet. She doesn't get too mad at him for drinking, she takes a drink herself. Tampa has gotten real fat, too, since she came over to Grassy Branch, putting on about ten pounds with each child: Alice, now fifteen; Freda, ten; and Buck, nine. And of course they've got Little Virginia living with them, Virgie's child. She's already sixteen.

That Virgie! It's like all the fire went out of Tampa and straight into Virgie, who is thirty-two years old now but don't appear to know it, or have a lick of sense. She's bad to drink, too, and bad to take up with a man. She's done this several times in fact, but so far it hasn't worked out too good, because Virgie's picky, too. Not to mention real vain and high-strung. She takes medicine for her nerves right now. Virgie is the only one of the three women who was just as excited about this trip as R.C. She jumps out of the car, smoothing her dress down over her hips. Virgie looks like a souped-up, more intense version of her mother: black-haired, skinny; big dark eyes, pouty red mouth. Everything that has gone soft in Tampa is sharp as a razor in her daughter Virgie.

Tampa hands Bill out to Virgie. Then Tampa and Lucie get out. Then Lucie takes Bill, and the rest of them get their instruments out of the back. "Oh, Lord," Lucie says as it hits her what they are about to do. She looks all around at the city buildings, the city cars. She's got beans to put up, back home.

"Come on, come on," R.C. says. He shepherds his women around to the side of the building, past some fellers that are having a big loud argument on the sidewalk, through the door, up the dark staircase to a little landing, then through another door with a pane of frosted glass in it. R.C. doesn't even knock. He just walks in like he owns the joint.

Ralph Peer is there waiting for them, leaning against a table covered with papers, pens, notes, coffee cups, drinking glasses. Blankets have been tacked to all the walls.

The women hang back, looking around, but R.C. crosses right over to Ralph Peer and sticks out his hand. "I'm R.C. Bailey," he says, "and these here is the Grassy Branch Girls."

Mr. Peer makes an elegant little half-bow in their direction, "Ladies, I'm so pleased to make your acquaintance," he says. "I understand you've traveled some distance to get here today."

Virgie and Tampa both start talking at the same time, then stop.

"We sure have," Lucie says.

Mr. Peer walks over and tweaks Bill's cheek. "Now that little feller is not likely to cry, is he?" he asks.

"Not if we go right ahead on," Lucie assures him. "He'll sleep for an hour at the leastest. I will just make him up a pallet right over here in the corner iffen you don't mind," she says, and Ralph Peer nods, and she does it while he says to R.C., "Now you, sir, are the manager of this group, as I understand it?"

When R.C. says that this is so, Ralph Peer motions him to the table. "Well, if you will just take a chair, then, Mr. Bailey, we will conduct our preliminary business with as much dispatch as possible while that little feller is asleep. You ladies just make yourselves comfortable over here." He indicates several benches and chairs, where the women settle. Tampa takes the autoharp out of its case while Virgie gets out the archtop guitar that she's been favoring lately. They start tuning up while R.C. discusses business with Mr. Peer.

The terms are simple. Mr. Peer, representing the Victor Talking Machine Company, will pay fifty dollars per selection plus royalties of about two and a half cents per side. To R.C. Bailey, this is a lot of money.

Mr. Peer seems especially happy to learn that R.C. has written two of the numbers the Grassy Branch Girls plan to sing this afternoon: "Melungeon Man" and "Down by Grassy Branch." The other numbers, R.C. assures Mr. Peer, feature his own personal arrangements and may be copyrighted as well. The fifth, "Shall We Gather at the River," is an old hymn that has been recorded many times previously, by many artists, but R.C. assures Mr. Peer that theirs is a brand-new styling. Mr. Peer nods.

A dapper, refined gentleman with hooded eyes and a fleshy, florid face, he has little regard for most of the "hillbillies" he deals with. Nor does he like their music much, but a man has to make a living, and this hillbilly music is making him rich. Ralph Peer is no fool. He realizes that R.C. Bailey is smart, a cut above most of the hillbillies who have come in here, and treats him with consequent respect. Many of these hillbillies have never heard of copyrighting songs, for instance, which is "the basis of the music business," as Mr. Peer tells R.C. now.

"You know, I have been recording nigger music for many years," Mr. Peer says, and mentions some of the Okeh 8000 series of "race" records he's made: Mamie Smith's "Crazy Blues," recorded in Memphis; Louis Armstrong's "Gutbucket Blues"; minstrel acts such as Butterbeans and Susie, recorded in Negro vaudeville theaters throughout the South. But Mr. Peer is always looking for original material, he tells R.C., and "niggers can't write." So he's turned to hillbilly now. Mr. Peer gives R.C. the necessary papers to sign and R.C. reads them through carefully, as befits the importance of this occasion. Some of the hillbillies Mr. Peer has signed can't even write their own names. The illiterate fiddler G.B. Grayson signed his contract with an X.

While R.C. reads over the contract, the two sound engineers come in carrying cold Coca-Colas in a box and hand them around. The engineers are introduced as Mr. Eckhardt and Mr. Lynch, and Virgie immediately begins to make eyes at Mr. Eckhardt. R.C. writes his name across the bottom of the contract in his habitual large scrawl, embellishing the capital letters with a flourish. Mr. Peer nods approval. He appreciates style in a man. Ceremoniously, Mr. Peer folds up R.C.'s copy of the contract and hands it over to him; R.C. deposits it carefully in his vest pocket. He stands up and shakes hands again with Mr. Peer.

"Now then, girls," R.C. says.

The engineers are rigging things up.

Mr. Peer shows them all over to the platform where they

are to sit, since they'd rather sit than stand. "It's more like home," as Lucie says, and Virgie wishes the rest of them would quit acting so country. Mr. Eckhardt adjusts the microphone, brushing up against Virgie's shoulder. "Excuse *you*!" Virgie says. They grin at each other.

"All right now," Mr. Peer says, and nods to Mr. Lynch, who flips the switch that starts up the electrical equipment, made by Western Electric. When Ralph Peer first went out into the country recording for Okeh, the heavy revolving turntable, covered by an inch of wax, was run by a mechanism involving weights and pulleys, like a cuckoo clock. This modern electrical equipment, which ensures a far superior product, fascinates R.C., who crosses the studio to observe its operation at close range while the women sing.

They start out with "Shall We Gather at the River," and after the first verse, Mr. Peer nods, a barely perceptible nod, to Mr. Eckhardt. Lucie plays the little Gibson guitar that R.C. got her so long ago, Tampa the autoharp, Virgie the big archtop guitar. Their harmony is perfect. It is a simple, direct, appealing sound.

"That's just fine, ladies," Mr. Peer says when they get done. "Now let's run through it one more time, and *you*"—he nods to Virgie—"back off from the microphone a bit. That big guitar is drowning out the other one." Virgie pouts but does it, scooting her chair back, and they sing it again, flawlessly.

For the next number, "Melungeon Man," R.C. joins them on the fiddle, sad and shrill on the refrain: *Melungeon Man don't know where he's going, Melungeon Man don't know where he's been*. This is an unusual, mournful tune, and it has a special sound to it, something different. Ralph Peer gets a hunch about this one. He snaps his fingers. *Done*.

On "Down by Grassy Branch," R.C. stays on the fiddle and Virgie switches to the banjo, which fascinates everybody. Girl banjo players are a rarity. This is a rollicking dance tune, and it will require four takes to get it right. Then R.C. sings bass with the girls on "Down in the Valley," which adds to the song's deep, sad resonance. *Down in the valley, valley so low, hang your head over, hear the wind blow.* Bill wakes up crying, so everybody takes a break while Lucie retires to the ladies' room to nurse him.

Tampa and Virgie smoke cigarettes out on the fire escape landing with the engineers while R.C., filled with that energy he just cannot control sometimes, strides wildly up and down State Street like a crazy man, running his hands through his hair. The afternoon has grown darker, hotter. It will rain soon. Back on Grassy Branch, R.C.'s crops need rain, but he can't think about that now. Alone among his carload of kin, R.C. understands the importance of this day, of this new recording equipment, of this infant industry. It is always R.C.'s blessing—and curse—to understand a little too much about everything.

When the session resumes, Lucie and Tampa sing a duet on "The Cuckoo Song," accompanying themselves only on autoharp and guitar, while Virgie reluctantly holds Bill.

For Lucie, this song will always bring back the fresh open faces of Lizzie and Sally, who taught it to her years ago. Tears come into her eyes then but do not fall, and her voice takes on a deeper shading of emotion, a tremor, that renders the simple old song almost unbearably poignant. Mr. Peer raises an eyebrow at Mr. Eckhardt. The last note lingers and lingers on the still, hot air, falling finally into silence. Even Bill is quiet, sucking his thumb, gazing raptly from face to face. Finally Mr. Peer clears his throat.

"I cannot say at the present time how many of these numbers the Victor Talking Machine Company will release as recordings," he announces formally. "The final decisions always involve factors beyond my control. But I can certainly tell you that this has been a productive session here today, and I feel that we have gotten some fine tunes out of it. I will be contacting you shortly." Mr. Peer shakes hands with R.C., then with each of the women in turn, except for Lucie, who is walking the floor with Bill.

Head down under pretext of tending to the baby, Lucie cries softly. For it seems to her that they have just given up something precious by singing these songs here to these strangers, and she feels a sudden terrible sense of loss. She knows it's silly to feel this way, but somehow that doesn't help. Mr. Peer notices and comes over to pat her, awkwardly, on the back. "Artists are real temperamental," he says to R.C. "I've seen it a million times."

R.C. nods. He puts his arm around Lucie and the baby and steers them out the door, saying he'll come back in a minute for the rest of the instruments. Mr. Peer nods. He takes a swig of excellent brandy from a silver flask the minute they are all out the door, then hands it over to the engineers, then to R.C. when he comes back up alone. R.C. tilts his head back for a long swallow. The liquor goes down fiery but smooth. He has never tasted any liquor like it. "Mighty fine," he says to Mr. Peer, handing the flask back, and Mr. Peer says again that he'll be in touch.

It's already thundering by the time R.C. gets his instruments and women packed back up into the Model T; it's already raining by the time he finds Durwood exactly where he thought he might find him, in Bull Boyd's saloon down by the railroad tracks, dead drunk. Bull is happy to help R.C. load Durwood into the car. The thunderstorm has passed by the time they start for home in a gentle rain, with the windshield wipers beating time to R.C.'s thoughts. The women are first talkative, then querulous, then sleepy. R.C. doesn't pay them any mind. He's too busy thinking over the events of the past few days.

R.C. first learned about these recording sessions nearly a month ago as he sat reading the newspaper in a Bristol barbershop, waiting to get his hair cut. The advertisement was small. It stated merely that Victor would have a recording machine in Bristol for ten days commencing in late July. Interested acts and persons were urged to apply in writing. An address was given—the same address that is printed on the letterhead at the top of the contract now in R.C.'s pocket.

At the time, R.C. tore the advertisement from the paper and took it home to show his family, but only Virgie was interested. "It's too far to go," Lucie said flatly, and even Tampa called the plan a "wild-goose chase." Both women were mad at him anyway. They reminded R.C. of the money he had just lost on a disastrous land speculation involving a gold mine in North Carolina. R.C., chastened, gave up.

But then on July 28, with the Victor sessions already in progress, R.C. came across a reporter's account of watching Mr. Ralph Peer record local star Ernest Stoneman and Eck Dunford singing "Skip to My Lou." The article read: "The synchronizing is perfect. Ernest Stoneman playing the guitar, the young matron the violin, and a young mountaineer the banjo and mouth harp. Bodies swaying, feet beating a perfect rhythm, it is calculated to go big when offered to the public."

The last paragraph, the one R.C. kept reading over and over, revealed that Pop Stoneman was paid a hundred dollars per day; his sideman, twenty-five. It further stated that Stoneman had received thirty-six hundred dollars in royalties the year before.

R.C. read this article while sitting at the soda fountain in Sutton's Drug Store in Cana. He rolled up the paper, put it under his arm, and went to the back of the store, where he used Homer Sutton's telephone to call the number given. Mr. Peer would return the call in an hour's time, he was told.

R.C. smoked and paced while he waited, refusing to tell the curious denizens of Sutton's soda fountain what he was up to.

Finally the phone rang. R.C. rushed to answer it. The appointment was made. Then all R.C. had to do was convince the women, but this was accomplished more easily than he'd thought. Tampa was impressed by the amount of Pop Stoneman's royalties; Virgie was ready to go anyplace at the drop of a hat anyway. Lucie had been feeling bad because she'd been so hard on R.C. about the gold deal (after all, he *was* a good man; he was a good provider; he did take care of them all), so a little sweet-talk did the trick there.

Now, driving them all back home, R.C. is still full of excitement. He feels like he might explode. He doesn't see how in the world they can all be asleep, in spite of the fact that they left home before dawn. *How can they sleep like that*? R.C. rolls the window of the Model T down. The night air is cool and mysterious, full of possibility. The rain comes in on his face. R.C. drives them home through the rainy night, on fire with thoughts of the future.

3

Flowers in the Meadow

I've been gatherin' flowers in the meadow
For to wreathe around your head,
But so long you have kept me a-waitin',
They're all withered now and dead.

I've been gatherin' flowers on the hillside
To bind them on your brow,
But so long you have kept me a-waitin'
The flowers are faded now.

Oh, many a mile with you I've wandered,
And many an hour with you I've spent,
Till I thought your heart was mine forever,
Now I know hit was only lent.

Now I will seek some distant river,
And there I'll spend my days and years,
I'll eat no food but the green willow
And drink no water but my tears.

1

Rose Annie Bailey Rush

Well, I know Gladys was only trying to help out and clean up around here, I know she didn't mean any harm by throwing it away, and I just jumped all over her anyway—I swear, sometimes I don't have no control over what I do. And now she has took off mad in the car. I don't blame her. But Buddy'll have a fit when he hears it. "Just don't be mean to Mamma," he always says. "You know how much she does for us," he says. Well, I *do* know it, and Lord knows I'm thankful. I can't stand how I act half the time. But I swear, I can't seem to do much better, no matter how hard I try. I do go to church, and I read the Bible and *The Upper Room* and *Good Housekeeping* and the *Reader's Digest*, I try real hard to be as good of a wife and mother and citizen as I can (Buddy is in the Toastmasters), but things get away from me somehow. I'll be washing the dishes one minute and crying in the garage the next. It is like a black cloud comes up out of noplace and smothers me down to the ground.

And poor Buddy—Buddy's so *good* about it all. If he sees that

I really *can't* get up sometimes, that I just *can't* take the kids to school or to church or go down to the ceramics shop or do whatever it is that I'm supposed to do that day, he just does it himself and doesn't say *one word* about it either. Buddy is a modern-day saint. He'll do it himself, or he'll call Gladys if he can't. Of course now *Gladys* has got some things to say, believe me! But at least she does it and she's got the decency not to say them to my face. Don't you think I haven't heard her, though!—telling everybody that I'm just spoiled. I've heard her say this to Buddy a million times too, and worse, but Buddy is just so *good*, he'll say, "Now Mamma, I've always told you that Rose Annie is real delicate. You know how artistic she is." Buddy is *proud* of this!

Why, he still tries to get me to sing sometimes, even though he knows I don't have any heart for it now. I feel like it is somebody else that used to sing, and not me. But Buddy grew up right down the road here, the other side of Holly Springs, so he knew all about my family and the Grassy Branch Girls—why, Gladys still has these scrapbooks, you ought to see them. She's got one on Virgie and the girls too—Mamma Rainette and the Raindrops, *excuse me!* Gladys is more interested in the Raindrops than she is in her own grandchildren, if you ask me. Of course she's got a Hank Williams scrapbook too, and never tires of telling how she saw him in person at the Armory in Knoxville in 1952, "not a year before his death," she always says. She's got an Elvis scrapbook now too, she particularly likes Elvis because he's so good to his mother, who is also named Gladys.

Gladys is a lot more interested in music than Daddy is, even though it used to be his whole life. He don't have no more heart for it either. I don't know if he just can't stand it since Mamma died or if he got pitched off at Virgie going off like that without so much as a by-your-leave, not asking him no advice. Daddy always ran the show when it was the Grassy Branch Girls, you know. It was him that thought of it being a sister act in the first place, and him that found the songs. Now he won't talk about those days at all. But he's still got that old record player from the Sterchi furniture store out in the shed, in what he calls his office, and you can hear him out there sometimes all night long, playing their old records—"Melungeon Man" in particular—over and over.

The Grassy Branch Girls made nineteen recordings before the Depression brought it all to a halt, and they could of kept on if they'd been willing to pick up and move someplace else to be on the radio, like the Carters went down to Del Rio, Texas, and got on that border station. But Mamma didn't want to leave home—she loved this place so—and Aunt Tampa wouldn't leave Uncle Durwood, and that was that. But Virgie was always hot to trot, so nobody was surprised when she done so. I was glad when Virgie left, she used to give me a headache trying to boss everybody around. Of course back in those days I used to have a lot of headaches anyway; this was part of my nervous breakdown which I don't remember too much about, to tell you the truth.

To this day Buddy tells me he doesn't want me to overdo, he thinks I might have another nervous breakdown. He knows all about my nervous breakdown, but he doesn't know anything about the baby, of course. Nobody did but Daddy and Aunt Freda, and Freda's dead now.

Actually Buddy has always seemed kindly *proud* of my nervous breakdown in a funny way. He never knew anybody else to have one, so he says. He thinks I'm special because of it.

Sometimes he still takes my hands in his big old hands and says, "Looky here, how little you are! Looky here how little," and he likes to run his big old finger real gentle along my collarbone. "You are like a little doll," he says, "a little old china doll," and since he has done so good in the contracting business, he just keeps on giving me things like I *am* a real doll—two diamond rings and a diamond lavaliere, a cashmere sweater set, a whole lot of fancy underwear and negligees, a nutria coat, that big white Buick out there in the drive. He loves to give me clothes. Then he likes for me to get dressed up and model them for him, while he sits in the recliner of an evening, taking a drink. I don't mind. I haven't got anything better to do.

Buddy is real good to me and I know it. I can't imagine what would of happened to me if he hadn't come along and married me when he did. It saved my life, I reckon, and God knows I'm grateful, and I try to be the best wife I can, as I said, but I swear there's this black empty place right down inside me ever since Johnny left. I don't say anything about it, *ever*, but I know it's there, and sometimes I think Buddy knows it too.

I believe Buddy thought a baby would fix me right up. Well, a lot of men think that. And when it *didn't*, when I had the postpartum depression as Dr. Baxter called it, he said it is common as dirt, why, Buddy just couldn't take it in for a time.

Then he said, "What we need around here is a little girl," and so we had Sugar right away. There is fifteen months between Buddy Junior and Sugar, her real name is Lucie, for Mamma, but that didn't do it either, pep me up I mean, although I go to great pains to raise my children the best I can and I do love them, and I do love Buddy. I do. I love how smooth and feathery his crew cut feels on the top and how he takes such good care of a car. I love that line which comes up between his eyebrows when he's really concentrating, looking at somebody's house plans on a table. I love how excited he gets over a ball game. Buddy was picked "Most Likely to Succeed" in the high school yearbook, and he has.

I was not in that high school yearbook because of my nervous breakdown, but that's also the year that my cousin Katie was Miss Holly Springs High. Buddy could have had her, or anybody, for his girlfriend, but instead he went in the army and then came back here and married me, all of it real deliberate the way he does everything, like he is following a blueprint.

I know I'm lucky to have him, and our two children, and this lovely brick home. I'm lucky that Gladys lives right down the road and doesn't mind helping out so much.

Buddy is the one that insisted on setting me up in the ceramics shop too, after Dr. Baxter told him I ought to have something to do, and get out more. I must say it's been a real big success, no thanks to me in particular. Everybody else around here needed something to do too, it looks like. I believe about half my customers like to come in to talk and gossip just as much as they like to make Christmas trees or frogs or mushrooms or whatever. It's kind of like going to the beauty shop, I reckon. And when I don't feel like going down there myself, why, Tammy Burnette runs it just as good as I do.

Tammy Burnette is my business partner and was just ahead of Buddy and I in high school, only she's never married and keeps house for her brother, he never married either, so she's glad to get out and do something too. She ran the shop by herself last summer when me and Buddy and Gladys took the kids to Florida. When we got back, Tammy had washed the windows and took in a hundred forty-five dollars and started making these little clay animals to use in macramé wall hangings, she got it out of a magazine. Everybody just went wild about Tammy's wall hangings. "These are great!" I said. "I wish you would do us an orange and brown one for the family room." But at that, Tammy started crying. "I wish I had a *family*," she said, and she just cried and cried and cried. Her mascara ran all over my white shell top.

"You just don't know how lucky you are," Tammy said to me then.

People tell me this all the time. Whiny old Aunt Alice won't shut up about it, for instance. "If I had me a new ranch-style house on top of a hill with a General Electric kitchen and a nice husband like you," she says, "I believe I would be able to get up out of the bed." Lord, there's times when I miss Mamma so much! For Mamma would of understood. I can't hardly stand to think about Mamma as it puts me in mind of the old days, which I generally try not to think about either, since I get so blue.

But it's *hard*, you know, still living right here where we all grew up.

When I stand in this living room and look out this picture window, everything I see reminds me. *Everything.* Of course, Daddy was real generous to give Buddy and me this big piece of land to build on, and it's real nice to be up here on the ridge, where you catch every little breeze and can see for miles all up and down Grassy Branch bottom, clear to the fork where the P.O. and the store and the Pure Oil station and my ceramics shop is. Right down there is the house we all grew up in. Daddy has put that nice new aluminum siding on it now; Buddy gave him a good deal on the siding. And there's all the outbuildings, and Daddy's office, and the barn where we played on rainy days, and the burning bush by the gate, and Mamma's hollyhocks which come up every year along the fencerow. Mamma used to love those hollyhocks.

There's Durwood and Tampa's house down the road, and then that little house that Daddy gave Aunt Alice and Uncle Ray, and then Robert Floyd and Ellen's place, and then that A-frame that Clarence built for his first wife.

Everything I see reminds me of everything else.

I see the road where I learned to drive a car, and setting up there on cinder blocks back of Daddy's is the car I learned on. There's the field where I kept my pony, there's the clothesline where Sally stood when she died. Mamma told it again and again, how Sally died. Seems like I remember everything that happened to me, and everything that happened to the rest of my family too. Seems like I am a walking memory, sometimes.

There's the creek where we played and the swimming hole Robert Floyd made by dynamiting the sycamore tree—that is where Johnny taught me to swim. Oh Johnny. *Johnny, Johnny Johnny*, I see him everywhere I look, I reckon this is the problem. Maybe if I had got away from here somehow, things would of been different. But as it is, when I stand here and look out this window, it is like I am looking at myself and Johnny, at a hundred little mes and Johnnys all up and down this valley. I can't get away from me and Johnny. Maybe I'd go crazy if I did. I don't know.

Back when it all happened, I did what Daddy said, because I couldn't think what else to do. Then when he said, "You couldn't hardly do no better than Buddy Rush," I said, "Yes. Yes, Buddy. Yes," because even I knew that was true. I had to marry *somebody*, didn't I?

Now Buddy knows some of this, but he don't know all of it. He is not even real interested in the past; the past don't drag on him the way it does me.

For instance, when I look out this window and see my children—there's Buddy Junior now in the driveway on his little bike with the training wheels, and some neighbor kids from down in the bottom too, they all come up here because it's the best place around to ride; Buddy is right when he says you can't put too much concrete around a house—when I see all these kids out the window, what I really see is me and Johnny and Georgia and Katie, oh we ran these hills around Grassy Branch like little animals, wild and free. We didn't have any concrete then—nor any grownups watching us out the window.

See, in those years the grownups were gone so much, off

singing someplace, that many's the time we children were left to our own devices, and many is the game we played.

Now, Aunt Virgie was Johnny and Georgia's mother, but Johnny never did know his father, who was nothing but a voice in the night anyway, according to her. Aunt Virgie was actually married to Georgia's daddy, though, for six months, and had a piece of paper to prove it. When she left him, he set their house on fire. This is true. Burned it to the ground. Virgie came back to Grassy Branch for good after that, and here she's been ever since, except for the occasional excursion, as Daddy calls it, such as the time she went off to Arkansas for a while with a married man.

So me and Johnny and Georgia grew up like stairstep brothers and sisters, Johnny three years older than me, Georgia two years older than Johnny. Then there was my cousin Katie that I loved so, just my age.

We were a *gang*, the four of us, a club, me and Johnny and Georgia and Katie. Alice and Freda were supposed to watch us but they didn't of course, silly Alice too busy reading magazines and painting her toenails, mean old Freda working her fingers to the bone doing the work of ten, as she liked to point out to us frequent. She could of had a hired girl—Daddy told her to hire one—but she'd rather do it all by herself and complain about it, that's the way she was. Pancake was pretty much running the farm by that time, though Daddy took a big interest too when he was home.

Now here's the thing I've tried to explain to people ever since—having the Grassy Branch Girls in our family just didn't mean that much to us at the time. We didn't hardly notice it, for a fact. It didn't change our life none. Oh, I'm sure we had more than most had during the Depression—but then there was Mamma putting up beans every summer with Freda, same as always, and saving string, and putting extra money in an old sock. And there was Daddy out in the fields with the boys, working like the devil. Or out in the barn building some new gadget like as not, the way he'd always done.

In summertime, we all worked the fields every day until four, hoeing corn in ground so rocky that our hoes would ring out like bells, right down there where Clarence is tilling now, riding the new tractor which nobody had then.

Oh, it was hard, hard! Your back would hurt till you couldn't hardly stand it, and you'd get blood blisters on your hands. We used to fight to get to be the one to stay back at the house with Mamma and cook for the rest.

But then, at about four o'clock, just when you thought you really *couldn't* stand it any longer, Pancake would clap his hands and let out a whoop, and off we'd run for the creek, shedding our clothes as we went, till we got to the big old swimming hole where Robert Floyd had dynamited the sycamore tree. Oh, that water felt so cool and good! Nothing has ever felt better to me, before or since. And the sunlight flashing greeny-gold down through the trees set spangles in the water.

It was Johnny that taught me to swim. It was Johnny that taught me everything I knew, and try as I might, I can't remember a time in my childhood that he wasn't there. "Rosie" he called me. Cousin, brother, heart of my heart, best friend—"Johnny is my best friend," I told them all as soon as I learned to talk, and they laughed and laughed. They thought it was cute back then.

One time Daddy bought Johnny and me little red cowboy suits just alike, with shiny badges and white fringe and white hats and boots, and let us sing together on the show. We were a big hit. We sang "Red River Valley," holding hands, and everybody said we were the cutest thing. I've got a whole bunch of pictures of us in our cowboy suits, right there in the dresser drawer, if Gladys didn't throw *them* out too, that is. We'd sing

"Home on the Range" and then I'd curtsy and Johnny would shoot off his cap gun. The crowd went wild.

But when he taught me to swim it was summertime and hot, and the water back then was so clear you could see straight down to the bottom, to your feet all white and wavy and your funny wobbly legs. "Just relax, Rosie," Johnny said, "don't be afraid," but I *was* afraid, then as now, of so many, many things. "Just relax, Rosie," Johnny said. "Hold your breath and put your face in the water," he said. "You'll never learn to swim if you won't put your face in the water. Close your eyes and hold your breath," he said, which I could not do for a long time, as the world went away then and this scared me. Later I would feel that it was happening all the time. Also, I did not know what creatures might be down there in the water, coming up to get me. One time Katie put a crawdad on my shoulder, and I screamed and screamed. I screamed bloody murder. "Trust me," Johnny said. "Lay on your back now, now you will learn to float. Just relax, Rosie, I've got you now." He had one hand under my shoulder, the other hand under my butt. "Just lay back in the water," he said. "Look up at the leaves, aren't they pretty, Rose Annie? Trust me," he said, and so I learned to float and to swim, but I would never dive down like the rest of them did into the dark scary places under the fallen tree. We used to play tag in the water and duck each other. I remember one time Clarence got me so good that Johnny jumped in to pull me up and he really scared me, coming on me down in the deep water that way, so I lashed out and hit him in fear, but he grabbed me around the waist and pushed up from the bottom kicking like crazy. We burst up into the sunlight like gangbusters and I was thrashing and kicking I was so scared. I can recall that day so good even now, it is more real to me than *this* day is—the green-gold sunlight, the squishy warm mud between my toes on the bank, Georgia's red bathing suit, and the water running down Johnny's chest as he held me out at arm's length and looked at me. He was getting muscles even then. "You are all right now, Rosie," he said.

Oh, they all took care of me to some extent, I suppose, for I was the littlest one and sick a lot as a child, while Georgia and Katie were both tomboys, fearless from the word go, Georgia with her spiky black hair and heart-shaped face like Virgie, Katie with those big blue eyes and straight yellow hair and a big build like a strong boy. I had light, light hair, sort of like it is now, I reckon, and real pale skin; they would not let me out in the sun without a hat for I sunburned so easy.

Mamma used to run after me, carrying the hat, and make me put it on. I was Mamma's little flower, so she said, her last child, born to her in old age after so many boys. They all doted on me, Mamma and the boys—Daddy too. They spoiled me something awful—Gladys is right about *that*! But I was a colicky baby, so they said, born early, and real nervous. "Lucie's womb just plumb gave out," is how Tampa described my birth. She said it was a wonder I lived at all, little as I was. But always, from the first day I remember, there was Johnny who stood in his special place between me and the world, protecting me, giving the world to me bit by bit so it wouldn't scare me.

For I scared easy, easy—

I remember one time when Daddy and Mamma took me way over on the other side of Cemetery Mountain, where her people came from, to visit some cousins I didn't know. There were so many kids around the table I couldn't look *anywhere* without looking right straight at one or the other of them.

But it was their daddy, my Uncle Anse, that scared me so. "Let us bless this food," he said in a loud voice, and we all bowed our heads and he started to pray. But right in the middle of the prayer, there comes this real loud knocking. I looked up quick, to see if somebody was at the door, but the door stood wide open and it was a nice sunny day outside. My uncle went on praying just like nothing was happening, and everybody else kept their heads down too, although some of the kids were fidgeting and Daddy seemed to be trying not to smile.

"Amen!" Uncle Anse said finally, and all the kids started eating. But I couldn't stand it. I leaned forward and said, "Uncle Anse! Uncle Anse! Didn't you hear all that knocking? What was that?"

"Oh, *that* knocking!" my uncle said. "You see, Rose Annie, we're so used to that knocking up here that we don't hardly notice it. But I can tell you what it is, of course. You see that pie safe over in the corner?" With a jerk of his thumb, he indicated the big cupboard in the corner, with its tin door.

"Yes," I said. I still hadn't started my chicken and dumplings.

"Well, about a hundred years ago," Uncle Anse said, "there was a little girl from the other side of the mountain who came over here to visit. Just like you, come to think of it. I believe I have heard tell that she was a little blond girl, just like you. How old are you, Rose Annie?" he asked.

"Nine," I said.

"Why, bless my bones if she wasn't nine too!" Uncle Anse leaned forward and looked at me good. He had hard, piercing eyes like bits of flint. "Well, this little girl got to playing in the old pie safe there, and didn't nobody know she was in it, and when it come time to go, they couldn't find her noplace. Oh, they looked high and low and couldn't find her, and it was not till a week or so later that her pore little body was found right in there, where she had smothered to death."

I looked at the pie safe.

Then I looked all around the table and they were every one looking at me real solemn, round eyes like marbles. At that quiet moment, the dreadful knocking started again, real loud. I jumped up.

Uncle Anse continued speaking over the noise. "And now," he said, "every now and then if we have a visitor, especially if it is a nice little blond girl just her age, why, she sets in knocking to get out and play. She's been so lonely in that pie safe without a playmate," he said. He stood up. "Should I let her out to play with you?" he asked.

"*No!*" I screamed, and jumped up from the table and ran out the open door into the yard sobbing. Behind me I could hear all the kids just about to die from laughing.

I wouldn't go back in my cousins' house then for love nor money, but set out there in that hot Studebaker crying my eyes out until they took me home, where I was sick in bed for two days.

And even though I knew it was a joke, somehow I could not get her out of my mind, that other little girl who looked so much like me, who had been smothered to death for a hundred years. I kept expecting to see her behind every big tree, in every cave on the mountain, down at the springhouse—I thought she'd be waiting for me up in the hayloft. Sometimes I did catch a glimpse of her, just ahead of me on the road to Holly Springs, for instance, going around the bend, I'd see her blond hair or her blue dress so plain for just a minute. Or she'd be out in the schoolyard playing with the other children, as I walked over the hill—then I'd look again, and she'd be gone. One time when I went down in the root cellar to grabble some turnips for Freda, there she was, my little girl, standing real still in the dim light.

"Play with me," she said. Her voice was my voice.

"I can't right now," I said. Then I ran lickety-split back up the stairs, and told nobody.

Over time, I came to love that little girl as much as I feared her, and she has been with me ever since, just out of sight. "Play with me," she says.

The only person who ever knew about her was Johnny, and

she didn't scare *him* at all. He used to laugh about her, and one day he stood right out in the middle of the road and hollered at her to show herself, but she did not. Johnny could make me laugh about her too. But he did not laugh *at* me, you understand, he never laughed at *me*, but at *her*, and this kept me safe, I believe.

Johnny saved me from the hogs too, which was another scary time. We all used to go sanging along about October, when the sang turned yellow and got easier to find. Now this is something Johnny was real good at, for he never was much on school and laid out of it half the time, traipsing the mountains by himself. There was big money in gathering sang then—still is, though there's few now that'll go as far back in the hills as that. Anyhow, this was a wet October, and Johnny took me with him.

We went way up on Cemetery Mountain and then over toward Craggy Knob, where I hadn't ever been, and when we got up there the sun came out and started burning off the mist, so we could see a whole beautiful valley spread out like a quilt before us. I do not know the name of that valley, never have, nor have I ever been back there. I was thirteen that October.

"Over here, Rosie," Johnny said, and I went around back of some big old rocks where he was already digging out those weird little roots that are shaped like a man. He had brought along a spoon for me to dig with, and I did, and we dug in silence awhile, putting the roots in a gunny sack, while the sun shone hot and everything took on a spanky-clean shiny look.

My back started hurting finally and I stood up and looked around and was surprised to find Johnny not digging at all right then, but staring at me real serious. Johnny looked like an Indian, with his big dark eyes and that floppy black hair which he wore too long. Johnny had brown skin and high cheekbones and a sticky-out Adam's apple. That fall he was real skinny. But Lord! I bet he grew up to make a handsome man. Johnny was wild, though, and everybody at school was a little bit afraid of him, but I wasn't.

"What are you staring at so hard?" I said, and he said, "You."

I was wearing some of Bill's old jeans. "I guess I look awful," I said. I believe it was the first time I ever thought about how I looked, one way or the other.

"You don't look awful," he said. "You're real pretty." Then he came over and took my hand and drew me to the edge of the craggy knob itself. He stood right behind me, so close I could feel his breath on the back of my neck.

"I believe I could fly," I said, and Johnny did not laugh at me.

"I bet you could too," he said.

His breath on my neck went all over my body, and though he did not put his hands on me that day, or kiss me, this is when it began, that part of it.

I felt like I was on fire all over. I had not felt like this before, ever, nor would I again—not even much later, with Buddy or the few boys I went out with before I married him.

So you see the problem. I had it all, everything there is, I think, when I was just a little girl, and it has ruinced me for men ever since. Or for *life*—I might as well say it. Johnny ruined me for life by making me feel so much *then*. Why, I was more alive at fourteen, at fifteen, than anybody has got a right to be ever, and I haven't got over it yet. I can't get over it.

That necklace—the one Gladys threw out, that I got so upset about—this was the necklace of scarlet haws he made for me once, and I reckon it *did* look like some kind of dried-up mess to Gladys, but whenever I saw it laying there in the dresser drawer, just for a minute I felt again the way I felt when he put it around my neck. I felt *alive*, I mean. We were over at Indian Grave Gap when Johnny gave it to me, sitting buck naked on a burying quilt that he had stole out of Virgie's cedar chest and she gave him hell for it later. The necklace scratched when he placed it around my neck.

But you know what? I would rather have it now, all brown and crumbly, than the diamond lavaliere Buddy gave me last Christmas, or the graduated pearls he gave me the year before that. I reckon Gladys *has* got my number all right—I *am* spoiled! But not like she thinks. It is a hard thing to peak out so young and then have to live out the rest of your life the best way you can. Everybody around here thinks, *Oh, she is so lucky, she's got a push-button door on her garage*, and this is true too. I *am* lucky.

But I was telling about the day we went sanging over to Craggy Knob, and then how coming back down we slipped and slid down the mountain till we came to lodge muddy and laughing against a big hollow stump that'd been hit by lightning. It was right after that that the hogs came scrambling out of the laurel slick and headed toward us.

"Run!" Johnny yelled, but I could not even get up; my feet kept slipping on the wet leaves. All of this was happening so fast, but like it was happening to somebody else.

In a flash Johnny was up and had his knife out, and when one hog ran at him, he stuck his knife right into its eye. Whereupon that hog gave a terrible squeal and started raring up and down pawing at its head, and then the other hog faltered and backed off.

Johnny grabbed my hand and we ran like crazy back up the hill to the path. The hogs did not follow us, though I did not feel safe until we had crossed the footlog over Grassy Branch at the very bottom of the mountain.

Of course we lost our ginseng in the process, and arrived back at Grassy Branch so muddy and torn up that Mamma looked at me real funny and said she thought it would be best if I didn't go off with Johnny Rainette anymore, that I was too big for such adventuring and ought to start acting like more of a lady. Mamma was not fond of Johnny, who got into more and more trouble as time went on, although she said she felt sorry for him as his mother was letting them grow up so wild. You know, Mamma never did get along with Virgie, or approve of her, though they sang together all that time. Mamma also used to say she feared that Johnny Rainette was born with a criminal nature. But she didn't mind for us to sing with Johnny as long as we stayed around the house, so many's the night he'd come over with his guitar and sing with us—around the fire in winter, out on the porch in summer, singing up the moon. This was all right with Mamma, and what Mamma didn't know didn't hurt her.

For we were on fire in those years, and just as determined to let no one know, and we got away with it too, so that to this very day no one knows the extent of it, nor when it started nor how long it went on.

I'll tell you, a thing like that will mark your life. For all my days then were spent in thinking, *Now where is Johnny today? Where is he right now? What's he doing? Will he be at school today?* or *Did he go into town with Daddy?* and *When will I see him next?* Yet when I saw him, I took such pride in *not* looking at him, nor appearing to notice him special in any way, and he did the same.

In church every Sunday I used to sit at an angle behind him, and look at the curve of his cheek and the hollow of his neck just below the ear, and it drove me wild—I couldn't hear *one word* Preacher Roebuck said, not one! As a child I was pretty religious—well, we *all* were, or we were *supposed* to be, Daddy saw to it that we went to church every time they cracked the door, and I was baptized when I was twelve—but after me and Johnny got so thick, I lost my religion, for a fact. I just couldn't keep my mind on it. In the same way that Johnny stood between me and the world, he stood between me and God. And although I have asked God for forgiveness since, and I have prayed over it, and I take my own children to church, I don't have any real feeling I'm getting through to Him. I have not had any personal response, I mean.

I made a god out of Johnny Rainette, and I've been cut off from the other one ever since.

We formed a little gospel group about this time—it was me, Johnny, Georgia, and Katie. We called ourselves the Grassy Branch Quartet and started out singing at a revival at our own church, where we were such a big hit that we got asked to come around to several other churches too. Mamma and Freda made us girls some blue dresses just alike, with big white collars. Johnny wore a black string tie and a white linen shirt. He looked so handsome. This was before his voice changed, and he sang a tenor rendition of "Wayfaring Stranger" that broke all hearts. There was not a dry eye in the churchhouse when we finished, and all the girls were eyeing Johnny, and I was *not* looking at him on purpose, for I had my secret to keep. We sang at several revivals and talent shows and once at the United Mine Workers' Fourth of July celebration up in Welch.

But soon after that, Johnny dropped out of school and got in trouble for "borrowing" a car, and Georgia got a job taking tickets at the movie theater, so we just stopped singing. The Grassy Branch Quartet was officially over. And I have to say, I was glad when we stopped. For I felt bad standing up there with Johnny and singing in front of everybody else, I felt like we were just *flaunting* ourselves, and asking for trouble.

I remember one of the last times our quartet sang together was in our own church at Chicken Rise, on Easter Sunday. Me and the other girls were wearing white dresses, we had outgrown our blue ones by then. Johnny had wet slicked-back hair but he didn't look so good, he looked like he might of been out someplace drinking the night before, which he was bad to do. Oh, I had tried to talk to him about his behavior, and Daddy had threatened to kick him off the place. But all Johnny said was that he had to do *something*, didn't he, because of course he couldn't be with me, I was not allowed to go out with boys yet. Everybody was real careful about me, since I was the only girl in my family.

Johnny had a wildness in his bones. He used to say to me, "Listen, honey, whatever I do when I ain't with you don't have a thing to do with me. It don't have a thing to do with *this*. This is it, honey. This is the only thing that's real in all the world to me right now, and you are the only one that matters."

I was afraid this was true. For Johnny never had gotten along too good with his mother, nor with his sister Georgia, who was a real bossy goody-goody. After Johnny dropped out of school, everybody—Daddy and Mamma included—was after him to go in the army like all the other boys done. Nobody could understand why he hadn't enlisted right off, why he stayed around here quitting one job and then another, hanging out with trash, and acting so generally wrought up all the time.

"I just don't understand what's wrong with Johnny," Mamma would fret more than once.

I didn't say a word.

But singing in the choir that Easter Sunday, I got awful afraid that pretty soon, somebody was going to figure it out, just by looking at us. We were singing "Wondrous Love." We also sung a lot of the gospel hymns and spirituals, but not at Chicken Rise of course. We had to stick to the old tunes there, and I must say, I do love them. Nothing else sounds quite like *church* to me even though now of course me and Buddy go to the Methodist church over in Holly Springs and sit on velvet cushions and sing to an organ playing.

See how my mind wanders? I can't seem to do a thing about it, I know it drives everybody crazy.

Anyway, it was Easter Sunday. We stood up in front of the congregation in a row and sung, "*What wondrous love is this, that caused the Lord of bliss to bear the dreadful curse for my soul, for my soul.*" There sat Mamma with Freda and Alice and the rest of the women, on their side. *Can't they tell?* I wondered. *Can't they see it all over me, like paint?* But they just sat like always, and Mamma had her eyes closed, swaying to the music.

Then I looked at Daddy, face as stern as God Himself, and at all my brothers, ranged about on the men's side. *Lord!* I thought all of a sudden. *They would kill him*, which was something I had not thought of before. But of course it was true, Robert Floyd in particular, with that hothead temper of his. We sung, "*To God and to the Lamb, who is the great I Am, I will sing.*"

I felt awful. After meeting was over, I went straight home and laid down in the bed, and did not stay for dinner on the ground. Mamma insisted on going home with me, and pulling down the shades, and rinsing out a cool cloth to put on my forehead. I felt terrible letting her take care of me like that, and making her miss dinner, which she always enjoyed so. I laid in the dark and cried.

But even this didn't stop me, and as time went on, me and Johnny got crazier and crazier, and the crazier we got, the more we did it. I am not saying it was *right*, mind you. All I am saying is, we did it. It was almost like we were trying to get caught. Rainy days in the hayloft in the sweet-smelling barn, with the horses below, rustling and sighing in their stalls, the rain on the pitched tin roof, and my little-girl ghost peeping in at us between the wide boards. Or out in the woods, we'd make sure nobody was around and then we'd drop in place like we'd been shot.

The last time my family ever had a stir-off up here on the old place, why, right down there, it was—Johnny and me did it outside not a hundred yards from where my daddy stood fiddling in the field. Not a hundred yards! Something broke in me that night, and it has not gone back right ever since.

Daddy had got Uncle Durwood all wrapped up in quilts and blankets and put him in the armchair, and had the boys carry him like that out from the house, and place his chair right close up to the fire and the trough, so he could supervise the whole operation—see, Durwood was the one that loved a stir-off so good. He was the one that planted the cane each year and decided when the stir-off would take place, and went up and down the valley telling folks to come. After he died, nobody planted any cane, and the stir-offs were over and done with. That last year, Daddy had them put him right up in the middle of the action, and bade them fetch another chair from the house to put his feet on, so Durwood was real comfortable when the folks started coming.

To tell you the honest-to-God truth, I remember all of this like it was yesterday. Maybe because it was the last big old time we ever had around the place, for it was soon after that Durwood died, and then Mamma, and Tampa went off her head. So that stir-off has come to stand for a lot in my mind, all the good times we had growing up here, and all the things we done together, all that hard work and fun and music, I mean, the way we lived then. The last time I saw Katie, she said she felt the exact same way about it, she said that stir-off stood out in her mind too.

For I'll tell you, folks are not the same anymore, *families* are not the same anymore. Of course I am grateful that Buddy has done so well and all, but a big family night at our house these days is when Buddy and me and Gladys take the kids and ride over to Bristol and eat at Jack Trayer's Restaurant. Gladys always gets the same thing at Jack Trayer's, spaghetti, and Buddy always gets the twelve-ounce rib-eye steak. Then we go to a movie. These family nights are not a thing like a stir-off, for instance, although of course they are more modern. I don't expect that Sugar and Buddy Junior will remember them in particular either. I wouldn't if I was them. It is nothing like standing out in the meadow in the forty-degree cold, clapping your hands together to keep warm, waiting on it to get dark, watching them press the cane.

When Mamma called us in to supper, I couldn't eat a bite. Mamma looked at me closely. "You can't go back out there if you don't eat something," she said, but when she turned her back I put my plate on the floor for a minute and let the dogs have it all.

By the time I got back up to the meadow, trailing Bill, who could run like the wind, the other boys had brung Durwood out and placed him to watch the syrup bubbling over the fire. *Where was Johnny?* Folks took turns stirring the syrup and skimming the green foam that rose to the top. The sky got darker and darker and a wind rose up. The hoot owls started hollering. *Where was Johnny?* More and more folks came walking up from the valley, carrying lantern lights and little pans or crocks to take their own molasses home in, and them that played an instrument brought it, so that it wasn't long before music rang out on the chilly air, and set everybody to singing, "*I'll eat when I'm hungry and drink when I'm dry, if a tree don't fall on me, I'll live till I die.*" Some of the younger ones were running a set on the ground. *Where was Johnny?* I looked from face to face. Folks were dancing up a storm. Soon they started skimming the molasses. You were not supposed to eat the green foam, which would make you sick for sure, but all the kids were allowed to dip cane stalks down in the stir-off pan to get some sweetening, as Mamma always called it. You'd have to wave your stalk around in the air to cool it off before you licked the sweetening, or you'd burn your tongue. Every year, some little kids did that. Every year, old man Rupert Lowe got knee-walking drunk, for by the time it got full dark, there was some drinking among the men, though we were not supposed to know it.

But that last year, I remember Pancake putting the bottle right up to Durwood's lips for all to see. Durwood was too weak to take much of a drink by then, yet he loved it so. He grinned his big old grin when the liquor hit him, and a great whoop went up from the boys. Durwood said something, and they whooped again. He was everybody's favorite, always. But *where was Johnny?* The fiddles went faster and faster. I started dancing with Hollis Boyd from up the road, a little old freckly boy just my age. *Oh get around, Jenny, get around, long summer day.* All of a sudden I got so hot I couldn't stand it, and had to run to the edge of the circle and try to breathe.

Then—sudden and sly as a cat—there was Johnny behind me.

"Did you miss me?" he said.

My knees went funny. But by the time I turned to talk, he was gone, dancing with Katie, his feet going double time. Oh, nobody could dance like Johnny! He never once looked my way while he was dancing, but later, when Daddy and them was taking a break and the Baldwin girl clapped her hands and yelled, "Hide-and-go-seek!" then hid her eyes and started counting out loud, Johnny grabbed my hand and pulled me halfway out in the dark meadow, catching me once when I stumbled.

"This is too far," I said.

"Too far to play games," he said. "But looky here. Oh, come here," and he pulled me down in a pile of frosty hay that the boys had missed somehow. From where we lay out in the cold dark field, we could look back at the stir-off and see it all as a dream, the black figures moving to and fro in the orange firelight.

We could scarce hear the Baldwin girl counting—"eighty-five, ninety, ninety-five, one hundred, coming, ready or not!" Then Johnny was all over me. *"Oh honey oh baby oh honey,"* he went, real loud, and I did not care. I did not care if they heard us or not. I did not care if they found us or not. *"Bushel of wheat, bushel of rye, all still hid, holler I!"* the Baldwin girl yelled finally, but we kept quiet, and we must have stayed out there another hour, loving each other up, and looking back at the circle of light and fire.

When Durwood died it was early evening. Tampa laid with him all night long and refused to let them take him from her to make him ready. The preacher had to talk her into it, yet then she insisted on sitting up by the open coffin all night long the *next* night, so that by the time they buried him, she was talking plum out of her head. I don't believe she has ever got back in her rightful mind since, to tell the truth. Daddy was just about as torn up as she was. I guess we were all so focused on Durwood's death that we did not remark how Mamma was dragging around; she had worn herself out as always, doing for everybody else.

It was three nights later, after supper, that she dropped a dishtowel on the floor, left the dishes in the sink, and went to sit down in her rocking chair. She sat real still and upright in her chair, like she was listening out for something.

"Why, Aunt Lucie, what's the matter?" asked Little Virginia, who was helping out in the kitchen.

"I believe I am just tired," Mamma said. "I've been feeling tired all day."

"Well, you sit right there," Little Virginia said, "and don't mind a thing. Come on, honey," Little Virginia said to me, and I went back in the kitchen to help her, so I missed what all happened next.

"Now Royster!" Mamma called out all of a sudden in a faint voice. "Royster, you quit that!"

But Royster Hall, Mamma's favorite little first cousin, had been dead for thirty years.

Everybody in the room stared at Mamma for a second, then leaped to her side, but by then she was dead. She sat bolt upright in her rocking chair with her head drooped over to the side, looking for all the world like a little robin. This was the first thing I thought when they brought me in there to see her, and then I don't remember a thing for a good while after that. I remember the night of Mamma's laying-out in little bits, like the bright splashes of color in a crazy-quilt. I remember how much makeup Virgie had on, and the purple plume in Tampa's big hat. I remember the argument over whether to bury Mamma with her wedding ring on or not. Usually you take a ring off, and give it to the kin. But Daddy insisted that Mamma keep her wedding ring *on*, and he further insisted that her little Gibson guitar be buried with her, so they had to dig an extra-big grave hole up there in the Chicken Rise graveyard where she lies. At the burial, Tampa and Virgie sang "Bright Morning Stars," standing together under a black umbrella in the gentle cold rain while the boys shoveled on the dirt.

I did not stand with Johnny, of course. He was over on the edge of the group, clenching and unclenching his hands, his face a black study. Whenever other folks got sad, Johnny would get mad. That's the way he always was. Daddy stood all by himself, it was like his grief had caused an invisible space around him. He stood with his hat in his hands and his face tilted up to the rain, and stared out across the valley with a look in his eye that you don't want to see. Rain ran down the wrinkles in his face. I got wet clear through, myself, and caught a fever. Freda bade me go to bed right afterward, which I did. By now they had built that little room onto the house just for me, since I was getting to be such a big girl, Daddy said. Daddy had brought me a fancy little vanity table and mirror, edged in gold, back from one of their trips.

The night after Mamma's funeral, as I was laying in the bed with a fever, I heard a knock on my window. I jumped like I was shot. At first I thought it was Mamma, coming back to lay a cool cloth on my forehead, then I thought it was my own little girl, as I'd been wondering all day where *she* was.

But it was Johnny.

I started crying when I heard his voice. I raised up the window and he pulled off the screen and climbed in, all wet and warm. I was so glad he was there! His hair smelled real funny when it got wet. I don't know how to describe it except to say it is a smell I have never smelled since. I would know it anywhere. Johnny kept his clothes on. He just lay on top of the covers and held me, and every time he said he'd better go, I held on for dear life and wouldn't let him.

Of course we fell asleep that way, to be discovered by Freda when she came in the next morning to wake me up. Freda always tried to take over when anybody died.

As soon as the door opened, I was suddenly, terribly awake. It was cold in the room, for we'd left the window open, and the sun blazed a bright path across my pink coverlet. In the vanity mirror I saw us, me and Johnny, intertwined.

Freda gasped like she was dying. "Well, I *swan*!" she said to herself, and came over to the bed and peered down close at us. Johnny lay on his side in deep sleep, mouth open, breathing regular as a judge. I acted like I was still sleeping too. But I was just about to wet my pants with Freda standing there over us, watching us. What was she going to do? One thing I remember thinking is how crazy it was to be found like this, when we were *doing nothing*, and yet all those other times . . . but Freda was shaking my shoulder real rough. "Wake up, huzzy!" she said.

Johnny woke up in a flash and leaped to his feet by the bed. "Now it ain't like you think," he said to Freda, with his hair all down in his eyes.

"I don't think nothing," Freda said in her flat hateful voice. "You get out of here now, John Rainette. Go!" But when Johnny made a move toward the door, she stuck out her bony hand and grabbed his jacket. "You go out the same shameful way you got in here," she said. "I will not have you upsetting that poor man further," meaning Daddy. "I don't never want to see your face over here again neither," she yelled after him. "Whyn't you go on in the army and make a man?"

Then Freda shook me so hard my teeth rattled. "I know what you've been doing all along, and don't you forget it," she said. "You little whore. Now you get up out of that bed!"

And it was a funny thing. It was like whatever had got loose inside me that night at the stir-off started spinning, then spinning faster and faster, until pieces of me were flying off in every direction, to the ends of the earth. It's the only way I can describe it, I believe. But it would be a while yet before I had my flat-out nervous breakdown. By the time I had it, there wasn't hardly anything in me left to fly away. By then Johnny was scared to death, for he knew something awful was wrong with me, yet he could tell no one.

In the end, I told Freda. I believe she had guessed anyway.

I was four or five months pregnant when I told her. I was real sick, and flunking everything at school. They all thought I was just upset over Mamma dying. "Rose Annie has always been high-strung," Mrs. Matney, my math teacher, said to Mrs. Peace in the office one day when I was calling Freda to come and take me home. "I reckon she gets it from her daddy," Mrs. Peace said.

Things speed up in my mind after this. I know—it's like that kaleidoscope Robert Floyd brought me from Germany when he was stationed over there. When you looked in it, the colors whirled faster and faster until the shapes flew fantastic and out of control.

Johnny and me were going to get married, though. That was one thing. We were going to run off and find somebody that would marry us as soon as Johnny got his two-week paycheck from the mill. But instead of that, I told Freda. I still don't know why I did it. I told her on a Wednesday afternoon, two days before we planned to run off. Then before I knew it, Daddy was driving me and Freda to Bristol in the dark of night, smoking cigarette after cigarette and throwing the butts out the window. He took us to the train station and threw my stuff out on the platform.

"Tell Johnny," I said. "Tell Johnny—"

But Daddy slapped my face, hard. "Forget about Johnny. Johnny is as good as dead," he said.

The train came and Daddy put us on it. I was so glad to see my little girl among the others. She wore a hat, which hid her long blond curls, but I knew who she was, and though she sat in another car so Freda wouldn't see her, I knew she was with me, and she would stay close by me in the months to come, when she was the only one I could really talk to.

Freda made herself comfortable on the train. She put her hat on the rack and folded up her coat and my coat just so, and then got out a white box she'd brought along, and untied the string and started eating fried chicken and deviled eggs. "Would you like some?" she said to the man across from us, who said he wouldn't mind, and then she gave it out to all and sundry like she was queen of the train. But I couldn't eat a bite.

I guess, thinking back, this trip was a big event for Freda, who never got to travel with the others but had to stay home all the time. If it hadn't been for my nervous breakdown, she never would have gone *anywhere*, so she ought to have been nicer to me, I think. But I know it's mean to speak ill of the dead.

We went to a place in Chattanooga where Freda was not nice, and I was sick, I couldn't eat, and Freda was not nice but I was too sick to stand up for myself and Freda was not nice at all and I don't know, to this day, what I would have done if it had not been for my little girl, who wasn't a bit scared of Freda and talked right back to her, saying the meanest things, things I'd never say, right to Freda's face! But my little girl was right, Freda should not have kept the door locked, she should not! and then there was a tiny little baby, my own tiny baby girl, she came too soon, though, she was in a tent, I never got to hold her, she never had a name. "I want to name her Lucie," I said to Freda when I could, but, "It is too late," she said. "The baby is dead," she said. "Thank God." I was very sick then and I stayed in the hospital a long time having my nervous breakdown and my little girl stayed with me all the while, and she watched out for me then too, and spoke right up to the mean ones. I had a blue bedspread there and a white iron bed and my window looked out on a fountain. We did arts and crafts. When I left, it was Daddy and Pancake that came to get me, dressed up like lawyers.

"You're a lot better now, Rose Annie," Daddy said. "We've come to take you home."

But my little girl stood right behind them, making terrible faces.

"We don't want to go back to Grassy Branch," I said. "Please no," I said.

"Oh, Rose Annie," Daddy said. He was crying. He hugged me and then I remembered how he smelled, cigarettes and something else, a traveling-man smell. "Freda will not be there," he said, and said he was sorry about Freda, who had gone to live in Johnson City now. She died there, several years later. Of *meanness*, I imagine. I imagine Freda's death like this—that she dried up from inside, more and more, until she was finally an empty, rattling husk.

When I got back to Grassy Branch, Johnny was not there and nobody mentioned him, and Virgie had gone off too, to make her fortune, though later she would come back for the girls. Virgie didn't know or care where Johnny was, though—nobody did. Tampa was gone too, but Little Virginia had taken over housekeeping for Daddy, and she was real nice to me, and so was Katie's mamma Alice, and so was Katie, and Georgia. *Everybody* was real nice to me. Little Virginia took me and Katie to Myrtle Beach, where I got real sunburned and the boys looked at us and we danced at the casino in the salty night air. We dated some boys from Ohio that talked real northern. We ate pizza, which I had never seen before. Then when we came back home, Daddy said that Louise Rickers had a little job for me over at her store The Family Shoppe in Holly Springs, and she did, and I got a discount, I got a lot of new clothes, and then some of the guys in Holly Springs started asking me for dates. At first I wouldn't go. I set aside an hour or so each night just for thinking about Johnny, remembering him, but this got harder and harder to do. It was like it had all happened a million years before, in another country. Finally I had some dates. I have to say I enjoyed flirting, and looking pretty again. I liked to make them want me.

Then Buddy Rush got out of the army and came around. "I always loved you," he said. "Don't you remember when we had homeroom together in eighth grade?" he said, and I said, "Yes," a lie.

One thing about Buddy is, he does things up right. For instance, this house. He wanted to get this house completely finished before we moved in, down to the last detail, so I wouldn't have to do a thing. Gladys got a decorator from Sherwin-Williams in Bristol to come over here and help her pick out the wallpaper and the carpet and even the light fixtures. The only thing I ever said about the house is, "I want a big picture window in the front so I can look up and down the whole valley," but I never said *why*, of course. The reason is that I've always somehow had this idea that Johnny might come back here sometime looking for me, just to see how I'm getting along, you know. Daddy told me that Johnny was only too glad to take off and escape his responsibility, and then later several people said they heard he was in prison somewhere, but I can't seem to get it out of my mind that he might want to look me up. It's crazy, I know. If he was going to, he would've done so a long time ago. I like this window, though. I like to sit right here and see people coming up the road, and watch them pass by and disappear. I like to watch my children playing. I like to watch the weather. Up here, I can see a rainstorm coming from a long way off. This window is real nice. This house is real nice. Oh, I *am* spoiled! I feel bad about acting so awful to Gladys. I'm going to call her right now and tell her I'm sorry, before Buddy gets home, and then I'm going to go put on my new turquoise mohair sweater and some fresh makeup, and fix Buddy a bourbon and Coke.

2

Tammy Adele Burnette in Her Prime

I didn't think a thing about it at the time.

Now, in light of what all has happened since, this sounds crazy, but it is true, so help me God! It was a day like any other day, a morning like any other, though prettier than most, a Thursday morning in the tail end of October, with the sky as blue as it ever gets, and red and gold leaves blowing ever whichaway across the road as I drove to work. I thought to myself, I will have to get a high school boy to come over this weekend and rake, because I knew for sure that Herbert—that's my brother, Herbert—would not do it. He won't lift a hand around the house. My daddy was like that too, bless his soul. A woman's work is never done. But a man can't even see what all needs doing, around a house. Herbert would be living in wrack and ruin if it wasn't for me. But I am happy to say I keep our house in a way that would make Mamma proud, poor little thing. She weighed under a hundred pounds by the time she died, but you could eat off her kitchen floor. Any drawer you pulled out, anyplace in the house, was a work of art. Of course Herbert is not a bad hand to bring home the bacon, I will say this. He is a real genius of electrical engineering. He went to State and got a degree in it, in *three years*. But like a lot of geniuses, Herbert does not do great in the world. He is not loaded with the social graces. In fact, over the years Herbert has run off several very nice women, such as Helen Warren who still teaches home ec at the high school and pines for him. She ought to count her lucky stars she didn't get him, is what I think. For Herbert, it is sad but true, has such a taste for lowlife that I'm not sure any wife could put an end to it. Herbert has been this way since he was a boy, when he broke our little mamma's heart many times.

Some people never grow up, you know. They just get older. Rose Annie Rush is another one.

I had to unlock the ceramics shop that October morning when I got to work, of course. Every evening, Rose Annie always *said* she'd do it, that she'd be in early tomorrow, and she'd open up, but I can count on the fingers of one hand the times this actually happened. Even though their house was right up the road there, practically in shouting distance, while I on the other hand had a nine-mile drive. But I was used to it. I didn't think a thing about it on that particular morning either, fumbling around in my purse for the keys, watching my breath turn white in the chilly air. While I was standing out there in the gravel lot in front of the shop, several people I knew went by and tooted their horns and waved at me. I waved back. I have lived in this area all my life and am real popular. But I was freezing to death standing out in the cold grabbling around for my keys. You know how hard it is to find anything down in your pocketbook. This is when it hit me—*key rings!* I thought to myself, Now I bet I could make a key ring with a doodad big enough to grab onto real easy, so a person would not have to stand around in a parking lot fishing down in their purse forever.

By the time I finally got in the shop, I was all fired up about it. I sat right down and did several preliminary drawings. First I decided to make some big alphabet letters, such as T for "Tammy," and then I realized that some of the Christmas ornament molds we already had would work *too*, such as the pussycat mold and the frog mold. A bright green frog keychain would be real cute. Then I remembered this book we've got with pictures of everything in the world in it, and I found some daisies which would be darling, and an antique car for the hubby. I was deep into my plans by the time Rose Annie finally showed up, looking dragged out as usual, and remarked that I had not made the coffee.

"Do it yourself!" I said. "I've got an idea that's going to make us some money." Of course *I* was the one that thought up the macramé wall hangings which have done so good, and the lamps which Herbert wires without charging Rose Annie a cent, so what could she say? She made the coffee that morning and then to my surprise seemed real interested in my key-ring idea. Rose Annie herself does not have a flair for ceramics. It was all Buddy's idea. Of course she would have had to close up shop a long time ago if not for me, I know it, Buddy knows it too, although of course he can't say it. But as long as he knows it, that's all right with me.

I'll tell you, there's not much I wouldn't do for Buddy Rush, who has always been one of the finest people on God's green earth in my opinion. I have known him ever since ninth grade, when I started coming over to the consolidated high school at Holly Springs, after finishing junior high at Raven. All through high school, I loved Buddy Rush from afar. He played football and basketball and was president of the Tri-Hi-Y and the Key

Club. I was the recording secretary of the Tri-Hi-Y while he was the president, which he does not remember, and I would not remind him of it for the world, he would be so embarrassed. In the Senior Superlatives, I was voted "Most Responsible," which made me cry.

I was very self-conscious then. Mamma used to drive me all the way to Bristol to buy my bras at King's Department Store, so nobody around here would know what size I took. Now I realize that you just cannot expect high school boys to appreciate a big girl like me. It takes a man. I will never forget how surprised I was when I was cleaning house right after Mamma passed, and found these dirty magazines under Herbert's bed, one of them named *British Plumpers Show All!* Let me tell you, lots of those girls were bigger than I am. And I realized then and there that some men like a large woman, which has turned out to be true. Russell Longmyer, for instance, worshipped the ground I walked on. I broke his heart. This is why he moved to Charleston, West Virginia.

Now that I am in my prime, I arouse plenty of interest. In fact, if I gave in to their base desires, I'd have to beat the men away with a stick. I'm proud to say I'm smarter than that. I'm still sitting on my treasure, so to speak. "Don't handle the merchandise unless you're fixing to buy it," I say, and I *mean* it. I'm in no hurry either. A woman with my assets can pick and choose. I am still saving myself for Mr. Right, in spite of Herbert who said, "I don't know that I'd be quite so economical if I was you!" just to make me real mad. Herbert can be so mean. But I know that somebody man enough for me will come along by and by, or else somebody I already know will suddenly see me with new eyes, as in books. This happens too. In the meantime I am content to bide my time and let Buddy Rush overpay me to keep his wife's business going.

Don't get me wrong—I *liked* Rose Annie, everybody liked her. I just don't understand what in the world is wrong with her. The Baileys are all a little off, in my opinion. This goes for old R.C., who has always been either real smart or real crazy—often, you know, you can't tell the difference. It goes double for Tampa, who has been flat out of her head ever since they buried that old drunk husband of hers. And don't even get me started on Virgie, always putting on the dog and acting so stuck up, but common as dirt all the same. However, Rose Annie's mamma was a real nice woman, and the boys are all right by and large except for Robert Floyd, who got in a lot of trouble over a woman and had to leave here. Then there was Freda, off her rocker, and then Alice, who turned into a religious nut after Ray died. She's just a *nut*, I'm not kidding. Of course religion has always run strong in that family, like red hair or cross-eyes in others.

This reminds me of something my sweet little mamma said about Rose Annie not long before she died. I mean Mamma died, not Rose Annie. But it was on Easter Sunday, back when Rose Annie and them had that little quartet, and they sang in church. Afterward, Rose Annie was sick or something, and her mother drove her home. For some reason this sticks in my mind, Rose Annie and her mamma getting in the car, and *my* little mamma saying, "They is something *wrong* with that child," as we watched them drive off down Chicken Rise.

As usual, Mamma was right.

Plus, Rose Annie did not care a *thing* about ceramics, or have any true feel for it at all. One time Mrs. Leroy Maupin had worked for *weeks* on this little gnome family. It took her a real long time because she has such bad bursitis. Old Mr. Maupin used to drive her over here every Monday, Wednesday, and Friday, then pick her up an hour later. She made a mother gnome, a daddy gnome, and six little ones. It was her pride and joy. Then don't you know, Rose Annie overbaked them. Just sat there staring out the window at the road, forgot to set the timer. It was a tragic thing. Every one of those gnomes was shot clear through with spider-web cracks. Mrs. Leroy Maupin never has come back to the shop, of course. And do you know, I don't know if Rose Annie has even *noticed*—she's like that. No business sense whatsoever.

Well, this particular morning in October, the day that I got the key-ring idea, here's who all was in the shop: me; Rose Annie; Beatrice Crowder, working on a garden lamb; Florine Pogue, one of our best customers, who is really talented but nosy as can be, she'll ask you *anything*; and the Sizemore sisters, Belle and Shirley. They live together and do everything together. Belle never says a word. She doesn't have to. Shirley will say, "Belle wants a Coke," or "Belle never misses *Arthur Godfrey*," and Belle just smiles and nods. She used to be real pretty, you can tell. In Herbert's words, Shirley is "built like a brick shithouse." She runs their farm as good as a man. Everybody around here respects her. Belle is the one that likes ceramics, so Shirley brings her over. It gives Shirley a chance to put her feet up and smoke a cigarette.

I showed Shirley how I was going to make the keychains, and she ordered two on the spot, an S for herself and a B for Belle, although Belle doesn't drive and I couldn't imagine her carrying any keys around. It was my first order on keychains.

So we were all there in the shop drinking coffee and doing our various projects and listening to the radio—Patti Page was singing "The Tennessee Waltz"—when the bell on the door jingled and here came Little Virginia bringing Tampa for us to watch while she, Little Virginia, took Alice over to Cana to get a permanent. Alice doesn't get out much since Tampa lives with her. She doesn't mind, though—too busy praying, I reckon!

"Now she shouldn't have to go to the bathroom for a while,"

Little Virginia said, settling Tampa into a chair in the corner across from Shirley Sizemore. She gave Tampa a *Glamour* magazine to look at. Shirley Sizemore started laughing, she kind of snorts when she laughs. "Won't do *her* much good!" Shirley snorted. Tampa smiled at us all. She's got a face like a pudding now, real soft, with her features sort of sunk down in it. She has fuzzy white hair like a halo standing up all over her head.

"God bless you all," Alice said from the door. Her voice has gotten real annoying since she got so religious. It is *too sweet*, if you know what I mean.

The bell on the door jingled again and Little Virginia and Alice were gone. Then the rhythms of the shop took over—somebody asking a question about paint color, somebody ready to bake, Patsy Cline on the radio, yellow maple leaves blowing against the window, Shirley smoking her Marlboro cigarettes, Tampa looking at *Glamour* magazine like she knew what she was doing, the good smell of coffee throughout.

"Why don't they put her in a *home*?" Florine Pogue asked. "Or over at Marion?" which is where the insane asylum is.

"Are you kidding? Daddy would rather *die*," Rose Annie said. "He wouldn't hear of it."

"Plus it gives Alice something to do," I said.

"I bet they're a sight up there," Florine said, meaning Tampa and Alice at home, and Shirley Sizemore snorted. "It Wasn't God Who Made Honky-tonk Angels" was still playing on the radio.

"Do you think I ought to make these lamb eyes brown or blue?" Beatrice Crowder asked. She can't ever make up her mind about anything.

"What's that?" Rose Annie said.

"What, honey?" I asked, and then I realized she had her head cocked, listening to the radio.

"That song," she said in a funny voice.

"I think *blue*," Florine said.

Tampa's magazine slid off onto the floor and she started to breathe real fast and make that "hunh-hunh" sound.

"No animal in nature has blue eyes," Shirley Sizemore said, lighting another Marlboro. I went over and picked up Tampa's magazine and got her to looking at it again.

"But for a *garden*," Florine said. "Everybody knows it's not a real lamb, Shirley."

"Of course they know it's not a real lamb, Florine," Shirley said. "*I* know that."

"I think you ought to make them blue if you want to," I told Beatrice. "It's only art," I said. I try to be diplomatic. Belle went right on working on her own plaque, like nobody was saying a word.

"I think you ought to make them blue if you want to," I told Beatrice. "It's only art," I said. I try to be diplomatic. Belle went right on working on her own plaque, like nobody was saying a word.

"What *is* that?" Rose Annie asked.

The song on the radio *did* sound kind of familiar, I had to admit. "I believe I've heard that before," I said.

"Hush," Rose Annie said.

"Now isn't that a old hymn-song?" Beatrice Crowder spoke up, and she was right. It was hard to tell with the drums and all, but it was "Wayfaring Stranger" basically, though sung like you never heard it, with a real big sound. Some of that pop gospel stuff.

"Why, I know who that is," I said then. After all, I am the one who stays in the shop all day long and listens to the radio, so I am generally the most up on popular music. "It's that new star, the one that sung 'I'm a Five-Card Stud.' It was a big hit a while back," I said, figuring they wouldn't know. "His name is Blackjack Something."

"I don't like all this newfangled music," Florine Pogue said, "do you? I don't know what they see in it, myself."

"I *like* a beat," Shirley Sizemore said.

Tampa let her magazine go again, but then she sat up real straight and started humming along to the radio. She was smiling.

"Why, look at that!" Beatrice Crowder said, pointing at Tampa.

"I don't think they ought to do a hymn-song that way," Florine said. "Do you?"

But before anybody answered her, the song was over, and Swap Shop of the Air came on.

Then Belle Sizemore, who never *says one word*, as I said, surprised us all by speaking right up. "Hit sounds a little bit like that boy that used to live around here, don't it? You all know the one I mean." Her voice is as squeaky as a rusty old gate, from her not using it.

"Oh, I don't think so," I said, because it didn't at all.

Tampa said, "Durwood bought me a raccoon coat in Cincinnati, it was a big surprise," sounding real conversational.

Beatrice Crowder said, "I think I'm ready to bake my lamb."

"Rose Annie," I said, "you turn on the timer while I help Beatrice get this lamb," but when I turned around to look for her, Rose Annie was gone. "Rose Annie?" I called.

"I'm on the telephone," she hollered from the back of the store.

Now I'm absolutely *sure* that this is when she called the radio station and found out how to get in touch with Johnny!

Anyway, I got Shirley Sizemore to help me put Beatrice's lamb in the kiln, and *I* set the timer. At least that way I could be sure it wouldn't get burned up like those poor gnomes. Rose

Annie stayed in the back of the shop for a while, then she kind of fiddled around with the alphabet letters I was starting on, then she went up to the house and didn't come back. Buddy came by and helped me close up. As I said, this was a typical day. I didn't think a thing about it at the time.

4

Rockabilly: Get Hot or Go Home

I've got a way with women,
And an ace or two up my sleeve,
I'm a five-card stud, baby,
I'm all the man you'll ever need.

1

Blackjack Johnny Raines and the Pig-Brain Theory

Loretta's Club outside Shreveport, Louisiana, on a Saturday night in late spring, and it's raining the way it seems to do most of the time in Louisiana, a pee-warm drizzle that don't do much to cool things off, at least in Blackjack Johnny Raines's opinion but hell, what does he know? What the fuck does he know, anyway? He's the entertainment. He grinds out a Camel butt under the heel of his boot and lights another and washes two pills down with a shot of vodka. Vodka don't have no taste, it's just like nothing, nothing at all, but you can feel it in your system going all the way down, it'll keep your blood running good and get your arteries cleaned out. For some years now, Blackjack Johnny has relied heavily on vodka. He likes to buy it in those little pint bottles; he's got about thirty of them out in the trunk of his car right now, wrapped up in an old army blanket. Those little pint bottles fit real easy in your hand and other places too; in fact, Johnny knew a man one time that always kept one down the inside of his boot, but this does not strike Johnny as a real good idea, what if you got in a fight or something, and it busted up in there, it could cut your foot pretty bad, maybe you couldn't even get your foot out of your boot. That could get bad. Johnny prefers to keep his bottle right here, in the inside pocket of his western jacket, his trademark black Nudie jacket with silver piping, silver studs; it's that dark dangerous look the women like, that's what Johnny's going for, kind of a cross between Porter Wagoner and an undertaker.

He's worn all black ever since his big hit, "I'm a Five-Card Stud," two years ago. Shit. Two years is a lifetime in music. He's dead, in other words, dead in the water right now, only those girls don't know it, those three girls over there at that table by the jukebox, big old factory girls out on the town, giving him the eye. They think he's hot stuff. So do the older women at the booths in the back; they're here because he's here, they don't come out to a place like this every night, you can tell. They think he's hot too. This young bass player that Vic lined up for him, this Gene. Somebody local, he don't know no better either, waiting so respectful by Johnny's elbow, clearing his throat, trying to get up enough courage to say something.

"They told me to tell you it's about time for the third set, Johnny," the boy says finally, and Johnny nods real businesslike and hands the pint bottle out toward him, but the boy looks down and shakes his head fast, declining. Well then, fuck it. Johnny takes another hit and screws the top on the little bottle and puts it back in his pocket. This boy ain't but about sixteen years old, never mind what he told the management to get hired, and he's good. Damn good. He don't even know how good he is yet. He don't know shit, in fact. If he knew anything at all, he'd know enough to take a drink. If Johnny still had his band, he'd take this boy along, he'd show him some things.

Of course if you ain't hot, you ain't got your own band, and the Deck of Cards—see, it used to be Blackjack Johnny Raines and the Deck of Cards—is shot all to hell now, Lewis doing session work, whatever he can find, living pretty much hand to mouth in Nashville, Dewey back in the auto parts business with his brother in Memphis, Dewey flat gave it up. Well, Blackjack Johnny Raines ain't gonna give it up anytime soon, that's for sure, he ain't got what they call a secondary skill, all he took in about electronics in the army is exactly what he needs to know to run a sound board, to fix an amp, to wire a mike. He ain't going to wire nobody's kitchen, forget it. He ain't gonna hook up nobody's stove. Shit. The only other thing out there waiting on anybody's horizon is some land someplace, seems like everybody else is always singing about going home. Well, forget that too. Because Blackjack Johnny has fucking *been there*. He hates farms. He hates dirt. He hates waking up in the middle of the night out in the country and when you look out your window it's all dark, man, no lights. Blackjack Johnny likes a lot of lights. He also likes a woman like that woman who just took a seat at the bar over there, a substantial woman with a little flash to her, big blond hair and pointy tits.

"Johnny?" the boy says again, and Johnny adjusts his black cowboy hat and follows the boy to the bandstand, nodding as he passes through the crowd. The drummer, what's-his-name, this boy's buddy, is already over there behind his drum set, real hyper; he's real young too, got a ducktail, trying to look like Elvis. They're all trying to look like Elvis these days. Well, fuck him.

The Cajun gets up from a table when he sees them coming. The Cajun is drunk, but Johnny knows he's the kind of player that stays drunk all the time to function, and what the hell business is it of anybody else's, he's good on steel. Some towns, you can't get nobody on steel, it's a definite loss. This little old Cajun kind of tickles Johnny anyway: he's dyed his hair, you can tell, it's real flat on top and real black; he's got a round little belly and skinny little old legs, like some kind of a Cajun bug. "Doodlebug," Johnny names him in his mind, which sounds kind of good, and so he files it away someplace up there in his head away from the vodka, it's always another song, another hit on the way. You never know when it might come to you either. Doodlebug. Johnny grins at the Cajun's whole family, he's sure that's who they are, they fill up a table.

He picks up his all-gold Fender Telecaster electric guitar off its stand, look out now, here's a star guitar even if he ain't a star at the moment. Johnny had to pawn this guitar one time in Nashville, it like to gave him a heart attack. Johnny hits a lick or two, then fiddles with the Peavey amps while the rest of them settle in. Diddly-shit amps; it figures. He nods and starts out with some old Lefty Frizzell tunes, then "Jole Blon" for the Cajun, then hits it hard on Bill Haley's "Rock the Joint," now the kid drummer and the kid bass player are really grooving, this is what they wanna do, and before you know it, the whole joint is rocking. Even those big old factory girls are up there shaking it around, dancing in kind of a circle with each other, they don't need a man, they don't give a damn. Blackjack Johnny runs right on into "Mystery Train," which he does more like Junior Parker than Elvis, and then slows things down some with Thomas Wayne's "Tragedy," always a surefire number for getting everybody up on the floor and rubbing up against their woman and groping her some. Not that a man in his right mind would want to grope most of these women. About a third of the dancers are the kind of beat-down old couples that keep a place like Loretta's in business, the kind that like to go out dancing on a Saturday night two or three times a month, and even though they don't look like they're having any fun right now, they are. This is the most fun they *ever* have, in spite of how flat their faces look. They're having a great time. Johnny reflects that if *he* ever gets this way, this sad-ass and beat-down, he hopes somebody will just shoot him in the head and put him out of his misery. Hell, he'll shoot *himself.*

The crowd also includes some oil riggers in from the shore, throwing their money around, and some girls they've got with them, the kind of girls that know exactly what to do with this money, and then of course your basic poor old drunk here and there, and a couple of guys hanging out on the edges of things, looking for something—maybe a woman, maybe something else. Johnny doesn't like the looks of one of these guys in particular, you can't be too careful, which is why he carries a little .32 stuck in the back of his belt right where he can grab it real easy if he wants to; he doesn't like to go without a gun. The guy he doesn't like asks the blonde at the bar to dance but she says no, so maybe she's married, having a fight with her husband, just drove over here to piss him off, maybe he's waiting outside in his truck with a deer rifle right now, out in that warm Louisiana rain. Just getting more and more pissed off. You never know. You can't tell by looking. You never know a damn thing about women.

These young boys ain't familiar with Bob Wills, so Johnny and the Cajun do pretty much of a duet on "Cotton-Eyed Joe" and then get into some stuff they're all more comfortable with: Pee Wee King, Ernest Tubb, Webb Pierce, some boogie, some nigger blues. By then Johnny isn't feeling too good, he hasn't been sleeping much lately, he's breaking a bad sweat. It ain't the heat, it's the fucking humidity. He needs a drink. Or something. He needs something.

So he ends the night (maybe a little early, but hell, they got their money's worth) with the song that got him this rinky-dink gig in the first place, the record that will always be identified with him, "I'm a Five-Card Stud." As soon as they hear the intro, people here and there all over Loretta's start clapping. Cheers ring out. Shit, why not? It's a damn good song.

Like most good songs it came easy, came one day when Johnny wasn't doing shit but riding around in his car with a girl, and she said something about her daddy being a compulsive gambler or something, and all of a sudden he remembered playing blackjack around the old claw-foot kitchen table in Lucie's kitchen with R.C. dealing, him and Rosie and Georgia and Katie and Pancake and all the rest of them, and everybody else throwing in while the ante went up, and him saying to R.C., "Hit me," and "Hit me again." Well, R.C. hit him all right. Shit. He sure did. Then right out of the blue, just riding in the car feeling of a girl's leg and remembering stuff he didn't want to remember, right out of the blue, the words of a song started coming to him, he heard them in his head. "I've got a way with women, and an ace or two up my sleeve." He pulled right over to the side of the road and said, "Have you got a pencil, honey? and something to write on?" which pissed her off, as she thought they were pulling over so he could pay more attention to her assets, which were considerable.

Then she got *really* pissed when he took her straight home so he could go get his guitar and finish the song. Didn't take long either. It was done by sundown including the bridge, which gave him the most trouble. By dark he was running through it with Dewey, who kept saying, "Where'd you say you got that song, Johnny? You bought it offa some guy, didn't you? Come on, man, come clean."

But the song was *his*, and as soon as Sam Phillips heard it, he knew they had something too. "All right, boys," he said, poker-faced as ever. "Let's get you some drums." The rest is history: Number One in Memphis, Number One in the South. But hell, there's no figuring it. "Wayfaring Stranger" didn't do shit; neither did the novelty tune Sam talked them into putting on the back of it, "The Robert E. Lee Rock"—it was kind of funny but it just didn't catch on. Plus there were several other records you might as well forget about, everybody else has.

But "Five-Card Stud" is over, and Johnny needs a drink in the worst possible way. He gets the boys in the band to take a bow, they haven't done too bad for a pick-up band, and Johnny tells them all that they can get their money from Loretta and does not say, *Because Vic don't trust me to keep the fucking money, that's why.* They shake hands all around. Johnny feels like he'll be seeing the young bass player before long, but for some reason he doesn't tell him that. Doesn't want to give him the big head.

Finally Johnny gets to the men's room, where he takes several long, slow swallows from that little pint bottle, so he's *ready* when he goes back out to the bar and sits down next to the blonde. He orders a beer and a double shot of bourbon on the side. She doesn't turn around, but she knows he's there. Johnny can tell from the way she holds herself, a woman who knows when a man's around.

Johnny's order comes, and he takes a long drink of the beer and leans forward and taps the blonde on the shoulder. "Excuse me, honey," he says, "but I got to tell you something. You look just like my sister. My favorite sister, honest to God."

The woman swivels around on the bar stool and he sees that she's older than he thought, but still nice, real nice-looking close up, big blue eyes with a lot of makeup. There's no point in a woman that looks like a man, Johnny has always thought.

"Really?" She sounds a little wary.

"Yessir," Johnny says. "She died when I was twelve. You look just exactly like her."

This line has never failed to have the desired effect, and now it's no different. She bites her pouty red bottom lip and says, "Oh, that's awful," then "I'm so sorry," sucking in her breath.

"So I reckon you'll just have to have a drink with me," Johnny says.

"I reckon so," she says. Her name is Sheila Calloway and she was supposed to come over here with a girlfriend who couldn't make it at the last minute, but since her sister had already planned to baby-sit for her, Sheila came on anyway. "I'm a big fan of yours," she says shyly to Johnny, who doesn't ask her how big of a fan can she be on the basis of one hit. Instead he orders her another gin and tonic, she looks like she's had one or two already, and then she tells him that actually it's her anniversary, that's why she and her girlfriend were coming over here, it's been exactly six months since her husband left her.

"Where is he?" Johnny asks. You can't be too careful.

"Alaska," she says. "He went to Alaska on a pipeline. He's kind of crazy," she says.

Johnny moves over so that her thigh is touching his. "He must be crazy if he left you," he says.

By the ragged way Sheila sucks her breath in, Johnny can tell she's hot. Real hot. She probably hasn't been laid in the last six months. They get some more drinks and Sheila tells him she's in dental hygiene, and Johnny says he could use some dental hygiene himself; then he imagines her leaning over him in a dentist's chair someplace, wearing a white dental hygiene uniform, brushing her tits up against his arm, putting her pretty fingers inside his mouth, rubbing his gums. Oh shit.

While Johnny pays the bill, Sheila looks at her face in the mirror of her compact, puckering her lips up and wrinkling her forehead as if she's asking herself some question, to which the answer is obviously yes, since when she turns back around she's got fresh lipstick on and she's smiling a big red smile. Johnny keeps his arm around her waist as they go out, and he's relieved to see that she speaks to nobody, nobody knows her in here, so nobody's going to worry about her. It's drizzling outside and some people are having an argument over in the corner of the gravel parking lot. The yellow neon lights spell out "Loretta's" against the warm wet darkness. Johnny opens the passenger door of the blue Ford for her. "Now you just make yourself comfortable," he tells her. "I'll be right back."

"Where are you going?" She's thick-voiced, maybe a little drunker than he thought, a little drunker than he likes them.

"I got to get my guitar and stuff," Johnny says, and when he goes back into Loretta's for it, the kid that's trying to look like Elvis gives him the high sign. "Man," he says. "That didn't take you long."

"Hell, it's nothing but pussy," Johnny says. "It don't mean a thing," and he leaves the boys thinking that one over.

Loretta herself comes by to say, "Glad you made it this time, hoss. You were real good too. Mighty fine." Now if Johnny failed to make it some other time, he can't remember the occasion. He doesn't know what Loretta's talking about, but she's pissing him off pretty bad.

"Honey, you must have me confused with somebody who gives a shit," he says, which makes Loretta's jaw drop down about a foot and her fat cheeks sag. Johnny goes out the door while she's just standing there with her hands on her hips, so scratch Loretta's, it's a dump anyway.

Meanwhile, Sheila's gotten kind of nervous in the car. "Listen," she says when Johnny returns, "maybe I'd better follow you or something. I forgot about my car. My car's right over there."

But Johnny's lost them this way before. "Aw, honey," he says, nuzzling into her big blond hair, "we won't be out long. I just want to get to know you a little bit." He puts a hand under her chin and turns her face toward his, to kiss her.

Just at the wrong moment, she jerks her head. "This car's a mess," she says nervously. "I don't see how a star like you can let a car get like this." The car is a 1950 Ford flathead V-8 which contains most of what Blackjack Raines owns in this fucking world, since he was evicted from his apartment just two days before the start of his tour. So he pretty much lives in the car these days, plus Vic's got him on this financial program to cover those bad checks and pay for the van he totaled last month, which wasn't his van actually, Vic is handling all this so maybe Johnny won't have to fuck around anymore with his parole officer.

"Honey," he says now, "I've gotta come right out and say something to you. When I saw you sitting in that bar back there, I can't tell you what come over me, the way I felt, I mean. You look just like my sister, I swear you do. You look just like she would of looked if she'd ever of growed up, I mean. And I felt like, well, I . . ." Johnny hesitates, running his hand almost absentmindedly over her tits, while Sheila listens real hard to what all he's saying. He'd better be careful now; he'd better get it right.

"Well, you know I've had some trouble with the law," Johnny says then.

She nods. Anybody who knows a thing about Blackjack Johnny Raines knows this. In fact, Sheila thinks she's probably taking her life in her hands to be sitting out here in a parking lot with him right now; she must be out of her mind.

"But it's all because I was a little orphan," he says. "After I found my mamma dead in the snow, I just didn't see no sense in being good," he says. "So I became a wayward youth, you might say. I went all over this country, honey, hopping freights, working here and there, picking apples, you name it. Sure, I got in trouble, but now some of what you've heard is publicity, to tell the truth. I served my time. And I'm good inside, honey, I really am, only I ain't had nobody to bring it out in me. When I saw you sitting in that bar, why, it just came all over me like an ocean wave."

Now that he's got his hand under her sweater, Sheila's having trouble following. "Uh, what did?" she asks. She didn't get the part about the ocean wave.

"*She's the one*, I said to myself. She can see your true nature, I said to myself, she could bring out the good in anybody, and she looks just like an angel with all that pretty yellow hair." Johnny is rubbing his face in her hair, which is kind of gluey, actually; she's got it all sprayed with something. He holds a breast in each hand.

Although Sheila has not exactly thought of herself as an angel before, she likes the idea fine. "I can tell you're a good man," she says to Johnny.

"Let's go, then," Johnny says. He's about to bust his pants.

"Go where?" Sheila tries to pull back enough to look at him.

"Why, your place," Johnny says.

Now she really gets nervous. "Shoot, we can't go to *my* place," she says, "I told you, my sister's there, staying with the boys, why, we couldn't ever go over *there*! Where are *you* staying?" she asks, peering at him. Sheila can't see Blackjack Johnny too good in the dim light of this parking lot, plus they've steamed up the windows now, messing around in the car. Sheila got married at seventeen; it's been years since she's messed around in a car. There's something sexy about it, for sure. Married people never do a thing in a car.

Johnny realizes he'll have to give up the idea of getting her to put on one of her dental hygiene uniforms for him. "I was real late driving into town," he says, "so I just came straight over here. I was going to check into a motel after the show. Let's you and me go find us one with a Magic Fingers bed," he says.

"Well, it is real late," Sheila says thoughtfully, "but I think there's a motel out on the highway that stays open all night. Everything right around here is closed. I don't know about the Magic Fingers, though."

Johnny starts the car and backs up, spinning gravel.

"Wait a minute! We never did decide where we're *going*!" Sheila's real loud; it's obviously true that she doesn't do this in the regular run of her life.

"I got to get me a room somewhere, honey," Johnny says as patient as he can. "So why don't you come on and stay with me, just for tonight? I'm real lonely, and you're the best thing I've ever seen," he adds, but Sheila has got her hand on the door handle anyhow.

"I *told you*, my sister's over there, I can't stay out *all night long*!" Sheila's voice is shrill, and Johnny realizes that he may have misjudged her a little bit, she's not as easy as she looks. Plus her eyes are too close together. But her tits were as big as grapefruits in his hands.

"Just pay me a little visit, that's all," Johnny says. "I'll drive you right back over here. One hour, I promise. Scout's honor," he says, shifting gears, edging out into the street.

Sheila hesitates. Rain patters lightly on the hood of the car; all the neon lights blur together in the rain-streaked window. The thing is, her married sister likes Blackjack Johnny Raines even better than Sheila does; she knows her sister would understand her having a little date with a star. After all, you can only stay heartbroken for so long, and speaking of heartbroken, Sheila can't even remember what her husband, Ralph, looks like. Of course that's her *ex*-husband, might as well call a spade a spade. Johnny's profile is real handsome, but she wishes he wouldn't smoke so much in the car, of course she won't say a word about it. It's clear that this man has suffered so much. He's got kind of a big nose, hasn't he, and that wide mouth, but he looks more sad than mean, she thinks, in fact he doesn't look mean at all, just handsome in a mean way. "Turn left," she says, then, "Turn right." She lets him keep his hand on her thigh; it's the least she can do when clearly he's led such a tragic life.

He doesn't take hardly any luggage when he goes to check in at the Moon Winx Motor Lodge, but apparently this is all right with the clerk, who is mostly asleep anyhow. Sheila looks all around the lobby carefully because of course *anybody* could be here, anybody from her church, or any of Dr. Gold's patients, or *anybody*, but nobody's around at all except for a Negro vacuuming the lobby. The Moon Winx is a fairly new stucco motel with a mostly tropical motif. Suddenly Sheila feels sexy.

"Honey?" Johnny is asking. "Have you got any cash in your purse? I just got a big check from Loretta, but of course they can't take it here, and my wallet's someplace out in the car."

That messy car! He'll never find it, it'll take hours, and they don't have much time. Sheila giggles. "Here, you can pay me back later," she says. "I just got paid yesterday," and she gives him what he needs out of her billfold. Sometime between when she got in his car and the time they got here, she realizes, she's decided to go ahead and *do it*. It would be stupid to come to a motel and *not* do it. Everybody would think you had, anyway, so you might as well. Actually, she'd give anything if Ralph could see her right now, it'd serve him right.

Johnny keeps his arm around her all the way down the brightly lit sidewalk, until they get to room 34. "Here we are," he says, turning the key in the lock.

"Excuse me just a minute," he says once they're inside, and he goes in the bathroom and pees and takes two pills so he'll be sharp, and then wraps the rest of the pills and the gun in a towel and stashes it all under the sink. It hurts to pee. He breaks the seal on a new pint bottle of vodka and drinks some and goes out and gives Sheila some, and then turns off a couple of the lights she's turned on. She's sitting on the room's one chair with her legs crossed at the ankle, like she's in church or something. She still looks pretty good, even if she is older than he thought at first, why, those boys of hers could be twelve, fourteen years old, and he notices she's not saying. Her cheeks have got that dumpy little sag on either side of the mouth that you don't see before thirty, thirty-five. But that's okay. In fact it's better. Johnny doesn't want a real young girl, or a beautiful girl, or a rich girl. He wants a *grateful* girl, and he might of just lucked out tonight. She's chugging vodka from the little bottle like a pro too. Johnny hangs up his expensive cowboy suit carefully before he falls to his knees naked in front of Sheila on the orange shag Moon Winx carpet. "I can't tell you how I felt when I saw you there in the bar." He rubs his face against the tight denim crotch of her jeans. "I swear, honey, I just worship you."

At the moment, this is true.

But even if it were *not* true, Johnny would say it anyway, and not feel bad about saying it either, because he firmly believes it doesn't matter what you say when your blood runs south and you're trying to get a woman to fuck you. Hell, you can tell her any damn thing that works. This is okay. A man turns into an animal at such times, his brain turns into a pig brain, he's nothing but a walking dick. He's not responsible for anything he says or does. And no pussy is bad pussy either. Because when you get their clothes off it's worth it, it's always worth it; in a lifetime of fucking women he's only seen three he'd just as soon not look at, and this is definitely not one of those, great big fat titties with saucer nipples, fine white dimply thighs, squeals like a cheerleader when she comes. Or *acts* like she comes, anyway—you can't ever tell if they're acting. The last thing she says, right before she rolls over on her side and starts snoring this sweet little whiffly snore like a puppy, is, "Please wake me up in fifteen minutes, you know I've got to get right on home." Johnny lays there beside her for a while and then he walks around the bed so he can watch her sleep. Everybody's so nice when they're asleep. And women in sleep fascinate him, their sweet slack-jawed faces, the random passions and griefs that pass across their loose features, how they'll twitch or startle sometimes and wake up all flustered. Sleep is active. It's not like death. It's not a thing like death, death is the only thing like death, and the way you can tell you're not dead is if you're fucking somebody, or if you just fucked them, or if you're fixing to. He watches Sheila sleeping for a while. Light from the open bathroom door falls in a path across her. She looks real young in that light. After looking at her for a long time, Johnny gets up and goes in the bathroom. It hurts like *hell* to pee. Shit. If your dick goes, you might as well kill yourself. Johnny looks in the mirror and is startled by who he sees there, that hollow-cheeked dude, you can count his ribs. Shit. He's got a free bed now for the rest of the night, but of course he can't sleep, he did all those pills tonight, he'll be good till noon. Shit. Might as well get on the road, get on over to Monroe. Maybe he can catch some Zs over there before the show. Johnny dresses carefully, quietly, takes his stuff out from under the sink, pulls one of the three fifty-dollar bills out of Sheila's billfold and puts the billfold back in her pocketbook, puts the bill in his breast pocket, a little transfer of funds you might say. Johnny might need some cash, you can't be too careful driving at night, especially driving alone at night. The roads of America are full of crazies.

Johnny sits down on the edge of the bed to pull his boots on; this gets harder all the time. Right now he's got a shooting pain that fans out from his dick all over his body. These women have broke down his health. Hard living and juke-joint food. He's not thirty but looks forty, maybe forty-five. Finally on his way out the door, Johnny pauses and then goes back to get Sheila's purse again. He takes it to the bathroom and dumps it out on the countertop by the sink. It's just awful what all a woman will carry around in her purse. Johnny paws through the mess until he finds her lipstick, Fire Engine Red. Then he writes across the mirror with it in big block letters, THANKS A MILLION, LOVE JOHNNY, and leaves.

It's three a.m., the dead of night, lonely enough to spook you, but at least it's quit raining. It's not hot or even warm now, but Johnny's sweating by the time he pulls out of the Moon Winx parking lot, and he starts sweating more when he looks in his rearview mirror and sees a long black Oldsmobile coming along real slow behind him. Now what kind of a person would be out driving around in the middle of the night? Somebody up to no good, that's who. Some maniac.

Johnny unwraps the Moon Winx towel from around his gun and lays the gun on the seat beside him. When he turns onto the highway, heading east, the black Oldsmobile turns too. *Shit.* Then for about an hour, it follows right along behind, just pacing him, keeping the same speed. If Johnny speeds up, the Oldsmobile speeds up. If he slows down, the Olds slows down too. Johnny drinks some vodka to get ahold of himself. He never could stand suspense, he always hated cop shows. Then, after about an hour of this, he looks in his rearview mirror and he can't see the Olds. The Olds is gone. This ought to be some relief, but oddly enough it's not, somehow. It's worse. Johnny is sure the Olds is still back there even though he can't see it. He thinks it's turned invisible or something, following him. His shirt is soaked through with sweat and he's feeling kind of light-headed by the time he gets to Arcadia, sometime in the last puny hours of the night. He decides to stop for breakfast if he can find any place that's open. Probably not, though. Arcadia is some kind of a college town, look at all these fucking columns, white and ghostly. Johnny hates college towns and college girls, smart-ass, got-it-all and know-it-all rich girls, he had him a run-in with one of those lately. *Greer.*

Only he didn't *know* she was one of them right at first,

she looked just like anybody else at the Hilltop in Nashville, where he was opening a show for Gene Vincent, last-minute replacement but what the hell, pretty high cotton for a country boy. Well, there she was, shiny straight brown hair rippling all down below her shoulders like a waterfall, and he couldn't take his eyes off of her. Eventually he got it around to where they struck up a conversation. She had this friend with her, which should have tipped him off, but she was so pretty, somehow it didn't. A good old girl does *not* take her friend along when she gets in a car with somebody, he'll remember this.

But somehow it all seemed pretty natural at the time, they'd been drinking a lot of beer, the three of them, till their mouths got all drawed up and they were talking funny. Her name was Greer, she said, and he said he'd never met a woman with a name like that. "No, you wouldn't have," said the friend, who was one of them straight-up-and-down washboard kind of girls with no waist and no tits. "Hush, Buffy," Greer said. The friend's name was Buffy or maybe Muffy, one of those names.

They were driving in Greer's car out to her parents' house to go swimming, the parents were out of town, and damn if it didn't turn out to be one of them fucking *mansions* out on Belle Meade Boulevard with a stone gate and a gatehouse and a lawn big enough to keep a Negro busy all the time just mowing it. If it was *him* now, Blackjack Johnny Raines, he wouldn't put all that energy into grass. He'd grow him something worthwhile, or he'd up and *pave* the sucker. Or maybe he'd put in a par-three golf course.

Anyway, the sight of this house, Greer's house, had sobered him up right fast, but no sooner did Greer park (nice car, baby-blue convertible) than she and Buffy were headed for the pool, dropping clothes as they went. It was the prettiest thing you can imagine, Greer buck naked in the moonlight thataway, poised like one of them art-museum statues before she dove headfirst off the board. It had not occurred to Johnny that they'd be swimming naked, but hell, he was all for it. The only problem was, once he got in there with them, it wasn't really sexy, it made him kind of *sad*, in fact, for some damn reason. It *ought* to've been sexy, the pool had lights in it and everything, so he could see the girls all the way down, every bit of them, even the dark triangles of hair which always embarrassed him somehow. It seemed like a shameful secret, for girls to have so much hair. This pool was painted aqua, so the girls' bodies looked kind of aqua too, aqua and insubstantial, dreamy mermaid bodies, nothing a man can grab ahold of and fuck.

Although by that time Johnny was beginning to get the idea that they weren't going to fuck anyway, him and Greer, he's not sure exactly when he figured this out. She wanted to talk too damn much, for one thing. She wanted to kid around. And that friend of hers, that Muffy or Buffy, stayed *right there*. So being naked in the water like this was no turn-on at all, in fact it was the opposite of a turn-on, in fact it put Johnny in mind of the swimming hole that Robert Floyd dynamited in Grassy Branch, it made him remember how long it took him to teach Rosie to swim and how little she looked in the water. She was just a kid then. At first, she was scared to put her face in. Later, she was scared to lean back. She never did learn to swim very good, not like these rich girls who seemed to be part fish; they could tread water for hours and ask him innumerable personal questions.

And for once, that night, Johnny just told the truth, fuck it, it was pretty clear he wasn't going to get any off of Greer anyway, so what the hell. He told them about leaving home—although he left out the part about *why*—he told them about the freight trains and the oil fields, he told them about the army, where he met a huge black man named Rufus Main who played nigger blues on the guitar, with a lot of string pushing and choking, and how Rufus Main taught him all his licks and runs, real patient, niggers always act like they've got all the time in the world, which is one thing Johnny likes about them, he hates hyper little white dudes like the kind that run everything in this fucking country. He'll take a big slow nigger anytime. He told them about the stolen cars, the petty theft, the bogus checks.

"This is amazing," the girl named Buffy or Muffy said, treading water.

"Have you ever been married?" Greer asked him then, and Johnny said, "Yes," which was true, in fact he might be married right now only he wasn't sure if he was or not, it was some Tijuana thing, it might or might not be legal, there's no way of knowing, and yes, he has a child. A boy he thinks, he's never seen him, though. L.A. They live in L.A.

Now at this point Greer got real serious; she went into some kind of a major dog-paddle and came over real close to Johnny, her hair floating out on the water like a giant lily pad. "How can you do that?" she asked, she was *too* fucking serious. "How can you treat them like that?"

By "them" Johnny guessed she meant the boy and old bucktooth, big-ass Ruth. Ruth was a terrible mistake caused by too many margaritas, although it's true that Johnny has always liked a woman with an overbite.

Greer dog-paddled around him in a circle, it was a fucking water ballet. "How can you justify doing this?" she asked in a tight little bitch voice.

Truth was, Ruth had been Johnny's landlady, free rent at a time when he needed it, but she was a mean drunk, she came at him with a kitchen knife, with a hoe, with a teakettle full of boiling hot water. A fucking *dangerous* woman, hell could freeze over before he'd get tangled up with Ruth again. But Johnny had a feeling he'd said too much already, he didn't want to get into it with these rich girls. He didn't even mention Sandra, the first one, which was not enough of a marriage to *count* anyhow, some crazy kid thing.

"*Well?*" Greer demanded, floating right in front of him.

Johnny didn't know what to say.

"Men are shits," he said finally.

"This is amazing," Muffy or Buffy said, after a little silence. Then she started swimming fast splashy laps like she was trying out for the Olympics, and while that was going on, Johnny grabbed Greer and pulled her over to him in the shallow end and kissed her hard, which she *allowed*, it seemed, but she did not kiss him back or put her arms around him. It was weird. It pissed him off.

"What the fuck is the matter with you?" he asked her, his breath coming hard. "You brought me over here, didn't you? You took off all your goddamn clothes, didn't you? What did you *expect*, sugar? I'm a *man*, in case you haven't noticed."

Greer was kneeling on the bottom of the shallow end of the pool, head and shoulders above the water, hair floating out, keeping her pretty body entirely to herself. She stared at Johnny with her big dark eyes. "I guess I wasn't thinking," she said. "I'm sorry."

Johnny could tell she meant it, he could tell she was really sincere. The thing about rich girls was, when they were nice, they were *so goddamn nice*, but you couldn't touch them, you couldn't just fuck them if you felt like it and they didn't, and this kind of a girl could break your heart.

"Come here," Greer said, and then she leaned forward in the water and Johnny leaned forward and she kissed him softly on the lips, a little kiss like a prayer. No tongue.

Then she stood up, all white and beautiful with water running down off of her, and got some keys and opened up the poolhouse and went in and came back out with three big soft towels, the softest towels in the world. She brought some damn fine bourbon out too, and they all wrapped up in the towels and laid in the pool chairs sipping the bourbon and smoking dope, getting a little wrecked, until the sun came up. Then they got dressed and drove out to the Loveless Café in Greer's car and ate breakfast. All in all, it was not such a bad night, even considering he didn't get to fuck anybody.

But the day after that, when he'd found out her last name finally by driving out there and getting it off the mailbox, and then called her up, it was nothing doing.

Her damn friend answered.

"Can I please speak to Greer?" he said.

"Just a minute," Buffy said like a little song, all insincere, and then there was some kind of a muffled conference going on; he could tell she had her hand over the phone. Then she came back on the line.

"Who is this, please?" she said.

"This is Johnny Raines," he said. "You know, from the other night."

"Oh!" Muffy sounded giggly and flustered. "It's Johnny Men-Are-Shits," she said to Greer with her hand over the phone, but Johnny heard her. First he thought, Johnny Menarshitz, what kind of a goddamn Jew name is that? Then he got it.

So when Greer finally came on the line, Johnny was damned if he'd say a word. He was Blackjack Johnny Raines, he would *not* be made light of.

"Hello?" Greer said, sounding sweet. "Hello? Johnny?"

"Fuck you, lady," he said. "And your friend too."

He hung up on the bitch. College girls are a pain in the ass. But now, remembering it, he grins, driving right on through this goddamn college town until he hits a place out on the highway that looks more like his kind of a place. Square cinder-block building, trucks in the dirt lot outside, MAMA'S GOOD FOOD it says, well all right. God, he's starved. Johnny parks but does not lock the Ford, fuck it.

He goes in and it turns out to be a nigger joint, working men in dark green uniforms heading off to some plant, a couple nigger traveling men in flashy suits, some guys on a highway job, one little coal-black dude with glasses and a dark suit, looks like a fucking undertaker, niggers have to have undertakers too, they have to lay out their own kind. Probably that little dude has been up all night draining nigger blood out of somebody, some fat old woman, fixing her up so she can get blessed and hollered over.

Two of the waitresses look like sisters, high-hipped friendly coffee-colored girls. Johnny likes this place. He orders eggs, ham, grits. When the food comes, it's real good, but it's funny how he's not too hungry by then. His head still feels light but it's something else; it's like somebody else is singing him a song in his head. Johnny pulls the Daily Special sheet off the plastic menu, turns it over, and writes on the back:

I've got a need
I've got to feed
The beast inside of me.

Then he pays and leaves a big tip for the pretty waitress, courtesy of, what was her name? *Sheila.* Thanks to Sheila, and he writes two verses while the sun comes up as he drives across the flat fertile farmland between here and Monroe, with all of Louisiana laid out before him like the future. Way, way back, the black Oldsmobile keeps its distance, then disappears.

He finishes the song in his motel room right before the show; it's a Holiday Inn but a real dump. Lula made him go in his room to lay down. "You look like hell, honey," Lula said; she ought to know. So Johnny lays down like she said, but sleep is fitful when it comes, scary and full of bad dreams, he can't ever get quite to sleep. He wakes up in a sweat and finishes the song and eats some of the cheeseburger Lula left in there for him. By the time he has broken the seal on a new pint bottle of vodka and taken a pill or so, he's feeling pretty good. He's feeling *right*.

There won't be no stopping Blackjack Johnny tonight—everything will be so right. When you're hot, you're hot, and by God, you *know* it, and there ain't nothing like it in the world. And after the show it'll be just like a dream when that long-legged redhead comes up to him and says "Five-Card Stud" is her all-time favorite song. She smiles, she's gorgeous, she's got an overbite.

"Honey, it just tickles me to death to hear you say that," Johnny will tell her. "You know, I've been looking at you all night, in fact I couldn't take my eyes offa you, honey. You look just like my baby sister," Johnny will say.

2

Mrs. Gladys Rush

People ask me all the time, "Gladys, didn't it just *gall* you when Rose Annie Bailey ran off with Blackjack Johnny Raines and left your son, after all you had done for her over the years? After all the time you'd spent taking care of those grandchildren, so she could lay up in the bed? Now tell the truth—couldn't you just *kill* her?"

And my answer is yes and no.

Yes because it liked to broke Buddy's heart, of course. I was not sure if he would get over it or not.

And no because Buddy *did* get over it, and he has got Tammy now, who is turning a profit in the ceramics shop and takes real good care of him and the kids in a way that Rose Annie did not.

And no because after all, you can't really blame Blackjack Johnny Raines (now this is nobody but little old Johnny Rainette, Virgie's boy, that other's his stage name, of course) for coming back here and doing what he done. He is a big star now, and everybody knows how stars act. You couldn't expect him to have decent behavior anyway, because his genetics was terrible—why, look at his mamma! They say he won't have hardly a thing to do with her now, and I for one don't blame him. She is just trash. And as for Rose Annie, well, Rose Annie was dazzled, I reckon, and she's always been soft in the head. So I was not as sorry as you might think to see her go. Buddy and the kids was my only concern all along, and they're better off, as I said.

But let me back up now, and start at the beginning, I mean the *real* beginning, which of course me and Buddy didn't know a thing about until it all came out in the papers. But now everybody is saying it, that they have loved each other since a child. I reckon it's true, too. Look here. This is the front-page story in the *Enquirer*, "Blackjack Johnny Steals His Queen of Hearts." That's them standing in front of the getaway car, that new Cadillac which was totaled when he wrecked it on the way into Nashville, speeding of course—Johnny Rainette never kept to a speed limit in his life. See, that's them shielding their eyes from the cameras, Rose Annie looking a lot better than she's got any right to under the circumstances. That's his car crashed into the tree behind them. This happened along the Cumberland River on I-40 outside of Nashville, which is how come they were recognized, because it was Nashville. See, his record "The Beast Inside of Me" had just gotten into the Top Ten when this happened, and then naturally with all the publicity it shot right up to the top of the charts and stayed there, oh I don't know, eight maybe ten months. It was a big hit.

Now here's a picture of Johnny holding it when it went gold, that's his first gold record, and the album went gold too. See, here's a picture of both of them holding up the album at the disc jockey convention. I think this was the first summer after she ran off with him. That's Chet Atkins over there to the left, and I'm not sure who that is next to him.

But I'm getting ahead of myself.

Now this clipping here is also from back when it happened—"Childhood Lovebirds Coo Anew"—and this one is, too—"Written in the Stars," which is real romantic the way it's written. It's from *Parade* magazine. See, they've even got an old picture of Rose Annie and Johnny in their little cowboy suits, singing with the Grassy Branch Girls.

I was the one that gave *Parade* that photo, actually. See, I've got all these old scrapbooks over here, the Grassy Branch Girls, going right back to the thirties and the late twenties even. Get a load of that *hat*! Tampa always looked good in a hat. She had a way about her, all right. She had some real style. *Now*, the way they do it, so many of the stars dress up real country. The Minnie Pearl look, you might say, or the cowgirl outfit. But really, way back in the beginning, the Grassy Branch Girls and all the rest of them, too, such as the Stonemans and the Carters, they wore their Sunday best to record or perform, either one. Look at R.C.'s nice suit right here, for instance, look at his starched white collar. I always like a man in a suit, myself. Now here's Lucie. Look at those dimples, all those curls. You can tell how sweet she was. I'm certainly glad she never lived to see Rose Annie act like this, I'll tell you. It would have killed her.

It has almost killed R.C. He's always been kind of funny anyway, and since this, you don't hardly ever see him. He just stays in the house. The first week or so after it happened, he wouldn't come out at all, and hollered out the door at the reporters that if they took one step closer, he was going to shoot them. I believe he would have, too. He shot one feller's tires out. Finally Pancake and Bill took turns keeping a watch down by the gate, sending folks away, until things died down some. Now they've put that big sign down there. NO TRESPASSING. Because, I'll tell you, the Bailey farm has become a regular tourist attraction around here now. There's not a day passes but two or three cars will pull up outside the gate and people get out and go to snapping pictures.

They come by the ceramics shop too, but Tammy doesn't mind, she's always real nice about it. She says it's good for business, which is true. What I think is, they ought to sell something in there that would be kind of like a souvenir, that folks could take back with them to wherever they came from, like for instance a plate with Johnny and Rose Annie's picture on it, especially now since they've gotten married and they've got a new hit record and folks have started calling them "The King and Queen of Country Music." I don't know whether Buddy would like that or not, though. Sometimes he still acts sensitive about the whole thing, especially about the new record, which I believe he takes personally. I'm sure you've heard it. It's that duet that goes:

She used to be somebody's sweetheart,
She used to be somebody's wife,
She used to own
A new brick home
And a subdivision life.

Ever since it was released, the people in the cars have started taking pictures of Buddy and Tammy's house, up on the hill there. Buddy is not too crazy about this, but what I say is, *Heck*. If you can't stop something, then you might as well cash in on it. A buck is a buck, I say. But I haven't said it to Buddy yet. However, I do believe he'll be fine when this song is not quite so popular. Right now you can't turn on the radio without hearing it. I guess it's one thing to have your wife leave you, and another thing to have to hear about it all day long on the radio.

I'll never forget the day she left!

Buddy was at work, of course, like he is every day, and the first I caught on to anything at all being wrong was about three-fifteen that afternoon, when Sugar called me and asked would I take her to ballet. I was cleaning out the hall closet when she called. "Well, of course I will, Sugar," I said, "but where's your mamma?"

"I don't know," Sugar said. "She's not here."

"Well, where's Buddy Junior?" I asked then, and Sugar said he'd stayed at school for play group. It was November 9, I'll never forget it—five days before Buddy's birthday! Some birthday present! Anyway, this meant that somebody would have to pick up Buddy Junior at school before long, too, then go back and get Sugar from ballet.

The first thing I did was call down to the ceramics shop, thinking that maybe they'd gotten real busy and Rose Annie had just let the time slip away. You know she's always been flighty.

But Tammy said that Rose Annie had not been in that day.

"Not at all?" I said.

"Nope," Tammy said. "I've been wondering where she was."

So I just threw on my car coat and took off, with a funny feeling in my stomach, I must say, although nothing quite as definite as downright ESP, which I have never actually experienced. I'm not sure why I was worried—things like this had happened plenty of times before, Rose Annie not being where she said she'd be. But when I got up there, I parked and went in, instead of just honking for Sugar to come out. I thought I'd take a look around, to ease my mind. Sugar sat on the kitchen floor lacing up her shoes. She's the prettiest child. It looked to me like not a thing had been touched in the kitchen since breakfast, in the way of cleaning up, I mean—dishes everywhere, a whole half-gallon of milk left out, cereal spilled on the floor. But this was not so unusual.

"I'm ready, Mamaw," Sugar said, standing up.

"Just a minute," I said. I walked down the hall and into the master bedroom, I'm not sure why. Sure enough, clothes were strewn everyplace from here to Kingdom Come. The dresser drawers were open, with clothes spilling out. The big walk-in closet door was open, too, and I could see from where I was that her side of the closet was almost empty. The king-size bed was unmade. I heard Sugar coming softly up the hall behind me, humming a little tune. I knew I didn't want her to see this. So I backed out and closed the door behind me. Later we would find that Rose Annie had left every piece of jewelry that Buddy ever gave her piled up in a sad glittery pile in the middle of the bed, including her wedding ring. But I didn't know that then.

I turned around. "Let's go, sweetheart."

But children are so smart, they never miss a trick. "What's the matter?" Sugar said right away, she could see something wrong in my face.

I kissed her on the top of her curly blond head. "Not a thing, Pumpkin," I said. "Let's go." I drove to Cana like a robot. Then I sat in a state of shock in Miss Bound's ballet class at the Masonic Lodge, watching those cute little girls bend and twirl like so many flowers, and trying to figure out how I would break the news to Buddy. But as it turned out, I didn't have to. By the time I had picked up Buddy Junior and driven back over to Grassy Branch, Buddy already knew it. He was laid out in the middle of the floor when we got home.

Now here's how Buddy knew it, which just goes to show how awful Rose Annie was—I say this because there's a lot of folks around here now who have changed things around in their mind since the two of them got so famous, who think it's all *sweet* now, who say you can't blame her. Well, I can still blame her, not so much for *what* she done, mind you, but for *how* she done it. Okay, I'm getting to it! Here goes.

They stopped, her and Johnny Rainette, someplace on the highway between here and Nashville, and she called up Buddy's secretary collect from a pay phone. *Collect!* Talked to June Osborne. Didn't even have the decency to talk to Buddy's own face, talked to June Osborne instead, the secretary at the cement company. Rose Annie said for June Osborne to tell Buddy that she was going to Nashville to live with Johnny Rainette, her childhood sweetheart, that she had never stopped loving him in all these years, or vice versa, that Johnny Rainette would have come back and taken her away long before this except he thought she was dead. Then Rose Annie said, "Tell Buddy he can ask Daddy about that!" sounding all wrought up. June Osborne said you couldn't hardly make sense out of what Rose Annie said, she was crying so. And then June said you could hear them talking, the two of them, and traffic going past on the highway, and then Blackjack Johnny himself got on the phone. June said she almost died!

"Miss Osborne?" he said, real polite. "This is the only message you need to give Buddy Rush, and you be sure to give it to him. You tell him this is Blackjack Johnny Raines calling to tell him that Rosie is all right, and she is going to be all right. And you can thank him for taking such good care of my girl all these years. You tell him I appreciate it."

Then, *click!* Johnny hung up the phone, and they got back in the car and headed off to Nashville, where Johnny would wrap that Cadillac around a pin oak tree overlooking the Cumberland River not three hours later, and they'd both walk away from it, lucky as ever.

But meanwhile back at the cement company, June Osborne

was having a fit. You can imagine! And not a minute after Johnny hung up, here comes Buddy's truck pulling up in the lot, and Buddy gets out, all smiles as always. He's got the best disposition. He walks in the door and there's June Osborne just sobbing like her heart is broken.

"Why, June, what's the matter?" Buddy says.

But June just cried harder. She couldn't stand to tell him.

Poor Buddy, think how innocent he was, standing there real awkward in his own office, covered with cement dust, patting June Osborne on the shoulder, not knowing what was up. People were starting to cluster around. Guys in from the different jobs, old Mrs. Spicer who does the books. Finally, since June either couldn't or wouldn't say what it was, Mrs. Spicer took her back in the bathroom to wash her face and calm her down some, and *then* June told it. To Mrs. Spicer! So Mrs. Spicer was the one who told Buddy finally, right there at the cement company, right outside of the ladies' room door, with June boo-hooing behind it. She didn't tell him *all* of it, just enough to let him know that Rose Annie was gone, and who she was gone with. The part about thanking Buddy "for taking such good care of my girl," well, June Osborne saved that for the *Midnight Star*. Here she is, saying it right here on page 2, wearing those harlequin glasses. Oh, it was June's heyday, all right! June is just lucky Buddy didn't fire her, but of course he wouldn't do something like that. He's fair, Buddy is, above all.

That day, though, he went clean out of his head. Everybody said so, everybody who was over at the cement company at the time. He tore up an electric typewriter and a floor lamp, and kicked a hole in the office wall. I find this hard to imagine. By the time I saw him, he was just brokenhearted, sweet as ever, but I must say, I was glad he broke all those things at the office instead of up at the house, if he had to break them. Anyway, by the time I came in the door with Sugar and Buddy Junior, he was laying out full length on the orange shag carpet in the den, crying like a baby! He wouldn't quit, either, or talk to me or the children either one. Finally Sugar went ahead and turned on the television and they sat there watching it, leaning up against their daddy, who wouldn't get off of the floor. I cooked everybody some fish sticks, and burned them, and started over and cooked some more. I was real rattled. The kids came to the table and ate, but Buddy wouldn't eat a thing. He sat up, though, after a while, and drank a beer, still crying. After the kids went to bed, Buddy's best friend, Leon Hurdle, came over with a bottle of bourbon, and while he was still there, I went to bed in the guest room. I felt like I'd been run over by a truck, I'll tell you!

But Buddy was up early, pale and set-faced, in the morning. He went to work and then came back to the house and started crying again, so I called my brother Roman to come over here and talk some sense into him. Now Buddy has always been real close to his Uncle Roman, not having a daddy around here and all. Roman was the one that learned Buddy to hunt, that bought him his first gun, that I called to come over here and thrash the devil out of him the time him and Toy Biggers got so drunk and wrecked my car when they were not but fifteen, didn't even have a driver's license.

Roman was Buddy's best man when he married Rose Annie Bailey. I will not forget how handsome the two of them looked standing up so straight there at the front of the Chicken Rise church which she had picked to be married in, both Buddy and Roman wearing tuxedos we'd rented in Holly Springs. The whole front of the church was filled with flowers, mostly dogwood and sarvis and redbud from the mountains all around, which is what Rose Annie wanted. Rose Annie always got what she wanted, I reckon. Well, it never struck me as a problem at the time. Because she *did* seem real fond of Buddy then, and so pretty and sweet, and Buddy was just wild for her, I'll say that. He was crazy in love.

And as any mother can tell you, whatever your son wants, this is what you want. You want him to have whatever it takes to make him happy, above all else in the world. As Buddy and Roman stood in the front of the church that day waiting for R.C. to bring Rose Annie down the aisle, Buddy's face shone like the sun. He stood real tall and proud, and looked toward the front of the church, at the door she would come in. His eyes were bright and shining, like he could see his whole life laid out before him and it was fine, and he just couldn't wait for it to start. Then when the door finally opened and she came out, and everybody else in the church swung around and started saying "Ooh!" and "Ah!" over how pretty she looked, I just kept my eyes on Buddy, for a look came over his face then that I can't even begin to describe. It gives me goose bumps right now, to think about it. It was *too much*. He loved her *too much*—I guess something was bound to go wrong. For it is best to stay in the middle of the road, I reckon, in all things.

Anyway, I called Roman and he came over. Now Roman is a big, slow-talking man that inspires confidence, this is how he's sold so much insurance over the years. He makes you feel like you *can* plan for the future, like you *can* see the years ahead. Well, Roman came in the door that day, took one look at Buddy, and then said to me, "Gladys, why don't you go on down to the ceramics shop and check on things, see how Tammy is making out down there with Rose Annie gone," and I was glad to do it. I know they needed to talk man to man. Because no matter how close you are to a son, there's times when you can't say a thing, when he needs to talk to a man. I knew that. So I went down the hill with butterflies in my stomach, and the awfullest sinking feeling. For at that moment, I feared Buddy would not be able to take it, and would lose everything—his heart, his business, his whole life that he had worked so hard to build for Rose Annie. And this meant that *I* would lose everything, too, for I have built my life around that boy.

And I admit, as I drove down the hill that morning, I had *no faith*, none whatsoever, that things would work out in the end. For a moment there I had forgotten that God works His own mysterious will on the earth, and it is not up to us to understand our life, or complain about it. It is up to us to pitch in and do the best we can, no matter what happens. For God knows more than we do—He does! And it is not up to us to question why, but to bite the bullet and get on with it. I myself thought I would die when Henry did, when he ran his car off that mountain twenty-five years ago, on his Jewel Tea route, July 17, 1934.

Oh, how I questioned God then, and moaned my fate, for I loved Henry with all my heart. He had the bluest eyes. But God never does something like that without giving you the strength to bear up under it, and I'm sure my eternal soul has been improved as a result—for I was a flibberty-gibbet girl when I ran off with Henry, truth to tell. Then I thought I would die when he died. But I did *not* die, for I had Buddy to raise, and God gave me the strength to go on, and a good job at the courthouse in Cana to boot. So I adjusted. I got along. I raised that boy and did a good job of it, too. If you look right over in this corner cupboard, you'll see some of the little statues Buddy got for sports, and the awards he won. He did just fine in Korea, too. The single-minded way he set to courting Rose Annie after he got back was almost like the way he went after these here trophies, and I don't think it ever occurred to him that he wouldn't win her in the end. Oh, I was all for it at the time, the Baileys being naturally the most famous family in this valley, and one of the most well-to-do. I'd been keeping my scrapbooks on the Grassy Branch Girls for years. Right here is when they got in the paper the first time, and here's when "Melungeon Man" was a hit, now notice Lucie's nice suit. Lucie was a good woman through and through. It is just too bad Rose Annie did not take after her more, is all I've got to say. And you have to wonder—if Lucie was still alive, would Rose Annie have done what she done? Somehow I doubt it. For I believe Lucie was the civilizing influence in that household, as a woman often is, and things just went to hell in a handbasket when she died. But that's all water over the dam. What happened, happened. But anyway, as I said, I got Roman to come over that day and try to talk to Buddy.

When I went back up to Buddy's house, he was gone, and Roman was fixing to go, too. Roman stood leaning against his car in the driveway, having a smoke, and waiting for me I reckon.

"Well, Roman?" I asked with my heart in my mouth.

Roman shook his head. "I tried to talk some sense into him," Roman said. "I told him a grown man with a business and two children can't just up and go all to pieces. 'Son,' I told him, 'as I see it, you've got two choices. You can go over there to Tennessee and get her back, or you can shut up and go on with your life.'"

"And?" I asked.

"I reckon he went," Roman said. "So we'll see what happens." He got in his car.

"We'll see, all right," I said. I had the darkest feeling about all of it.

So Buddy went—he tried—but he never has said *one word* about that trip! Naturally I stayed up at his house the whole time he was gone, keeping Sugar and Buddy Junior, but then Tammy came over and took them to the PTA carnival over at the high school, and that Saturday night when Buddy came back from Nashville looking all beat down, like he'd lost his last friend, why, here came Tammy and the kids in from the carnival not ten minutes later.

"Daddy, Daddy, looky here!" Buddy Junior was squealing. He had won a sword cane from Japan, which looked like a walking cane but had a sword stuck down inside it.

"Let me see that, son," Buddy said, and went and made over the sword cane like it was really something, and like Buddy Junior was really something to win it. Buddy Junior told how he had won it by throwing baseballs, how he kept getting so close and then kept having to pay again until finally he won it.

"So," Buddy said, standing up, you could see he was bone-tired, "so where did you get the money for all this baseball throwing?"

Buddy Junior looked at Tammy, who turned bright red and looked down at the rug. Buddy looked hard at Tammy, too. Tammy has that kind of blotching complexion that does not look good when she blushes, plus she is such a large girl, but that Saturday night she was wearing a navy blue overblouse and her red hair had come loose from the ponytail she wears it in, and she looked almost pretty, I swear she did.

So Buddy looked at her, too. "How much?" he asked.

"You don't owe me a thing," Tammy said.

"Now Tammy," Buddy said.

"Nothing. I won't take it!" When Tammy makes up her mind, it won't do to argue with her. All the Burnettes are that way, famous for stubbornness.

Finally Buddy grinned. "Well, thank you, then," he said.

Tammy was fixing to leave, but Sugar chose that very moment to burst into tears because she had gotten her cotton candy all stuck in her hair, and only just realized it. It was a mess, too. So Tammy stayed long enough to wash out Sugar's hair at the kitchen sink. Buddy Junior was fighting a private duel over in the corner with his sword cane. "On guard!" he hollered. He is so smart for his age. While all of this was going on, Buddy paced the kitchen like a wild animal in a cage, back and forth, back and forth, smoking one cigarette after another. I sat at the table drinking ice tea and watching him. I knew this was a real important time for Buddy—either he could be heartbroken forever, or he could go on to something else, and up until *that very moment* it wasn't clear to me which one he would choose. But as I watched him, while Tammy was toweling off Sugar's hair, something shifted in his face. It was as clear as day. Something changed, you could see it change. Buddy stubbed out his cigarette and went over and picked up Buddy Junior.

"Come on, cowboy," he said. "Time for bed."

"I ain't a cowboy," Buddy Junior said, riding high on Buddy's shoulder, "I'm a knight."

"Time for bed anyway," Buddy said, carting him off.

Tammy said good-bye then and left, and as I put Sugar to bed, a great thankfulness came up in me, for until that moment I did not really understand how much I'd feared that Rose Annie's leaving would *destroy* Buddy. But now Buddy had *given her up*, just like that, and it would be the saving of him. For whenever Buddy does something, he does it all the way, he puts everything he's got into it. And when he gave her up, he *gave her up*—just like when he was a boy and he worked so hard raising that little goat for the 4-H competition, but when she lost, he never said another word about it, and took just as good care of her as he had before the contest.

He can *adjust*, Buddy can. This is the most necessary ingredient for a happy life, I read it in *Reader's Digest*.

And now he's downright happy, even if he's gained until he's close to being as big as Tammy. They're big as a house, the two of them put together, and happy? They're happy. You bet.

I can't say the same about the King and Queen of Country Music, however. Oh, they're rich all right. After the first album went gold, the second one zoomed right on up the charts the minute it was released. That's the *Two Hearts* album, with them on the cover in that big red heart, I think it's tacky myself. Look at Rose Annie with her bosoms hanging out. Obviously she's wearing one of them push-up bras. Anyway, this is the album which Johnny's song "If Drinkin' Don't Kill Me, Your Memory Will" came off of, and of course they all said it was written while he thought Rose Annie was dead, and made a big thing out of it. People are just so curious. They love to gossip, they love to learn the private lives of the stars. This drives Buddy crazy, all the publicity about Rose Annie, but I understand it. It's purely natural, I say. People don't mean any harm.

Still yet, Buddy would not let Buddy Junior and Sugar go to the wedding, which took place at Johnny's agent's house in Nashville, outside in the garden, next to the kidney-shaped pool. See, here it is. Look at those matching white cowboy wedding suits with the sequin fringe. Johnny and Rose Annie had their picture in every newspaper in the country, wearing those suits, and she wore a rhinestone tiara. This is when everybody started calling them the King and Queen of Country Music.

The only people from the family that went were Virgie, naturally, trying to get some of that publicity for her own self, and Little Virginia. Little Virginia snuck off and gone over there, and R.C. got so mad at her when he found it out, he liked to kicked her right out of his house. As if he could even *function* by himself, hateful and old as he is! R.C. ought to thank his lucky stars every day that Little Virginia is willing to put up with him, and run that house, and cook for him. They say he won't eat a thing but ham biscuits. Anyway, none of the boys went, not even Bill, who always appeared to have such a soft spot for Rose Annie. They stuck right by their daddy, to a man.

I really thought that Buddy ought to have let Sugar and Buddy Junior go to the wedding, I really did. I still think he made a mistake. For it is something that they would have remembered all their lives. It is history.

Rose Annie called up on the phone and cried, begging Buddy to send them. But he stood firm. I told Buddy that I would have been glad to go over to Nashville with the children, and I would, too. I would have taken them to the wedding. I wouldn't have minded a bit to be there. I told Buddy this. But nothing doing. He and Tammy took the kids to Rock City for the weekend, and that was that, leaving me here to read about it in the news. See, look here at the stars that was present—Eddy Arnold, Ferlin Husky, Porter Wagoner—why, I think it was practically criminal not to let Sugar and Buddy Junior go, they would have had little white suits of their own and been in the ceremony, and then they would be in these pictures, too. It is a part of their heritage which has been denied them, the way I see it. Of course, I never have said this to Buddy, not in so many words.

And Buddy *has* softened up some. Last summer, after Rose Annie begged and begged, he let me take the children over there for a visit. Pancake drove us, and then disappeared the whole time we were there, only showing up in time to drive us back home. He *said* he was going to be staying at the Holiday Inn, but I don't know where he was. When I'd call over there, he was never in his room, not even real late at night. But naturally I didn't mention this to his wife, Loney, after we got back. The closer you get to the Baileys, the worse they look. I have learned this over the years.

There is not a one of them that is normal.

Well, Rose Annie and Johnny had just moved into their new house on Old Hickory Lake, and there was workmen all over the place finishing up. They were putting that famous wrought-iron gate up while we were there, in fact, the one with the notes from the first line of "Five-Card Stud" on it. It's been photographed a million times since—see here? and here? Anyway, the house was perfectly beautiful, I have to admit it, even to one like myself that is not really a fan of modern architecture.

The whole back of it was glass, looking out on the pool, with the lake beyond. All the living room furniture was blue velvet, blue being Rose Annie's favorite color, and I must say I enjoyed sitting there on that long blue velvet sofa looking out at the pool and the lake and the mountains beyond, and thinking about all the other stars that live around Old Hickory Lake, too, wondering what *they* were doing right then! You couldn't keep Sugar and Buddy Junior out of the pool, they were just crazy about it. And Rose Annie was with them every minute, you could tell how glad she was to see them.

She had bought them some little ponies, as a surprise—Sugar's pony was named Miss Pat and Buddy Junior's was Charley—and cowboy boots for riding. You should have seen Sugar's eyes light up when she first saw Miss Pat! Sugar has read every horse book in the library, I reckon. She's always been wild about horses, like a lot of little girls are. Rose Annie even had a boy down at the stable hired to teach them how to ride, and stay right by them, and Rose Annie herself stayed down there, too, watching them. It was like she couldn't get enough of watching them. I got tired of it myself, and went back up to the house and sat down on that blue sofa and got the Filipino boy, Ramon, to bring me a 7-Up. I wouldn't have minded bringing Ramon back home with me, I'll tell you!

Anything you wanted, he couldn't get it fast enough. I was enjoying myself.

I knew Buddy wouldn't like it about the ponies, he would say that Rose Annie was trying to buy their love. This is what he said whenever she sent them presents, too, even those sweaters from Scotland. He made Tammy put them all in the basement to give to the Kiwanis gift drive at Christmas. So Sugar and Buddy never saw their gifts, and Rose Annie never inquired about them. She didn't inquire even when we were over in Nashville visiting; it was almost like she didn't want to know.

Well, as I sat there watching Ramon bow himself backward out of the room, I made a decision. I decided *not to tell* Buddy about the ponies. People don't need to know everything. I would tell the children that the ponies were a secret between them and me, and that way they could ride them whenever Buddy let them go visit again. So this is what I did.

And as for Rose Annie, that visit was an eye-opener for me. I went over to Tennessee prepared to hate her, but I couldn't hate her any more than I could when she was married to Buddy and laying in the bed. I thought she would be *changed*, I guess, since she had become the Queen of Country Music and all, but the only thing changed about her was the size of her bosom on that album cover. In the flesh, she was the same Rose Annie as always, with something about her that made you want to hug her and tell her it would be all right. She looked young as ever, and pretty as ever in a frail kind of way, like a wildflower.

This is what came to me that day as I watched her walking up from the stables with a child on each hand—*like a wildflower.* I don't know why I thought that, but you know how wildflowers are—they die if you try to transplant them or bring them inside. Her hair was still as pale and flyaway as dandelion fluff, and the color still came and went in her cheeks. Her eyes were that cornflower blue—oh, it was not possible to stay mad at Rose Annie!

We stayed in Nashville for four days, and on the second night she took us to the Grand Ole Opry, where we actually got to go backstage and meet Hank Snow who I have always admired so much, and Little Jimmy Dickens, he is not but four-eleven foot tall, and Kitty Wells and her husband. The biggest thrill of the whole night was when Kitty sang "It Wasn't God Who Made Honky-tonk Angels"; you never heard so much applause. I was proud to be there. Minnie Pearl was on the Opry that night, too, and I was so surprised to learn that in real life she is from a fancy family, and not from up a holler someplace. Her real name is Mrs. Sarah Ophelia Colley Cannon, and she is rich, can you believe it? Another time, we saw Webb Pierce in the street! Out of the car window! Walking down Broadway big as life! When we saw him, Rose Annie got so tickled at me because I'd been saying, "Now is *he* a star? or *him*? or *her*?" Looking for stars, you know. So when we really saw Webb Pierce, I liked to died.

Anyway, Rose Annie kept us so busy, showing us Nashville, that it was the third day before it really hit me—why, where was Johnny?

"He's on tour right now," Rose Annie answered, but the color came up in her cheeks and I thought to myself, *There is more here than meets the eye.*

But then what I thought was, she and Johnny had decided that for this first visit, it might be better for the children if he wasn't around; that way the children could get used to their mamma again, and *then* him. So I thought they had planned it that way out of decency. But it would not have bothered *me* a bit to see him, and I said as much to Rose Annie. I told her flat out that I and the children would sure love to meet him, and mentioned that I had promised the women in my Circle to get his autograph if I had a chance.

"Well, next time, for sure," Rose Annie said, smiling at me. "He's in, let's see, Tulsa right now."

But this turned out not to be true, as the phone started ringing off the hook later that afternoon, people looking for Johnny. He had *not* showed up in Tulsa yet, even though the show was not but about four hours away and his band had already run a sound check. Oh, I heard it all. Did Rose Annie have any idea where he might be? No, she did not, but she had to talk to the boys in the band and the people that were booking the concert, and I don't know who all. Then their manager, Billy Bodine, and two other men came out to the house and went in the office with Rose Annie and stayed for over an hour.

Meanwhile the sun was shining and the children were splashing in the pool with the boy from the stables up there watching out for them, and a snooty decorator out from town was measuring for drapes in the dining room, and workmen were finishing up the mirror walls in the foyer and putting the wrought-iron clef note on the gate.

I had not seen so much activity in the whole rest of my life up to that point, I'll tell you. I was about to wet my pants from all the excitement, but when the men left and Rose Annie came back into the living room, she seemed real calm, considering.

"Oh, there must have been some kind of a mix-up," she said. "Billy will get it all straightened out." Then she said she wanted us to eat early so she could take the children into town to this special old-fashioned soda parlor for ice cream, since it was their last night with her, and she knew they'd need plenty of rest for the trip home.

Rose Annie was trying to act like nothing at all was wrong about Johnny being missing, so I didn't say a word. We ate some kind of delicious chicken cooked by Ramon, with almonds in it, and then Rose Annie put the kids in her Cadillac and headed off for town. See, this is a picture of her and them in the soda parlor that night, it's just made to look like olden times.

Anyway, that left me there alone to pack and try to get Pancake on the phone, which I could not do. I just hoped and prayed he'd show up the next morning, when he said he would.

After I finished packing my clothes and the children's, I got to feeling sorry for the ladies in my Circle because I couldn't bring Johnny's autograph back to them. So I got up and went into Rose Annie and Johnny's bedroom—the master suite—to see if I might find some little souvenir. I couldn't get over the bed, kingsize, but with a canopy—you know it had to be built special. It was *Gone With the Wind* all the way. Blue satin sheets and floor-length mirrors everyplace, double mahogany dressers and gold brocade drapes, even gold fixtures in the bathroom, and blue towels with gold monograms. She had about a million pictures of Buddy Junior and Sugar on her dresser and her vanity, plus a beautiful huge color picture of Johnny which he had signed "I have allways loved you my Darling." Both Johnny and Rose Annie had a cedar closet as big as my own bedroom to keep all their clothes in. Johnny had at least twelve of those black cowboy suits he always wears, with different kinds of silver and sequin designs on them. Some of them had silver and turquoise designs, I bet they are priceless. Johnny's closet was real messy, though, compared to Rose Annie's. The whole floor was covered with piles of stuff, so I picked up a souvenir or two for my Circle girlfriends, just some things it was clear he would never miss, a little cigarette lighter shaped like a gun, a string tie—he had a million string ties!—some belt buckles, etc. Then I packed those and went in the kitchen and told Ramon I would like some kind of a sweet little after-dinner drink to settle my nerves. Tía María, I think it was. I sat out by the pool and sipped it, watching the lights come on one by one all around Old Hickory Lake.

I certainly could get used to that life, I thought to myself riding back home in the truck the next day with Pancake and the kids.

But clearly all was not kisses and Tía María with the King and Queen of Country Music, so I was not too surprised when these stories started coming out in the papers recently. Stories like this one, I mean. Tulsa is not the only engagement he's missed, not by a long shot. Dallas, Richmond, Knoxville—it goes on and on. Why, they are now referring to him as Johnny No-Show! And look here how skinny he is. For a while after he and Rose Annie got together, Johnny was looking a lot better than he used to, but now he looks awful again. I bet it's not just drinking. I bet it's drugs. See how he's dropped off, look at him from the side in this one. He's nothing but a shadow. You know, you can't expect to change a man by marrying him. You cannot. People don't change when they get married, no matter how much they swear they're going to. They just *don't*. I don't know if Rose Annie thought about that or not before she run off with him. I can't imagine *what* she was thinking about, to tell the truth. Sometimes I wonder if she's *all there*, if you know what I mean, but I wouldn't say it to a soul.

Now here's the worst one, I saved it for last, I just can't get it out of my mind. It says that Rose Annie was picked up by the police in Gainesville, Florida, wearing a negligee, incoherent, with a bleeding lip—well, read it yourself, it's just terrible. This event took place "following a disagreement with her husband, the well-known singer Blackjack Johnny Raines, who apparently locked her out of their motel room." Although another article said that *she* had left, trying to get away from *him*. So you can't tell what to believe. Anyway, I just hope and pray that Buddy doesn't see these—I don't think he will, because folks around here realize how sensitive he is about Rose Annie, especially now since "Subdivision Wife" is such a big hit.

And you can't ever tell, all those problems might have just blown over by the time I'm supposed to take the children to Nashville for the Christmas visit, which Buddy has finally agreed to. Pancake volunteered to drive them and just drop them off and wait on them and then bring them on back, but while I can't say anything to Loney about Pancake's motives, I naturally feel that it would be best for all concerned if I go along, knowing what I know about the whole situation. Plus I certainly wouldn't want the children to witness any *scene* in that house between Johnny and Rose Annie, and as I told Buddy, I don't mind going a bit.

3

Blue Christmas, 1959

Rose Annie Talking

I'm trying. I'm trying to tell you. I'm telling it as fast as I can. But I have to get this tree trimmed right now, you can see that, anybody can see that, don't you know this is Christmas Eve? The children are coming tomorrow. *Sugar and Buddy Junior*, of course—my children. *My children.* So if it's all right with you, we'll just talk while I trim this tree, if you don't mind, I mean.

Ramon! Where is Ramon? Could you hand me one of those boxes sitting on the sofa next to you, please? Could you maybe take the cellophane off of it first? Thank you so much, Officer, I hate to ask you, I just don't understand where Ramon is.

I got the idea for the tree out of a magazine, I always wanted an all-blue Christmas tree. Then Harry Russo, that's my decorator, found this beautiful blue tree for me. He also found the angel on the top, she's French porcelain, I don't know where he bought her, but isn't she perfect? I think that little star she's carrying is so cute. Well, it's a little light bulb, actually, but it's *supposed* to be a star. And her lovely blue dress is in the

Empire style, Harry says. Isn't she beautiful? She looks just like my own little girl. Oh no, not Sugar. *Not Sugar!* My *own* little girl. I don't know. She was here just a minute ago. When you came in. She was the one who let you in, I believe.

Yes, *doesn't* the yard look pretty? Tour buses have been coming by here about six times a day ever since we got it set up. It took them five whole days to set it all up, and then when they turned it on, why it just took my breath away!

It *does* look like a real baby, doesn't it? But it's just a doll. Just a doll. That's what they used to say to me, "Rose Annie, you're just a doll."

The way they do the tree is, they wrap each limb around and around with strings of the tiniest little lights, it takes *forever.* And then of course when they turn on the electricity you can see every branch, every twig. I think they look like lightning.

I used to live up on Grassy Branch in a house on a hill where I could look out and see a storm coming up the valley from a long way off. The leaves on the trees will turn inside out, this is how you know a storm is coming. Inside out, they look all silvery in the wind. That happens first. Then the wind picks up. The clouds get dark. Then lightning stands up like a tree in the sky. I used to sit there every day, looking up and down the valley, watching the weather, watching my children play, watching the cars pass by, waiting for him to come. Why, Johnny Rainette, of course! Laying right over there on the rug. I bet Ramon has gone out to get a carpet shampooer, I certainly hope so.

How about handing me that box of little blue stars? This is what they sang when Mamma died, Tampa and Virgie standing under a black umbrella in the graveyard in the rain. *Bright morning stars are rising, bright morning stars are rising, bright morning stars are rising, day is a-breaking in my soul.* Their voices made puffs of smoke in the air, it was so cold that day, they buried Mamma in the cold rock ground, which does not matter for the soul will leave the body and rise like smoke to meet Jesus in the air. And didn't we lay in the freezing hayfield, me and him, oh did we not? in that cold dark field looking back at the fire and all the figures dancing, it was all of them a-dancing, dancing in the fiery light while we laid out in the night and watched them, and stars as big and wild as fireworks filled the sky. Johnny. It was always Johnny. He never loved nobody but me, never in all his life, no matter what he done. No matter what any of them said. No matter what *she* said.

Why, the one that was here this afternoon, I mean, that said she was having a baby. His baby, she said. Oh, I had his baby too, I told her. It was little and blue and it died, I told her, with its little fingers curled up in a tiny blue fist, I told her, it lived all by itself in a little tent in Chattanooga. We will wait for him to come home, then, I said. He will want to do the right thing, I said. Come sit by me, I said, on this sofa here we can look out the window and see all the lights come on, it is almost dark, it's time to turn them on, anyway. Just sit here beside me, I said. I've been so lonesome lately. But she started crying and ran away. I saw her go stumbling and crying through the shepherds and the Wise Men, away into the dark. It gets dark so early now, don't it? Don't you just hate it?

When we were growing up there were so many of us, there was always somebody to be with, it seems like, I never got lonesome like I do now. Christmas smelled like pine and oranges then. I must tell Ramon to buy oranges. We will stick cloves in them just like Little Virginia does every year, we will make fudge like Mamma. Ramon will be so surprised.

Where *is* he, anyway? I need some help with this tree. I am not well, I've got bad nerves, you see, I had a nervous breakdown as a girl. Officer, if you wouldn't mind, I need somebody tall to put these icicles up on the top of the tree. *Yes. Oh yes.* It is so pretty.

Well, then I sat here in this dark house waiting for him to come, of course, and looking out the picture window at the manger scene and all the lights, and then at the cars that came by on the road to see it, and I could not help thinking of those other windows, the one in Chattanooga that looked out on the little fountain which splashed so, and up on Grassy Branch where I sat for so long as the seasons passed, while I waited for him to come.

Why, then he *did* come, of course, as I knew he would, and as soon as I saw his car I knew it was him. The funniest feeling came all over me, I can't describe it. I knew I would do whatever he said, I'd go with him wherever he went. Oh, and when he parked and got out of the car he was wearing a black cowboy hat and mirror sunglasses, but I knew who it was immediately and I ran outside and he took me in his arms and kissed me and kissed me. "What took you so long?" I said, and he laughed and kissed me some more. And when I drew back what I saw was myself, Rose Annie Bailey, in his mirror sunglasses, and then I remembered who I had been all along, Johnny's girl, and so I was alive then, and I left with him as soon as we could load my stuff in the car. For we are one, you see, him and me. I'd been waiting for years and years. And now here I am waiting again, he's been gone for days, and it's Christmas. Families ought to be together at Christmas. Christmas is a family time. And I get so lonesome, for he ought not to go off that way and leave me, not at Christmas, he *ought not*, or to do the things he has done to me. Oh, awful things. But then my little girl came and sat beside me.

Right there on the sofa where you are now. By then it was really late and so she brought me that little .32 Johnny gave me for my protection. Oh no, she is *not* good, my little girl, she is willful and bad, but she takes good care of me, and I have to be taken care of. I do. Somebody has got to take care of me.

Well, when Johnny came in drunk and he was so mean, she—Hand me that string of little silver balls, won't you—*There.* Oh yes. Now if you'll plug the lights in, it's right there behind you, behind the sofa. Oh yes. Yes. *Yes.* Now isn't that beautiful? It's exactly the way I dreamed it would be, just exactly.

5

Katie Cocker Tells It Like It Is

I got a double bed
In this double-wide,
And a double shot of gin,
But I'm a single girl
In a one-horse town,
Layin' here alone again.

1

Mamma Rainette and the Raindrops

Aunt Virgie used to say, "Be good, girls, and if you can't, be careful." Then she'd give us a big sly wink and close the door behind her, real soft-like. And even if we didn't know where she was going exactly, we had a pretty good idea of what she was going to do when she got there. We'd sit on the old iron bed in the boardinghouse in Richmond and giggle, me and Georgia, and not say out loud what we were thinking. Or at least I didn't say out loud what I was thinking, and I *know* what I was thinking. I reckon I've always had a dirty mind, or at the very least a mind which is *down-to-earth.* I will call a spade a spade. I will tell it like it is. I can't kid myself, or not for long, anyhow. Oh, I guess we all kid ourselves a little bit.

Actually, I'm not sure why I remember this so good, Virgie going out the door in Richmond and winking at us that way when she left. But I do. I remember her dark red lipstick and how she wore her hair pulled up in back with combs, like a Spanish dancer, those dyed black curls like bedsprings all around her face. Virgie still had a hard country Kewpie-doll prettiness about her at that time. Twenty more pounds and she would lose it, her cute little turned-up nose and pouty mouth squeezed in by those big old cheeks.

This must have been right when we first got to Richmond, me and Georgia, ready to hit the big time, fresh off the farm. But it wasn't long before we were going out too, with our own boys. I hadn't been much interested in the boys around home, to tell you the truth, or vice versa. I was related to most of them, and I believe I was just too big and definite for the rest. I spoke my mind a lot in school, maybe because I had to keep so buttoned up at home, for reasons which I'll get to. But oh Lord, those Richmond boys! I hadn't ever seen nothing like them. Slow-talking, big-spending rich boys in vanilla-ice-cream suits and open cars; fast-talking, chain-smoking young salesmen in plaid pants just on the verge of making it big; boys that worked in stores; boys whose families owned some of that flat rich black land right outside town, that land so different from where we'd grown up on Grassy Branch. I knew a rough boy from Oregon Hills that worked in the ironworks down by the river, I knew a pale sweet boy that was in school to be a lawyer, I knew a boy with a glass eye that shot pool for a living. I didn't discriminate too much among them, to tell you the truth. I liked them all. There were more boys in Richmond than I had ever dreamed of, twiddling my thumbs up on Grassy Branch—this is one reason I jumped at the chance to go off with Virgie and be a Raindrop.

The other reason is that I was just dying to leave home. Even when I was a senior, Mamma wouldn't hardly let me out of her sight, not that I had any particular feller to go off with, either. So I got this idea that if I could find me a husband in Richmond, I wouldn't ever have to go back home. Doesn't that sound crazy now? What a reason to want a husband! But that's what we thought back then, us country girls, that's the way we were raised. We thought we had to have a husband to do anything. This sounds especially crazy to me now, since I've had several. Oh Lord. If I could just know what I know now and feel like I used to feel! Anyhow, I was wild to leave home, I was wild to get me a husband—I guess I was wild in general, but ignorant as a post.

Two of my best friends, Dessie Hudson and Shirley Bell Cameron, had gotten married before we finished high school, and I'd never even had a real boyfriend. Dessie was the head majorette. She got married one week before the whole band went to Roanoke to compete in the Battle of the Bands, so then she had to drop out of school, and naturally the band didn't win. Dessie Hudson was the best head majorette we ever had at Holly Springs High, but it didn't stop her from getting married. We all thought it was romantic, of course. Dessie and her boyfriend, Jerry Lindsay, ran off to South Carolina in a school bus, because he was a school bus driver. The board of supervisors voted not to prosecute him, though. Then there was Shirley Bell Cameron, who was pregnant and dropped out to marry Roland Jolly, and then brought her little tiny baby girl to graduation. Only a few people in my class—mostly the town kids, like the doctors' kids from Holly Springs and Cana—planned to go on to college, which really hadn't even been mentioned in my case. I thought I would probably try to get a job working for the veterinarian in Holly Springs, since I'd always liked animals and I couldn't think of anything else to do. Mamma had already said flat-out that there was *no way* she was going to ever consent to me trying to be a singer, which was what I really wanted to do. "They is enough singers in this family already," Mamma had said absolutely. "Too many to please God," she said, for she was convinced that most singing was a sin.

So I wasn't doing much of anything except baby-sitting

for people when Virgie called up and asked me to go off with her and Georgia, to be a star. A star! As soon as she said it, I jumped on it like a dog on a bone, for I wanted something more than what I had. I've *always* wanted something more than what I had, it seems like. This has been one of my big problems in life. Until Virgie said it, I didn't know how bad I wanted it. But I loved to sing, better than anything, and always had.

When I was a little girl, my favorite times up on Grassy Branch were when all of us sat out on R.C. and Lucie's porch singing while the moon came up, listening to the little babble of the creek in that sudden hush that fell sometimes at the end of a song, sneaking a burning sip of whiskey out of one of the grownups' glasses, drunk already on the sweet-sweet smell of the honeysuckle vine. I'd stay up there all night, any night, if Mamma would let me. But no, here she'd come walking around the hill from our house to get me, wearing Daddy's old green cardigan sweater with the holes in the elbows, which she always wore around the house. I hated that sweater. It made me so mad to see her wear that awful old sweater around, just like it made me so mad to hear her high wavery voice quaver out, "Katie? Katie? You come on home now, honey." For a minute I'd just sit there, knowing she couldn't see me in the dark, imagining what she'd do if she thought I'd run away from home and she'd never see me again. But then Little Virginia or somebody would say, "Katie, you go on home with your mamma now," and I'd go. I wanted so desperately to live there in the big house with Rose Annie and not in my own house, where things went on that I knew I couldn't mention, even young as I was then.

I had always loved to sing. I was crazy about the little gospel quartet we had for a while, me and Rose Annie and Georgia and Johnny, and when I won Miss Holly Springs High, I sang for my Talent even though I had lied and told Mamma I was going to use sewing as my Talent and model two outfits

I'd made in home ec. (This is actually what Darlene Jewel did, who came in third. And I *had* made a really pretty red sheath dress with a matching jacket, and another dress with a circular skirt and cap sleeves that were awful to put in right.) But I didn't model these outfits. Instead I wore an electric-blue strapless dress with a ballerina-length skirt loaned to me by Dessie Hudson (Mrs. Jerry Lindsay!) and sang "I Want to Be a Cowboy's Sweetheart," accompanying myself on my guitar. I belted it out, too, just like Patsy Montana on the radio.

The audience loved it. People all over the auditorium jumped up and whistled and clapped and yelled when I finished. It went to my head, I guess. I felt hot and tingly all over, a feeling I *still* get, believe it or not, at the end of every show. And every time it's just as exciting as it was that first time, honestly. It gets in your blood, you know. Finally you can't live without it. I was probably *born* with it in my blood, but I didn't know it until that night I was crowned Miss Holly Springs High.

Then when Helen Ann Breeding, who had been Miss Holly Springs High the year before, came forward with my tiara and put it on me, I just burst into tears—I couldn't help it—and the crowd clapped and yelled even louder. They always love it if you cry. The applause echoed off the green tile walls of the auditorium.

I was hooked.

Mamma wasn't there, thank God. She had stayed home with Mamma Tampa, who'd come to live with us for good by that time. I just hated it, too. I felt like I was in a cage with the two of them there—Mamma Tampa talking out of her head all the time, and Mamma praying over everything. So there was that, *that* somehow, behind me that night as I sang, the knowledge of Mamma Tampa and Mamma back home in the kitchen sitting on those old straight chairs stringing beans, looking awful and acting creepy. It made me wild, I'll tell you.

And also I could not quit thinking about Rose Annie, who was not in the audience but in a hospital someplace in Tennessee, having a nervous breakdown. Rose Annie was a whole lot prettier than me, and could sing better, too. I never would have won Miss Holly Springs High if she'd been in the contest. The thought of Rose Annie in the hospital filled me with a crazy sadness I could not contain, a feeling that I would *burst* somehow, and I think all this stuff found its way into how I sang that night. It always does, but I didn't know that then. It made me want to dance and jump and strut my stuff all over the stage and sing louder and better than anybody else ever had. I wanted to pep up Mamma and Mamma Tampa. I wanted to give Rose Annie a voice, a body, a self in the world again.

So I won. I got a rhinestone tiara and a steam iron and a check for fifty dollars.

Mamma cried the next day when she heard it at the beauty shop, even though everybody told her how good I was. She didn't care. All she wanted to do was marry me off as soon as possible, so she wouldn't have to worry about me anymore. She acted like I was some big wild animal in the house, but at the same time she wouldn't let me go out anywhere or do anything. "How do you think you're going to marry me off," I asked her one time point-blank, "if you won't let me go out anyplace to meet anybody?"

This made Mamma's weak chin quiver, and her pop eyes fill up with tears. "Oh, Katie," she said, "you'll understand when you're older, honey. You will." And because I knew how much Mamma loved me, and how hard her own life had been, I tried hard to do like she said, and be good and bide my time, trusting that things would work out somehow in the end.

For I had always been a good girl, always done what they said to, and I guess in a way I was as alarmed as Mamma was by this new personality that seemed to be trying to take me over right then, right about the time of the Miss Holly Springs High contest. Do you remember that movie *The Three Faces of Eve*? That's what I felt like, like several girls in the same body, all of a sudden swept by the wildest desire for something I couldn't even name. I wanted to be good, I wanted to be bad, I wanted to get a husband, I wanted to sing my heart out. I loved Mamma but I hated her, too, hated her whiny voice and lack of gumption, the way she'd make you say the blessing over *everything*, even a piece of pie and a glass of milk. We were driving each other crazy by the time Virgie came to get me, but even so, Mamma refused to let me go with her.

I went anyway.

I didn't tell Mamma I was going until the very afternoon I left, a bright hot day in June. I didn't figure there was any point in telling her any earlier and getting her all wrought up about it. I'd known I was going the very minute Virgie called up long-distance and asked me. "Yes," I said immediately. I didn't even have to think about it.

"And I'll be *just fine*," I said to Mamma when I told her. "Georgia's going too." Mamma thought a lot of Georgia, who was responsible to a fault, not a thing like her mamma.

"Honey, you don't know what's out there," my mamma said, her chin quivering as she followed me around while I packed my clothes. "You don't have a clue."

"I don't know what you mean, 'what's out there.' *Out where?*" I said just to devil her. I couldn't help it.

"Out in the world," Mamma said. "You just don't know, honey, what all a girl can get into. It's mean people out there, it's not like here."

Not like here where your own husband ran around the county drinking until he died of it and beat you up whenever he felt like it, I didn't say. *It's so damn nice here*, I didn't say. I understood that Mamma wanted to keep me here because she couldn't think of what else to do with me. She couldn't imagine any other kind of life, or any other place to live.

But I *could*, throwing clothes into my cardboard suitcase that I hadn't used since 4-H camp. I packed my jeans, my church clothes, my winter coat. I didn't plan to come back for a while. Then I looked out the window and there was Virgie's car, the long white Oldsmobile. She was right on time, and Georgia was with her. They didn't get out of the car. I put the rest of my clothes in my suitcase and sat on it to get it shut.

I looked around my room good before I left, at the pictures of Gene Autry I'd taped over the fading wallpaper with its repeated pattern of little lattice squares and curlicues and violets—oh Lord, how many afternoons, how many hot nights had I laid on my bed and stared at that wallpaper and waited for something to happen! Well, it was happening now. All my yearbooks stood in a stack on the floor, my dolls filled the top of the closet, my blue-and-gold cheerleader pom-poms hung on either side of my mirror. All around the inside of the mirror frame I'd stuck school pictures of all my friends, each one across from the boy she liked. I looked out my window and saw Aunt Virgie out there smoking a cigarette in the car. But for some reason, I still took the time to make up my narrow bed, something Mamma usually had to *force* me to do, and smoothed my pink chenille spread over the pillow carefully. Then I unplugged my radio, which Mamma had bought me with Green Stamps. Lord knows how many nights I had stayed up until one or two o'clock in the morning, listening to *Randy's Record Shop* out of Gallatin, Tennessee, singing along.

I carried my radio in one hand and my suitcase in the other when I went back in the kitchen to kiss Mamma Tampa good-bye. She sat at the table where Mamma had put her, stringing beans. She loved to string beans, it calmed her down. Mamma Tampa's white hair stood up straight all over her head, like a crew cut growing way out. Her dress was buttoned up wrong. This was the kind of thing I just couldn't stand to see, for I could still remember when she dressed to kill, and took so much pride in her looks. "Bye-bye, Mamma Tampa," I said, hugging her from behind.

"Durwood Bailey was born during a thunderstorm," she said. "His mother ran off with a midget." Mamma Tampa was always telling some kind of a big story.

"Now Mamma, you know that's not true," my mamma said.

"Bye-bye, I love you," I said. At this point I couldn't even tell if *that* was true or not, I was so dead set on leaving. I dragged my bag down the hall—it was a little dog-trot house we lived in, around the side of the hill from R.C. and Lucie's—and pushed open the screen door and went down the steps and out the walk, blinded by the sunshine. Bees were buzzing around, a little soft breeze was blowing. I felt like I'd come out of a cave and into the world. Mamma followed me down the walk twisting a handkerchief in her hands and blinking at the light like some kind of underground animal flushed from cover.

"Honey," she said, twisting her handkerchief, "honey, I just want what is best for you."

"I know it, Mamma," I said. I realized this was true.

But then she had to say, "I just pray that God is looking over your shoulder as you make this decision, honey," and I could hear Mr. Erwin Bledsoe, our preacher, in the tone of her voice. Personally I didn't like Erwin Bledsoe, because he always stood too close to me when he was talking, and touched me too much. He did this to all the girls. I need a lot of room.

But I went back and bent down and hugged Mamma good before I got in Virgie's car, and as I hugged her, all of a sudden, a little movie of Mamma went running through my mind—Mamma sewing tiny little stitches to make the smocking on my Easter dress when I was nine; Mamma taking all her saved-up money out of the old sock when I was twelve, to pay the doctor bills; Mamma down on her knees with a ruler, her mouth bristling with a line of straight pins, hemming up our cheerleader skirts for us while we drank Coca-Colas and talked silly and acted for all the world like Mamma was some kind of hired help; Mamma nailing the oilcloth over my window and reading out loud to me so my eyes wouldn't get ruined when I had the measles; Mamma trying her best to explain it away when Daddy would get so bad, and telling me he had a good heart really, and that he never meant to hurt anybody and he never would again, she was sure of it, but that life is full of trouble, and I'd understand when I got older. . . .

All these pictures of Mamma ran through my mind when I told her good-bye, and right then I wanted desperately to be everything she wanted me to be, and more—better than she ever dreamed, for this is the awful curse which is naturally laid on an only child, you have to go forth in the world bowed down by all your parents' hopes and dreams as well as your own.

"Don't worry about me, Mamma," I said, hugging her. "I'll be just fine." But I was crying my heart out by then. Mamma felt as little as a grasshopper when I wrapped her up in my arms and held her tight, I could feel her little fast-beating heart. I watched her turn and stumble a little as she went back up the walk. She did not turn, nor wave. I knew she was crying. Then I got in the car with Georgia and Virgie.

"Well, good Lord!" Georgia said when she got a good look at me. "It's not like we're going away *forever!*"

Virgie handed me a Kleenex and a cigarette and a silver lighter. "Here you go, honey," she said. Then Mamma went back into the house, and I hauled off down the road with my cousin Georgia and my wild Aunt Virgie, a high school education and a rhinestone tiara and not a clue as to what lay ahead.

But before I get into what all befell us as Raindrops, I feel a need to go back for a minute and tell how we got to this point. I chalk it up to biology, myself. I think it's in the genes. Me, I never wanted to do anything but sing. I used to read those early clippings about the Grassy Branch Girls over and over. . . . I used to wish I *was* them, that I'd been born twenty years earlier, so I could have been one of the Grassy Branch Girls too, and lived in a simpler time. At the very least I wished I'd been born into the other side of the family, and got to live in the big house and have lots and lots of brothers, and stay up late singing on the porch, and drink as many Nehi orange drinks as I wanted to out of the old red cooler R.C. kept in the barn, a cooler just like they had at the store. I thought this was wonderful.

But our life was different from that. Now it seems to me like Mamma was all the time going around the house turning off lights, to save electricity she said. When I think of home, I think of darkness. Mamma also saved every scrap of food, so that our refrigerator was full of little jars covered with tinfoil. Every now and then she'd go through and clean them out—they'd have gray stuff growing on them by then. Daddy used to kid her about this habit, saying, "Now who in the hell is going to eat those three tablespoons of corn, Alice?" but she'd spoon the corn into the little jar anyway, and he'd wink at me. Mamma saved string, pieces of tinfoil, buttons and ribbons and rubber bands. She even saved the inside cardboard part of toilet paper rolls. I bet she *still* saves them. "You're a pack rat, Alice," Daddy'd say, winking at me.

Mamma was crazy for washing dishes, too. When we were

through eating, she couldn't let a dish set on the table without jumping up to wash it. Then *I'd* have to jump up, too, because Daddy would say, "Katie, help your mamma."

Actually, Daddy seemed real fond of Mamma; even the things about her that drove me crazy were okay with him. I never heard him say a word against her in my life. But it was like he wasn't quite *up* to Mamma somehow.

Here's what I mean. This happened about a year before Daddy died. He had been out on a drunk for a week or more, which was not uncommon, for after Grandaddy Durwood passed away, Daddy just cut loose. It was like he'd been holding back in order to please Grandaddy Durwood. Anyway, Daddy had been off someplace for a while. Mamma and Mamma Tampa were squabbling in the kitchen that morning over how to cook an egg (Mamma Tampa liked hers fried hard as a rock, Mamma always gave it to her runny, then Mamma Tampa said that Mamma was just trying to torment her and run her off). Well, I heard this discussion every morning of my life, *every* morning! And that day I wasn't even hardly listening to it, I was going over the multiplication tables in my mind, for we had a big test in Miss Bell's class. I grabbed my books and sweater, hollered, "Bye!" and set off down the hill early to catch the school bus down by Grassy Branch. It was a pale misty morning in early spring.

I had not gotten but about a hundred yards from the house when I saw a man's legs sticking out of the brush by the side of the road. Mist was all around me, nobody else on the road. At first I thought it was a dead man, of course. A *body.*

I dropped my books and screamed.

Then Daddy set up and said, "Hush, Katie, you'll scare your mother to death!"

"You scared *me* to death!" I said. I was crying and laughing both. "What are you doing over there, Daddy?"

"I was just taking me a little rest," he said with a lot of dignity under the circumstances. "I'll be going on home shortly."

"Mamma's been real worried about you," I said, which was a lie—Mamma never said one word about his disappearances.

"She has, has she?" Daddy peered out at me from under his bushy eyebrows and his beat-up hat. I could hardly see his face. Then all of a sudden he gave a huge, deep sigh, as if all the life was going right out of him. "Well, she's a good woman," he said sadly. Daddy sat in the brush staring out through the mist on the road, looking like he'd lost his last friend, and I stood there holding my books and looking at him.

"Come here, honey," Daddy said after a while, and so I went over and held out my hand and he took it and got up. He had a hard time getting up. Then he leaned over and kissed the top of my head. "You better get on down the road, doll," he said—he always called me "doll"—"you'll miss the bus."

"No, I'm early," I said, but I went on, while he turned toward home.

As I walked down the hill, mist swirling all around me, I felt like I was all alone in an uncertain world, and like the last thing on earth I ever wanted to be was a good woman.

Still, it was easy for me to see how Mamma got that way. In her own family, Freda was mean and Virgie was wild, so Mamma was good. Everybody has got to be *something*, and it was the only thing left to be. Mamma grew up as the kind of little girl who'd cry if you said "Boo" to her. But she loved her father, my Grandaddy Durwood, with all her heart, and so it fell to her to take care of him a lot of the time when he was sick, while Mamma Tampa and Virgie and the others were on the road. Freda's job was to do the housework. Mamma's job was to nurse Grandaddy, and she went about it like an angel, keeping it up even after she got married and I was born. Often she'd take me over there with her, and oh how I loved to play on the log-cabin quilt on the brass bed where Grandaddy stayed—they had put the bed right out in the sitting room so he could see everyone that came by, for Grandaddy loved people, he loved a joke or a song, right up until the last. After he got so thin, Mamma used to make him boiled custard all the time and get me to carry it over there in a mason jar. Her boiled custard was about the only thing he'd eat.

Now I wonder if my own daddy didn't resent all that attention Mamma lavished on Grandaddy—and on me, and on our church, too, the little old church on Chicken Rise, for honestly she was the most church-loving woman I ever knew. She has a beautiful voice still yet, even though the only songs she'll sing are the old church songs. And Mamma was home-loving to a fault. Didn't want to go anywhere else, or do anything else, the complete opposite of Virgie. Mamma wanted to *stay put*, and for everyone else to stay put, too, and for everything to always stay the same.

Of course, that is the one thing that never happens.

Grandaddy died in 1941, Daddy drank himself to death in 1943, and I left home in 1947 with Virgie and Georgia, heading for bright lights and hard times, only I didn't know about the hard times yet.

You know, in my whole entire life I have never heard Mamma say one word about drinking, Grandaddy's drinking or Daddy's, either one. Mamma believes that if you don't mention something, then it's not happening. I do remember one time, in about fourth grade, I came home from school and repeated something I'd heard on the school bus, that Tillie Dew said her mamma said that my grandaddy was an alcoholic. I asked Mamma what that meant. She just looked at me for a minute with her blue eyes blazing. Then she slapped me so hard across the face that I fell against the wall. I had the marks of her fingers on my face for a week afterward. "Don't you ever, *ever* let me hear you say such a thing about your grandaddy again," Mamma said. "It is bad manners."

And as for Daddy, I never even saw him take a drink, because Mamma wouldn't allow a drop of liquor in the house, and it was *her house* after all, the little old dog-trot house that Grandaddy gave them after they married so young without a penny to their name. I still can't figure out why they did it, got married I mean, since Mamma wasn't even pregnant. One time I asked her, and she just said, "Well, Katie, he *asked* me," in her whiny way, but a funny little smile played around her lips. So I give up! You can't tell what goes on between people, you can't figure it out in a million years. By the time I got old enough to think about it, my mamma was certainly not what you would call an object of desire. But Daddy was no prize, either. I spent my childhood being generally embarrassed about one or the other of them, and sneaking over to stay as long as I could at Rose Annie's or any of my other friends' houses—anything to keep from sitting in the dark in my own house and acting like I felt sorry for Daddy laying in bed with the flu when I knew better all along. So I got real good at covering up things, and not letting anybody know how I felt.

I learned to lie like a rug.

I remember one time when Mamma had a bruise on her upper arm, and I knew how she'd gotten it, and she knew I knew, but of course we had not discussed it. Well, there was a Ladies' Circle meeting set for our house, and Mamma was determined to have it anyway, and so she wore a long-sleeve dress and acted like she wasn't even *hot*, in the middle of August.

We were sitting out on the porch with the women from the church, rocking and fanning, and Mamma was passing around a tray that had ice tea with lemon and mint in it.

"Now where's that Ray?" Mrs. Branham asked, and Mamma answered smoothly that he was working on a construction job in West Virginia, which was the first I'd heard of it.

Then, "Alice, aren't you just burning up in that dress?" my Aunt Freda asked.

"Why, no," Mamma said, beads of sweat standing all along her upper lip. "I think it's right pleasant out here." Freda and some of the other women were peering at Mamma's face.

"*I* don't think it's a bit hot!" I said real loud, rocking my chair so violently that I broke a geranium pot on the porch, and then we had to clean *that* up, and the moment passed. I got good at things like this, and in a funny way I didn't even mind so much. A person can get used to anything, you know, and also I loved Daddy. I did. I loved him more than I loved Mamma. I know this is hard to understand. I felt guilty about it, too. But when Daddy died, I just couldn't quit grieving—nor could Mamma, to be honest.

Mamma and me did not have near as much in common after he was gone, it was like our sad secret had held us together, and with him gone, there was not much left between us. Oh, we tried. We both tried.

But even the way I walked around a room bothered her. She just didn't know what to do with me, as I said. Then when Mamma Tampa came to live with us, it all got a lot worse. Now Mamma Tampa was never what you would call *sweet*, even before she went crazy, so she was real hard to deal with. Everybody said Mamma was a saint for putting up with Mamma Tampa, and I reckon this is so, but I just went straight up the wall. I'm no saint and never have been. I felt like I'd never get out of that house, like I was going crazy, like I'd *die* there. I believe I would have died if I'd stayed any longer.

I felt like we'd always be sitting in the front room, just the three of us, watching the night come on. In a funny way it seemed like the men had never really been there at all, Daddy and Grandaddy, like they'd been just passing through and only *this* was real, the sunlight fading on the old flowered carpet, the shadows growing under the furniture until I felt that something dark was hiding under everything, just waiting to come out and get me, absorb me into that room, those lives.

I left.

Even then, I knew it was a turning point in my life. Sometimes you can see a turning point when it comes, sometimes you can't. Sometimes it is only later, a lot later, that you realize what was important and what was not. I know Mamma didn't understand that it was as hard for me to go as it would have been for me to stay. It hurt her, my leaving like that. She thought I was picking Virgie over her. I wasn't though. I was just doing what I had to. But it would never be the same between me and Mamma again, for she was bound to disapprove of what I was bound to do. Riding around the bend in the big white car with Virgie and Georgia, I did not look back. I took a long hard drag on my cigarette and rolled down the window to let the wind blow my hair.

2

I Have a Baby

If I thought I was hitching my wagon to a star when I hooked up with Aunt Virgie, I was dead wrong. It was more like getting soldered onto a comet. Aunt Virgie didn't really have a great voice, nor any particular skill on that old gutbucket guitar. What she did have was *energy*, I mean electricity just sizzling out of every pore, enough to turn on every light in the whole city of Richmond. There's something real attractive about energy, pure and simple—it took me a while to catch on to the fact that nobody else took Aunt Virgie quite so serious as she took herself, nor have quite so high a regard for her talents as she did.

Why, back home on Grassy Branch, we all thought she was a big star, and read over and over those clippings and programs she sent back to us from the faraway places she was working, places like Texas and Iowa and the state of Washington. Now I know praise is cheap. Paper is even cheaper, and advertising is the cheapest thing there is. Those posters and programs didn't mean as much as we thought. Anybody can go to a printer, or hold a show. But back then, we thought Aunt Virgie was a big star, and that big white car she drove every time she came home proved it.

Come to find out, but this was lots later, that a man who turned out to be married had given that car to Virgie, to keep her from paying a call on his wife. Come to find out, too, that Virgie left Grassy Branch because R.C. made her, after he had to go over to Big Al's Café in Bristol and bring her back home one time too many, Big Al calling up real respectful on the phone to say that he knew Mr. R.C. would want to know that his kin woman was laying drunk in a room upstairs. R.C. and Virgie really got into it after this, and she finally left home in a pickup truck with a man that none of us had ever seen before or would ever see again, hanging out the window calling R.C. names.

But then she won some kind of a talent contest over in Kentucky, and first thing we knew she was on WHAS out of Louisville, and somehow ended up on the Renfro Valley Barn Dance, which was mighty high cotton indeed, with the likes of Red Foley and Aunt Idy Harper and Little Clifford, and the Coon Creek Girls. Virgie never sang solo on there, but she did have a little comedy act she'd do with the rest of them, and she sang in the cast, and on the *Sunday Morning Gatherin'* show too. Virgie hated Lily May Ledford, though, one of the Coon Creek Girls, and she got to telling tales about her, and eventually John Lair fired her.

Virgie bounced around from one radio station to another for a while then, not staying anyplace long, until she decided that an all-girl comedy act was the way to go, and came back to get me and Georgia. By this time she had got a reputation in the business as being difficult, which is the kiss of death, as there is always another girl from up in a holler somewhere just waiting to take your place, with a big country grin all over her face. She's nicer than you. She can sing better, too. So it don't do to be difficult. But Virgie was, and she was known for it, although me and Georgia didn't know it for a while.

At first we went right along with all of Virgie's ideas, since we surely had none of our own. Mamma Rainette and the Raindrops really *was* something different in the world of radio right then, I'll say that for us. For her role as Mamma Rainette, Virgie wore a funny hat with a huge black feather on it, a fancy red and black satin dress pinched in at the waist to where I didn't see how she could even breathe, red leather high-heel boots with silver toes, and a ton of makeup, including the longest false eyelashes you ever saw. Her dress was cut real low. The running joke in the act was that Virgie was trying to marry us (the Raindrops) off, so *she* could get a man before she was too old (not such a joke!), but our role was to be too stupid for marrying off. In fact we were supposed to be just short of retarded, and our act consisted mostly of telling dumb jokes to each other, such as the knock-knock jokes and Little Moron jokes that were real popular then. Our radio names were Bitty and Elvira.

ELVIRA: Bitty, do you know why the Little Moron threw the clock out the window?

BITTY: Why, Lord no, Elvira, I can't imagine nobody doing a dumb thing like that! Why *did* the Little Moron throw the clock out the window?

ELVIRA: Why, shoot, honey, he jest wanted to see time fly!

In all the Little Moron jokes, the Little Moron came off smarter than we did! There was a couple of skits that were right funny, though, one in particular that got us in hot water with the station. It featured me and Georgia as Old Farmer

Brown and his Old Wife, and it went like this. (We were supposed to be sitting out on the porch talking.)

FARMER BROWN: Well, wife, I paid off the mortgage today. Now we own this here farm free and clear.

WIFE: (*Sounds real mournful*) Well, that's good, I reckon.

FARMER BROWN: You reckon! Why, what in tarnation's the matter with you, woman? Hit's what we always dreamed of, ain't it? Ain't you happy?

WIFE: Hit's jest hard fer me to be happy about anything when I think about our two daughters a-layin out there in the cemetery.

FARMER BROWN: Well, wife, ain't it the truth! I know I oughtn't to say it, but to tell you the truth, sometimes I'd a heap rather they was dead!

We were country as they come. At first, I didn't know any better. Later, I came to hate it, wearing those crazy getups she made us wear, straw hats and bloomers and big black clodhopper lace-up boots, our red-checkered dresses buttoned up wrong.

But I had to admit, the crowds at the Old Dominion Barn Dance just ate us up, and I do love applause as much as anybody. We were a big hit. The Barn Dance even took a bunch of publicity photos of us to promote the show, and put up four big billboards with our pictures on them twenty feet high, grinning like the fools we were. Georgia and me made Virgie drive us out Monument Avenue in Richmond every day to look at ourselves on our billboard, we just couldn't get over it! We were as big as General Lee, and lots more important!

Naturally, as I said, the boys started coming around, and it wasn't long before I was going with one of them in particular, Hank Smith, and it wasn't long before we were rubbing up against each other on the dance floor until I couldn't breathe right, and it wasn't long until I was sneaking out with him after hours, into the dry cleaner's where he worked, that he had a key to, and laying with him across those big old soft tables where you press men's shirts, and the streetlights came in the windows all pale and ghosty where the shirts hung on hangers all around. Maybe I knew, in some part of my mind, that this was wrong—I can't say for sure if I knew it or not, though. I can't say for sure if it was wrong or not, either. I was not real sure I wanted to be a good woman, anyway, as I said. Look where it had gotten Mamma!

When I thought about Mamma and Mamma Tampa up on Grassy Branch, it all seemed so long ago and far away, like somebody else's life in another country. I liked Richmond, where the streets were full of people and the streetcars ran up and down and you could get your fortune told or buy a piece of hot chicken on the street corner or see a Negro tap-dance in a big box of sand.

I didn't think about Chicken Rise church at all, despite how much time I'd spent there, for Virgie didn't care if we went to church or not, and Hank Smith and I liked to borrow a car and take a picnic out to the James River on Sundays. Or sometimes we'd go to Hollywood Cemetery, which I loved, it was all cool and beautiful in there. One little girl's dog had died right after she did, pining away for her, so there was this beautiful statue of the dog right beside the headstone. It was so sad. There were dead babies, too, lots of them, with little lambs or roses or angels on their graves. This is where I got the idea for my song "The Littlest Shepherd" from, you know it is about a baby angel that shepherds the lambs. We used to sit right on the graves in the soft mossy grass, and then I'd lay back, and then he'd kiss me. Hank Smith was a great kisser for his age.

Which was my age exactly, seventeen. He lived with his uncle and aunt, and sent half of his wages home to his mother, a widow in Danville. His daddy had been killed in the war, and Hank was an only child. His mother couldn't work, she had palpitations of the heart. When his aunt and uncle told her how much time he was spending with me, she had a cousin drive her to Richmond to talk some sense into Hank. Of course she couldn't, and went home mad, and when I'd missed three periods in a row, Hank and I got married.

I didn't have the nerve to ask Virgie to come. Georgia was the only family member present, arriving by taxi at the very last minute. We were married down at the big courthouse by Judge Roy Reardon, solemn as God Himself.

Hank wore a blue suit and I wore a beautiful pale green wool suit with a matching green hat and a little illusion veil, all of which Hank had borrowed from the dry cleaner's. Later he took them back and ran them through again, and no one was the wiser. I often thought about the people that owned those clothes, how surprised they'd be to learn they'd been in a wedding! I have two pictures taken on my wedding day by a Negro photographer down at the courthouse who did this all day long. Here we are with Georgia. Here we are just the two of us, holding hands. We look like children. We *were* children.

And yet I have to say, Hank Smith was sweet. He was no city slicker, but a nice boy whose whole heart showed in his eyes. He was not a boy for the long haul, but how can you tell?

Georgia married not long after, and she's still married—shoot, she's a grandmother now! Live and learn.

After the wedding ceremony, which took only about a minute and a half but was one of the nicest wedding ceremonies I ever had, I have to say, because we were so young and so full of hope I reckon, we walked outside to find that it had started to snow like crazy, not a car was moving, and they had turned on the streetlights early. It seemed like a blessing, that snow. It made Georgia and Hank and me act like kids, running down the street throwing snowballs at each other in our fancy wedding clothes, giggling and whooping all the way home, the longest walk in the world, all across Richmond, to come in dripping and giggling and exhausted finally at the boardinghouse on Floyd Avenue, where Virgie had gotten real worried about us by this time.

"I got married!" I hollered, and then me and Hank fell in a pile in front of the fire laughing.

Virgie was not a bad sport. She took a good long look at us and said, "Well, I'll be damned!" and then, "Congratulations!" She went upstairs and got some rum, and Mrs. Marblehead, who ran the boardinghouse, got out some fruitcake and made coffee, and one by one the others in the house came down, until we had a real party going on. It was my new husband Hank and me; Georgia, Virgie, Mrs. Marblehead; Mr. Ralph Johnson, a traveling salesman who wore a toupee; Miss Harriet Lumpkin, a registered nurse; a Mr. and Mrs. Livingston Hall from Baltimore, who were in Richmond on temporary business; old Mrs. Wright, who had lived there for years and years; and the pale little clerk, John Umstead, who never spoke a word. After a while we started to sing, naturally, and found that John Umstead had a wonderful bass voice, even better than R.C., and that Miss Lumpkin was a trained soprano. Miss Lumpkin really showed off on "Mighty Lak a Rose," which Virgie played to everyone's astonishment on the piano. I didn't have any idea Virgie could play the piano like that.

The snow piled up outside, higher and higher, until the streets were filled with people marveling at it. It was the most snow Richmond had had in twenty years. Hank and I fell asleep on the rug in front of the parlor fire, and Mrs. Marblehead covered us up with a quilt sometime in the night and let us sleep there.

It was a fine wedding night, to my mind. We woke early on Sunday morning to the blinding glare of sunshine off the snow, and the wild ringing of every church bell in Richmond. I looked over at Hank to see if he was awake, and he was laying there grinning at me. He had floppy brown hair, and a cowlick that fell down over one eye. "Why does the Little Moron take off all his clothes and run out in the snow?" he said.

"I don't know," I said.

"I don't know either," he said, and then he kissed me.

When Mr. and Mrs. Livingston Hall left, Mrs. Marblehead gave me and Hank their bedroom, the biggest and nicest one in the house, overlooking the gaslight on Floyd Avenue instead of the back alley. The curtains in that room were made of Irish lace, and the light from the bay window coming through them at night cast a flowery pattern across us in the big old four-poster bed and across the whole room. It looked beautiful. It was the prettiest room I had ever been in, anyway, that's for sure, with its antique chest-on-chest and a real oil painting of some castle in another country.

I didn't tell Virgie I was pregnant until I had to, until I just couldn't button up the front of my red-and-white-checkered dress. Then she guessed it. Backstage after the show one night, she lit up a cigarette and squinted at me shrewdly through the smoke. "Well, when's it due?" she asked me.

"May, best I can figure," I said.

"Goddamnit!" Virgie looked like she was going to cry, a

sight I had never seen. "Goddamnit, Katie, why did you have to go and do *this*? You could have made it, you've really got something, something I would have given my eyeteeth for." She gazed off through the smoke, tapping her foot. "You're a damn fool," she said.

Virgie kicked me out of the act two weeks later, replacing me with a Richmond girl named Ernestine Dodd, naming her "Petunia" for the act. Petunia wore my clothes and learned my jokes in no time flat. It was the strangest feeling, sitting out there in the studio audience watching her.

I was too big to work anywhere by then, so I just mostly laid on the bed with my feet up, reading magazines and fooling around with melodies on my guitar, picking things out. I wasn't writing songs yet, but I was getting close to it. The bigger I got, the harder it was to sleep, and I'd often wake up in the night with a tune running through my mind so loud and clear I'd have to get up and write it down. No words, just the tune. I couldn't go back to sleep if I didn't write it down, the tunes were as demanding to be born as the baby herself.

Annie May came on the last day of May, with the weather so hot I'd done nothing but sit in a tub of cold water the day before to keep cool. Hank was at work at the cleaner's. Thank goodness it happened to be Miss Lumpkin's day off. She went with me to the little hospital over on Stuart Circle, where we had arranged to go, and I was in labor for nearly twenty-four hours before Annie May was born. It was awful. I named her Annie for Rose Annie, May for her birth month. In spite of my long labor, she was beautiful, not red or twisted like some of the other babies in the viewing room.

I held her out to Hank, who had not been in the room when she was born; they didn't use to do that back then. I think the modern way is the best way, myself—let the men see how bad it hurts! Maybe they'll keep that thing in their pants a little better after that. Anyway, Hank did not take to Annie May then or later. Maybe he was still too much of a baby himself to want another baby around. I don't know.

"Looky here," I said, lifting her little pink gown to show him all of her toes, little round perfect toes like pink pearls.

Hank looked out the window, sucking in his breath. "I reckon I'll call Mamma," he said.

"Well, tell her that her granddaughter is just beautiful," I said.

"I sure will." Hank sat and twisted his cap in his hands.

"What is it, honey?" I said then, for I could tell something was wrong.

"Nothing," Hank said.

But still he sat there. Then he said, "Well, Katie, I reckon we are about down to our last nickel for sure," not looking at me. "When do you reckon you can get up from there and go back to work?"

"Why, Hank, I just don't know!" I said. He surprised me. I had been figuring on spending some time with the baby while she was so little and all. Then after a while, I thought, I'd try to get a job singing someplace around town. I wasn't too big on joining back up with Virgie and the Raindrops again. But I couldn't for the life of me see how we could be down to our last nickel, anyway, it didn't make sense, for I had been saving up all those months while I was sharing a room with Georgia and pulling in that good radio money.

"Here," I said. I handed him the baby, and he sat there stiff as a post.

"Mamma had to go to the doctor," Hank said. "She's been getting these headaches every day." Well, I should have known! Mamma this, Mamma that. Mamma had to have the furnace fixed, Mamma had to buy new eyeglasses. Of course, Mamma was not but forty years old when she was widowed, but she had yet to show one sign of going out and looking for a job—believing, as Hank believed, that she was "not that kind of woman," and holding fast to those palpitations of the heart.

Hank handed Annie May back to me in a hurry. "I'm late for work," he said. "I've got to go." He put on his cap and left in a rush, and the hospital nurse, a big Scottish woman who was right there in the room and had seen all of this, came over and hugged me. "My wee girlie," she used to call me.

By the time Annie May and I came back to the boarding-house, things had changed. Hank was different. He had a worried, tight look about the eyes now, and he went out a lot. He wouldn't talk to me. He did not love to lie beside me in the bed as he had once, tracing the patterns of the lace on my body as I sang the old songs for him. Now when he made love to me it was a hard, fast act, almost as if he was giving in to something and wanted to get it over with as soon as possible.

I remember that summer now as a long bright stretch of time with me and Annie May alone in our room, yet I was not unhappy, because a baby is the best company in the world. I would sing to her all day long, the cuckoo song being her favorite, as it had been mine. I lay in the bed for hours just daydreaming, while Annie May pulled on my nipple. During the afternoon we'd sit at the bay window and I'd watch the life of the street, which I never tired of—the vegetable man from out in the country with his wagon full of corn, watermelons, beans, and tomatoes; his mule wore a floppy hat. "Sweet corn! Sweet corn!" he'd holler. He'd play a blues tune on his old flatbox guitar for a nickel. The three old-lady sisters across the street fanned themselves slowly in the heat all day long, all dressed up for nobody. Children, wild at being out of school, ran up and down the sidewalk with sticks and bats and balls, headed for a game someplace. The thin old man who lived on the corner was said to have been in the Civil War. He walked back and forth to the other end of the block every day, wearing a white linen suit. It took him an hour.

I'd play and play with Annie May, or just look at her for hours as she slept—her little fingers and toes, the tiny birthmark on her upper arm, her funny flyaway hair. She was just perfect. I wondered how she'd look as a six-year-old, or when she was ten, or twelve. I wondered what kind of a teenager she'd be—not like me, I hoped! I wondered what kind of a woman she'd be, where she'd live, what she'd do.

I loved that summer I spent in the boardinghouse with Annie May. I love thinking about it now, summers and summers since. Of course now I wonder if I knew somehow, in the back of my mind, what lay ahead, if that's why I treasured it so very much. . . . Anyway, it ended in the fall. Hank kept pushing me to go back to work, as his mother needed this and that, so finally I just joined up with the Raindrops again, since it seemed like the easiest thing to do. Mrs. Marblehead found me a Negro woman named Sophrina Little who took care of Annie May along with her own children. Actually, I still got to spend a lot of time with Annie May since we didn't have to be down at the studio until five p.m. for the Barn Dance, this was every weekday afternoon.

Sometimes Hank would stay with Annie May then, but usually I took her to Sophrina Little's, which I always felt better about, for Sophrina's children loved babies as much as she did, and Annie May got so much attention over there. Hank didn't pay enough attention to her, I felt, just leaving her in her playpen or on a blanket while he read the papers or studied for a class. Hank was taking a self-improvement class that fall, he was real serious about it, and another class in accounting.

He was determined to make something of himself, so I reckon he has. People usually get what they go after. Whether they end up wanting it or not is another matter.

I always took Annie May to Sophrina's on the mornings we did the *Breakfast Club* with Ed Barr, which was real popular.

We were getting real popular, in fact! Ernestine Dodd—Petunia—stayed on when I came back, so it was Mamma Rainette and three Raindrops now instead of two, and we sounded a lot better. Ernestine Dodd was a natural cut-up on the radio, in a way that Georgia and I were not. Later she went on to be Sally in Sally and Clyde, which was a famous variety act. They were on *Arthur Godfrey*, *Ed Sullivan*, you name it.

This was the fall that Mamma Rainette and the Raindrops made a record featuring "Git Along Home, Cindy," which was our lead-in song, on one side and R.C.'s song "Living on Love" on the other. We got a lot of play around Virginia and the Carolinas, so much that Virgie started getting invitations for us to come and play different events, shows and fairs and such, on the weekends. Of course this involved traveling, and I hated so to leave Annie May.

But Hank would say, "Go, go," for we needed the money, he said, and I went, for I was still trying to be a good wife even though I was having my doubts by then.

I will never forget that Friday night when we got back to Floyd Avenue real late, it must have been three a.m., back from doing a show in Roanoke, and I tiptoed over to peep at my baby, switching on the light in the bathroom and cracking the door just a little bit first so I could see where I was going without waking her up. I was surprised to see her turning her head back and forth, and kicking her feet—usually she slept like a little log. Her breath was coming in tiny shallow gasps. I leaned down and felt of her forehead. It was burning hot.

I pulled on the overhead light and grabbed her up out of her crib. Hank sat up in bed. "What the hell are you doing?" He was rubbing his eyes.

"Annie May is sick," I told him. "She's just as sick as she

can be. Get up, Hank, we've got to take her to the hospital. I think she's *real* sick," I said.

"Now just hold your horses, Katie," Hank said. "She hasn't got a thing but a little cold."

"How do you know?" I said.

"I got Miss Lumpkin to come up here and look at her," Hank said. "It's nothing. Go to bed, let her sleep. She'll probably be just fine in the morning."

"I'm going to take her to the hospital if I have to walk," I said.

"You are not! You spoil that baby to death, Katie, that's probably what's the matter with her anyway. It's *nothing*, I'm telling you. Get in the bed. I've got to get up at six o'clock and go to work, in case you've forgotten."

"I've just *been* working, in case you've forgotten," I said, knowing it was a mistake, for I made more money than Hank, which he hated. "Go get the car keys from Virgie," I said. We still didn't have a car.

"Goddamnit, Katie, shut up! I'm telling you for the last time, we're not taking this baby to the doctor for nothing. Nothing, you understand me? We ain't got the money for it. You wait and see how she is in the morning, I'm telling you. There's nothing wrong with that baby. "Hank never called her by her name, Annie May. He always called her "that baby." He had a fixation that going to the doctor was a big waste of money—for *us*, that is. His mother went all the time, and furnished us with full reports—what she said, what the doctor said.

"If you don't get up and take me and Annie May to the doctor right now," I started, but then I didn't know what to say next.

"*What?*" he yelled, bounding up out of the bed to stand in front of me. "*What?*" He pushed me into the wall, so that I stumbled back and nearly dropped her. I got real light-headed and scared, it was late and I was so tired.

"Nothing," I said. I backed off, and he pulled the light chain and lay back down.

"Get in the bed, Katie," he said, but I wouldn't put her down, and in a minute I could tell by his breathing that he'd gone back to sleep.

I took Annie May in the bathroom and put her blanket down in the tub and let her stay there with me sitting on the bathroom floor beside her, sponging her whole body off with a damp washcloth from time to time to try and bring the fever down. This seemed to work. Finally she started resting easier after a while, and breathing better. Finally it started getting light outside, and then the alarm went off and Hank got up and dressed for work in a hurry. He came in the bathroom and leaned over and kissed me. I could tell he felt real bad about how he had acted, even though he didn't say anything about it, men just can't sometimes.

"I think she's some better," I said.

"Well, you'd better get Virgie to drive you to the doctor anyway," Hank said, so then I *knew* he was sorry, and I said I would.

But the first thing I did after he went out to catch the streetcar was go upstairs and get Miss Lumpkin, who came to the door with her gray hair hanging down to her waist, and I realized that she must have been real pretty, years and years ago. This shocked me.

I asked Miss Lumpkin if she would come and take another look at Annie May, and she said, "Why, what's wrong with Annie May?" and then I knew Hank had been lying.

"She's sick," I said, "she's been real sick." And not five minutes later, Miss Lumpkin was there, all professional-looking with her gray hair wound up in a bun now under her starched white cap. I was embarrassed to have her see the unmade bed, yet she walked past it without a glance and picked up Annie May, who was sleeping deeply by then, a good sign, I thought.

Miss Lumpkin looked at me with her clear gray eyes and said, "This baby needs to see the doctor. Now I'll just sit right here with her"—she sat in the rocking chair—"while you gather some things together, Katie, and we'll take her right down to the hospital. It's always best to see the doctor." Her voice was bright, false, professional.

I couldn't hardly think. I packed up a sack with baby clothes and toys, diapers, the blanket Mamma had crocheted and sent in the mail, Annie May's little silver cup from Hank's mamma. Then I picked up my purse and my guitar case.

"You won't need that, honey," she said. "But get yourself a sweater or a coat," which I did, and we left.

They took her away from me at the hospital and did some tests, which took about two hours. I sat in the waiting room and bummed cigarettes from the other people waiting there too, and vomited twice in the bathroom. It didn't even occur to me to call anybody, Virgie or Georgia or Hank.

Finally Miss Lumpkin came back out with two doctors.

Annie May had polio.

They said she would need to stay in the hospital for some time, and it might be months before we would know the extent of the damage. They said a lot of other stuff too, but I couldn't take it all in. Then they led me back to where they had put her in a crib in a room with three other babies in it, under a bright white light that stayed on, I would learn, day and night. There was a chair beside her crib. I could stay for a while. There were certain hours every day when I could visit, and sit in the chair, and hold her. I couldn't hold her that first day, though. I sat there and somebody brought me a cup of coffee and a newspaper. I looked at the date on the newspaper. December 18, 1948. Annie May was nearly seven months old.

I sat there until they told me I had to leave, that I could come back in the afternoon, and again at night if I wished to.

So I went and called Virgie down at the radio station, where I knew they'd be just finishing up Ed Barr's *Breakfast Club*.

"Where the hell have you been?" Virgie said. Then I told her, and she said she'd be right there.

It was cold, but I sat out on the steps of the hospital and waited for Virgie, watching people go in and out of the door. I felt light-headed and funny, like everybody was staring at me. Once an ambulance pulled up with its bell clanging, and they wheeled a bloody man on a stretcher in through the double doors. Once a big young Negro man nearly knocked me down, pushing a wheelchair into my shoulder. Some boys about my age walked past on the sidewalk and paused to light a cigarette, staring at me. They *were* staring at me! Then, just as Virgie squealed up to the curb in the big white Oldsmobile, I looked down at myself and realized why they were all staring at me—because I still had on my Raindrop outfit, the red-and-white-checkered dress buttoned up wrong, those big black clodhopper boots. I looked like country come to town. Behind me, in the hospital, my little Annie May lay sleeping beneath those bright-bright lights. Virgie slammed out of the car and ran up to hug me tight. She smelled, as usual, like cigarettes and perfume and gin. "Oh Katie, it'll be all right," she said, but I knew it would not.

3

The Last Barn Dance

The Raindrops busted up in Charlotte in 1953, when we were working the old Dixie Jamboree radio show out of WBT. Now I have to say, I had not been a Raindrop for that whole time. Hank left me as soon as he found out that Annie May had polio, he never even went to see her in the hospital. He went back to Danville, and his mother sent me a check for three hundred dollars along with a little note on her monogrammed notepaper which I did not bother to read, and this is the last I ever heard from either of them, although later a Danville lawyer sent a piece of paper to Mamma saying that I had been annulled. I didn't care. I was *glad* to be annulled!

Anyway, I did try to work while Annie May was in the hospital, but I was just too wrought up, so finally I quit trying, and as soon as she was well enough, I took her back home to Grassy Branch, where I thought we could live with Mamma and Mamma Tampa, and they would help me take care of her. It was all I could think of to do.

But I had not been in that house two months before I saw that it would never work, that I'd go stark raving mad there.

Nothing had changed. Not one thing.

It was Mamma and Mamma Tampa still sitting around in the dark stringing beans, and Mamma going off to church every time they cracked the church door, and trying to get me to do the same, and then, when she was out of the house, Mamma Tampa would follow me around and tell me endless crazy stories in her whispery old voice.

I loved some of them, though, I have to say, like this one she told me about her and Durwood driving all the way down to Key West, Florida, years ago. She said they swam off of a pink sand beach and drank rum out of coconuts with people from New York City. Then she held up her finger like a warning. "Wait a minute! Wait a minute!" she said, all excited, and before you could say scat, she was digging in the bottom of the closet and darn if she didn't come up with a big old conch shell I had never seen before. "Ssh!" she said. She pressed it up to her ear, listening hard, and then the most beautiful look came over her face.

"Mamma Tampa, what do you hear in there?" I asked.

"Why, honey, hit's the ocean!" she said. "Here. Listen to it."

But when I pressed the conch shell up to my ear, I couldn't hear a thing. Nothing.

I left her there in the bedroom listening to the ocean while I carried Annie May down the hill and caught a ride with Pancake on down to see Rose Annie and Little Virginia. Little Virginia always pepped me up, but Rose Annie just didn't seem to be as happy as she ought to be. That nervous breakdown had left her with some permanent brain damage, or depression, or something. She seemed so sad all the time, like a washed-out version of the girl she used to be. I couldn't adjust to the new

Rose Annie. It depressed me, along with everything else up on Grassy Branch.

When I told them about Mamma Tampa and the conch shell, they just nodded. Everybody knew what Mamma Tampa was like. "I don't know if I'll be able to stay up there or not," I said, and they nodded again, and Rose Annie came over and hugged me. I could feel her shoulder blades sticking out like little wings underneath her shirt.

So leaving was on my mind already when the postcard came from Virgie saying that her and the Raindrops had moved from Richmond to Charlotte to be on the Dixie Jamboree, and Ernestine Dodd was quitting the act, and wouldn't I like to reconsider.

I started thinking about it. I started reconsidering.

For one thing, by that time I was not so scared about taking care of Annie May. She was a year old then, and though she had never talked and we didn't know if she ever would or not, she was crawling all around and pulling up on things with her good arm, and had even taken a step or two. She wore a little brace from the knee down on her bad leg. I was taking her to the hospital at Holly Springs every three weeks so they could change the size of the brace as she grew. And I have to say, every time I took Annie May over there, or anywhere else for that matter, everybody marveled at her, at how sweet she was, all smiles and giggles. See, she didn't *know* she'd had polio. She didn't *know* she was crippled.

That summer I'd sit out with her for hours on end in this little red plastic wading pool, and we had a big time. I began to realize that she'd *live*, that she would grow up, that I could raise her after all. I started thinking more about Charlotte, about the fine hospitals I was sure they must have there. You know they'd beat Holly Springs Memorial!

One summer day I was sitting out in the wading pool when Buster Yates came around in a truck to install a washing machine. I used to know him in high school, now he worked for B. T. Goforth Appliances. Anyway, Buster got out of the truck and said, "Hey, sweetie," to Annie May, who looked up at him and giggled. Then he asked me right out if I'd like to go hear some music over at that new place on the highway outside of Holly Springs.

"Aren't you married?" I asked.

"Not really," he said, and when I kept on looking up at him he sort of ducked his head and blushed. "I'm kind of transitional," he mumbled.

Well, that was good enough for me. All of a sudden I was sick of that house, and ready to have some fun. Buster had a handlebar mustache and sideburns, which I have always liked. I like a lot of hair on a man. So we made our plans, but when Saturday night came around, Mamma flat-out refused to baby-sit for Annie May. She announced that she had talked it over with Mr. Bledsoe her preacher, and that in his opinion—and hers, she was real clear about this—Annie May's polio was a direct judgment on me from God for what I'd done.

"What did I do?" I asked.

"Why, *you know*," Mamma said, pinching her lips together.

Mamma Tampa was not in on this conversation—she sat in the other room, listening to the radio.

"I don't know either," I said, feeling all of a sudden like my old feisty self again. "What do you mean, Mamma?"

"Why, leaving home thataway," Mamma said, "and living in sin. Don't you reckon I can *count*, Katie?" meaning, she'd been over her counting the months, seeing how long it was between Christmas when I got married and May when Annie May was born. "I'm not about to help you get up to none of your old tricks again, Miss Priss, not with this poor cripple baby to take care of."

"Very well," I said, and then I called Buster and told him I couldn't make it, and then I called Little Virginia and asked her if she'd give me a ride into Holly Springs to catch the bus to Charlotte.

"Shoot, I'll *drive* you to Charlotte," Little Virginia said. "I have always wanted to go to the Dixie Jamboree myself. Don't you reckon Virgie can get us tickets?"

So we went.

Mamma Tampa stuck her face right up close to mine just before we left and said, "Remember, honey, don't ever buy nothing but silk hose, and sing the old songs for me."

"That's not bad advice," Little Virginia said when we got in the car, and it's *not*, either. But I could see Mamma praying on the porch as we pulled into the road, and it made me mad as fire. I knew for sure that I would never come back home to live again.

"How do you stand it here?" I asked Little Virginia, but she said R.C. was real easy to take care of these days, and she did all his business for him, mostly buying and selling land, and she enjoyed that. She said she'd gotten real good at it. She also said that she planned to start living with her boyfriend, Homer Onslow, if his mother ever died, that Homer was going to move in up there with her and R.C.

"I wouldn't *marry* him, though," Little Virginia went on to say. "Not for two or three years, anyway. I'd wait and see how things went. I'd want to keep my own room, too, of course. You know, you get used to doing things the way you want to do them, and not having to worry about somebody else. Whether they like salt or whether they don't. Whether they like to leave a light on at night."

I looked at her good, for it was the first time I'd ever heard a woman say a thing like that. "What do you think R.C. will say, though, if you move Homer in?" I asked.

"What *can* he say?" Little Virginia snorted. "He don't even know how to fry an egg."

We got there in time for the show and just loved it, and so there I was, a Raindrop again!

Virgie found me a real nice baby-sitter for Annie May, actually she was the station manager's daughter, so that worked out good, but this was the *only* thing that worked out in Charlotte.

The act was just plain *flat* without Ernestine Dodd. Georgia and me tried hard of course, but neither her nor me could really fill the gap. Ernestine was a natural cut-up as I said, real antic, and without her, Georgia and me just looked *dumb*. Or this is how I felt about it, anyway! Georgia had started dating a real nice Charlotte businessman who was somewhat embarrassed by our act, and so she was losing interest fast. She wasn't ever really cut out for show business, anyway—I mean it wasn't just flat-out *in her blood* the way it was with me and Virgie, the way it had been with Mamma Tampa when she was young. For me, I reckon it had something to do with my sad short marriage and with Annie May getting polio—but the fact is, I just couldn't act corny and silly anymore.

But Virgie refused to change the act. "Oh hell," she said, "somebody's got to give folks a good laugh. That's what they hired us for, honey, in case you've forgot it."

In the meantime I'd been writing some songs of my own, up on Grassy Branch during the time I had not been working, but they were not songs that Mamma Rainette and the Raindrops could sing. I wanted to sing them myself—I wrote them for *me*, and I dreamed of this—but Virgie said nothing doing, even though me and Georgia both begged her on it. Nor were we allowed to appear on our own outside of the act. I begged her and begged her, for I could have used the extra money, believe me! But she said no.

Of course Virgie was drinking a lot by then, vodka mostly, she thought we couldn't smell it on her breath, and sometimes she was kind of mean-tempered, and other times she was confused. Another thing that was going on right then was a rumor that they were fixing to put the Jamboree, or part of it anyhow, on television, and so everybody was wondering who would make the cut for TV. I knew for a fact that Virgie had been worrying about it, and with good reason, because she'd already had a few run-ins with the management, and the fact is, she'd actually been fired off of WRVA in Richmond because of coming in drunk one morning on Ed Barr's *Breakfast Club* and cussing everybody out on the air. They didn't use to have that three-second time delay, the way they do now. Live was *live*, you'd better believe it! It would of been funny if it hadn't of been so awful.

Anyway, there was a lot of tension in the air, and finally it all blew up, right in the middle of a show.

Now the Dixie Jamboree had kind of a recipe, you might say—all the old-timey radio barn dances did. The only difference among them was the sponsor, and who the emcee was. At the Dixie Jamboree it was Colonel Jack Kyle, who allowed more horseplay onstage than some, and featured more comedy. Why, a new singing group was likely to smell smoke and look down to find lighted matches in the soles of their shoes, which just tickled the audience to death. They loved stuff like that. They loved it when Shorty of Shorty's Crazy Hillbillies let his pants fall down around his feet, or when me and Georgia did the one about walking over the air vent and the wind blew up our crinoline skirts to show our bloomers. Not that you could see much, with those big old bloomers!

Georgia's boyfriend had told her that he found this joke

demeaning (he had gone to Davidson College), which made Virgie see red. So Virgie had blessed him out, up one side and down the other, and because of this, Georgia had decided to quit the act. Only, she hadn't told Virgie yet. This was the secret she was trying to keep until the end of the month, when they planned to announce their engagement.

Anyway, here's how it went. First you'd hear the Jamboree theme song, "Hot Time in the Old Town Tonight," and then Colonel Jack would start out by welcoming everybody, saying, "From the Queen City of the South, in the heart of the Carolinas, it's eight-thirty Saturday night . . . time for all the boys and girls at the Dixie Jamboree to gather round the microphone and sneak into your hearts with a song or two. Now the first little ditty coming atcha is one the fiddlers kinda shine on . . . and the rest of the fellers twang their guitars and slap the bass fiddle while Ma and Pa and all the younguns join hands and circle round for an old square dance. . . ." Then they'd let loose with something like "Pretty Little Pink" or "The Arkansas Traveler." Then after that we'd have a western number—you had to have a western number, they were real big then—and then the first Crazy Water Crystals spot.

I swear, I was on the Jamboree for a couple of months before I ever figured out what Crazy Water Crystals actually do—it's a laxative! Only they didn't ever come right out and say it. Oh no, Colonel Jack was real high-toned, coming on like this: "Since the beginning of civilization, hydrotherapy—now this is nothing more than the treatment of illness with the element of water—yes, hydrotherapy has been regarded as indispensable in the treatment of physical and mental ills all over the world. For nature has endowed mineral waters with healing properties. In our own America, that water, so richly endowed, is found only in the Crazy Wells in Crazy, Texas.

And now, these crystals, formed by evaporation from Crazy Water itself, are available at a price everybody can afford. Simply dissolve Crazy Water Crystals in your drinking water, and let Nature do the rest. If faulty elimination is causing you to suffer from arthritis, bad nerves, upset stomach, liver disease, or kidney problems, the least you can do is rid the body of these toxic impurities that may have accumulated. *See for yourself what Nature can do!*" Colonel Jack would holler at the end of every Crazy spot. Then he'd always say, "Pucker up your face and keep smiling!" which didn't make a bit of sense to me. Seems like you would *either* pucker up your face *or* you'd keep smiling.

I mentioned this to Virgie one time, but she looked at me hard and said, "Just shut up, Katie Cocker! I don't know what you're talking about, and it's not good for a girl to think too much, either."

Then there'd be a gospel act, maybe an instrumental after that, and then *us,* after which there would be another Crazy Water Crystals spot.

Well, this particular Saturday night, me and Georgia were getting real nervous because we'd already had the first spot, and now the Johnson Family was gathered around the microphone singing "Tomorrow May Mean Good-bye," and still Virgie had not showed up. She was often late, but she had never been *this* late before, or not since I'd joined the show.

Colonel Jack came up to us while the Johnson Family was singing. "Well, girls, where *is* she?" he asked, puffing like mad on his cigarette. He smoked all the time.

We had to say we didn't know.

"I'm sure she'll be here momentarily," Georgia said. Now she had started putting on airs to match her businessman boyfriend.

"Momentarily, my ass!" Colonel Jack stomped his cigarette out on the floor and squeezed the ends of his mustache into little points, another habit of his.

"I tell you what I'll do, girls," he said. "I'll run Arthur in here for a extry act. Then I'll do the next Crazy spot, and you all can foller it. But I tell you what. If she ain't here by the time Arthur gets done, you're history. Am I making myself clear?" He lit another cigarette.

"Yes, sir," I said.

"Oh, I suppose so," Georgia said in that new way of hers.

Colonel Jack looked at her good. Georgia held out her hand and looked at her manicure.

"My nerves is bad," Colonel Jack said to nobody in particular, "and the women in this business is about to kill me."

"Why "don't you drink you some of them Crazy Water Crystals then?" somebody in Shorty's band called out, and everybody laughed.

"Hellfire," Colonel Jack mumbled into his mustache, stepping back over to the microphone. "And now, neighbors, here's that general handyman around the old Jamboree, Arthur Smith! and when I say handyman, I mean just that. One week Arthur plays his banjo, and the next the mandolin, and he's even done a little singing, too. Seems like whatever you folks ask for, it don't matter much, Arthur's always ready with a bang-up good tune like the one he's going to play right now. Folks, here's Arthur Smith's big hit from 1946, the world-famous 'Guitar Boogie.'"

The studio crowd went wild, because this act wasn't listed on the program, and Arthur Smith was the biggest star in Charlotte at that time, and a real nice man to boot.

Georgia had gone over to stand by the studio door with the red light above it. When Arthur Smith was nearly done, I looked over at her and she shrugged her shoulders. No Virgie.

All of a sudden I got an idea. I stepped up to Colonel Jack and grabbed his elbow. "Let me and Georgia go on by ourselves, Colonel," I begged him. "Please, sir. We can do it."

He stared at me with his little beady eyes, blowing out smoke. "A duet, huh?" he asked. "A sister act?"

"Yes, sir," I said. "We sing together all the time," which was a lie, we didn't do hardly anything together since Georgia took up with that boyfriend.

I swear I don't know what came over me. I just couldn't stand to give up the spot. I couldn't stand not to be on the air!

Colonel Jack got out his pad of paper. He wrote something down. "So what're you going to sing?" he asked.

"I'll have to talk to Georgia first," I said with my heart just bumping away.

"Honey, I ain't got time for that," Colonel Jack told me, for sure enough, Arthur Smith was done.

"Just announce us, then," I said. "We'll come on and say what we're going to sing."

Colonel Jack nodded and wrote it down. I flew across the room to tell Georgia as, behind me, Colonel Jack started in on the second Crazy spot. "Isn't it pitiful?" he said into the microphone. "That as conditions get better all over the world, as we recover from those lean war years, and dare to look back on our misfortune, still thousands in our own country remain hungry to this day, unable to eat due to chronically upset stomach. I ask you, is there anything more pitiful than to sit at a table loaded with good things, and watch others regale themselves, yet not be able to eat?"

I had Georgia by the sleeve, dragging her through the gospel group, across the studio.

"What in the world is the matter with you, Katie Cocker?" she was sputtering. "Virgie's not even come yet. Now let go of my arm!"

"Colonel Jack said you and me could go on anyway," I said, "just the two of us. We can sing anything we want to." By then we had made it over to where our instruments were, and I was getting my guitar out of its case.

"*Without Virgie?*" Georgia's face turned white.

"Sure," I said. "Let's do 'White Linen.'"

"Unh-unh!"

"What do you mean, unh-unh? Let's just do 'Living on Love,' then." We had done that one so much, we could have sung it backward and blindfolded.

But Georgia folded her arms and stood fast, tapping her foot. "I'm not about to make a fool of myself," she said. "We're enough of a fool already."

"Pucker up your face and keep smiling!" Colonel Jack hollered out.

"Then don't," I told Georgia. "Just *don't*. But I am. I'm a-going to do it." I took off my straw hat and fluffed up my hair, and unbuttoned the top button of my red-and-white-checkered dress. I decided to sing one of those songs I'd been writing up on Grassy Branch, a real sad number named "It's Either Her or Me."

"And now, folks, another unexpected treat for you tonight, two beautiful sisters from the Virginia hills, those Virginia Raindrops!"

Georgia and me just looked at each other. "I swear I can't do it," she said.

I stepped up and grabbed the microphone like I'd been doing solo acts on radio all my life. "Actually it's just me by myself," I said into it. "My name is Katie Cocker." Then I stopped cold, for I just couldn't do it, I just couldn't sing "It's Either Her or Me." I had never sung it for *anybody*, much less for thousands of people on the radio. Nobody but me had ever heard it. I swallowed hard. Then I heard myself saying, "And

I'm going to entertain you tonight with a real old song that my family has been singing down through the years. We call it 'The Cuckoo Song.'"

Then I put my guitar down and sung "The Cuckoo Song" flat-out with no accompaniment, not daring to look over at Colonel Jack. In fact I didn't look at anyone. I closed my eyes and clasped my hands behind my back and sang in the old style, and a hush came over the crowd. I still don't know what possessed me to do such a thing, to sing this song which I had not sung in years, but I just felt like it all of a sudden, and so I did it. When I got done, you could have heard a pin drop. Then everybody started clapping and hollering, and Georgia was hugging me.

"I can't believe you did that," she said. "That old thing. Whatever got into you?"

"Whatever it was, she'd better get shed of it real fast," a familiar voice said then, and I looked over Georgia's shoulder to see Virgie, red-faced and bleary-eyed, with her hair falling down in the back.

"What the hell is going on here, Jack?" she asked Colonel Jack in the most hateful voice, over the noise of a little Cherokee Indian doing "Pan-American Express" on the harmonica, it sounded just like a train.

"Now Virgie," he said, "let's you and me get together after the show, honey. We've got some serious talking to do." Then he put his arm around her and kissed her on the cheek, meanwhile winking at Georgia and me. Colonel Jack was smart. It was the only way he could have got her to shut up while the Jamboree was still on the air.

"And I've got some things to say to *you*, too," Virgie told me, but she was getting a little wobbly on her feet by then, and some of the fire had gone out of her. One of the Jordan Brothers led her over to a chair, where she snoozed for the rest of the show. When it was all over, she woke up with a jerk and looked straight at me.

"You're fired," she said.

It was hard to believe that somebody who could be as nice as Virgie could be so hateful, too.

"All right," I said.

"And I quit." Georgia had her coat on, ready to leave, with her boyfriend probably waiting outside.

"I don't give a damn," Virgie said. "You think I can't get some more Raindrops? Hell, girls ask me all the time if they can be a Raindrop. I've got my pick of Raindrops." Colonel Jack appeared then, offering his arm, and Virgie arose regally, wobbly as ever, to take it. "Raindrops are a dime a dozen," she said.

4

I Act Like a Fool

Lord, I hate to even tell this next part, it makes me look like such a fool. Well, I *was* a fool. I might as well say it. But I was real young. I am not the first person to fall for a smooth line and a handsome face, either. And Lord! Wayne Ricketts *was* a good-looking devil, I have to say. He certainly didn't look mean as a snake or downright dishonest, which he was. The first time I set eyes on Wayne Ricketts, I couldn't quit staring at him, he had this effect on everybody.

It was just about dusk when I drove into that trailer park in Shreveport, bone-tired, looking for a trailer to rent. A nice woman over at the Hayride, where I had just been hired to sing backup, had told me to go over there. A trailer was a lot cheaper than an apartment, she said. She was older than me and kind of beat-up-looking. You could tell she'd been around some. She was trying to take care of me, to give me some good advice. I hadn't ever thought about renting a trailer before. It sounded like a good idea at the time.

I was driving that green Buick I had saved up for by working clubs and juke joints in Charlotte, and I thought I was headed for a new life. That's what I was after—a new life. I was young enough and foolish enough at that time to really believe there was any such thing. I had cut all my ties to the past—I wasn't ever going to speak to Virgie again, or Mamma or Mamma Tampa, and Georgia was too involved in keeping house for Mr. Right to pay any attention to me, and Rose Annie was busy having babies with Buddy Rush, and she was just so weird now, anyway—well, I got in that green Buick and took off.

I was determined to make it on my own.

I went to Louisiana because I liked the sound of it, *Louisiana*, it sounded pretty and frivolous, like a party dress. It sounded like fun.

And Lord knows, I needed a little fun!

I was not but twenty-three, yet I felt ancient. I felt as old as the hills. All I'd done for the longest time was sing and take care of Annie May. I was tired of it. I felt like a dishrag, wrung out and hung up to dry.

Wayne Ricketts was standing right by the trailer with the yellow awning and the sign that said OFFICE. He was leaned up against a tree, smoking a cigarette. Something about the way he was standing suggested that he had all the time in the world. Now this was certainly attractive to me, since I felt like I'd been rushing around for several months like a chicken with its head cut off. He just stood there. No shirt, great tan. Wayne Ricketts was the only person I ever knew in my life that had truly green eyes.

"Yessum," he said, stepping up to my car window. "How can I help you?"

I believe we both knew the answer to that question immediately.

But what I said was, "I'm looking for a trailer to rent," and he said he thought there was one available. He leaned against my car, looking in the window, and all of a sudden I felt faint, like I was having a heatstroke.

"Oh," I said. "Oh, I . . ." I felt awful.

"Here, honey," he said. "Why don't you and this precious baby child come inside with me for a minute, and relax and put your feet up. Then we'll talk about the trailer."

Now it *was* hot and humid that day in Shreveport, but not *that* hot and humid! Not enough to make a girl lose her natural mind. Which I proceeded to do. It was like I'd been charmed, the way old Cooney Hart up on Grassy Branch used to charm snakes. Of course, what old Cooney always said about the snakes could be said of me: *Ye can't charm a snake if it don't want to be charmed*, he'd say. So I reckon I was ripe for charming.

I got out of the Buick and picked up Annie May and walked with Wayne Ricketts to his trailer, which was *not* the manager's trailer, he wasn't the manager of course, he'd just been acting like it, to impress me. We went in his trailer and he fixed me a bourbon and Coke without even asking did I want one or not, and I sipped it while Annie May went lurching all around. The trailer was a mess. Wayne Ricketts apologized for it, saying his wife had left town several months before, and he wasn't much of a hand at cleaning up.

"I never knew a man who was," I said. Then I asked him if he had any children.

"No," he said, but his face darkened, or saddened, or something, so I wondered if he was telling the truth. He started to say something else and then did not. Instead he put some more bourbon in my Coke and got Annie May a deck of cards to play with and came over and sat down beside me on the sofa with its stuffing coming out.

"You're awful pretty," he said. "What do you do?"

"I'm a singer," I said. "What do you do?" By now I was feeling better.

"I'm an independent contractor," he said.

"Contractor for what?" I asked. Some little voice in the back of my mind—it sounded a lot like Mamma—was saying, *Be careful, be careful.*

"Anything you want." Wayne Ricketts smiled a big outdoors trust-me kind of smile, and I shut that little voice off.

"I just got me a job over at the Hayride. I was real lucky," I said. "They just happened to have an opening. A girl quit today. That's what I came down here hoping for." Naturally I had noticed the guitar case propped up in the corner. "Is that yours?" I asked.

"Yes." Wayne Ricketts moved over closer on the couch.

"You sing?" I asked.

"Used to." Now his leg was touching mine. I couldn't look at him. I couldn't hardly breathe, to tell the truth.

Neither of us said anything for a minute. The sun was setting over this little putrid lake that was right next to the trailer park. Dust went around and around, slow and lazy, in the last red rays of sun that came in through the dirty glass on the trailer door. Annie May's hair was shining like real gold in that sun where she sat on the floor and played. All of a sudden she looked up from her deck of cards and said something that sounded like, "I'm hungry."

I started crying.

Wayne Ricketts stood up. "You reckon she'd like some cheese and crackers?" he asked. "I don't keep much of a house."

I pulled Annie May up on my lap and held her tight. "You don't understand," I said in between crying. "She hasn't ever talked before. She can't talk. She had polio."

"Well, I did notice that little limp," Wayne Ricketts said. "But I'd swear I heard her say she was hungry." He went over and knelt down in front of us and turned Annie May's little face toward his. "Honey, ain't you hungry?" he asked.

Annie May bobbed her head up and down so hard her curls bounced.

"Well, then." Wayne stood back up. He was so tall his head grazed the top of the trailer. He crossed the trailer in one stride and opened the little refrigerator, which didn't have a thing in it but beer and Velveeta cheese and half a package of hot dogs. He got the cheese out and cut it up in little square pieces with his pocketknife, then put them all in a saucer and brought it over to Annie May where she sat beside me on the couch. "Sorry, no crackers." He grinned at me.

Annie May started eating the cheese one little piece at a time, real dainty like she was at a tea party.

"Come on," Wayne said to me. He pulled me up.

"Come on where?" I said. I couldn't think straight, I couldn't get over Annie May talking.

"Let's go get your stuff," he said. "You're beat. You all can stay over here with me tonight."

I followed him out the door like a zombie, out into Louisiana. The lake was red in the last of the sun. Strange birds swooped overhead. Any direction I looked in, I could see distance—the swamp across the lake, the little twinkling lights of the cars way out on the highway, a blue blinking neon sign. I was used to mountains, hemming me in, holding me back. But Louisiana stretched out as far as I could see. Wayne Ricketts pulled me to him and kissed me hard.

We lived right there in that trailer for the whole time we were in Shreveport. I took Annie May's starting to talk as a sign of good luck, and for a while it appeared to be so. Things were going my way at last. In those days, getting on the Hayride was a surefire way to get to Nashville, and I felt like I was on my way. I was aiming for the top. Webb Pierce had been here—shoot, he even played the Hayride for *free* at first, just to be on it! Even the late great *Hank Williams* had played the Hayride, plenty of times. It thrilled me all over just to stand on the floor where Hank had stood. And I did real well, catching the eye of Horace Logan right away. Horace started featuring me regular, and then he moved me up front—always a good sign.

Of course Wayne Ricketts took full credit for everything, everything I did, since he had elected to be my partner, my manager, and change my image to boot.

Sometimes when I think about my life, it all comes to me in pictures of the images I've had and gotten rid of—that dumb country girl in the Raindrops to start off with, and next, the girl I became with Wayne—a honky-tonk honey, which did fit the times. Wayne Ricketts was somebody who always knew what was happening. He lived on the cutting edge. He stuck me into a push-up bra and four-inch heels and the fanciest low-cut outfits you ever saw. He got my teeth fixed. At first I balked when he suggested the wig, it was so big, but then I started wearing it, too. I learned real fast, it's a lot easier to wear a wig than it is to fix your own hair up good all the time, I have to say.

"People don't want you to look like their neighbor," Wayne told me, "or their wife. They don't want you to look like their sister, either. They want you to look like all their dreams," Wayne said.

It was Wayne who pushed me into asking Horace Logan if I could sing one of my own songs, after I'd only been on the Hayride for four or five months. I never would have done it myself. But Wayne rode me and rode me to do it, and eventually, of course, I did everything Wayne wanted.

And when I finally did ask Horace Logan if I could sing a number, he said, "Sure, honey," like I had been doing it all my life. Well! I decided to sing a new one I'd just finished writing.

I'd been fooling around with it for a long time. At first I called it "I Don't Know What You See in Me but I Hope You Don't Go Blind," which was the first line but too long for a title. I got the idea for it one time when Wayne just happened to say this to me right out of the blue, and I started laughing and couldn't stop. So it was a kind of funny-sweet rocker, you might say. Later I started calling it "New Eyes."

So I was running through "New Eyes" the afternoon before the show, nervous as a cat in a roomful of rocking chairs, when Wayne came home and took off his work shirt that said *Wayne* on it and threw it out the trailer door.

He stood there in the middle of the trailer in his undershirt with his muscles rippling. He stood there looking at me. Annie May was over at his sister's, so I could practice. But of course he was distracting me.

"Honey," I said, "You're distracting me. Also I wish you wouldn't throw your shirt down in the dirt thataway," I said. That old red Louisiana dirt was so hard to get out.

But Wayne continued to stand there in the middle of the trailer flexing his ropy muscles, so I said, "You're home early, aren't you?" which he was.

"Honey, I ain't going to be wearing that shirt no more, for I have bid that job a sweet adieu." Wayne always had such a way with words, this is one way he charmed me, I know, for Hank Smith never had hardly a thing to say. "I have told them to kiss my pretty ass good-bye," Wayne said.

"Oh Wayne, *why*?" In the six months I'd been with him, I'd learned fast that "independent contractor" really meant "no steady job." Oh, he'd lay carpet for a week or so, paint houses for a while, you name it, he could do it, there wasn't anything Wayne Ricketts couldn't do—but he never stuck at things. The people at work didn't appreciate him, or they tried to cheat him out of some of the money he had coming, or something.

It was always something. I had really hoped he'd stick with this new job at the Western Auto store. They gave benefits and everything.

"What happened?" I asked, getting that familiar funny feeling in my stomach, as we had just gotten a bunch of new stuff for the trailer, none of it paid for, of course, all of it bought on time.

Wayne hugged me. "Aw, I figured I'd better help my baby out," he said. Then he reached for the guitar case in the corner, and my heart sank.

For our first night on the Hayride, Wayne had gone all out and bought a flashy western suit, a secondhand Nudie. When he unbuttoned the jacket and flipped it back, it said *Hey Babe* on the lining in sequins. The first thing that popped into my mind when he walked out of the bedroom wearing it was, What in the world would R.C. think of *this*? Or Miss Lucie? Or Durwood? For the Grassy Branch Girls had dressed plain as dirt by today's standards. Sequins was not an item in that act.

"But you ain't up on Grassy Branch no more, honey," Wayne pointed out when I told him what I was thinking. "You left Grassy Branch. You are down here in Louisiana. That's the whole idea."

I see I have not said too much as yet about sex. But sex is a factor here, let me tell you. So is talking. A big talker who is great at sex can have his way in this world.

Wayne kissed me some more and then we went out and got in the new Chevrolet convertible he'd come home with the month before, and drove over to the Hayride.

When we walked in the door together, everybody turned around to look at us. Horace Logan walked over to me and said, "All right, Katie, who's the cowboy?"

I said, "Horace, I'd like for you to meet my husband."

So there wasn't a darn thing Horace could do but let him sing.

We went on right after Del Wood. I was scared to death, but we were a big hit. Wayne was so natural on a stage, it was like he owned it—flashing that *Hey Babe* sign and flirting with this old lady in the front row who liked to have died from the sheer excitement of it all. The folks at the Hayride purely loved "New Eyes," and they seemed to love us, too. "Katie Cocker and Wayne Ricketts" was how Horace Logan introduced the act.

After the show, a beady-eyed little fat man came up and proceeded to engage Wayne in intense conversation, ignoring me altogether, and then on the drive back out to the trailer park, Wayne told me we were going to cut a record.

"Honey, that's great!" I said. Of course, I was just beside myself, this was my dream. "Who was that guy you were just talking to?" I figured it was bound to have something to do with him.

"Nobody you'd know," he said. "Forget him, he ain't important. The important one around here is Wayne Ricketts."

Sometimes it was hard to tell when Wayne was kidding and when he wasn't

"Well, is he a producer? a scout?" They showed up at the Hayride real frequent.

"Just relax, baby," Wayne said. He put two cigarettes in his mouth and lit them, and gave one to me. "He's just some little Jew with big ideas."

"What big ideas?"

"Some ideas that Wayne Ricketts is going to *adapt*, you might say." Wayne was staring real intently out into the night, his cigarette hanging off his lip. "With a little bit of initial investment, I believe we could have a hit on our hands."

"I don't know what you're talking about, Wayne," I said.

"No, you don't know," Wayne said. "You don't need to know, either. All you need to know is what to do with this," Wayne said, unzipping his pants and taking it out.

"*Wayne,*" I said.

"Come on, honey," he said, all husky-voiced, waving it around.

So I went down on him, right there on the interstate highway. I always did everything Wayne Ricketts wanted.

Everything.

Wayne's big idea was to put up all the money we had and borrow the rest in order to finance the recording of "New Eyes," and then travel all over the South with it ourselves, from radio station to radio station, which we did, talking them into putting it on the air, which they did, and then getting the local record stores to order it when the requests for it started coming in. We also sold the records ourselves, of course—we had the whole trunk of that Chevrolet full of "New Eyes." Louis Carbone, the little fat guy, was our mail distributor. And I have to say, all of this happened just like Wayne said it would. We were still in that period when everything that Wayne said would happen did.

It was a crazy, close time, those months in the Chevrolet with Wayne, crisscrossing the South. I don't believe it is possible for two people to be any closer than we were in that car, which came to be our home, eating in it drinking in it fighting in it, sleeping on the side of the road. I remember waking up real early one morning someplace in north Georgia and looking up to find a grinning Negro's face pressed right up against the window looking in, and my skirt hiked up to my waist. I just kept on acting like I was asleep, because to tell you the truth, I was too tired to care. I lost fifteen pounds on that trip and missed Annie May something terrible even though I knew she was having the time of her life with Wayne's sister Rhonda, who was real fat and never had been able to have children and therefore loved Annie May to death.

Sometimes I puzzled over how Rhonda's husband had acted when I took Annie May over there before we left, how he sat me down in a reclining chair and said, "Now are you absolutely sure you want to go off with Wayne Ricketts thisaway?"

"Why, yes," I said. "I mean, I reckon." I looked at him, he was a man that drove a Merita Bread truck and went to church regular, you had to respect his opinion. "What do you mean?" I said.

Rhonda was hovering around us like a big old moth. "Now Don," she said.

"Well, dammit, Rhonda," Don said.

"This is a *big girl*," Rhonda said, punching him. "She knows what she's doing."

"I just think you ought to tell her—" Don said.

"*Tell her what?*" Rhonda snapped. "You leave her alone, Don. Wayne deserves a chance in life just like anybody else." Rhonda thought Wayne hung the moon, and that he had been dogged by bad luck and bad women. Later, both Don and I would find out how much of their life savings she had put up for Wayne's and my trip. "Now you all have fun, honey," Rhonda said, and hugged me. "Send us some postcards. Annie May, come over here and hug Mamma, she's a-fixing to go, honey," and Annie May did.

I sent her about a million postcards from that trip, and Rhonda helped her put them all in a scrapbook which Annie May has kept to this day, it's real sweet.

I got to missing her awful bad one time in particular after we had been traveling about a month. It was raining, we were driving, and I started crying and telling Wayne I just wanted to go back on the Hayride and get that steady check again and forget it, forget this whole thing. Without even slowing down or changing his expression, Wayne reached over and slapped me hard. "You don't seem to appreciate what all I'm doing for you, girl," he said. I fell against the door, and then I just grabbed the handle and flung the door open and leaped out, right as Wayne pulled over on the side of the road, zigzagging like crazy. Car horns were blowing everyplace, Wayne was yelling, then I went sliding down a wet leafy bank, and then I was out for a minute, and when I came to, Wayne was down there with me, saying, "Honey, are you all right?" over and over, and the soft summer rain was falling on my face. A couple of other men, truckers I guess, stood up by the road looking down. "Everything all right?" one of them hollered.

"Fine! Just a little accident, door came open," Wayne hollered back.

Later that day, when we stopped for coffee, he let me call Rhonda. "Lordy, I'm so glad you called!" was the first thing she said. She went on to tell me that a special doctor had said that if Annie May could have two operations in Houston, she would be able to walk just fine. The operations would cost around twenty-five hundred dollars, Rhonda said, but that was cheap because it was a new procedure and they needed candidates for it. Annie May was an ideal candidate, the doctor said. The operations involved some kind of a nerve transplant.

I walked back out to where Wayne was drinking coffee, and told him I was sorry I'd got upset, and I did appreciate what all he was doing for me, and I wanted "New Eyes" to be a hit just as much as he did.

Well, it wasn't a *big* hit, but as a result of that trip it did get picked up and reissued on the Four Star label out of Nashville, and it got a lot of airplay, enough to where Wayne and me started getting plenty of requests for club dates and dances and such, and we went on to cut another one of mine, "Call Me Back When You've Got Time," which did all right for me, but *really* hit when Dawn Chapel recorded it. That's the one most people have heard, Dawn Chapel's version.

Shoot, I didn't care! Annie May had those two operations in Houston, and they were a big success, and then she went into regular school at Pearson Town Elementary in Shreveport, just like anybody else. I don't know what I would have done without Rhonda during this period, as Wayne had us working all the time.

"When you're hot, you're hot, when you're not, you're not," he'd say. "Come on baby, get with it."

Wayne had kind of a genius for getting good bands together, he could talk anybody into anything, as I said. When we cut "Call Me Back When You've Got Time," we had a great steel guitar player, Ralph Handy, and Emory Marlowe on the bass, and Roy Hart on drums. Later we had Little Billy Burnett. We had several different fiddlers. Now all of these were real nice guys that had been around the Hayride for years, and Ralph Handy was particularly nice. He was a big, solid man whose daddy was a preacher over in Arkansas, and he was still real close to his daddy and to his whole family in fact. He talked about them a lot, things they'd done growing up, pranks they'd pulled, and all of this made me think about Grassy Branch. I got to missing everybody, even Virgie and Mamma Tampa!

But I was not about to call—I couldn't, I knew exactly what Mamma would think of how I was living down there. I knew what she would think of Wayne. I couldn't stand to think about her praying over me. Wayne Ricketts and I finally did get married, though I don't know why we bothered.

By then it was becoming real clear to me how bad Wayne was to drink. It took a long time for me to understand this, because he was not a spree drinker like Grandaddy had been, or a falling-down drinker like Daddy, but a daylong drinker who gets to a certain point and keeps it there all day. Wayne used to refer to this point as his "plateau." He used to say he was "plateaued out" when he got to where he wanted to be.

I couldn't do anything about it, because by then I was drinking, too.

And if you think that is awful, then you don't know anything much about life, or understand anything at all about this business. You get real tired, so you need a lift—you've got to get up for a show—then after the show you're real wired, you can't sleep, so you need a drink to come down. Then you start feeling bad, so you need pills, too. At first you get your pills from this doctor that a friend has recommended, then you just find yourself a pharmacist who will sell them to you when you want them, then you find yourself a man who will bring them around to your house. You get to where you need a lot of help. Don't tell me! I know all about it. I will never pass judgment on anybody. Believe me, I know all about it. It just happens, it all seems real natural at the time.

During this period Wayne went down to New Orleans and bought us a tour bus from a Cajun family, the Matilles. I *knew* we didn't have the money, but Wayne said we had to have the bus, it was an investment in the future, and he had already taken care of the financing. "How?" I asked him point-blank.

"Trust me," Wayne said. Then he said, "Come here, baby, I want to show you this bus," and he smiled that big smile and took my hand and led me outside to see it, and I had to say, it *was* nice, not really much of a bus by today's standards, but it did have nice maroon plush seats and a bar and bunk beds and the cutest little bathroom with a mirror that had lights all around it.

I was looking in the mirror when Wayne flicked the lights on.

"These here are *star* lights," he said. "Just for you."

"Oh, Wayne," I said, looking at myself and at his face behind me in the mirror. "Oh no, honey," I said, because then he reached around and started unbuttoning my shirt.

"I've got a bottle of champagne in this here little refrigerator," he said, "just waiting on you."

I followed him back in there and we got drunk in that trailer at two o'clock in the afternoon, me wearing nothing but capri pants and a bra.

This is how we lived.

So it was not altogether a surprise when the federal agents finally caught up with Wayne. It seems like he had been doing some real creative financing, under several different names, for a period of years. Well, to make a long sad story short, Wayne was given ten years. I got a suspended sentence and a fine. They seized the tour bus, our new Cadillac, the Chevrolet, our house, even Annie May's prize pony, Boots. Annie May just cried her eyes out when they took Boots. For four days, she was too upset and embarrassed to go to school. Annie May and me had to move in with Rhonda and Don, and then I had to go in the hospital for a while, as I was suffering from nervous exhaustion.

Most of this sad time is a blur to me. I remember two of these days real good, though.

One is while I was still in the hospital. I had been refusing to cooperate much with the nurses. To tell the truth, I had been just mostly laying there thinking about Wayne and trying to figure out how I had let him get such an awful hold over me, for I had to admit, in my own heart, that I *had* known, someplace deep down where I was not admitting it, that he was up to no good. I knew he was breaking the law. I reckon I had come to think Wayne was above the law, or beyond it someway. But I also knew better. You always know *everything*, don't you? Only you won't let yourself know you know it, a lot of times you *can't* let yourself know it, because you can't stand to know what you know. You can't stand what that knowing might tell you about yourself. And I was flat up against it there in that hospital. Every day I'd let myself know just a little bit more. This was what I was doing in my mind, opening a door, inch by inch.

I was also drying out, which is what is meant by "recovering from nervous exhaustion."

So I already had plenty to deal with when the lady doctor came in my room very early one morning—our room, actually I had two roommates, it was the state mental hospital if you want to know—and said, "Miss Cocker? Miss Cocker? Look at me, please."

I looked at her. She had gray hair and looked like a fireplug. "Miss Cocker, are you aware that you are pregnant?"

"Pregnant?" I said.

"Yes, ma'am. Absolutely," the lady doctor said.

I started crying. I believe I had known this, too.

"Well, what do you want to do about it? Do you wish to abort?" she asked. She had a northern voice but she sounded kind.

I shook my head. "No," I said. "No, I don't," for in that moment it seemed to me like *something* had to come out of all this, all this pain and craziness which had been my life with Wayne Ricketts.

For a minute she put her hand, cool and smooth, on my forehead. She stroked my hair. "I'll be back," she said. "I will urge you to reconsider. It's time you thought about yourself, I believe, Miss Cocker."

So I lay there for a while, and then all of a sudden, the truth came to me. *Katie*, I heard a voice as clear as a bell. *Katie, sit up.* So I sat up. I looked around but nobody was in my room except my roommates sleeping their drugged sleep. The sun was coming up outside. *Katie Cocker,* I heard. I could tell it was a voice from home, from up on Grassy Branch. It sounded something like Little Virginia, a woman's voice, but it was not anybody I knew. It was a voice I had not ever heard before, yet it was as familiar to me as my own. Maybe it *was* my own, in some crazy way which is past understanding. I listened for more. *Katie, girl,* I heard. *You can either lay in this bed for the rest of your life, or you can get up and make something of yourself. It's up to you. You've got some more singing to do. Get up.*

So I got up. I got out of there. Of course it took me a little while. I had to convince the lady doctor that I was not going to have an abortion, and I had to convince everybody else that I was all right. I reckon I had been so far gone that this took some real effort on my part! But finally they let me go, and Don came and got me, driving the Merita truck. It smelled so good in there, he had just picked up the bread for his route.

When I got back to the house, everybody had something to show me. Annie May showed me a picture she had drawn of a horse, and I have to say it was real good. It was wearing a crown hat. "He is the king of all the horses," Annie May said. "His queen is named Judy." Annie May showed me some more horses she'd drawn, and then a bunch of drawings of houses with smoke coming out of the chimney, and I started crying. I was still weak from the hospital, and still taking tranquilizers. Rhonda brought out some of Annie May's writing, too. It was just as even and pretty as could be.

"She's smart as a whip," Rhonda said proudly. "And now sit down, honey"—meaning me—"*I've* got something to show you, too."

"You mean you ain't showed her yet?" Don said, standing in the doorway.

"I'm fixing to," Rhonda said, and Don started chuckling.

"I can't imagine what you all are up to," I said.

"That's right, honey, you *can't!*" Rhonda said, and then she came over and laid several *Enquirers* and magazines and such as that in my lap, and sure enough, there was Rose Annie and Johnny, big as life. "The King and Queen of Country Music," it said.

"I bet you could of gone to the wedding," Rhonda said, "if you would of told anybody where you was at."

I read the articles again and again, I just couldn't get over it, me in a hospital in Shreveport while Rose Annie and Johnny turned into the King and Queen of Country Music! Rose Annie looked so pretty in the pictures, lots prettier than she had looked the last time I was home. I started thinking back on all the time her and Johnny had spent together as children up on Grassy Branch. Now they were saying they'd been "childhood sweethearts." I couldn't get over it. Everybody that ever knew Johnny Rainette knew he had a screw loose someplace. I always figured he'd gone off and got in the army or else in trouble—for sure I'd figured that, like me, he was long gone from Grassy Branch. And I swear I'd never connected him with Blackjack Johnny Raines, whose songs I had heard on the radio, of course. "Five-Card Stud" is considered a standard.

"Well, what do you think?" Rhonda stood over me grinning like crazy.

"Lord, I don't know," I said. "I can't hardly take it all in," which was true. I sat there looking at the clippings and playing paper dolls with Annie May while Don went back out on his route and Rhonda made a German chocolate cake.

After that, me and Rhonda saved all the clippings about them that we could find, for I kept thinking that as soon as I had my baby and got back on my feet a little bit, I'd call Rose Annie up. I knew she'd be glad to hear from me. I wasn't too anxious to see Johnny again, to tell the truth, because of this one time I remembered when he tried to come on to *me* when we were kids, and I slapped him good for it. But it was so long ago, maybe he had forgotten the whole thing. I certainly hoped so. I certainly hoped Rose Annie was as happy as she looked. She was the only person in my family I could imagine calling up at that point. Of course I realized that if Wayne Ricketts had not been in prison, he'd of had us up in Nashville in a New York second, to "take advantage of the situation," as he'd say. I could just *hear* him saying it! But I wasn't going to do that.

I was real big by then, and I needed to have this baby before I even thought about what to do after that. I wasn't so sure I wanted to go back into music, anyway. I really liked the job that Don had helped me get, keeping accounts at Merita, and they'd said I could continue to work at home when the baby came. This part of me was thinking, *Why keep knocking yourself out? Why kill yourself?*

But another part of me was still writing songs, staying up late at night to do it, picking them out on my little old Gibson guitar.

This is what I was doing the night my water burst, in fact, and made the biggest mess in Rhonda and Don's TV room. "Listen, don't you touch that mess, I'll clean it up as soon as I get back," is the last thing I remember saying to Rhonda as they wheeled me into the delivery room, for the baby had started coming so fast.

"Forget it," Rhonda said. "You just go in there and have your baby, and don't worry about a thing."

This time the baby came easy, as second babies often do. It was a seven-pound, six-ounce girl, just as bald as she could be, but real pretty in the face. I had hoped she would have her daddy's green eyes, but hers were big and china blue like mine.

The saddest thing is that Wayne Ricketts didn't even know

she'd been born, because late that same night he was killed by another inmate at the prison, stabbed repeatedly in the chest with a six-inch knife. The argument was over a poker game, and I privately have always been sure that Wayne was cheating, knowing him as I did. Rhonda did not comment on this one way or the other, but his death was harder on her than it was on me, I'll tell you.

It may sound awful to say it, but I've been through so much that I just say what I want to now, and the truth is, Wayne's death let me off the hook. I knew I didn't want him back when he made parole, but I hadn't gotten around to telling Rhonda that because I knew it would just kill her, and now I'd never have to tell her. Now she could make believe whatever good things she wanted to about Wayne. She could change him all around in her mind, and turn him into something better than he was. Rhonda grieved hard, let me tell you! Even Don was surprised. It was like Wayne's death had caused a dam to break. Rhonda would cry nonstop, then she'd talk nonstop. She went on for a week or more, and liked to wore us both out, especially me with a new baby. I learned things about the Ricketts that I'd never heard before, such as their daddy went out for a pack of Camels one day when Wayne was three and never came back, and their mother killed herself. Blew her head off with a shotgun, and Wayne was the one who found her with her brains all over the kitchen floor. And now Rhonda was the only one left.

No wonder she was so crazy about Annie May. No wonder she and Don got so excited about the new baby, who I named Louisiana. Louisiana Cocker.

Little Lou was only seven months old when I got a personal call at the office from Miss Dawn Chapel at BMI. She said she had had the hardest time getting my number. She said that "Call Me Back When You've Got Time" had been her all-time favorite record ever. And then she asked did I just by chance have any other tunes that they might look at. She said she was getting an album together. I couldn't believe it—there I was, in the Merita Bread office, talking to *Dawn Chapel!* I didn't even have to struggle with my answer. All my good intentions of staying out of music flew right straight out the window, just like the Little Moron's alarm clock.

"Yes ma'am, I sure do," I said.

"Honey, when you get to be my age," Dawn Chapel said, "you just purely hate it when anybody calls you ma'am. My name is Dawn," she said.

"Well, sure, Dawn," my voice came out real chipper and professional from someplace deep inside me, "I sure do appreciate your interest, and I'll get a tape to you right away. I hope you'll like at least one of the tunes."

The song which Dawn Chapel put on her album was "Two Lefts Don't Make a Right," which nobody has ever heard of although that album went gold. I didn't much like her version of the song myself. But selling a song to Dawn Chapel gave me the nerve to start singing in public again, with some of the boys from our old band backing me up, and before long I took it in my head to move to Nashville.

I will never forget the moment I decided it. It was real late and I was driving back alone from some juke joint or other where I'd been singing; I was smoking a cigarette and drinking a long-neck beer and enjoying the feel of the night, when all of a sudden it just popped into my head that I was going to Nashville, that I'd been headed for Nashville all my life, only I'd got sidetracked by first one thing and then another.

Now it was time to get a move on.

There's some things you can't do later.

The next night after supper, I told Rhonda and Don.

Rhonda just looked at me for a minute with her chins shaking, and then she looked at Don, and then she said, "Well, when are we going to move?"

I jumped up and hugged her, and hugged Don, who said he could live anyplace and drive a truck, he reckoned, but he wouldn't have no little baby girls anyplace else to drive him crazy. Then Rhonda went in the kitchen and made us another pot of coffee and we sat down and planned our strategy. I would go on up to Nashville by myself, and look for work, and find us a place to live, and then Rhonda and Don would come up bringing the girls.

When I told the boys in the band that I'd be leaving, I was surprised at how choked up I got, and how emotional they got, too. Everybody hugged me, and I told them all to look me up if they ever came up there, which was not likely, I knew, as they were all family men with day jobs in Shreveport.

Ralph Handy was the hardest one for me to say good-bye to. He pulled me to him so hard that I knew his bolo tie clasp was making a bruise on my neck, then he held me back out at arm's length to look at me, then he hugged me again.

"Just keep it country," he said.

I left soon after, driving a blue Dodge that I had bought cheap from Emory Marlowe's mother-in-law, packed to the top with everything I owned in the world. It was so hard for me to say good-bye to Annie May and Louisiana. But as things turned out, it was nearabout a year before I could get established to where Rhonda and Don could bring the girls up to Nashville, and by then, it wasn't only Annie May and little Louisiana that they brought.

They brought Wayne Ricketts's son Tommy, too.

The first that any of us ever heard of Tommy was about six

months after Wayne's death, when a tacky redheaded woman from New Orleans came knocking on Rhonda and Don's door in Shreveport, hauling a mean-looking kid along. Rhonda said that the kid's lip was stuck out a mile, and he wouldn't look you in the face. The woman was obviously a whore, according to Rhonda, who claims to be able to spot this instantly. She calls it a "hoor." But the woman in question, Wayne Ricketts's legal married wife as it turned out, claimed to be an exotic dancer, an *artiste* is what she said, who called herself the Fabulous Flame Woman and did some kind of an artistic fire dance. Her name was Suzanne Claudette Jones Ricketts.

"But you can call me Felice," she told Rhonda. She said Felice was her professional name.

"What's your professional *last* name?" Rhonda asked, trying to be friendly, you know, and the woman looked at her like she was crazy.

"I don't *have* a professional last name," she said.

Since they had about exhausted that subject and it was fixing to rain, Rhonda said, "Well, you'd better come on in, then," and they did, and she gave them some pound cake right out of the oven, made from scratch. Felice ate one bite and then burst into tears, green eye makeup running down her cheeks like the River Nile. She had loved Wayne, she told Rhonda, she had lived with him in sin against her church (she was a Catholic, she said, which made Rhonda wonder what the Church thought of her profession, but of course Rhonda didn't ask, not with Felice there crying buckets of green tears in the TV room), then married him, then had little Tommy (little Tommy was just about six feet tall already, at thirteen), and then you could have knocked Felice over with a feather when Wayne went out one day to get a haircut and never came back home. "Of course people disappear all the time in New Orleans," Felice said, "but still."

Rhonda said she just couldn't say a word at that point. All

she could think of was their own father and what he'd done. She said she got the spookiest feeling there for just a minute, as the thunder boomed and the rain fell in sheets outside. Then Tommy, who had not said one word up to that point, asked if he could have some more pound cake, and Rhonda said, "Sure you can, honey," realizing in that moment that Tommy was hers now, that Felice had brought him there to stay.

Sure enough. It took all afternoon to get to it, but Felice had read in the *Times-Picayune* about Wayne's murder in the penitentiary, and had been real sad about it, and meant to go down there and find out all she could from the records, as she knew Wayne had a sister (Rhonda) living someplace, but somehow she had never gotten around to it, not until just lately, when suddenly beyond her wildest dreams she had become engaged to a pilot at American Airlines, and frankly she'd really like to be able to start her new life out from under a cloud, and so she had thought that maybe Rhonda and Don would like for Tommy to come for a visit, just to get to know him, while she and her pilot husband honeymooned in the islands and they started their new life.

"What islands?" Rhonda said.

But then all of a sudden Tommy said "Shit" and rushed into the kitchen, where he started to play with a knife in a dangerous way. Rhonda went in and took it away from him, and marched him back into the living room with his arm twisted behind his back. When Rhonda wants you to do something, you do it. Rhonda is six feet tall and weighs two hundred fifty pounds.

"Tommy and me will be just fine, won't we?" she said, twisting Tommy's arm until he nodded and gritted his teeth. "You go right on, I think the rain has about quit now," Rhonda said to Felice, who took this opportunity to get out while the getting was good.

Later, Rhonda and Don would find out about the shoplifting and the other things. Right then, the main point seemed to be that Felice wanted to get him out of her pretty red hair. Then Don came in. He took Tommy out in the backyard and pointed at the old Chevrolet resting there with the weeds growing up around it. "You want to help me tune that thing up?" Don asked him. "Then I'll teach you how to drive."

When Tommy turned back around to look at Don and see if he really meant it, he had tears in his green eyes.

5

Knocking on Doors

I'm not going to tell the next part of this story in too much detail, because this here is where my story gets to be just like everybody else's. There's a whole lot of knocking on doors up and down 17th Avenue, a lot of following up leads that go noplace, a lot of living on one meal a day at Linebaugh's, a lot of people that run out on you. There's a lot of nursing beers at the Exit-Inn, hoping you'll meet somebody important. And then there's always a producer who listens to your demo and takes you out to dinner and tells you how much he can do for you and then takes you out on his houseboat at Percy Priest Lake for the weekend and tells you some more about what he can do for you, and gives you a margarita.

I know all about that.

I've been out to Percy Priest Lake.

Any woman who makes it in this business has been out there, no matter how sweet and down-home and pure as the driven snow she comes off sounding in an interview ten years later. She's been out there, too. She's had that margarita. She's had several. But finally she's figured out that this don't help much. Nothing is going to happen overnight, in spite of what you read. Finally it's all a combination of good luck and good timing, not talent, not looks.

This town is full of pretty girls that can sing their hearts out, it's full of country boys with a great song written down in pencil on a sheet of notebook paper folded up real little in their back pocket. Most of those pretty girls will go back to singing in their own hometowns eventually, and then they'll get married. They'll sing in church. Most of those boys will go back home, too, and get a job doing something else, and sing on the weekends for a while with some old boys they went to high school with, and then they'll quit, too. They'll think about Nashville some over the years, about the time they spent here, they'll make it out in their minds to be better than it was.

Because it was not fun, mostly. It was hard, hard.

The first thing you do, of course, is call up whoever you know, but when I tried to call Rose Annie I got a recording that said, This number is no longer in service at this time. I was sure it was the right number—I had written ahead to Rose Annie and she'd written back on the nicest notepaper with a color picture of their home on the front. So I kept trying from a pay phone, and getting that recording.

I was staying then in a room at the Parthenon Tourist downtown, right across from the park. When I went out to get some supper, I passed a rack of newspapers and saw immediately why I couldn't get Rose Annie on the phone. "BLACKJACK JOHNNY SHOT BY WIFE" pretty much said it all. I bought a couple of newspapers and a couple of beers and some nabs and went back to my room and read all about it. It was just tragic for Rose Annie, to have left Buddy Rush for *him* and have it turn out this way. I was sure he'd deserved shooting, since she'd shot him. I never thought otherwise. As I was reading, it occurred to me that Johnny Raines had been just waiting for that bullet his whole life long. I can't tell you exactly what I mean by that, but I know it is so. There's some men that are born to be killed. Johnny Raines was one and Wayne Ricketts was another, and every minute they're alive is borrowed time. Right then, in that dark back room at the Parthenon Tourist, I started writing my song "Borrowed Time."

The next day I went back out to the pay phone and called Mamma.

"Mamma?" I said. "This is Katie."

"Katie who?" she asked.

"Your *daughter* Katie," I said.

"I used to have a daughter," Mamma said, "but she went to Hell."

"Now Mamma," I started to say, but she had hung up on me.

I stood there in that phone booth looking at the Parthenon in the park across the street. You know it is an exact replica of the real one in Italy. It's real pretty, with perfect proportions, as this hippie fiddler would tell me later, who went to Harvard. He said the Parthenon was Art.

Right then I wasn't studying on Art. I missed my girls, and the money I'd saved up was going fast. I kept trying to get ahold of Dawn Chapel, but it was hard to get the call through, and then when I finally did get her on the phone, we had the strangest conversation.

At first she was real nice.

"You know I just *loved* that song you sent me," she said when she finally remembered who I was. "I still get requests for it all the time. I'm going to put it on my new album, *The Best of Dawn Chapel.*"

"Wow! Great!" I said. "I can't tell you how honored I am, Miss Chapel."

"*Dawn,*" she said. Then she asked me if I'd been writing

any more tunes. At this point in the conversation, she was still being real nice.

"Why, yes ma'am, as a matter of fact I have," I said.

"Dawn," she said. "Call me *Dawn*."

This is the point where, if I had played my cards right, I might have gotten someplace, at least I might have gotten her to listen to some more tapes. But I was still upset about Rose Annie, and more desperate than I realized. So I said, "As a matter of fact I have just recently moved to Nashville, and I'm trying to get somebody to listen to me sing. Do you have any ideas, Miss Chapel? Who is your agent, anyway?"

A silence as definite as a black blanket fell over the line.

I cleared my throat and went on. "I cut a record with Mamma Rainette and the Raindrops in 1952," I said, "and then I did 'New Eyes' for Four Star, and it did pretty good. Maybe you heard that one? I could bring it by," I said, "if you'd like to hear it."

Dawn Chapel's voice got funny and faraway, like I was a Jehovah's Witness that had come to her door, or somebody selling burial insurance. "That sounds nice," she said. "Call my agent, honey, why don't you?" And then she hung up without ever telling me who her agent was, and I stood there looking at the Parthenon.

No matter how big I get, I will always remember this moment. I will always try to be nice to the kids coming up in this business and treat them decent, not like Dawn Chapel did me. It's a great feeling to help another artist who's really struggling as a new-comer. And I know what it means to a new artist for someone else to just speak up for them a little bit.

So I will always be grateful to those people that finally did help me, especially Jim Reeves and Chet Atkins, and Tom Barksdale, who signed me with MCA and produced my first album, *Call Me Back When You've Got Time*, which featured "New Eyes" of course, but also the tune that turned out to be a surprise hit, "You Made My Day Last Night," which went on to be nominated by the Country Music Association for Single of the Year. So I bought the house on Harding Place and brought Rhonda and Don and the kids up here from Shreveport at last. They just loved Nashville from the start, all of them, taking to it like a duck to water! Tommy had his first drum set by then, so he could take lessons with the best. Rhonda ran into Patsy Cline in the grocery store at Green Hills the day after they got up here, and almost died she was so excited! Rhonda took over running the house and Don took over some of my business for me, as it was getting to where I just couldn't keep up with everything.

They were all right there when I got invited to sing "You Made My Day Last Night" on the Grand Ole Opry. This is a night I will never forget, April 10, 1964.

I can't even begin to tell you how much it meant to me because of all the nights in my life I had listened to those Grand Ole Opry broadcasts on the radio, dreaming of someday being there myself and meeting some of the greats, like Ernest Tubb, who turned out to be the *first person* I happened to run into backstage. I couldn't believe it!

"We're mighty proud to have you on here tonight, darling," he said. He seemed real warm and did not appear to notice my outfit one way or the other, which was good.

I was worried to death about my outfit.

The truth is that during the period while "You Made My Day Last Night" was climbing the charts, Tom Barksdale stuck onto me like a leech. He told me where to go, what to do, who to talk to. I gave in to him on everything, including image. So not only did my first album have a real smooth, contemporary sound, but I myself was no longer the same girl I'd been in my appearances with Wayne Ricketts. Tom Barksdale had me wearing my hair long and straight now, "California hair" he called it. I had on white cowgirl boots and the littlest white fringed skirt you ever saw. I didn't know what folks on the Opry would think of my outfit, but since that's what I was wearing on the album cover, it had become my trademark at that time. Tom said we were aiming for a bigger audience now, and that I'd be cutting my next album in L.A.

Tom said Nashville was dead and L.A. was where it was happening. He was switching all his operations to L.A.

Tom was *not* backstage with me at the Opry that night, though—I put my foot down. Tom Barksdale had long blond hair and wore things like turtleneck sweaters, and while I knew I was real lucky to have him produce my album and all, I just didn't want to let him come backstage at the Opry with me.

The Opry was for *me* in a way that I knew Tom would never understand, as he was a northerner from Michigan who had gone to the Berklee College of Music. "A technical genius," people were calling him.

Maybe so.

But I preferred to stand by myself at the right side of the stage, where I could see everything that was happening, and if anybody minded my outfit, they sure didn't show it. They were nice as pie, making me feel like it really *was* one big happy family, as it had always seemed to me, and for that night anyway, I was part of it. Lucile White asked me where I was from, and I got to hear Roy Acuff sing "Great Speckled Bird" and work his yo-yo. He's great with the yo-yo! Skeeter Davis was on that night, and the Wilburn Brothers. And Jim and Jesse, who I have always been crazy about, were making a guest appearance, too.

Standing back there waiting for my turn, I got real nervous for the first time in years. I wanted a drink so bad! Of course, I had tossed back a stiff one across the alley in Tootsie's Orchid Lounge before I went in the Ryman. That's what you do. You go in Tootsie's first. Because of course you can't have a drink at the Opry, those people are real straight-laced. The only thing you can get backstage is a Coke from a machine, or coffee and orange Kool-Aid, which they've got laid out on a table.

There was something like a *church* about the Opry in those days when it was still at the Ryman Auditorium—why, shoot, the Ryman used to *be* a church, come to think of it. It's got those pews, and the balcony, and stained glass in the windows. There's something solemn about the crowd, too—even now, over at the new Opry House—something worshipful, which has to do with how far the fans have driven to be there, and how long they've been listening to their favorites, which is *years*, in most cases. For you know, the country music fan is like no other, they'll follow you for years, through good times and bad, and never tire of hearing your old tunes one more time. They are the biggest-hearted, most devoted folks in the world, and they are the ones that have made the business what it is today. It is not the stars. It's the fans.

Standing backstage at the Ryman was when I really realized this, watching them get up and slip forward as their favorites came on, walking one at a time right up to the footlights to take their own photos to carry back home. It's exactly like people going up for Communion in a big Catholic church, if you ask me, the fans moving forward in a steady stream to pause and snap, pause and snap, and then move on, back to their seats, back to Ohio and Maryland and West Virginia and all the places they came from, where they will get these pictures developed and put them in frames where they can point to them and say, "I was there. I was right there." It was just wild when "Pretty Miss Norma Jean" and Porter came on, you never saw so many flash bulbs! It was like fireworks on the Fourth of July. Norma Jean must have been seeing spots before her eyes. You sure couldn't tell it from her performance, though. On her way offstage, she passed real close to me, and reached out and squeezed my hand. She was pretty as could be. "Good luck, honey!" she said. And I'll confess, I was star-struck! I felt like I was a kid again, instead of a grown woman with my own kids in the audience. I felt ridiculous in my outfit.

I could look out and see my own girls right up front, and Tommy who looked so much like Wayne Ricketts it spooked me, like he was a ghost sitting up big as life in the Ryman Auditorium, waiting for me to come on.

There was a Martha White commercial ("Martha White self-rising flour! The one all-purpose flour! Martha White self-rising flour has got Hot Rize!"), and then I heard them call my name.

As I walked forward with my guitar, I just couldn't believe it—the fans were streaming forward for *me* this time, the cameras were flashing for me. For *me!* So some of these were *my* fans. Mine! I couldn't hardly quit grinning long enough to sing my song. After it was all over with, everybody gathered around backstage to congratulate me and say how fine I did, and I left that stage feeling like I was walking on air.

But when I finally made it back to the dressing room—they have these big dressing rooms—to get my purse and my coat, there was Lucile White, taking off her wig. She looked awful without her wig. And she was not even all that old, fifty-five I would guess. But she looked like she had been rode hard and put up wet, as Virgie used to say.

Lucile White was once the most beautiful woman in Nashville—this is how everybody described her, as the most beautiful woman in Nashville. She still looked great onstage. She had the prettiest smile, which she smiled at me right then, in spite of getting caught with her wig and her blouse off, smoking a cigarette. The great stars are real friendly.

"You did so good," she said. "It's exciting, isn't it?"

Now Lucile White had been a child star, so she had been a member of the Opry practically since she was born, but she could tell what I was feeling.

"Yes," I said. "Yes, it is. It's been a long time coming," I said. "I got here in kind of a roundabout way." I was thinking about all the hard times I had had in Shreveport with Wayne Ricketts while Lucile White was an established star.

"Sweetie, let me tell you something," she said, leaning over so that I could see how folded and crepey the skin around her neck was. "There ain't no free ride. And a body can get tired. Real tired." Then she smiled her famous smile, and a twinkle came into her eyes. "You know, it ain't hard to figure out who to fuck to get *on* the Opry," she said. "The hard thing is figuring out who to fuck to get *off*." Then she just about died laughing, so I couldn't tell if she was serious or not. But I sat down and smoked a cigarette with her, and she put some bourbon in my Coke from a little silver flask she carried in her purse.

So this was another peak moment for me, sitting in the deserted Opry dressing room with Lucile White after the show, putting our feet up and talking girl talk.

Lucile White was always real nice to me after that, and gave me a lot of breaks. I opened for her several times, and sang on her *Forever* album. When she died of an overdose five years after I met her, I couldn't hardly get over it. She always acted like she was having a ball. But then it came back to me what she'd said in the dressing room that night, "There ain't no free ride."

The official cause of her death was heart failure.

6

California Is a State of Mind

Well, I'm not real proud of this next part of my life, nor do I feel awful about it, either. For we all go through phases and stages, as in Willie's song which is one of my favorites, "Phases and Stages." I did go out to California to cut my second album at Tom Barksdale's new studio in L.A., and I did let him do a lot of mixing and arranging and adding in strings and horns, and I did stay with him in his rented glass house that hung right out over the Pacific Ocean, halfway into the sunset, it looked like. While I was staying there I wasn't supposed to answer the phone, in case it was Tom's wife calling. She was rich. She was the real money behind Apollo Records. Tom had her picture and his kids' pictures all set out on the windowsill in the kitchen next to the cookie jar where he kept his drugs.

Tom's wife's name—her *first* name—was Brandon. She was one of those girls that went to a girls' school and now owns a big estate outside Nashville, in Brentwood, and runs the Junior League and plans the Swan Ball. I knew the type. I'd been seeing them around town for years.

Nashville itself has kind of a split personality—there's the folks in the music business, and then there's these old families with big houses and a lot of money they've had for generations. They belong to the Belle Meade Country Club. Most of them are kind of crazy. And since all of this is happening right here in Nashville, it's bound to get all mixed up together sometimes, as in the case of Minnie Pearl and the case of Tom Barksdale, who married a woman whose grandfather had been the governor of Tennessee.

Of course I never really thought for a minute that he was going to leave *her* for *me*.

So what was I doing, you might ask, drinking vodka on his deck in the sunset, wearing nothing but a pair of sunglasses? What did I think I was doing? Now when I look back on it, I swear I just don't know! You might say I got carried away by the times. I was just out there trying to make a living, I told myself, but it was more than that. I missed my family like crazy, the whole time. I reckon that really I was just trying to make it through the night, as in the words of Kris Kristofferson, who was a friend of Tom's. Just trying to make it through the night, and a long way from home.

It seemed like everybody else out there was a long way from home, too—everybody was from some little town, like me, and didn't know how to act in California, where there were no rules at all, where you could do anything you wanted to do, or be anybody you wanted to be. I couldn't get into it, actually, though I tried to for a while. I grew my hair out real long and got a tan. I was trying to please Tom, since he had been so good to me, and so good for my career, and I was grateful. But I couldn't get used to the way people moved in and out of the beach house, people I didn't even know, and sometimes Tom didn't know them, either. They were friends of friends of his. One time somebody brought a real young girl out there, and when I was showing her where the bathroom was, she grabbed me and started crying and saying all she wanted to do was get back to North Carolina, but this man she was with wouldn't let her out of his sight and she didn't have any money. I slipped a hundred-dollar bill in the back pocket of her jeans as they were leaving, but she was high then, and I never knew if she found it, or if she knew what it was for. I never knew what happened to her.

Another time a guy who really *was* a friend of Tom's, from college, came in and locked himself in one of the bedrooms and wouldn't come out for days, you could hear him in there talking to himself, having a regular conversation. Finally Tom called an ambulance to come and take him to the hospital, they had to break down the door. We had to get a cleaning service to come out and deal with that bedroom. I never knew what happened to this guy, either. It was so easy to lose people in California. I worried about him, but Tom didn't. Tom made it all into a great story, I heard him telling it to several people on the phone. Every time he told it, he'd add more to it, he'd make it more dramatic, he'd make the guy more weird.

"What a character!" he'd say on the phone. Tom lived on the phone.

"Listen here," I told him when he finally hung up, "Kevin is *not* a character. He's a real person, and he got real sick here."

"Katie, Katie," Tom said, stroking my hair, the way he did. "I know that. But it's a story too. You're too literal, babe. You need to take a more cosmic view."

At first when he used these big terms like "literal" and "cosmic" I just shut up, since he was so well educated, and so smart. Later I started asking him what this meant and that meant, and this is when he started trying to educate me, which is what finally broke us up in the end.

Anyway Tom *was* smart, and he was writing a novel, and

sometimes he'd get it out and work on it far into the night, then wake me up to have real intense sex, which at first I mistook for passion. But it wasn't. It was just intensity, which is what Tom wanted all the time, what he craved, what he lived for.

Some of this life was too much for me. I remember one all-day party in particular. It had mushroomed out of noplace, and I got trapped in the kitchen by this friend of Tom's named Paul Murray, who was a photographer. He kept getting right up in my face with his camera, snapping pictures. He wanted me to go outside with him to take some more. We were drinking vodka. "No," I said. I kept saying it, but he wouldn't leave me alone. I hadn't seen Tom for an hour or so.

"Listen," I said finally, pushing Paul away, "I've got to find Tom," but when I went into the big living room he wasn't there. He wasn't anywhere. Everybody was leaving, but nobody said good-bye. I went in our bedroom to get some aspirin, and was surprised to find the drapes all drawn, shutting out the great view of the ocean. In the shadows I could just make out the king-size bed all messed up, and a girl's rump sticking up. "Honey?" she said, hearing me open the door.

I shut the door. I went back out to the kitchen and got drunk with Paul Murray, and we went outside and I posed naked for him on the deck. It was sunset. I kept laughing. It all seemed real funny at the time. We kept on drinking, and I don't know what happened after that. But the next day, Tom was sweet as ever and said he didn't know who the girl in our bed was, if there *was* a girl, and he wasn't even jealous about me and Paul. I was kind of hurt because he wasn't. I was not sophisticated enough for Tom, I guess.

But for a while, it *was* kind of interesting. Tom got dead set on improving my mind and teaching me things such as history, which I have never been very crazy about. He also gave me a little book to improve my vocabulary, with a quiz at the end of each chapter. He wanted me to listen to a lot of strange music, too, and he tried to tell me unpatriotic things about the United States of America.

"Listen, this is my country you're talking about," I said to him once.

"Well, it's my country too," he said. "If I didn't care about it, I wouldn't criticize it, would I?"

For which I had no answer, as I have never been one of those people given to standing around worrying about the state of the world. I'm too busy figuring out when I can get to the grocery store, if you know what I mean. I believe it is mostly *men* that are given to this train of thought, anyway, and to that other kind which Tom Barksdale was prone to, such as the following.

One time when we were laying out on the beach in the sun and Tom was on his stomach, letting the sand run through his fingers, looking at it real close, he said, "We are nothing but grains of sand, Katie. Insignificant in the universe." Of course he was always smoking dope.

"Speak for yourself!" I said. I sat straight up, he made me so mad.

At that, Tom just cracked up, and laughed so hard I finally had to laugh, too. He was real cute when he laughed, and real good-looking, the way rich people usually are. I don't know why this is true but it is, they have these perfectly regular features.

By then I was starting to get tired of it, tired of Tom Barksdale's perfectly regular features, tired of having perfect weather every day in California, tired of the parties, tired of the great view, tired of dubbing and overdubbing, tired of not being able to answer the phone, and tired of him trying to improve my mind. I have to say, a person can stand only so much improvement!

One day I walked out of the studio crying, and stood there on the sidewalk in the bright hot sun looking at a hedge full of big red flowers.

Tom came out after me. “Those are hibiscus,” he said.

“I don’t give a damn,” I said.

“Honey, what’s wrong?” he said, putting his arm around me, pulling me close.

“I reckon I’m homesick,” I said.

That album has been called a crossover album, but I never felt like I crossed over anything, to tell you the truth. It was Tom Barksdale’s album, not mine. By the time he got done with it, it was *all* his, too. And who was I to complain? I’d gone along with everything, and now I was making money hand over fist, and I got asked to sing “California Is a State of Mind” on *The Ed Sullivan Show.* I flew up to New York City to do it, taking Annie May along.

7

Full-Tilt Boogie

Right after I got done singing on that TV show, a boy handed me a note that said:

> *Hey girl,*
>
> *I thought I told you to keep it country.*
>
> *Ralph Handy*

"Where did you get this?" I asked the boy. "Is he out there in the studio audience?"

When the boy nodded, I wrote on the back of it for Ralph to meet me outside after the show, which Ralph did, and this is how we got together.

He was up there touring with the New Cripple Creek Boys, a bluegrass outfit, so Annie May and me went over to the apartment where some of them were staying, and we had the biggest time, just like in the old days in Shreveport. Nobody has a good time in California, as I told Ralph, they are all too cool.

Ralph Handy laughed his big belly laugh at this, so I went on and told him about my drummer out there who was a Zen Buddhist and about how nobody eats meat or cooks their vegetables long enough. I told him about the food because I remembered how much he liked to cook and how he used to bring ham biscuits along when we traveled. One time he gave me and Wayne a marble pound cake for Christmas. "If you have a picnic in California," I told him, "they bring *whole things*. They don't know how to have a picnic," I said.

"What do you mean, 'whole things'?" he asked.

"I mean like a whole cooked chicken instead of fried chicken or chicken salad sandwiches. Or a big old slab of cheese instead of pimiento cheese sandwiches." All of a sudden I realized that I was making fun of Tom Barksdale's idea of romance, those picnics by the Pacific which had been the actual highlights of my time out there. Something like a light bulb clicked on in my mind—I felt smart again, and funny. But guilty, too—I'd been with Tom for about two years, off and on, by then.

"I don't mean to make fun of *Tom*," I said. "I know how lucky I am to have him producing my records. I owe him everything."

"Well, now, I'm just a old country boy," Ralph Handy said—he always said this!—"but I ain't so sure about that. What it looks to me like, *he* owes *you* a lot. He's in *your* debt, and not the other way around, and don't you forget it, honey. It's your songs."

I looked at Ralph Handy good. We were sitting in somebody's room someplace in Greenwich Village in New York City. There was a lot of smoke and a lot of people in the room, most of them musicians.

"Honest Injun," he said, and smiled at me. This was something I had not heard since I was a child, growing up on Grassy Branch.

I let it sink in. I smiled back at him. I had always been crazy about Ralph Handy, who was comfortable being a big man, who was not embarrassed to speak his mind—a man that didn't know he had a bad haircut, who'd been playing music all his life. He had a wide grin, and looked you in the eye.

"How's your family?" I said.

"We-ell," he said, drawing it out, lighting a cigarette. "That depends."

"Depends on what?" I asked.

"On what you mean by 'family.' The boys are fine—hell, one of them has gone and got married now! And Shirley's all right, I reckon. She's still in high school, so she's living with Jean."

"You and Jean split up?" I said stupidly. I couldn't believe it! I remembered back in Shreveport, how Ralph used to talk and talk about Jean and the kids. He thought the sun rose and set on Jean.

"First Jean started getting these headaches all the time. Then she decided she had stopped growing as a person because she was married to me." Ralph shook his head. "So I encouraged her, of course. I told her she ought to go back to school, do whatever the hell she wanted to do. Whatever would make her happy, you know. Whatever would make her grow as a person."

"What did she do?" I asked.

"Well, she took a course or two at the community college, and she started taking yoga lessons, and she stopped having the headaches so bad. So naturally I thought, Fine. Now we're getting someplace. But then come to find out she wasn't really taking one of them courses, the one I thought she was taking on Tuesday and Thursday nights. No, she was sneaking out to be with her yoga instructor, who is a wimpy little guy about ten years younger than she is."

"I can't believe it," I said. Of course the sixties was a new world, but this was less true in the business than in the schools, for instance. It seemed like every time you turned on the television, some kids someplace were burning their schoolhouse down. The sixties didn't happen to everybody, though. They didn't happen to me.

"How did you find out?" I asked.

"Hell, they came in together one night and *told* me!" Ralph sounded so disgusted. "Jean said that a part of her was sorry for what she was doing, but the other part of her felt she had a right to be happy. She said she knew she was causing me pain, and then *he* said he had some techniques he could show me to deal with the pain. I showed their ass to the door," Ralph said. "Now Jean and this yoga instructor are living in my house, and I'm living up over top of a Western Auto store. It don't make any sense to me. She don't look particularly happy either, whenever I go over there to see Shirley. But they've got a lot of nerve, I'll tell you that. Asked me for a loan the other day—can you beat it? Not to mention that I am still paying the mortgage on that house for Jean and her boyfriend to live in, until Shirley gets through high school. I must be some kind of a fool."

"Honey, is he telling you that old sad story one more time?" Mooney Yates, who is one of the best banjo players that ever was, came over and put his arm around Ralph.

"It *is* pretty sad," I said.

"You know what I tell him?" Mooney asked. "Me and the boys, we tell him he ought to get into some of this meditation himself, ain't that right, Ralph? Like this—*ommmmm* . . ." Mooney started humming and about three more of them gathered around real quick and took it up, just like they were some kind of a crazy barbershop quartet. "*Mmmmmmm*," they went.

I just about died laughing.

"Come on, let's get out of here," Ralph said when they had finally quit. "Let's go take a walk."

"It's raining," somebody said.

"Well, hell, hasn't anybody got a umbrella?" Ralph asked. "For this little lady?" meaning me, and so then we got one and took off, leaving Annie May up there with the rest, happy as a clam. She thought she was real sophisticated, being in New York.

"All right!" Ralph Handy said the minute we got out on the sidewalk. "All right!" He was standing out there bareheaded in the rain, he turned his whole face up to it.

Later I would come to understand that this was a man that you couldn't hardly keep in a house, a man born for the out-of-doors. Now it seems to me like I hardly even noticed the weather before I was with Ralph Handy, and then while I was with him I noticed everything—how cold it was, how hot it was, how the sun felt on my face, if the wind was coming up out of the east. It seems like we were outside all the time.

That first night in New York, we walked around the block in the rain, past queers and winos and hippies and Lord knows what all. Ralph Handy put his arm around me and kept me under the umbrella. I knew the rain was messing up my hairdo something awful, and I didn't even care.

"I'm glad I got up with you, Katie-bird," he said. "I always did think you were a fine woman, and I'll be damned if you ain't just as pretty as ever."

The street was full of people and slick with rain. Neon lights shone up at us everywhere out of the puddles, in a way that was just beautiful.

I knew I would see him again.

And sure enough it was not even a full month later that Ralph Handy called me up at eight o'clock in the morning. I was laying in the bed in my old house over on Harding Place not asleep but not awake yet, either, the way you do. Since I work nights I am not an early riser. I never take phone calls that early, either, but somehow Ralph had talked Rhonda into putting him through. Ralph could talk anybody into anything, and Rhonda purely loves to talk.

"Katie-bird, this is Ralph Handy," his voice came booming out of the receiver, too loud for the a.m. "I want to take you out to breakfast."

"That's real sweet," I said, "but I don't eat breakfast."

"What do you mean?" He sounded really puzzled. "A person has got to eat breakfast. I'll pick you up in half a hour. I know where you live."

Then he hung up, before I could say no. And he was *there* before I could get ready, so I just went ahead on without my makeup. It was a sunny, cold December day where the grass crunches down when you step on it, and you have to wear sunglasses it's so bright. I wore jeans and an old sweater, we went in Ralph's jeep. I have to say, it gave me a start to see those Louisiana license tags.

"I did a lot of living down there," I said to Ralph, pointing at the tag.

"Me too." Ralph wore a black Stetson hat that looked really good on him, he looked like he was born wearing it. "I reckon I just about drank that state dry at one time. But then you get to a point, you know you've got to cut back or die," he said. "I chose to cut back."

"Me too." I decided not to mention any of the big times I'd had in California, where I would have gotten in trouble again if I'd stayed any longer. I got in the jeep, which was nice and warm and smelled like cigarette smoke and after-shave. We drove out to the Loveless Café, where we sat at the front table by the window. Sun streamed in on the red-and-white-checkered tablecloths, and the waitress brought us big heavy white cups of steaming coffee right away. I was aware of Ralph's knees right across from mine under the table. I imagined the toes of his boots nearly touching my boots. *Girl,* I thought to myself, *you are a plumb fool.* For I had had plenty of men since Wayne Ricketts, and not felt so crazy and girlish about a one of them.

"What are you grinning at?" Ralph asked me.

"You," I said real bold. "I'm grinning at you."

Then the waitress came back and Ralph ordered for both of us, the biggest breakfast you ever heard of—scrambled eggs and biscuits, country ham and red-eye gravy. "I hope you're ready to eat all of that," I said. "I told you I'm not a breakfast person."

"You'll eat it," he said.

Which turned out to be *true*! But first Ralph got me to talking by asking me a lot of questions, and he was fascinated to learn who my family was.

"You mean the *Grassy Branch Girls*?" he kept saying. "The *original* Grassy Branch Girls?" He was just knocked out. He said he couldn't figure out why he never had heard about this before, down in Louisiana, and all I could say was, it didn't seem very important when I was with Wayne. There wasn't any past or any future when I was with Wayne, nothing but Wayne himself, only I didn't say this, of course. Then Ralph wanted to know what everybody was doing now, and so I told him how R.C. never got over Lucie's death and he was still living up there in his old house on Grassy Branch with Little Virginia and her boyfriend, and how Mamma Tampa lived with *my* mamma, who had been so mean to me, and how Georgia had put Virgie in a rest home, suffering from premature senile dementia. Then I went on to tell about Rose Annie, who was out at Brushy Mountain State Prison even as we sat there that morning in the Loveless Café. I told him how I went to see her as often as I could, and collected all that stuff for the prisoners last Christmas.

"Now hang on! Just hang on! Just hold it!" Ralph Handy banged on the table. "You mean that's your *cousin*?" And I said yes, it was.

"Well, I don't know whether to shit or go blind!" Ralph Handy said, signaling the waitress for more biscuits, which he poured sorghum molasses all over. He ate them with his fork.

I had never talked so much in my life. I had never felt so *interesting*, either—there was a way Ralph had of looking at a person that made them feel like they had a lot to say. It was this single-minded quality he had of paying close attention, and looking right at you.

This was the kind of breakfast they used to serve up at Lucie and R.C.'s. I had not tasted sorghum molasses in years, but one taste of it made so many memories come flooding back. I told Ralph all about the molasses stir-offs we used to have up on Grassy Branch when Grandaddy Durwood was still alive, and how folks would come from far and near, and how good that hot molasses tasted when you dipped it up out of the stirring trough on a little piece of cane, and how the notes from R.C.'s banjo rang out in the still cold air. And all of a sudden I could *see* it—see the great fire and the full moon, it was like I was *right there*. Suddenly I knew it was time. I knew I'd be going back to see them before long. Ralph Handy told me about how he used to help *his* grandaddy cure ham—packing it in salt, then hanging it up to cure from spring to fall. He said this ham at the Loveless was passable but not great. Too salty.

"I thought it was delicious," I said sincerely, lighting up a cigarette.

"I see that you did." Ralph grinned at my empty plate. "I'll cook for you sometime," he said. "I'm a great cook."

"I know that," I said. "What's your favorite thing to cook?"

"Beans," he said right away. "I put a little sausage in them, a coupla onions, maybe a little hot pepper. You ought to keep some beans going all the time." I remembered how Lucie used to do that, too, and then Little Virginia, on the back of the stove in the big house.

We were both smoking cigarettes by then, and looking at each other through the blue smoke that curled up to the wood ceiling, while the waitresses hustled around setting up for lunch. The sun coming in through the window felt warm on my face. I smelled ham and coffee. Our knees were touching, and I curled my foot around his like I'd been doing it all my life. I felt like I had known him all my life.

Ralph Handy moved into my house on Harding Place three days later, and we got married as soon as we could. He got along great with Don and Rhonda, and also with Annie May and Louisiana and Tommy, who became the drummer in the new band Ralph put together for me. This was the tightest, best band I ever had, with Ralph on steel, Tommy on drums, Mooney Yates playing the banjo, Frosty Duke on bass, and a fine young fiddler from east Tennessee. It was clear from the word go, without anybody saying it, that Tom Barksdale was not going to produce me anymore, and so I eventually signed with RCA. That's who recorded "Shoes."

I wrote "Shoes" because of something a girl said to me at the beauty shop one day while we were both in there getting our hair streaked, which takes forever. She said that her ex-husband had called up to ask her something about the kids, and then he just came right out and asked her if she'd been sleeping with other men. She said she wouldn't give him the satisfaction of an answer one way or the other, but wasn't that awful? She said he thought that no one else could fill his shoes. It rang in my head when she said that, the way a song will. Well, we all talked about her situation that day in the beauty shop, and then about two days later I sat down and started writing.

All you ever cared about was workin' night and day,
You didn't want home or family gettin' in your way,
I'll bet you're at the office now, your feet all hurt and sore
From some flimsy Italian shoes you paid too much for at the store.

Well, you know I've got somebody else,
And it ain't real recent news,
You still don't seem to think anyone else
Could ever fill your shoes.

Due to the big success of "Shoes" we bought a farm out in Brentwood and moved everybody on out there, none too soon as it turned out, because Ralph's daughter Shirley wanted to come up to live with us, too, since she hated this yoga instructor her mamma was with, and so of course we said yes. Then Ralph's son James and his wife Susan and their little boy Ricky Lee moved up from Texas—James is a soundman—and so we built them a house out at the farm, next to Don and Rhonda's. After I had the twins, we hired a full-time nanny named Ramona Smoot and converted the old tobacco barn into a house for her to live in. Ralph put in a pond so he could go fishing whenever he wanted. Then Don got interested in Arabian horses, so we had this special barn built and bought six of them. I admit I love to see them running around out in the field in front of the house looking pretty, but I wouldn't ride a horse on a bet. They are too big.

We got an interior decorator to come out and help us do over the house, and by the time he got done with it, it was just beautiful! They wrote it up in the Nashville *Tennessean*, in

Nashville Homes, and even in *Southern Living*. The only thing Ralph said, before the decorator started in on it, was that he wanted one room just for *him* that would stay undecorated, and have a reclining chair and a big TV and a refrigerator in it, so that's what he got!

Ralph and me were both just as interested in our new bus, because in this business you're on the road as much as you're at home. So we had it customized to our specifications, with a little kitchen in the back where Ralph would whip up all kinds of things for me and the boys. It relaxed him. He used to like to drive the bus himself, too, though we had a driver to do it. Many's the night I sat up in the front with Ralph, watching America roll by, and many's the night I lay with him in our special-built king-size bunk in the back, feeling the distance pass under us all night long, falling asleep in one state and waking up in another. The first year we had that bus, we put 250,000 miles on it. Then we took a kind of a break from touring long enough for me to have the twins and record the *Roots* album, and then we were back on the road again. Lord! It seemed to me that our life was like that endless highway, only the older I got, the faster we seemed to be traveling along it. I wished I could slow things down. I wished I could go back and travel some of those miles over again.

I remember saying something of the kind to Ralph one time, it was when I was pregnant with the twins. We were in bed on the bus, driving through the desert headed somewhere. I forget where we were going. I couldn't sleep. I sat up just for a minute and pushed the blinds up to look out at the flat silver desert drifting by. Moonlight came in through the space in the blinds and lit up Ralph's dear face.

"Honey?" I said. "Honey?"

"Hmmm?"

I could tell he was nearly asleep. But the moonlight—or

maybe just being pregnant, or something—had filled me with the most awful feeling, a feeling of time passing, of sorrow ahead. "Honey?" I said. "Will you love me when I'm old?"

"What?"

"When I'm old, Ralph. When you're old. Will you love me then?" I was crying.

"Katie-bird," Ralph said very solemn, feeling of my stomach, "as God is my witness, I will love you when you're old. I will love you till the end of the world," he said.

I felt better then. I tried to explain. "The thing that kills me is, I just wish we were both real young right now, honey, and had our whole lives ahead of us. I wish we were just starting out. I wish I could go back and meet you when I was eighteen, and live all those years with you. You know what I mean?"

Good old Ralph. He'd bring me back down to earth every time. "But you can't do it, sugar," he said then. "It don't work that way. The only way you can go is straight ahead, full-tilt boogie. There ain't no other way."

So that's the way we went, Ralph and me, and it was fine.

But we didn't get to grow old together.

Ralph and his son James were both killed in a head-on collision outside Knoxville in a patch of the thick Tennessee River fog which that stretch of road is famous for. Ralph was driving the bus, and James was sitting up there keeping him company. I was sound asleep in the back. So were Mooney and Frosty, and the others were playing poker. I woke up at the moment of impact, when the semi truck ran into us with a crash so loud I thought it was a bomb dropping—this was the first thought that ran through my mind. But then we were going down the bank backward, and then we were rolling, and I was flung out through the window.

I'm not sure how long I lay there passed out. When I came

to, I was laying on my back in wet grass looking straight up at the sky, where oddly enough I could see stars—the brightest, prettiest stars—just for a minute before the drifting fog and smoke covered them up.

You couldn't breathe. You couldn't see twenty feet in front of you. I was on a slant, and somehow I had a sense of the big river on down there below us, though I couldn't see it. A lot of people were yelling, but I couldn't see them either, only here and there a light or a flare through the fog, and then all of a sudden there came this tremendous explosion, this awful burst of flame which lit up the whole night, and I knew it was the bus, the bus blazing all over, end to end, I could see its outline in the flames.

And now lots of people were yelling, there seemed to be more people, though I still couldn't see them. I couldn't see *anything* but the brilliant burning bus, and I have been seeing it ever since, it burns like that forever in my heart.

Somehow I made my way over there closer to it, but they grabbed me and made me stay back. Nobody could get close to the bus. The heat was awful. By then there were sirens and blue lights everyplace, and somehow Mooney was there too, holding me back, but I kept screaming for Ralph and asking them, *Has anybody seen Ralph? Has anybody seen Ralph?* An awful, chemical smell was coming from the burning bus, that made everybody draw back and cough.

I don't know how much later it was when they got the fire out, more or less. By then I guess I was crazy. I broke free of Mooney and stumbled up to the bus, which you could see better now in the flares they had set all around. It lay on its side, the driver's side, like a big terrible toy. "Ralph!" I was screaming. "Ralph!" I burned my feet and legs on the metal before they could catch me and pull me back.

But I knew then.

I stayed there for hours and hours. I refused to leave until they had gotten Ralph and James out, which was well into the day I know now, though I had lost all sense of time. It seemed like there were hundreds of people down there by then, maybe there were.

When it got light you could see that the semi truck had gone all the way down in the river. Its driver, Sam Rasnake from Cookeville, Tennessee, drowned. People said it was a miracle that him, Ralph, and James were the only ones that died in such a collision, but it was not a miracle to me, it was a curse. I wished I had died, too. I stayed there until the crane came and lifted the bus and they got them out and put them on stretchers, and then I went forward to see.

I had to see.

"Don't let her go up there!" somebody was hollering, but it was too late. Ralph's whole face was gone, he was bloody and black beyond knowing, and the smell was terrible. One arm hung down off the stretcher bed, and there was the hand I had held so many times, and there was the turquoise wedding band we had bought in Gatlinburg, just like this one I'm wearing.

For some reason, I thought to get his ring. Crazy things will go through your mind at a time like that. I reached down for Ralph's hand, but when I touched it, all the flesh came right off and stuck to mine. I started screaming then, and couldn't stop.

You don't think you can live through a thing like that, but you do. You don't have any idea what all you can live through until you have to. And me, I was supporting about fifteen people not counting my band, *so I had to.*

I had to work.

When you get right down to it, there's not much in this life that we've got any choice about, is there? It is amazing what all a person can take, and still go on. I don't know what I would have done without my family, or my fans.

Little Virginia came over here for a while to help Don and

Rhonda, and they handled everything—the funeral, which I cannot even remember, the burial out at the farm.

I insisted on having Ralph buried by the pond, where he loved to fish, and where I can look out my bedroom window and see his grave. Of course now we've put in the memory garden all around the grave, so that makes it a very special place for me, and also it is nice for the children and for the fans. When the tour buses come in the turn-around, they always point out Ralph's memory garden. It is nice to be remembered. It is nice to have a memorial.

And I'll tell you, not a single hour of a single day goes by that I don't remember Ralph, and what a fine man he was, and how good he was to me. And fun? *Lord!* Ralph was *fun*, and a woman has got to have some fun in this life too, though many of us get precious little, it seems to me. I just wish every woman in the world could take a hit of what I had.

I may sound like I've got it together now, but this is not true either. One thing I *have* learned through my experience is that you never do get it really together, and you might as well quit waiting for that particular day to come. You'll die waiting to get it together. The best you can do is to keep on keeping on, and let the low side drag. I believe this.

But it took me a long while to learn it. I was so bitter at first, and so confused, and made several bad decisions that could have wrecked my life still more if God had not stepped in, in the person of Billy Jack Reems.

To go back to the accident itself, I had three broken ribs, a fractured bone in my ankle, lacerations on my face which required plastic surgery, and third-degree burns on my feet and legs. Mooney had a broken arm and a broken nose, the fiddle player had a broken collarbone, and Tommy was shook up but medically all right. Poor Frosty Duke got an injury to the spine that has made him gradually lose control of the whole right side of his body. This is heartbreaking to see, as it has made him give up music altogether. Now he runs a catfish farm in north Alabama, which is as good as anything else to do I reckon, if you get to where you can't perform.

God forbid I should ever get to that point, as it has become more and more my life, and especially since the accident. It was all I had left, so I threw myself into my work, bought a new bus, and Mooney helped me get a new band together of mostly young Texas boys.

I was neglecting my little twins, back home with Ramona and the rest of the family, they didn't even hardly know me. All I did was work. I was much more comfortable on the bus than I was at home.

I had a lot of men during this period of my life, because I was so angry, I know now, but none of them meant a thing to me. I needed somebody there with me in the dark, but as far as I was concerned, there was one side of the bed that would always stay empty. Right about then is when I wrote "What Happened to the Good in the Good Old Boys?" and "Single Girl."

It don't take a genius to figure out where those came from!

It was during the session when we were cutting "Single Girl" that Mooney took me aside by the elbow and said he thought I ought to lay off the rum and Coke until we got it down on wax.

"Just what do you *mean*, 'lay off'?" I got real mad at Mooney and made a little scene, which got blown up out of all proportion in the papers, of course, everything always does.

But it was not a month later that I wrecked my car on the way home from a party at a politician's house—I'm sure you know who, that made the papers, too—and ended up in Vanderbilt Hospital again, this time with a DWI and charges pending.

I agreed to go into a twenty-eight-day rehab program only after RCA made it clear that I had to. But I was mad as fire and would not participate in any of those dumb group things. I sat in my room and bided my time, thinking about Ralph Handy. I guess I still couldn't believe that there wasn't *some* way I could get Ralph Handy back, you see I had had my own way for so long. I was spoiled. I'd worked hard, but I had gotten everything I ever wanted. Ralph Handy was the first thing I'd ever wanted that I purely couldn't have, that had been taken away from me forever. He was the only thing I'd ever really wanted, the only man I'd ever loved.

Well, I was sitting in my room one day feeling sorry for myself and refusing to go to a group, when in pops the littlest preacher you ever saw. He put his umbrella down (it was early spring, and raining) and said, "Whew! What a downpour!" I got tickled at the way he talked, like a man in a cartoon. He pulled up a chair near the window where I was sitting and said, "Now. My name is Billy Jack Reems." He looked at me good. "You can go ahead and cry now," he said, which I did, literally *buckets* of tears, all those tears I'd held back because I'd been too busy working and drinking and messing around to cry. It was the first time I'd cried since I buried Ralph. I couldn't stop, either. I screamed and pulled on my hair.

When I wore out some, he held a big old-fashioned handker-chief out to me. "Blow your nose," he said.

"You act like I'm a child," I said.

"We are all children of God," he said, "and God loves us every one."

Naturally this made me furious. "If that's true, how come He treats us so bad? How come He would kill Ralph Handy for no reason at all? How come He would make me suffer like this?"

"He doesn't like to see you suffer, Katie," Billy Jack said.

"Your pain is His holy pain, and He will bear it all for you. He will take it all away from you right now if you will let Him."

"Bullshit," I said. "Pardon my French."

Billy Jack smiled at me like an angel. "I'll pardon your French, honey, and the Lord God who loves you will pardon your soul. As *well* as lift your pain, if you will only hand it over to Him."

I stared at him sitting in that orange Naugahyde chair. His feet didn't even touch the ground.

"Let go and let God," he said mysteriously.

"Oh yeah?" I said. "Well, just exactly how am I supposed to do that?"

"I'll help you," said Billy Jack Reems, and even though he was about as big as a Barbie doll, I believed him. There was something about him that made me believe him. Rhonda's opinion was that I was just ready to believe *anybody* at that point, but she took it all back after she met Billy Jack, and now she's a Minister of Care. But I'm getting ahead of myself.

Just then the nurse came in, and her face turned dark as a thundercloud when she saw who was in the room with me. "Mr. Reems!" she said. "You know you're not supposed to be in here! We've run you out of this unit before! This is a private hospital," she said severely, and shoved him out of the room, but not before he had handed me his card. It read:

BILLY JACK REEMS
CHILD OF GOD
HALLELUJAH CONGREGATION

"I don't know how he keeps getting in here," the nurse said as she left.

In the bottom right-hand corner of the card there were three telephone numbers, only one of them not crossed out.

When I got out of my twenty-eight-day rehab, I called that number.

Now I can understand that I was starving for God's love, that I had been denying that part of myself ever since I was a child, ever since I'd been cut off somehow from the love of God at the church on Chicken Rise. I'd *cut myself off*, to be exact—out of arrogance, out of pride, out of not wanting to be like my mamma. Anyway, I called the number, and I went to my first Hallelujah Congregation meeting without any particular hope, simply to have something to do on a Sunday morning, which used to be kind of a special time for me and Ralph, he would cook us a real big breakfast. You can just imagine.

Well, I went. The Hallelujah Congregation was meeting then in the YMCA on Hillside Drive, and as soon as I walked in, I knew it would be a joke. I had gotten dressed up like a person would normally dress up for church. But the other people had on every kind of thing you can imagine—blue jeans, shorts, overalls, work clothes, you name it! They were sitting in a circle of folding chairs. No sooner did I sit down than Billy Jack—for he was in the center of the circle—asked us all to hold hands.

Now this is the kind of stuff I just hate, and particularly with women. I don't believe I had held hands with a woman since I was a little girl playing Pretty Girl Station with Rose Annie and Georgia. I had never seen any reason to hold hands with a woman. But now I had gone and gotten myself in a situation where I had to hold hands, and I had a woman on either side of me, and one of them a Negro! Plus I had just recently learned that my nanny Ramona Smoot was one of *those*, when she asked if she could let her "friend" move in out at the farm and, to my surprise, this friend turned out to be a woman that Ramona Smoot went around holding hands with in public, in spite of being English! So you can understand how I felt about holding hands.

But somehow it wasn't too bad. I held hands with this little bitty dried-up woman on my right side and with the big heavy black woman on my left side, while we all sang "You Gotta Love One Another Right Now," and when we were done, the black woman reached over and hugged me, squeezing me into her huge soft bosom like I was a little baby. My own mamma had never hugged me at all, you know, and here I was, over forty years old before I realized how needy I was.

The big black woman, Roberta Boyd, would sing "The Rose" later in the service, beautifully, and she would turn out to be one of the Ministers of Care that help in the Laying On of Hands ministry, which closes every service in the Hallelujah Congregation.

The message which Billy Jack brought to us that day was perfectly simple—"God is Love, God loves you, no matter how unworthy you are, no matter what you've done, and all you have to do is let Him into your heart. Just relax and let Him in. He will do the rest." Then Billy Jack had us close our eyes, empty our minds, and just sit still for the longest time. At first this was hard for me. My head was spinning. And then it was like I felt something spiraling downward inside of me, down, down, down, and come to rest. I can't tell you how long it had been since I'd had a chance to just *sit down*.

Billy Jack stood in the middle of the circle and turned around as he talked. All the preachers I had ever seen before were old, and serious as death, and death was mostly what they talked about. But Billy Jack talks about life. He is young and full of joy. He cracks jokes. He laughs a lot. He wears a flowered gown with a rope tied around his waist, and sandals, like Jesus wore.

That day at the YMCA, the first thing Billy Jack said after we sat still was, "Everything we ever do in our lives has got something to do with the search for love."

This hit me like a bolt out of the blue.

It is the story of my life.

"And today, my friends, I've got some good news for you, and I've got some bad news. The bad news is, we can't find divine love in the backseat of a Camaro, nor in a Sara Lee coffee cake, nor in a new dress, nor in a fat bank account, nor in a ranch-style home, nor in a hit record"—I knew he was talking right to me!—"nor in worldly success of any kind. We can't find divine love in the faces of our friends, nor in our own beloved families. We cannot find divine love in the dark night with our earthly lovers either, because the key to divine love is a paradox—we can't find it at all, if we go out looking for it.

"But the good news is, *God* will find *you*. He's out there looking for you right now, you don't have to look! All you have to do is slow down and be quiet, and open up your heart to Him."

At the end of the service, Billy Jack had those who were ready to do this come forward and lay down while the Ministers of Care stroked their bodies to remove their pain and open them up to the Lord, and some boys strummed guitars in the corner. I didn't go up that time, I still thought it was all pretty weird, but I did sing with them and hold hands some more, and hug everybody at the end of the service. The hugging felt okay.

Billy Jack Reems came up to me outside and took my hands and kissed them. "I knew I'd see you here, Katie Cocker," he said.

The place on my hand that his lips touched burned like fire and then turned red. It stayed red for three days. I went home that Sunday and told Rhonda and Don about it, and we laughed at how crazy it all was, but during the next week I felt *better*, somehow, like a cloud was lifting.

When I finally went forward and laid down to receive the

Ministry of Care, I was ready for the cloud to lift even more, to be taken from me utterly, so God could enter in, and this is exactly what happened. I could feel my pain rushing up from all over my body, feel the shock when it hit the air, feel it shatter and blow away, nothing but dust in the wind. Then I felt God come into me, right into me through the mouth, like a long cool drink of water.

Since then, everybody has started saying how good I look.

Everybody has started saying my voice has never sounded better.

And though I continue to work too hard, I don't get so tired anymore, because God is an endless source of pure energy for me. What my God says to me is *Yes! Yes!* (which is what we have emblazoned on the hanging banners in the front of our new Building for Celebration) instead of *No! No!* which is all God ever said to anybody up on Chicken Rise, if you ask me! God wants us to express His love in our lives through using our creative gifts to the fullest, he wants us to *use* this life which He has given us. He wants us to be artists for Him. Of course the Hallelujah Congregation has grown like crazy, a lot of us in the music business, so it is like a great big family in a way.

I have furthermore come to realize that God never left me, I left God. I got dazzled by the things of the earth, while He stayed right there patiently waiting for me to come back and find Him again. This is basically the message of my recent gospel song "God Stood Waiting by the Side of the Road." It is doing so good now that we are thinking about doing an album of sacred songs.

My whole career has been affected by these changes. At first, without Ralph, I seesawed back and forth between producers. Tom Barksdale came sniffing back around, slick as ever, also Cowboy Jack Clark and Billy Romaine. I put everybody off. I couldn't make up my mind.

I couldn't decide who I wanted to sign with, what I wanted to sound like, what I wanted to look like—what direction I wanted my career to take. I had been a dumb hick Raindrop with Virgie, I had been a honky-tonk angel with Wayne Ricketts, I had been a California pop singer with Tom Barksdale, I had been a good country woman with Ralph. For the first time in my professional life, I didn't have an image. I was alone again. And somehow, because of my new faith, I felt suddenly open to the whole world, stripped of all these past images, in a new and terrifying way.

Billy Jack Reems counseled me to just take it easy for a while and listen for the Lord's opinion, so that's what I did. I quit touring for three months. I really got to know my little twins, Sean and Shane, for the first time. I had a big wedding for Annie May when she married Donnie Hart. I put Tommy in rehab. I bought a gazebo. Rhonda had a mastectomy.

Then one summer evening I was over visiting with Ramona Smoot and her friend Carole Bliss, down at the old tobacco barn which honestly they have turned into the cutest house, all ruffles and ducks, right when *Masterpiece Theatre* was just going off TV. Ramona never misses an episode of *Masterpiece Theatre*. She loves Alistair Cooke. Anyway, we were sitting there sipping on ice tea when all of a sudden Virgie Rainette came on the screen, big as life. I sat straight up in my wicker chair, spilling my ice tea.

"Good heavens," Ramona said.

"Hush," I said. "It's my Aunt Virgie."

And sure enough it was, Virgie being interviewed on public television by the nicest young long-haired boy. She told him all about living up on Grassy Branch like she had invented it. She told about working tobacco like she'd done it herself. She said it used to take them a day to get to a doctor, which was not true either, Cana was not that far. She told all about being a

Grassy Branch Girl without once mentioning R.C., who was the genius behind it all. When the boy asked her if she would favor them with a song, she was as ready as ever. "This song was brought into our family by my mother, Tampa Rainette," Virgie said, and then she sung "White Linen," accompanying herself on her old guitar. While she sang, the camera panned around so that we could see her audience sitting in a circle around her, paying close attention. One boy was writing things down in a notebook. Virgie didn't sound any better than she ever had, and she looked a lot worse. She looked old as the hills. When I said as much, Ramona said, "But she's *authentic*, Katie. That's what they're looking for now. She was *there*, after all. She's the real thing."

The idea of the *real* thing being a *good* thing was certainly something new for me to think about.

After "White Linen," Virgie did "The Preacher's Son" and then "Down by Grassy Branch," which got her a standing ovation. They didn't care about her voice, I realized. They cared about something else. Then the show switched over to Doc Watson, who was the real thing for sure. The minute that show went off, I called up Georgia long-distance, from Ramona's.

"You won't believe it!" I said. "Your mamma was just on ETV."

Georgia said she knew it, that her son, who goes to school up North, was actually *there* when they filmed it.

"I wish Mamma wouldn't act like this," Georgia said. She said that Virgie had been in a private rest home suffering from senile dementia when she was discovered by hippies who recorded her and then started carrying her around to all these festivals.

"It sounds like she's got a whole new lease on life," I said.

"Well, we think it's embarrassing!" Georgia snapped.

We talked some more, and when I hung up Ramona said,

"Virgie's a hoot, isn't she? Maybe you ought to put *her* on your next album. Actually it might be kind of interesting."

"Are you kidding?" I said. "Virgie will drive you crazy. I know what Georgia means. She's better off in the rest home."

"No, now *listen*," said Carole Bliss, a CPA with a real forceful way of speaking. "We've just been talking, Ramona and I, while you were on the phone, and we were wondering, why *don't* you get Virgie and your whole family together and make an album of all your old family songs? The time is right. People are really interested in that kind of thing."

"That's a completely crazy idea," I told her. "It's not commercial. Nobody would produce it."

"Then produce it yourself!" Carole Bliss snapped, and I just stared at her.

If it is possible for God to speak to Paul on the road to Damascus, it is possible for Him to speak to me in the voice of a crackerjack lesbian accountant. *Why not? Why not?* is the question to ask anyway, Billy Jack says, instead of *Why*?

So we are going ahead with it, and RCA has approved the idea.

I am the producer. Carole Bliss is the associate producer.

They've got Alan Rubin, one of these new young ones, to record and mix it. We are actually going to record it in the old Ryman itself, and some people are going to make a documentary film out of us recording it. That's kind of like the little girl on the Morton's salt shaker, isn't it? She's carrying a salt shaker that's got a picture of a little girl carrying a salt shaker. It all comes around full circle, don't it?

Like an album.

The name of the album is going to be *Shall We Gather at the River*. I knew I had to come up with something religious or Mamma wouldn't make the trip.

RCA is paying for R.C., Little Virginia and her boyfriend

Homer Onslow, Virgie and her hippie companions, and Mamma and Mamma Tampa to stay at the Opryland Hotel, which I bet they will just love. It is really something at Christmastime, with miles of lights. Mooney and all the boys will be in on it too, even Frosty, who's coming up from Alabama with his wife to hit a lick or so. Everybody I've ever been associated with except Georgia, who has given up music altogether, is going to be on this album.

And the best part is, they're going to let Rose Annie out of prison to sing with us! It has been at least twenty-five years since Rose Annie and me have sung together. I can't wait. I don't even care what she sounds like.

I have never sounded better.

And Alan Rubin is rounding up some young traditional singers to join us on the album anyway, such as Don Oakes and C.J. Barnes. I'm surprised I can get them so cheap, because I can't pay them what they're used to, but they seem to want to do it. So it's shaping up!

I'm starting to get real excited about it myself. For instance right now it's two a.m., the middle of the night, and I can't sleep a wink for thinking about this album. I've been tossing and turning across most of Arkansas, my mind is so full of music. There's *too many* songs, is the problem. The longer you live, the more songs you get attached to, they just get to be a part of you somehow. It's going to be hard to pick and choose. Maybe R.C. will help me out. But I love it, you know, I love riding along in my bus in the middle of the night, thinking about it.

To tell you the truth, I'd rather be here than home in Nashville, where there's always too much stuff that keeps happening, that you have to deal with. I got my fill of it last summer. I don't really want to go to Sean and Shane's lacrosse match tomorrow for instance, I'm *glad* we'll be in Little Rock! I never heard of lacrosse before I was forty years old, I am not going to get into it now. I am not into sports, anyway. Or sports cars. Or running. Or jewelery. Or real estate, or astrology, or therapy, or bonsai trees. I know other women in music that are just wild about these things. I never had time for a hobby, and I'm too old to get one now. When I was in Vanderbilt Hospital, they forced me to make an ashtray out of little mosaic tiles and I just *hated* it.

But don't get me wrong, I still know how to have a good time. I like to dance. I will take a drink from time to time. I like to have a date. There's nothing wrong with any of this. Billy Jack says that, above all, God does not want us to put ourselves under a bushel.

Right at this minute there's a young bass player from East Texas sleeping in a bunk not thirty feet from where I am right now. He's got a certain look in his eye. I believe I might want to get to know him a little better. It will probably be darn good for him, too! I also believe I might as well get up and put some beans in to soak, then I can cook them tomorrow in Little Rock. I have plumb spoiled my boys! They won't eat any but my cooking if they can help it, and I've certainly got time to put the beans in, Lord knows, tonight I've got nothing but time.

Shall We Gather at the River

The Opryland Hotel has got a lobby as long as a football field. Right now at Christmastime this lobby is decorated from top to bottom with fresh-cut evergreen garlands, poinsettias, a tree so big it can't be real—and maybe it's not, who cares!—red ribbon bows, lights, and all kinds of Christmas decorations.

Homer Onslow would never admit it out loud, but he for one is damn glad to be met at the door by these slick little boys from the RCA record company, still wet behind the ears but at least they seem to know their way around this goddamn hotel. The Grassy Branch group pauses just inside the lobby while the boys go to get a wheelchair for Mamma Tampa. As for Mamma Tampa herself, she is a sight to behold, as usual; today she's wearing a large green velvet hat, which Little Virginia has stuck a red bow on, for the season. Mamma Tampa must be closing in on a hundred by now; nobody seems to be sure exactly how old she is. You might think she looks terrible, but just remember—for her age, she looks great! Little

Virginia plops Mamma Tampa down in the wheelchair when they come running with it.

Homer is further impressed to learn that they don't even have to check in at any of the forty check-in desks, it's all been taken care of by RCA—now that's service! *The RCA boys are a little confused, they keep thinking that Homer is R.C., and frankly, Homer is just letting them think it, he's kind of enjoying the celebrity. He ought to get* something *for putting up with R.C. Bailey all these years!*

Little Virginia, a handsome woman by God, steps along right smart in her big plaid pantsuit, pulling whiny sour little Alice by the elbow. As for Alice, all the lines on her face go down. Her mouth looks like a shovel. Right now she's still trying to act like she's not here.

One boy from RCA is talking on a walkie-talkie. "I tell you what, sir," he says finally, deferentially, to Homer. "We're supposed to rendezvous at the Pickin Parlor in about thirty minutes, and then we'll take you on into town by bus. We've got a pretty tight schedule since your plane was late. Frankly, sir, I don't think we've got time for you all to go to your rooms now, if that's all right with you, I mean. I believe we'd better just send your bags on up there. It's too far to walk, sir, you'll see what I mean later. We'd better just head on over to the Pickin Parlor."

"Why, sure!" Homer says magnanimously. He has no idea what this boy is talking about.

Mamma Tampa smiles and nods and waves as she is wheeled along through the crowded lobby, exactly like a beauty queen on a float. She's got that beauty-queen wave down pat. They wheel her past a crowd of senior citizens from Columbia, South Carolina, past Santa, around a boys' choir singing "The Little Drummer Boy."

Then wow! They stop at the entrance to the giant Conservatory, and even Alice is impressed. "Oh!" she says involuntarily, and then immediately claps her hand over her mouth.

The Conservatory, crowned by a one-acre skylight, covers more than two acres. Although it's starting to sleet outside, it's always summer in the Conservatory. Even now, in December, it's full of palm trees and blooming flowers and giant ferns, little waterfalls and babbling brooks and grottoes and brilliant birds.

Tampa leans forward to touch a fragile pink flower. "Durwood Bailey and I went to Key West on the train," she says. "We bought a box stew in South Carolina."

"What's a box stew?" one of the RCA boys just can't keep himself from asking, but his question goes unanswered because right then the Singing Fountain starts up. This happens every hour on the hour regular as clockwork, and of course today it's a Christmas medley, with the spotlights shining red and green and gold and blue on the dancing jets of water. The jets shoot up, down, sideways, forming arcs, sheets, squiggles, spirals in time to "Deck the Halls." Then the Singing Fountain changes to "White Christmas" and an involuntary "Oh!" goes up from the crowd as a magic doorway high up in the courtyard wall opens and Lloyd Lindroth emerges onto a little balcony, majestically dressed in a white sequined tuxedo. He flips up his tuxedo tails, seats himself before his giant harp, and lifts his arms to flex his fingers in the air. "Irene, Irene, is it Elvis?" one of the ladies from South Carolina says too loud, they just knew *she would embarrass them all, they should have made her stay home.*

"Well, I swan!" Alice says mildly when the whole show is over with. It is as close as Alice has ever come to being impressed.

And now, here they go! With one boy from RCA pushing the wheelchair and another one leading the way, with the rest of them holding onto each other for dear life so they won't get lost, they follow the fancy path over the arched bridges, past the Seven Singing Dwarves doing "Muleskinner Blues," past cocktail lounges and fancy shops and special Christmas displays until finally they are completely exhausted and Little Virginia puts a heavy hand on the first boy's shoulder and drags him to a halt. "Now just a durn minute!" she says. "How much further is it?" Little Virginia is a big woman, she goes everywhere in a car and hates to walk. Also she thinks Homer might cardiac out on her at any minute, his chlorestol is naturally sky-high. "Nobody mentioned that this was going to be a marathon!" she says.

"The Pickin Parlor is just around here past the fireplace," the boy says. "I promise."

They make another turn and pass the enormous fireplace, big enough for a man to walk into, its blazing fire tended by elves, and then there they are at the Pickin Parlor, where Katie Cocker is waiting with Carole Bliss and some people from RCA. Katie jumps up and runs to meet them. "Oh, Mamma Tampa," she says, kneeling and taking her hand, "Mamma Tampa, I'm so glad you're here!"

"We've been on the road fer three days," Mamma Tampa announces. "Our radiator busted," which of course is a flat-out lie, RCA flew them over here in a private plane and had a driver pick them up. "It'll be hell to pay," Mamma Tampa starts muttering darkly, mysteriously, twisting her hands.

"Well, what do you think of the hotel*?" Katie asks brightly; real loud. Katie believes that the louder she speaks, the better Mamma Tampa will be able to understand what's going on. This is not true. Since Mamma Tampa keeps muttering and twisting her hands, Katie asks Little Virginia, "What does Mamma Tampa think of the hotel?" but Little Virginia is breathing too hard to answer.*

"Hard to say," Homer Onslow finally says, which seems to settle it.

"Why, where's R.C.?" Katie asks then, noticing his absence for the first time.

"Wouldn't come," Homer says. "Couldn't get him to come. Went out in the barn and locked the door behind him."

"Wait a minute," one of the boys says. "This isn't R.C. Bailey?"

"Nosir," Homer says, "this here's Homer Onslow, small-engine repair," and shakes his hand. It is the soft white hand of a boy who has never worked a day in his life.

"Well, here's Mamma!" Katie comes around to hug Alice. It might be just her imagination, but it seems to Katie that her mother has actually grown smaller, *shrunk by about three or four inches, really she's just this old tiny dried-up husk of a thing now, something like a cricket, too little to do any damage, too insignificant to make anybody miserable.*

"Oh, Katie," Alice says. It seems to be all she can say. But she came, she's here—wearing all black, like she's going to a funeral, but still she came. Katie hugs her mamma tight for a minute. Maybe Alice did the best she could, considering. Maybe we all do.

"Now I've got somebody I want you all to meet," Katie says, leading them up onto the porch of the Pickin Parlor. "This here's my daughter Annie May Hart and her husband Donnie, and looky here, this is my first grandbaby! This is little June. June, say hello to your great-grandmother, Alice Cocker!"

June doesn't say anything. She's not but two months old.

Alice can't believe it. She has to sit down right there in a rocking chair on the porch of the Pickin Parlor and fan herself with one of the fans they have thoughtfully provided, those old funeral fans like the kind they used to have in the church on Chicken Rise. Now here they all are at the Opryland Hotel and they've got these same kind of fans, don't it beat all? Same kind of rocking chairs, too, just like the ones on the porch at R.C. and Lucie's house, only those really are old, and these are just made to look old. It's hard to tell the difference.

"Grandma? Grandma?" Annie May is saying. "Don't you want to hold June?"

But Alice never liked babies. "No," she says, looking away, drawing up her face till she looks like a dried-apple doll. Annie May has got herself all fixed up like a huzzy instead of a mother, you'd think a cripple girl would know better, and her so-called husband has got on bell-bottom britches with silver-toed boots. Not to mention Alice's own daughter Katie, who is dressed like a hoor. Alice knew she should have stayed home. The way it is, they're going to miss church tomorrow, church which is the only thing Alice loves in the world anyway, fergit babies, fergit all that breathing and groping and rolling around in the dark, ain't no man alive that can hold a candle to God. A strolling trio of English-looking men in stovepipe hats comes by, singing "God Rest Ye Merry, Gentlemen," which is not even a Christmas song, in Alice's opinion. The Christmas songs she likes are the old hard high songs like "Wondrous Love." What wondrous love is this, oh my soul! oh my soul! *On Chicken Rise you can see your breath in the frosty air as you sing, see the actual shapes of the words in the air like souls rising up to God.*

"Honey, don't cry," Donnie Hart is saying to his wife.

"Get me one of them blue drinks with a little umbreller in it, and make it snappy," Tampa says to her RCA boy, handling him a quarter. But Katie has ordered coffee and cookies all around, brought by waitresses in black fishnet stockings and little aprons who are obviously hoors, while Carole Bliss

talks into her walkie-talkie and taps her foot and curses the day she ever had this big idea.

When Rose Annie arrives, escorted by two good-looking state marshals and her daughter Sugar, for a minute nobody recognizes her. The little group stops dead still in the midst of the holiday throng moving past the porch of the Pickin Parlor, where they all sit, until Little Virginia shrieks out, "Why, Lord, it's Sugar!" because they haven't hardly seen Sugar in the last few years while she's been off getting her Ph.D. in deconstruction at Duke University. Sugar may well be the only Ph.D. in the world named Sugar. When Sugar starts smiling and reaching out across the rail, Katie bursts into tears, she can't hardly stand it. Rose Annie has gotten old all of a sudden, the way women will at their age who don't take care of themselves, with wispy gray hair hanging down in her face, hunched shoulders, veiny blue hands sticking out the sleeves of her old coat. Katie wonders where Rose Annie could have possibly gotten that awful coat. Rose Annie will be up for parole next year but she might have to live in a rest home, this is what they've told Sugar, as she suffers from depression. Her spirit has been broken, as you can see. Still, the loveliest smile comes over Rose Annie's face as she recognizes Katie, and her beautiful eyes, still cornflower blue, are perfectly clear, a girl's eyes in an old woman's face.

What a reunion!

Flash bulbs go off like fireworks. Even Little Virginia is crying, and tough old Homer Onslow wipes a tear from his eyes.

"Well, set down!" *Tampa orders. "It's a real nice night. Looky here, you can see the Big Dipper." Everybody starts laughing and the waitresses bring more coffee. Carole Bliss is just beside herself, looking at her watch, tapping her foot. "Time is money," she says.*

Then Katie pokes her, pointing past the Merry Gentlemen, and here comes Virgie strolling along like she's got all the time in the world, accompanied by hippies. Virgie has gone all-out for this occasion, wearing a glittery gold western-style dress with a long skirt, gold boots, and a cascading black wig. She starts waving like crazy as soon as she sees them on the porch, and everybody waves back.

"Where the hell have you been? Dinner's waiting on you," Tampa says severely. "The men have already eat."

"Virgie, you look just terrific!" Katie hugs Virgie, who submits to this gingerly; she just spent forty minutes up in her room working on herself.

"Now I've been thinking about the lineup," Virgie tells Katie right off, taking a little notebook out of her purse.

Katie looks at Virgie good. Under the fake black eyelashes, Virgie's eyes are as bright as ever. She doesn't look senile or demented either one, and Katie wonders if it is just remotely possible that Georgia put her in the rest home so she wouldn't embarrass her and her big-shot husband.

"Don't sit down!" Carole Bliss directs Virgie's group. "This way, everybody! They're waiting for us." Carole Bliss's walkie-talkie crackles smartly as she leads them around the corner at exactly the moment when R.C., in the barn up on Grassy Branch, puts the barrel of his rifle in his mouth and sets the needle over on "Melungeon Man" one more time. R.C. has been thinking about his mamma, whose love for the Melungeon marked his life and made him a man always outside the closed door, waiting there forever in the outer dark. Then R.C. thinks of the night he and his Lucie, lovely Lucie, spent at that fancy hotel in Cana so long ago, how they took a bath in the big white bathtub with claw feet, how Lucie giggled.

There is a little wait before the fireplace while the driver brings the bus around, it went to the other entrance apparently. The elves are delighted, handing out Christmas candy.

"Jawbreakers," Tampa calls them.

"Mamma Tampa, doesn't this remind you of how you all used to tell stories around the fire of a night in the wintertime?" Katie asks.

"Lord yes, honey, it sure does," Mamma Tampa starts up. "I don't know if you've ever heerd the one about the fiddling woman and the preacherman, but it was always one of my favorites. And it's a true one, too! Took place over on Lone Bald Mountain, now that is about the lonesomest place you ever saw. They is a little cabin over there to this day, all overgrowed by big dark cedar trees, where it happened. You can still hear that ghostly fiddle music playing out in the dead of night. It'll chill your bones, I'll tell you. It'll put the fear of God in you."

"What happened?" asks one hippie girl, edging closer. Even the elves are listening.

"They was an old preacherman that lived in that cabin, and somehow, whether by hook or cook or the will of God, he convinced a beautiful young fiddle-playing woman to marry him and come over there to live. She just loved him, it is said, against all reason or common sense, and bore him three babies right away," Tampa says.

Virgie is not one bit interested in these old stories. "What's your *name, honey?" she asks one of the marshals. Virgie has always liked a man in a uniform.*

"Eddie Ray Cox," he says.

Rose Annie likes to look into the fire, she's always loved a fire, she laid out in the cold dark field one night looking back at a fire and all the people dancing in the fiery light, and Johnny was there too and she looked up past his head at the starry sky. "Come on, Rose Annie." Katie pulls gently at her arm. "The bus is here," which is all Katie ever sees in any fire, that burning bus. Katie leads Rose Annie past a tower of poinsettias. Katie wanted to plant burning bushes behind the benches in Ralph's memory garden, like Lucie grew by the gate up home, but the landscape designer said he didn't know what a burning bush was, he'd never heard of a burning bush which Lucie grew by the gate of the house up on Grassy Branch, where even now R.C. is dying. After they make this album, after a decent length of time has gone by to mark R.C.'s passing, Little Virginia and Homer will decide to go along with Gladys and Tammy's idea of opening up the barn to the general public, filling it with old family pictures and clothes and furniture. Little Virginia has been dying to clean out that old house, anyway.

"So he cracked that fiddle up against one of them cedar trees and forbid her to fiddle ever again, or to learn it to the younguns. And then he taken his walking stick to the younguns, one by one," Tampa goes on.

"Well, why don't you hand that baby on over here after all?" Alice says to Annie May right out of the blue.

"Eddie Ray, I believe I could use a hand here." Virgie follows them onto the bus.

"But the eldest boy would have none of it, he grabbed the stick away from the old preacherman and whacked him on the head with it, knocking his own daddy down in the dirt, and then ran off through the woods hollering that he would not be back, that he would never darken that door again."

"Come on now," Carole Bliss says. "Let's get her in the bus." The RCA boys and the other marshal lift the wheelchair.

"He ran like the wind through piney woods and laurel

slicks, he ran acrost the rocky top of Lone Bald Mountain itself in the pitch-black dark, but in his awful haste he ran right over a clift, and that was the end of him. . . ." The last thing you hear as they shut the door is Mamma Tampa, telling her old crazy stories one more time.

Notes

I would like to express very special thanks to Mike Casey at the Southern Folklife Collection of the Wilson Library, University of North Carolina at Chapel Hill, for his knowledge and advice; to Peggy Ellis for her editorial skill and help with information on contemporary country music; to Cathie Pelletier and Jim Glaser for their conversation, information, friendship, and for a trip backstage at the Opry; to Beverly Patterson for advising me on early Primitive Baptist hymns; to Gloria Wansley for inspiration; to Glenn Hinson for his medicine show expertise; to Bob Fagg for tapes and general encouragement; to Al's Garage of Chapel Hill for automotive advice; to Maggi Vaughn for her interest; and to Hannah Byrum, whose help was invaluable to me as I wrote this book.

Sources I consulted include:

The Bristol Sessions, available through the Country Music Hall of Fame and Museum, Nashville. Much information about the historic Bristol sessions comes from the liner notes of this double album.

Country: The Music and the Musicians, edited by Paul Kingsbury and Alan Axelrod, compiled by and published for the Country Music Foundation. New York: Abbeville Press, 1988. Alice Bailey's narration is based on Elmer Bird's recollection of listening to the Grand Ole Opry on a radio rigged up to a car battery, in chapter 2, "The Triumph of the Hills: Country Radio, 1920–50," by Charles Wolfe. I also drew from Wolfe's descriptions of radio barn dances, the section titled "Anatomy of a Barn Dance" in particular.

Country Music U.S.A. by Bill C. Malone, published for the American Folklore Society. Austin and London: University of Texas Press, 1968.

Ghosts of the Southern Mountains and Appalachia by Nancy Roberts. Columbia: University of South Carolina Press, 1988; originally published Garden City, NY: Doubleday, 1978. Ira Keen's narrative is based on the West Virginia hill country tale collected and written up by Roberts as "The Ghost Fiddler."

Lost Highway by Peter Guralnick. New York: Vintage Books, 1982.

Pilgrims of Paradox: Calvinism and Experience Among Primitive Baptists of the Blue Ridge by James L. Peacock and Ruel Tyson. Washington, D.C., and London: Smithsonian Institution Press, 1989. Whence comes the key phrase "This world is not my home," as well as information and background on many beliefs and concepts.

Primitive Baptist Hymns of the Blue Ridge, recorded by Brett Sutton, edited by Daniel Patterson. This album, whose liner notes are wonderful, is one of a series of American Folklore recordings edited by Patterson. The idea of Ezekiel Bailey's "gift hymn" comes from here, as well as background on other Primitive Baptist beliefs and practices.

The Singing Family of the Cumberlands by Jean Ritchie. Louisville: The University Press of Kentucky, 1988. Surely this is the best and most charming book ever written about growing up in a real "singing family."

The Spirit of the Mountains by Emma Bell Miles. Knoxville: University of Tennessee Press, 1975; originally published 1905.

The Stars of Country Music, edited by Bill C. Malone and Judith McCulloh. Urbana, Chicago, and London: University of Illinois Press, 1975.

The Vi-Ton-Ka Medicine Show, project director Glenn Hinson. New York: American Place Theatre, 1983. In the Southern Folklife Collection, Wilson Library, University of North Carolina at Chapel Hill. Several medicine show routines are described in this booklet.

We Wanna Boogie: An Illustrated History of the American Rockabilly Movement by Randy McNutt. Hamilton, OH: HHP Books, 1988. Available through the Country Music Hall of Fame and Museum, Nashville. The memorable phrase "Get hot or go home" comes from this book.

As I worked on this book, I was especially inspired by the music of Jean Ritchie; the novels *The Heart of the Country* by Bland Simpson and *Ruby Red* by William Price Fox; the music of the Red Clay Ramblers of Chapel Hill, North Carolina; and ballad singer Sheila Barnhill's tales about growing up in Sodom, North Carolina.

The author gratefully acknowledges permission to quote from the following:

"The Bad Girl" (no. 97) from Alan Lomax, *The Folk Songs of North America* (Doubleday, 1960).

"I've Been Gatherin' Flowers in the Meadow," "The Muskrat Song," and "The Old Ship of Zion" from Emma Bell Miles, *The Spirit of the Mountains* (University of Tennessee Press, 1975; originally published 1905).

"Bright Morning Stars," as arranged and adapted by Tony and Irene Saletan Copyright 1970 Hillgreen Music (BMI).

And thanks her friends:

Retha Danvers, for the lyrics of "Shoes"
Annie Dillard, for the song title "Two Lefts Don't Make a Right"
Susan Ketchin, for the song titles "You Made My Day Last Night" and "What Happened to the Good in the Good Old Boys?"
Rita Quillen, for the song title "If Drinkin' Don't Kill Me, Your Memory Will"

About the Author

Lee Smith is the author of fifteen works of fiction including *Oral History, Fair and Tender Ladies,* and her recent *Mrs. Darcy and the Blue-Eyed Stranger.* She has received many awards including the North Carolina Award for Literature and an Academy Award in Literature from the American Academy of Arts and Letters; her novel *The Last Girls* was a *New York Times* bestseller as well as winner of the Southern Book Critics Circle Award. She lives in North Carolina.